PRAISE FOR THE NOVELS OF
MICHAEL A. STACKPOLE

The DragonCrown War Cycle

Fortress Draconis

"What a splendid story; it grabbed me and wrenched me full force into a gripping adventure. And the wonderful thing is, there are two more books to come."
—Dennis L. McKiernan, author of *Once Upon a Winter's Night*

"I think that Michael A. Stackpole is incapable of writing a book that isn't imaginative, intelligent, and sympathetic. On top of that, *Fortress Draconis* is ambitious, even for him. It can hardly help being exciting and satisfying. When future readers name the writers who followed the Asimov-Clarke generation, and the Zelazny-Silverberg generation, they'll have to mention Michael A. Stackpole."
—Stephen R. Donaldson

"A compelling and engaging escape." —*Publishers Weekly*

"With a deliciously evil antagonist and some truly remarkable supporting characters, this is a terrific read."
—*Booklist*

"A powerful epic fantasy that is wholly grounded in the gritty realism of battlefields and sacrifices."
—*Ro*

When Dragons Rage

"Intriguing [and] complex . . . worth the wait."
—*Publishers Weekly*

"Addicts will devour [*When Dragons Rage*] swiftly and demand more." —*Kirkus Reviews*

"Enough sex, love, bloody battles, and high adventure to keep reading lamps lit well into the wee hours." —*Booklist*

The Grand Crusade

"This is fantasy on the most epic of scales, with plenty of bloody conflict and treacherous double-dealing."
—*Publishers Weekly*

AND FOR HIS LATEST TRILOGY

A Secret Atlas

"High melodrama empowers a cunning tale."
—*Kirkus Reviews*

"Making maps can be gripping work, as shown in this sweeping novel of grand schemes, imperial machinations and brave heroes who seek new lands, the first in a new fantasy series from bestseller Michael A. Stackpole. . . . This satisfying story has it all—wild magic, the excitement of epic fantasy and the adventure of exploration in the age of sail." —*Publishers Weekly*

"Stackpole creates a very interesting world that, while fantastic, mirrors our own in many ways. . . . The characters were quite alive, as was the world which they live in and are discovering. . . . A solidly entertaining story."
—sffworld.com

"A story of adventure, but it also has intrigue, grandeur, alien cultures and lots of action . . . The plot is tangled but fascinating, with politics, technology, love and ambition all threads being warped by past events and possible future disasters. The scenes of magic gone wild are very beguiling, with descriptions of lands where trees are living copper and sway like seaweed in water. New lands also add color, including a continent whose culture is obviously based on the great empires of Mexico and South America. . . . For the adventure, the magic, the exploration and the fun, you should try *A Secret Atlas;* it will be a discovery you won't regret." —*Fast Forward*

"A story rife with political intrigue, where everyone is vying to use his talents to get ahead . . . Definitely a new series to watch." —*Affaire de Coeur* (4 stars)

"Michael Stackpole has done a fine and clever thing with the first volume in his latest series. He has married famous moments from our own history during the classical period of discovery—say, the 15th through the 18th centuries A.D.—with a strong fantasy milieu, whose elements in turn mirror cultures we know, mainly Confucian China. This strong resonant underpinning, combined with ingenious fabrications and Machiavellian plotting, forms a rousing saga whose lineaments we are only beginning to grasp when this book ends on multiple cliff-hangers. . . . Finding romance in exploration and the acquisition of knowledge rather than warfare—although plenty of the latter still intrudes—Stackpole's novel resembles science fiction almost as much as it does pure fantasy, lending it allure for readers who might not otherwise be tempted by a mere Tolkien-style trilogy." —Paul DiFillipo, scifi.com

"With *A Secret Atlas,* [Stackpole's] tried to do something a bit different with the fantasy genre. Does he carry it off? Well, judging by this, the first book in what will develop into the Age of Discovery trilogy, the answer's a yes.... A fairly rich and agreeable stew... There are enough hints, clues, depth charges and bombs on slow-burning fuses placed in the story that you know the second volume is definitely not going to be short on entertainment." —sfcrowsnest.com

Cartomancy

"Adventure aplenty for those who like their fantasies big and bloody." —*Publishers Weekly*

"Stackpole handles these machinations masterfully and makes his plotters fully as intelligent as their plots... a powerfully compelling page-turner." —scifi.com

"Stackpole's unique voice makes this a pleasure to read." —*Kansas City Star*

"The fast pace continues in this exciting adventure, which has plenty of intrigue, mystery and passion.... This is a fun read, full of action, machinations and conundrums.

Different pieces of the past are exposed throughout the story, like bits of a broken mirror. There are times when it is not clear who are the good guys and who are the bad. . . . Stackpole demonstrates great skill in his character building, with even lesser players being fully formed. . . . Delve into this world and you will unearth a great *Age of Discovery*." —SFRevu.com

The New World

"[Stackpole's] tales have been compared to those by fantasy giants George R. R. Martin and Robert Jordan. . . . Think in terms of constant plotting by characters with hidden agendas, endless action, magic-fueled battles, ancient evils and epic heroism." —*Sacramento Bee*

"Stackpole writes on several fronts—political, military, familial—with a tincture of magical realism. That *The New World* holds together means he must have done some mapping of his own." —*Kansas City Star*

BOOKS BY MICHAEL A. STACKPOLE

BOOK THREE OF THE

BANTAM SPECTRA

Vastes

Deseirion

FELARATI

Iaras

Black River

Helosunde

MILES IN

DELAROTH

FUR

PECZISTOR

GRAN
MURROSO

The New World

Gold River

Nalenyr

GLOYSAN

AGE OF DISCOVERY

Erumvirine

Michael A. Stackpole

KELEWAN

Tyreoth

Eastern Sea

Miromil

1 = 150 miles

THE NEW WORLD
A Bantam Spectra Book

PUBLISHING HISTORY
Bantam Spectra trade paperback edition published July 2007
Bantam Spectra mass market edition / July 2008

Published by Bantam Dell
A division of Random House, Inc.
New York, New York

This is a work of fiction. Names, characters, places, and incidents
either are the product of the author's imagination or are used
fictitiously. Any resemblance to actual persons, living or dead, events,
or locales is entirely coincidental.

Bantam Books and the rooster colophon are registered trademarks and
Spectra and the portrayal of a boxed "s" are trademarks of Random
House, Inc.

ISBN 978-0-553-58665-7

Printed in the United States of America
Published simultaneously in Canada

www.bantamdell.com

OPM   10 9 8 7 6 5 4 3 2 1

To Al Gore,
To change the world you need vision and passion.
Thanks for sharing yours.

Acknowledgments

The author would like to thank Anne Lesley Groell and Josh Pasternak for their hard work on this novel; Howard Morhaim and Danny Baror for being the greatest agents in the world; and Brian Pulido and Kassie Klaybourne for their encouragement and support during the book's writing.

Turasyndi

Ixyll

ØPASLYNOT

Solaeth

Dolosan

TELARUNDE

SYLUMAK

Dreonath

EOLOTH

Irusviruk

Dark Sea

Iireath

Eurenyon

Tejanmorek

Ceriskoron

Ummummorar

(Five Princes)

Gloysan

The New World

Chapter One

4th day, Month of the Hawk, Year of the Rat
Last Year of Imperial Prince Cyron's Court
163rd Year of the Komyr Dynasty
737th Year since the Cataclysm
Voraxan

Ciras Dejote sighed and wished that the peace of Voraxan might once again infect him. Instead he wandered the empty onyx streets, passing between buildings carved from ruby and emerald, topaz, lapis, and citrine, and felt nothing. The architecture reminded him of the grand palaces of the Empire—relics of a time when heroes walked and epic tales were born.

He had grown up listening to such stories and had dreamed of someday becoming a hero. He knew the path to such immortality would require achieving *jaedun*—the magic that transformed an ordinary warrior into a Mystic. Through diligent study and practice, he could become a superior swordsman. But as a Mystic, he would be *supernaturally* gifted.

He had set out with his master, Moraven Tolo, on a quest into the Wastes, where wild magic still warped the land. Then his mission had changed. He and the inventor, Borosan Gryst, had set off deep into Ixyll, to find Voraxan, the resting place of the Sleeping Empress. They were to awaken her and bring her army back to the very Empire she had sundered over seven centuries before.

Ciras paused beside a small emerald building. He ran his fingers over the characters gently carved into the lintel: *Shan Tsiendao*. Within the building he could see her recumbent form, sleeping, dreaming, waiting to be summoned once again to war. Though *he* felt drawn back to the Nine Principalities, he regretted the necessity of awakening any of these warriors.

His quest to be a hero had brought him to this grand city of the dead, with tombs carved of gems, styled to be homes. It was not, however, a place of misery and remorse. The streets and buildings all combined instead to make it into a peaceful haven. Given that the warriors resting therein had fought the greatest battle in the history of the world, it seemed appropriate.

Ciras walked on, wending his way back toward the onyx courtyard of the ruby palace that had been the Empress' resting place. Trapped between the palace and a diamond fountain, Borosan Gryst sat tinkering with one of his magical machines. Despite the hardship of their journey together, the man remained overweight. He wore no sword and had neither martial skill nor sense. In Ciras' world, those deficiencies would have made the dark-haired man beneath contempt.

And yet, on the journey, Borosan had proven himself clever. *Almost too clever.*

Ciras' shadow fell over Borosan. "I cannot believe you hid the fact that Empress Cyrsa had already left this place." He opened his arms wide to take in the gemstone city. "We traveled across the known world, through strange lands and countless perils, and yet you kept that hidden from me."

Borosan smiled indulgently. "It was not a matter of trust, Master Dejote. I had been given a secret mission by the Empress. I did not tell my father. I would not have told Prince Cyron, had he asked. You should not feel betrayed."

The slender swordsman crouched beside his thickset companion, though he remained beyond the reach of the spiderlike *thanaton* on which Borosan worked. "I understand secrecy. Delivering the message to the people of Voraxan was very important. What would have happened if you had died on the way? The call would not have gone out."

Borosan shrugged. Both arms were elbow deep in the inner workings of the *thanaton*'s spherical body. "I would imagine I was not the only person the Empress sent with her message. I'm just the first one to make it. And . . ."

The *gyanridin*'s right hand emerged from the magical machine's bowels and tossed Ciras a small, yellowed ivory cylinder with delicate script carved on it. "If I died, there was always this."

Ciras caught it. The writing was in the old Imperial script and therefore taxing to read. "A poem?"

"By Jaor Dirxi. A meditation on the beauty of a

woman who became the Empress." Borosan nodded. "I was told he inscribed the ivory himself."

The slender swordsman twisted the top and slid the end off. A small scroll of rice paper fell into his hand when he upended the cylinder. He unrolled it. It contained the message Borosan had delivered. "Unsheathe your claws, spread your wings, and answer the call you have waited so long to hear."

The hand that had wielded the brush had been strong yet delicate. Something else struck him about the note, but he could not immediately identify it. Then he raised the note to his nose and breathed in.

Ciras' head snapped up. "The scent. This wasn't written by the Empress. This was written by the Lady of Jet and Jade. My master knows her. I caught the scent on his robes . . ."

Borosan shook his head. "You're too quick to jump to conclusions. You're correct in part. It *was* written by the Lady of Jet and Jade. Why would you assume that she is not also the Empress?"

Ciras rocked back and sat staring at the ruby palace. The Empress had led an army of Mystics to destroy the Turasynd horde raiding from the north. Their grand battle released untold amounts of magical energy, which swept over the continent, triggering the Time of Black Ice. The Nine Principalities had been devastated, and even now were only beginning to match their former glory and power.

The swordsman from Tirat frowned. "The Lady of Jet and Jade is a courtesan of incredible skill. She, too, is a Mystic, hence her longevity, but . . ."

"You must have known she became one of the last

Emperor's wives as a gift from a courtier. What did you think she had been previous to that?"

Ciras shook his head. "I know you people of Nalenyr think those of us from the islands are provincial, but we, too, have our houses of pleasure. I have no objection to the Lady of Jet and Jade, but she is no warrior, and yet, from the stories, I expected someone more like one of the Keru."

Borosan laughed and closed the *thanaton*'s body. "Yes, tall, strong, able to kill a charging elephant with a single spear thrust. Apparently skill at arms was not where her strength lay—and I don't intend that as a pun. She had the world's greatest warriors with her, many of whom are now being wakened from their Voraxan homes."

"And they will answer her call." Ciras shook his head. "I wonder what she will ask them to do?"

Borosan stood and brushed his hands off. "We will see when we return with them."

Borosan bowed past Ciras to a slender man with a bald head. Ciras stood immediately and bowed as well. "Greetings, Master Laedhze."

The warrior returned their bows. "I have news to impart and a favor to ask."

"Of course." Ciras answered for the both of them. "Whatever you need."

Vlay Laedhze waved a hand back toward the city. Throughout, people could be seen stirring within their jeweled homes. "We are waking our companions, and many are consenting to answer the call."

Ciras arched an eyebrow. "'Many'? I would have thought they all wanted to answer."

The tall man brought his hands together and hung his

head with resignation. "I have little doubt they all intended to answer when they first lay themselves down. Over the years a few of them have done their duty when wakened and have departed Voraxan. Others returned to their homes here, and embraced the peace of this city. You have partaken of this."

Ciras nodded. During his time in Voraxan he had slept very well. He had not once dreamed of violence or warfare. In dreams, he'd journeyed to far Tirat and visited his family. They knew nothing of his sojourns, but he was able to watch them and see that they were happy. That warmed his heart in a way quite beyond value.

Laedhze smiled gently. "The dreams are very seductive, and some will not awaken. And, alas, some of our companions have expired in their sleep. We know they have gone to a better place. They will rest happily in Kianmang, awaiting the call of another time to fight again."

"So how many will we have?"

"We have a battalion." Laedhze nodded solemnly. "We may have a few more."

Ciras' stomach twisted in on itself. "Two hundred forty-three warriors? Granted, they are all Mystics, but only three companies. How is that possible?"

Borosan caught Ciras' sleeve. "Ask him how many survived the battle."

Laedhze's expression became grim. "Just over four hundred."

"Not possible." Ciras tore his sleeve from Borosan's grasp. "All the stories . . . Even this place . . . How could four hundred have created it?"

The warrior from Voraxan clasped his hands at the

small of his back. "You have traveled past the battlefield. You have seen how the corpses continue to fight. Such was the violence of that day—the venom of each man, the strength of his will—that even death will not release them. Would you care to see the scars I bear from that day? To say we triumphed is an exaggeration—we barely survived. We were the Empress' Bodyguard. There were two thousand of us held in reserve."

He rubbed a hand over his face. "We were but a tenth of our army, and a twentieth of the horde we faced. The *vanyesh* had already been broken, but had bled much of the Turasynd horde. By rights, the nomads should have retreated; but they believed the Empress had brought her treasury with her, so they came on. And came and came and came. And we killed and killed and killed."

Ciras nodded, his anger ablated by the man's sober tone. "But this place, four hundred of you, how could . . ."

"You forget, Master Dejote, that this place was alive with wild magic. All of us were steeped in it. There were those of us who could work magic—not all the magicians belonged to Prince Nelesquin's *vanyesh*. They and a Viruk companion of ours shaped the magic and made this place. They made it to be our haven. If what you tell me of Tolwreen is true, then *vanyesh* survivors have done the same thing."

"But not as well." Borosan shook his head. "This place nourishes you, but Tolwreen is just a shabby mausoleum."

"I am certain they would just as soon call this place a mausoleum, too." Laedhze looked up, his face again a pleasant mask. "It is not a mausoleum, however, and we have not all just lain sleeping. It is with this in mind that

I need your aid, Borosan Gryst. You may come, too, Master Dejote."

Ciras agreed with a nod, his mind still reeling. The trio set off, with Borosan's *thanaton* pacing them. Its metal feet ticked loudly on the onyx road, reminding Ciras of the ringing of one blade against another. The peace of Voraxan was something he would know no more, and he felt certain none of those waking would ever return to it, either.

Laedhze led them into a bloodstone building and down a broad set of stairs. They emerged in what might once have been a natural cavern but had been shaped and carved into a stable of stone that extended into darkness. The nearest end had been transformed into a smithy, and though the fires were out, there was ample evidence that it had been very active throughout the ages.

Borosan gasped and drifted toward the nearest stall. "I don't believe it. I have dreamed it, of course, but . . ." He raised a hand and stroked a sleek metal muzzle.

The *thanaton* had wandered forward, and there was a clear kinship between it and the tall mechanical horse Borosan stood admiring. The *thanaton* had an insect's simplicity, but the steed revealed intricate gearing and springs, support pieces and joints. All the mechanical beasts had been decorated with plating, making them as beautiful as they were sturdy.

Laedhze pointed off into the darkness. "When we awakened to rotate through sentinel duty, we each assembled at least one of these creatures. We were given plans for how they were to be constructed and examples of the pieces. The original plans have long since been lost, though each of us has memorized them. We know each beast is meant to be ridden, yet each is immobile. And we know no magic to make them work, though we are certain some must exist."

Borosan moved into the stable and slowly made a circuit of the steed. He ran his hand over the flanks and along the neck, then reemerged at the head. He stared closely at it, then waved Ciras over. "Come here. I need your help."

Ciras frowned. "Have you forgotten I want nothing to do with your *gyanrigot*?"

Borosan looked back at him, incredulous. "This isn't mine. I mean, I dreamed it, but this is more refined. It . . . I can't explain, but I need your help."

Ciras approached reluctantly, and almost retreated when he saw himself reflected in the steed's dead ruby eyes. "What do you need?"

"Up there, by the ear, there is a spring-loaded catch. Press down and in."

Ciras did as he was bidden. Something clicked and he pulled his hand back fast, dropping it to the hilt of the sword at his waist. He reached out and tugged Borosan back with his other hand.

Borosan smiled, but did not laugh. "It won't hurt us."

With a hiss the faceplate tipped up near the ears and extended straight out, coming down near the muzzle. At the same time the steed's head dipped, bringing the cavity behind the faceplate into clear view. The fact that the ruby eyes still stared at Ciras did not make him feel any better.

Borosan stepped forward and poked at five narrow slots in a flat plate. "Of course. Brilliant."

The Voraxan warrior came forward. "What is it, Master Borosan?"

"The one useful thing I discovered in Tolwreen was an alloy of *thaumston,* which could store both the wild magic and directions for the operation of a *gyanrigot.* Made into command-slates and properly inscribed, they should power and direct one of these mounts. They work in the *thanaton,* so there is no reason they won't work here."

Ciras folded his arms over his chest. "I will not ride one of those things."

Borosan smiled. "On our horses we can go maybe thirty miles in a day. What if these will take us sixty, and in half the time? In a quarter of it?"

Laedhze nodded solemnly. "And think of these mounts in combat. Just their weight alone will shatter an enemy formation in a charge."

Ciras frowned. "And where is the heroism in that? It takes no skill and wins no honor."

The ancient warrior pressed his hands together. "Our final battle was not a matter of skill. There was no honor to be won. It was a war of survival, and we did what we were required to do. We won *because* we survived."

Ciras bowed. "I mean to suggest no dishonor."

"And I did not think you had." Laedhze smiled cautiously. "But the Empress has summoned us, and it is not to display skill or win glory. She summoned us because of dire peril. And so I will not hesitate to use whatever means are at my disposal to reach her side as fast as possible, and do her bidding with all the strength I possess."

Chapter Two

4th day, Month of the Hawk, Year of the Rat
Last Year of Imperial Prince Cyron's Court
163rd Year of the Komyr Dynasty
737th Year since the Cataclysm
Tsatol Pelyn, Deseirion

Keles Anturasi looked up at Tyressa. "Prince Cyron ordered you to kill me?"

The blond Keru warrior gave him a hard stare. "You are more valuable to Nalenyr than you could possibly imagine. You have knowledge of the world that would benefit *all* nations, including our enemies. I was tasked with keeping you safe."

"But in the event that I was captured, you were to kill me?"

"To keep the knowledge you possess from our enemies, yes." Tyressa nodded, then held out a hand. "Will you allow me to finish dressing your wounds?"

Keles shivered. When he'd thought Tyressa dead, he'd

realized how much he cared for her. When he learned she had traveled with a Viruk warrior over the length of the continent to rescue him, he'd fallen in love. He thought she'd felt something, too. Learning that her feelings were all that stopped her from killing him was disorienting, but still welcome.

"These orders from the Prince, do you consider them still in force?"

She closed her eyes. "No."

"Because . . ."

Her blue eyes opened again, but remained slitted. "Because I've seen what you have done here." She opened her arms to take in the expanse of Tsatol Pelyn and the armored warriors therein. "You resurrected this fortress from a midden, and you turned a rabble into an army. It is magic on a scale unseen. Not only is it paramount to get you back to Nalenyr, but it would be an abrogation of my responsibility if I killed you."

Keles frowned, but Tyressa did not let him ask the question forming in his mind. Instead, she took one of his broken and bruised hands and again began to wash away encrusted blood. "Keles, you have to understand the impossibility of any love between us. I am bound in service to the crown of Nalenyr. You are bound in service to your family, and they are likewise bound to the crown. In fact, your only chance at escaping the gilded cage that entraps your grandfather is for you to marry my niece. You could become the Prince Consort of Helosunde and have greater bargaining power over your position."

Keles sighed. "The problem being that your niece already has a husband. While I'm sure Prince Pyrust will be thankful that I've built this fortress back up, the troops coming after me have razed his capital. I think that might anger him."

Tyressa smiled. "There cannot be enough discomforts in Prince Pyrust's life." She dried Keles' hands and applied unguents to the abrasions. He'd broken them in frustration at his inability to save those who had followed him from Felarati when the Eyeless Ones came searching for him. He'd had an odd dream prior to the invaders' arrival, which suggested they'd been sent by Qiro Anturasi, his grandfather. Yet that was impossible, because creatures like the Eyeless Ones and their allies simply did not exist anywhere in the world. But even as he tried to take comfort in that, reality melded with the dream and made him think they *had* come from his grandfather.

And only my sister knew I was in Felarati. I dreamed of walking with her in a strange land. Was it a dream, or . . .

He hissed as Tyressa began cocooning his hands in silken bandages. "My hands are throbbing."

"They will for a while, but should heal well." She gently knotted a bandage off at his wrist. "Keep them clean and dry, if you can."

"I'll try." Keles sighed. "What are we going to do?"

"About what?"

"This place. These people." At the height of a storm, as the short, savage Eyeless Ones had closed on the ruined fortress, Keles had not only rebuilt the fortress, but had transformed the refugees. The eldest shed years, and children pulled them on. Armor and weapons had materialized, and the garrison could have fended off another assault. But they had no supplies. They could easily be starved out of the fortress.

"You should have filled the storerooms with rice and wine while you were rebuilding."

He raised an eyebrow. "You jest."

"I do, but I was also hopeful." She tied off the other bandage. "Could you not do that now?"

Keles shrugged. "I could if I knew what I had done. Rekarafi says this was the second time I did something like that. The first time I moved the cavern in Ixyll, but I have no real memory of that. Last night I felt urgency and frustration, and yet . . ."

"And yet, because it was not the same in Ixyll, you doubt that emotion has anything to do with it?"

He nodded. "I know of *jaedunto*. Moraven Tolo was a Mystic swordsman. The few times I saw him fight, he was almost emotionless. Since what I did last night required magic, I have to assume I reached a level of *jaedun*. In Ixyll that made sense: I drew a map because I'm a cartographer. But, last night? True, I had been working as an engineer in Felarati, but I have no significant formal training."

Tyressa dumped the bowl of water she'd used to clean his hands. "Not knowing what you did makes it difficult to repeat."

"There have to be common elements between the two situations. Both times I was singularly focused. I pictured things in my mind with incredible clarity." He shrugged. "That must be one piece to using magic, but I have never heard of anyone being able to do something like this."

"True." Tyressa looked around, then frowned. "If only you could conjure supplies. We cannot stay here. I need to get you back to Nalenyr, and I need to get Jasai away from Deseirion. Plus, we need to keep ahead of the Eyeless Ones. The sooner we can move out, the better. Don't you think?"

Keles thought for a moment, then realized Tyressa was asking him for permission to organize the survivors. "I trust your judgment. You have my support. How long?"

"By noon. We're in good shape. If the water supply holds, we'll be okay for a couple of days. There are villages we can hit for food. Once we get into Helosunde, we'll be among friends."

"I like the idea of being in Helosunde." Keles stood and offered Tyressa a hand. She took it gingerly and applied no weight or pressure as she stood.

"I will talk to Jasai about organizing the people. They are devoted to her."

"Good idea." He bowed to Tyressa and she returned it. As she walked away, various people approached her. They shot covert glances in his direction. A variety of them had drawn circles on their armor, or donned circular amulets.

To ward off magic. Keles shuddered and wandered toward the fortress' open gate. Over seven centuries ago, magic had caused a cataclysm known to all as the Time of Black Ice. Waves of chaotic magic had swept over the world, killing many and transforming others. Since then, any undisciplined use of magic was considered an abomination.

The people's reaction didn't surprise Keles. Right now they were all thankful for the transformation that had allowed them to defend themselves. Soon enough, however, they'd fear the power he had used. They would wonder if he could take away what he had given and why he hadn't returned them to their former selves.

But they were not alone in their fears.

He, too, feared what he had done. He could not control it. He couldn't even identify it. It was possible that he could accidentally do something even worse. He could become as bad as the *vanyesh*.

Stop it! Keles frowned as he walked down to the edge of the muddy moat. His whole life had been centered on learning how things worked, and yet here he was convinced he could never figure out how to control magic. Mystics respected discipline and training—both of which would sharpen a person's mind, free him of inconsequential thoughts, and allow him to concentrate on what needed to be done.

I need a task I can focus on. He squatted at the moat's edge and scooped up mud with his fingertips. He ran his thumb over it—something didn't feel right. It was cool and gritty, but not as rough as he would have expected. Not at all like the sand the Desei mixed to make concrete. It was the residue of the Eyeless Ones that had dissolved in the moat.

It didn't matter. Keles concentrated and recalled a memory of playing in the mud on the banks of the Gold River. His father had been there. Along with his sister, Nirati, he had been making castles out of the mud. While he and Nirati scooped out shapeless mounds, his father somehow transformed it into straight walls and tall towers.

He focused on that image and called to mind the conviction that the mud had a proper shape. He did not allow himself to entertain any other thought. He would make it into what it was supposed to be.

A tingle began at the base of his scalp and clawed its way up through his hair. Something shifted and mud dripped from his fingers. A castle loomed large in his vision. Suddenly he saw himself there, on the top of a tower, looking out over a vast continent. Mountains rose and fell. Clouds gathered. Fierce lightning crashed. Snow fell and winds howled.

Then the white curtain parted, revealing the slender figure of a man in a white robe, with flowing white hair. Around him, verdant grasses grew up through the snow. The man straightened, his gaze rising from the base of the tower.

A jolt ran through Keles. "Grandfather?"

Qiro laughed. "A tower? This is the best you can do? You thought you could supplant me, and all you can raise is a tower?"

"I never . . ." Keles shook his head. "Where are we? What is this place?"

Qiro threw his arms open, and mountains rose to stab through the clouds capping the valley. "This is Anturasixan. It is *my* world. I created it! I have done what you will never do."

"I don't understand." Keles leaned against the parapet. Though the stone appeared to be polished granite, it felt cold and wet, like the mud from the moat. "How did I come to be here?"

"You're not here. Not yet. But you will be. Soon. Come to me, Keles. You, too, can be a god."

Then the tower collapsed, reverting to mud, which splashed over Keles in a viscous wave. Something hard closed around his ankle, pulling him down. Keles kicked something solid, but the hold on his ankle only tightened.

Keles flailed his hands. They broke the surface. *The moat, it has to be!* His lungs burned, his flesh tingled. He kicked again, trying to swim to the surface, but the thing kept dragging him deeper.

Keles' lungs ached. To breathe was to drown, yet the urge was irresistible.

I've gotten my hands wet. Air bubbled from fiery lungs. *What a silly last thought.*

Then something plunged into the moat from above. The pressure on his ankle vanished as strong hands grabbed him by the back of the neck and thigh, then pushed him up through the muck. He broke the surface, sputtering, and sucked in cool air before landing hard and bouncing.

He tried to stop himself from rolling, but that only hurt his hands. He slammed into the fortress' wall and slumped over, swiping mud from his eyes.

A hulking creature emerged from the moat, mud sheeting off his body. The coating did not hide the bony plates on his arms or the hooks at his elbow. Mud dripped from clawed hands and water pasted long black hair against half his face. That face split with a grin that revealed an ivory phalanx of needle-sharp teeth.

"You must be more careful, Keles Anturasi." The Viruk's words came in a deep, gravelly rumble. "One of the Eyeless Ones caught you by the ankle."

Keles shook his head. "But there weren't any present."

Rekarafi brushed mud from his shoulders. "Not until you brought one to life."

"What?"

"I was there on the wall, watching. You scooped up mud, then let it drip back. The Eyeless One took shape. It grabbed your ankle and pulled you under."

Keles drew his knees up, the wall solid against his back. "But that wasn't what happened. I was trying to make a sand castle from the mud. All of a sudden I found myself in a tower, facing my grandfather. He wanted me to come to him, which was when the tower collapsed and I was dragged under."

The Viruk crouched and touched some of the mud to his tongue. He spat it out again and it steamed on the ground. "This mud is not from here."

"I had that same impression." Keles hugged his knees to his chest. "My grandfather created the Eyeless Ones. I think he shaped them from the mud of the land he created."

The Viruk's dark eyes widened. "He created life from nothing?"

"So it would appear."

"This changes everything."

"What do you mean?"

Rekarafi's eyes slitted. "If he can make life from nothing, he can just as easily make all life *into* nothing. And if you cannot stop him, that is exactly what he will do."

Chapter Three

4th day, Month of the Hawk, Year of the Rat
Last Year of Imperial Prince Cyron's Court
163rd Year of the Komyr Dynasty
737th Year since the Cataclysm
Wentokikun, Moriande
Nalenyr

Prince Pyrust of Deseirion wanted to laugh. There he stood, nine steps from the Naleni Dragon Throne. Prince Cyron, having lost half an arm to an assassin, sat there waiting to die. Yet, at the other end of the red strip of carpet running to the throne room's doorway, a small, dark-haired courtesan known throughout the Nine as the Lady of Jet and Jade had just *commanded* Pyrust not to kill Cyron.

The Desei Prince shook his head. "Beautiful and yet insane." He smiled at Cyron, stepping closer. "She'll not outlive you by much."

Cyron did not reply. He just stared past Pyrust, at the Lady of Jet and Jade, his eyes already glassy as if he were dead. Still, his nostrils flared with a heavy, irregular breath.

Pyrust intended to take another step forward, and another. With one strong blow he would decapitate his enemy. His sword would so swiftly pass through the man's neck that his head would remain in place until a bloody geyser vaulted it into the air. The head would land on the carpet, rolling to his feet, eyes staring up at him from a blood-dappled face. Then his greatest enemy would be dead, and Nalenyr would be his.

He sensed her at his elbow before she spoke. "Nalenyr will never be yours, Pyrust."

She had advanced silently and stood within striking distance. "You think it a rival nation, but it is merely another province in *my* Empire. I deny you the right to slay my provincial governor."

Pyrust spun, his sword poised to strike. "Prattle on about being Empress all you like, but it shall save neither you nor him. I am not a simpleton to believe in wishful tales. There is no protective matriarch who will return to save us."

The Lady of Jet and Jade smiled beguilingly. The courtesan's hand came up slowly, twisting, fingers opening as a lotus might blossom. The seductive gesture captivated him with its delicate ease. Then, there she was, right up against him, inside his guard. Her other hand rose up his rain-splashed breastplate and caressed his cheek.

Heat flashed through him, rising to his face. Sweat condensed on his brow and spilled down to burn his eyes. He remembered the sensation from his last coupling with his wife, Jasai. In the heat of passion he had gotten a child on her. The pleasure had filled him with warmth and peace.

Just as I feel now.

"No!" Pyrust went to shove the woman away, but she danced beyond his reach. He stepped toward her, but his left leg weakened and buckled. He went to a knee and a hand, still managing to keep his sword off the carpet. He tried to rise, but his right leg failed as well. He struggled to lift his head, then found himself on his knees before the Dragon Throne—a position he had imagined only in his worst nightmares.

His only solace was that Cyron, too, stared unbelieving at the courtesan. Had he moved, had he lifted his sword, Pyrust would have been at his mercy. The Desei Prince's limbs trembled uncontrollably.

The Lady of Jet and Jade bowed to both of them. "You have my sincere apologies for the fraud I have perpetrated. Since my return from Ixyll eons ago, I have known many leaders. You have given me the most hope—and caused me the greatest fear."

Cyron slowly shook his head. "It is not possible. You are not the Cyrsa of legend. You cannot be."

The woman smiled warmly, and yet with a superior air that almost made Pyrust believe her story. "Would this be because Cyrsa was the warrior empress who led the expedition to destroy the Turasynd?"

Both men remained mute, which drew a quiet laugh from her. "History remembers me as it does because I have spent a great deal of money bribing minstrels, storytellers, and playwrights to present me as a warrior worthy of the Keru. Many know that I was but a Pleasure Wife to the last Emperor; but since I led an army, they assume I had military training. But I was never a warrior, only a courtesan who was given to the Emperor to distract him. He dithered when decisiveness was needed to save the Empire, so I acted to save it myself."

Pyrust frowned. "Then you would be over seven hundred years old . . ."

"Closer to eight hundred, though I think the time I slept in Ixyll has not been counted against me." She brought her hands together at her waist. "I am a Mystic. Mastery of my arts has conferred upon me the customary longevity. You, Prince Pyrust, have had a mild taste of what my magic allows me to do."

Pyrust nodded slowly. He had not had an orgasm when she touched him, but his body responded as if it had. The intense pleasure, the exhaustion leaving him so weak he could not stand, the clues were all there. It was as if, with a simple caress, she could reawaken sensations to leave him sated.

Helpless.

He looked up at her. "You could have killed me, couldn't you?"

"Far more pleasantly than your Mother of Shadows harvests her victims, yes."

"Why didn't you?"

Cyrsa smiled. "It has never been my way to destroy assets which are useful to the Empire. *My* Empire." She looked past him to Cyron. "Prince Cyron has informed me of the situation in Erumvirine. The invaders, whoever they are, have likely taken Kelewan. From there, they can either strike south at the Five Princes, or north. But I have a feeling they've attacked in both directions and suffered for it."

The Desei Prince frowned. "Is their host that great?"

"I do not know, but the ego of their leader certainly is."

Cyron shook off some of his lethargy. "Who leads them?"

The Lady of Jet and Jade's face closed. "Prince Nelesquin."

"The *vanyesh* leader?" Pyrust weakly rubbed his half hand over his forehead. "He died in Ixyll."

"He did. I saw to it that he was entombed in the Wastes. Then the survivors and I—who had been bathed in so much wild magic that the miracles the *vanyesh* performed were as conjurers' tricks to us—retreated and built a sanctuary. We raised Voraxan with magic so the power could drain from within us. We did not wholly succeed and could not return here lest we destroy the Empire we fought to save.

"We slept, in shifts, and some of us went out on patrols. I was awakened and taken to Nelesquin's tomb." Her eyes focused distantly as she spoke. "It had been fashioned of black basalt and was flawless. We wrapped stone around it like thorned ivy. You could not look upon it and see it as anything but a fell place, a lair of vipers and poison. We hoped any who ventured into the Wastes would shun it."

Pyrust shivered, her words painting pictures in his mind of a dark place, twisted and obscene. The angles warped, the decorations grotesque and terrifying. There could be no mistaking the foul nature of what lurked behind those walls.

"But what we found rekindled terror in our hearts. Nelesquin had come on the expedition, bringing his *vanyesh* with him, but it was never his intent to save the Empire. His goal was to have the Turasynd and the Imperial heroes destroy one another. He had anticipated the Cataclysm and wanted his *vanyesh* to harvest the power. Then they would return to strengthen the Empire into a machine that would enable them to conquer the known world.

"And there, at his tomb, we found his ambitions had not died with him. His tomb had been burst open, *from within*." She stared at them intently. The chill running down Pyrust's spine tightened his bowels. "None of us had believed he would have the power to return from the dead. Apparently he did."

Cyron shifted slowly in his throne. "And this was when you returned to watch and wait. You built up your network of spies to alert you to his return."

"I had no choice."

The Desei Prince came up on one knee. "If you feared his return, why did you not work to reunite the Empire? As separate nations, we are at a disadvantage."

"I did not know *how* he would return. He might just as easily usurp a provincial throne as the Imperial throne. By maintaining the split, I denied him a significant power base. He, alas, found one elsewhere."

Cyron sighed exhaustedly. "Anturasixan."

She nodded. "I feared that to be the truth when you mentioned it to me."

"What are you talking about?" Pyrust looked from one to the other. "A land named after your cartographers? Did the *Stormwolf* expedition discover it?"

"No." Cyron's eyes narrowed. "Qiro Anturasi, it would appear, was able to achieve magic. He is a Mystic and, in the wake of his granddaughter's slaughter at the hands of a madman, Qiro lost his grip on sanity. He created a map with a continent drawn in his blood. He called it Anturasixan. The map warns 'Here there be monsters.' I fear that if the *Stormwolf* expedition did find it, they were destroyed there."

Blood drained from Pyrust's face, but he forced himself to his feet. "He has a continent to breed an army? How large is it?"

"A quarter of our landmass." Cyron looked off in the direction of Anturasikun. "I will show you the map, if I live that long."

The Empress shook her head. "There will be no killing. I need you both. Either one of you could have reunited the Empire. One by the sword, the other by gold. Prince Cyron, you have described Prince Pyrust as a wolf. That he is—ruthless and implacable. He may even be a match for Nelesquin in that."

Pyrust did not smile, determined not to reveal her flattery's effect on him. He could not be certain if the pleasure he felt was because of her magic, or the truth in her words. Either way, she was correct: two steps and he could still harvest Cyron's head, making Nalenyr his.

"And you, Prince Pyrust, you have rightly feared Prince Cyron's domesticating influence on you and your nation. Had the invasion not weakened Nalenyr, you would have been kept at bay indefinitely. Another disastrous harvest would have crippled Deseirion. Your nation would have become a Naleni client state. Soon thereafter, the other nations would have joined you, all bound with golden chains."

Pyrust would have bristled, save that Cyron appeared

to take no pleasure in her assessment. But what she said might well have been true. With Helosunde as a buffer between them, and its Council of Ministers willing to fight a proxy war, Nalenyr would have been ascendant.

So close. Pyrust slid his sword back into its scabbard, then stooped and recovered the lacquered wooden scabbard for Cyron's blade. "You need us both how?"

She smiled. "You each have your talents. You, Pyrust, will be my warlord. Naleni troops will march with your Desei warriors to destroy the invaders. You will crush Nelesquin."

Pyrust cocked an eyebrow. "And I leave my brother here to consolidate our nations with himself on the throne?"

"You forget, it is *my* throne, and I would have neither of you upon it. Political affairs I can deal with easily enough, but Cyron has special talents."

Cyron coughed lightly. "I fear, Empress, I will be of scant use to you in my condition."

"You will get better, I am certain." She crossed to him, accepting the scabbard from Pyrust, then freeing the sword from Cyron's hand and sheathing it. "You have never been a warrior, but your grasp of logistics is superior. This war will require as much organization as the Turasynd expedition, maybe more. Logistics were never Nelesquin's strong suit, and I mean to use that against him."

Cyrsa pointed the Naleni blade at Pyrust. "So you shall fight my war, and Cyron will enable you to fight it."

Pyrust's eyes narrowed as he looked past her to Cyron. The man still slumped in his throne, looking like an ashen-faced child trapped in an adult's armor. His grey pallor and the blood seeping through the bandages on his arm's stump suggested he was finished. And yet, in his light blue eyes, there now burned a spark, dispelling any notion that he was going to die of his wounds. He would survive.

He will thrive.

Pyrust nodded slowly. All his life he had prided himself on his heritage. The Desei had done so much with so little. He'd always wondered what he could do if given a tenth of his enemy's resources.

The Desei Prince rested a hand on his sword's hilt. "I have but one question for you, Empress."

"Please."

"You said before that you arranged for Nelesquin's demise. That he was a threat to you. How do I know that you do not see *me* the same way?"

Her eyes hardened, becoming at once cold and ancient. "I *do* see you as a threat. If I didn't, I'd not pit you against Nelesquin. If you were not a threat you'd have no hope of defeating him."

She leveled the sheathed blade at his heart. "You are a man of ambition. So is Nelesquin. I pit your ambition against his. When you succeed, you will be rewarded. Greatly rewarded, both of you."

"There cannot be two emperors."

"As long as I am alive, there may never be *one*." Her eyes softened. "But destroy this threat to my empire, and many possibilities may make themselves known."

Chapter Four

4th day, Month of the Hawk, Year of the Rat
Last Year of Imperial Prince Cyron's Court
163rd Year of the Komyr Dynasty
737th Year since the Cataclysm
Jaidanxan (The Ninth Heaven)

The god who had once incarnated as Jorim Anturasi fought to maintain a grasp on his human identity. It was a task worthy of a god, because a human life seemed so insignificant compared to the divine. What mattered the travails of the mortal when the very nature of reality was at risk?

Jorim—for this is how the dragon god Wentoki sought to identify himself—largely maintained a human form. At least in size and shape, though his skin had become scaly. From throat to loins, he had a rich golden hue, while the rest of his flesh had a supple ebon color allowing him to vanish into shadows, which almost made him laugh because, as a god, he could do so without effort.

He looked up, suddenly aware of other presences in his palace. Each of the nine gods had a palace floating above the mortal plane. White marble flowed in strong lines that abstractly defined his nature as a dragon. Gauzy curtains danced on breezes. The broad stairs led down to a balcony from which he could overlook the world.

Tsiwen, his elder sister, the goddess of Wisdom, all but flew down the steps. Her black robe bore the crest of a white bat on the wing and her sharpened features hinted at her thoughtful nature. Dark and beautiful, her wide eyes bespoke sagacity; she could be counted upon for good counsel.

With her came two other gods. Grija, grey and wolfish, let his nervousness betray him. He stank of death, the essence of his nature, and his appearance reflected it. His threadbare robe hung poorly on his gaunt frame. The fur covering his legs had fallen out in patches, revealing red and irritated flesh beneath.

Between them strode Chado, one of the eldest of the godlings. He moved deliberately, muscles rippling. He appeared human, in deference to Jorim's choice, but wore an orange robe with black tiger stripes. As the god of Shadows, he allied himself very closely with Grija and was the author of many of the world's ills. Yet while Jorim recognized the uses of disease and rot in fostering a renewal of the world, he still had little love for his brother.

Jorim opened his hands, allowing golden talons to sprout from his fingertips. "Welcome to my domain."

Grija snarled anxiously, almost tripping on the last step. "Have you given any thought to what I told you? Have you done anything about it?" He tensed, and might have leaped at Jorim had not Chado's hand landed heavily on his shoulder.

"Easy, brother, for he is still unused to his true nature." Chado smiled easily enough, but his predatory grin did little to ease Jorim's sense of doom. "I understand you wish to be addressed as Jorim."

"That serves its purposes, yes." Jorim ignored his brothers and embraced his sister. "You are always welcome."

"And always pleased to be here."

Jorim allowed himself to imagine her embrace as warm. Releasing her, he turned to his brothers. "I have spent the night thinking on what you said, Grija. I do not doubt you believe it is necessary for me to slay my mortal sister. It is a solution to a problem. I am not convinced, however, it is the *only* solution."

The god of Death bristled. "I am not stupid! When will you realize that?"

He would have lunged at Jorim, but Chado restrained him yet again. "I feared his reaction might be hasty, so Tsiwen suggested I might explain. Where should I start?"

"Grija told me that my mortal sister, Nirati, is causing a problem. She is dead, but *somehow* not dead. She has escaped Grija's realm. I can imagine such things, but what I find curious is that she is beyond his reach but not mine. How is this possible? We are gods. Is anything beyond our reach?"

The tiger god released Grija and began to pace. "Ultimately, no; but directly, most assuredly. It begins with the tree of creation. This reality we all share is the trunk of the tree, and many are the branches. We are all part of it. We are born of it, created by the one who created everything."

Jorim nodded. "Nessagafel?"

"Yes, our father." Chado waved a hand at the world below. "We are part and parcel of his creation. We, too, have created things. Some of us create things of substance, and others create things more ethereal."

Tsiwen laughed easily. "Leave your brow unfurrowed, brother. Nessagafel created the Viruk, and we are powerless to affect them directly. He protected them, at a cost to himself, which made him vulnerable. Chado has fashioned diseases, some of which we may blunt, others of which we cannot."

Jorim rubbed a hand over his jaw. "What did I create? Nessagafel incarnated as a Viruk. Did I create Men, then become one?"

Chado laughed. "No, brother. Men were a creation we, the Nine, collaborated upon. You have created other things, like the Fennych, but you reserved your greatest creation for the benefit of mankind."

Grija scratched at his arm. "This is what has caused the problem."

Tsiwen took Jorim's left hand between hers. "You have not let yourself remember much, but you are the youngest of us. As such, you sought the most to please our father. While we made mankind, you watched him and his Viruk. You saw him give them magic, and you resolved that a different type of magic would be your gift to Men. That is a most dangerous gift, however, and you were opposed in your desires."

"Why?"

"Because it ruins everything." Grija stabbed a hooked

finger toward the mortal plane. "We had seen it with the Viruk. Magic gives them an ability which should be ours alone: the ability to alter reality. You know what the unfettered release of magic can do in the world. Men are too limited to understand how to control such power. Even the limits you placed upon it are insufficient to preclude disaster."

Fear thrummed through Jorim. Grija's explanation, curt though it was, captured the dilemma perfectly. Magic allowed Men the ability to create. If they could create, they could presumably bar others, including the gods, from having a direct impact on their creation.

It would allow them to become gods themselves.

Chado nodded. "You see it, Jorim. We have always found ways to subvert the protections. Nessagafel created the Viruk. They enslaved our Men. You created the Fennych as a scourge upon the Viruk, and you denied Nessagafel the right to interfere with them. I created a variety of maladies that could attack all three. This allowed for a balance."

"But if there was a balance, how did it became necessary to destroy Nessagafel?"

"Events, one tipping into another; things unforeseen and unpredictable." Chado stopped at the edge of the balcony and leaned heavily on the balustrade. "When Nessagafel created the Viruk, he was still proud of us, his children. He made us gods among them, and we were worshipped. The Viruk thrived, and yet their enslavement of Men came to rankle. Tension grew, and Nessagafel realized two things. The first was that the Viruk were a superior creation to his own children. Second, and far more important, he realized that in creating us, he had granted us enough power that we could stage a revolt against him. He became determined to prune all the branches from creation, save for the Viruk. He would remake everything, and unmake us."

Jorim frowned mightily. "How do you know this?"

The god of Shadows laughed. "Through you."

"Me?"

Tsiwen patted his hand. "You loved our father and sought his attention. Yet you remained loyal to all of us, so when the true danger manifested, you opposed him."

Jorim laughed. "Sounds like my grandfather Qiro."

"In many ways they are linked." The goddess of Wisdom smiled easily. "Allow yourself to think on the name Talrisaal."

Jorim immediately recognized the name as being of Viruk origin, but his understanding stopped there. Yet concentration unlocked deeper memories. Before his mind's eye, a scene unfolded deep in the jungles of Ummummorar. Jorim swooped down, his vision piercing the dense veil of leaves. As Men saw color and heard sound, likewise foreign emotions resonated through him.

Below, a band of Viruk raced along a twisting jungle trail. Full-grown warriors, save for one, they fled. One crashed through the brush ahead of the juvenile, while the half dozen others constantly tossed glances back at their pursuers. The warriors mumbled prayers to Kojai, the god of War, thinking he might be more merciful than the mighty and terrible Nessagafel.

But the young one, Talrisaal, prayed to Wentoki. He sought courage so he would not dishonor himself amid the company of warriors. He feared dishonor more than he feared death, and the fervency of his prayer attracted Wentoki's attention.

Their pursuers boiled through the rain forest. Fennych moved in a vast band, low to the ground, teeth flashing and claws rending vegetation. When he had created the Fennych, Wentoki had made them gentle—a clownish crossing of small apes and bears. He did, however, imbue them with some magic, and it allowed them to change shape to adapt to new situations. In winter their coats might lighten, or if they hunted in caverns, their eyes would grow wide to sharpen their vision.

But in the presence of the Viruk, they lost all pretense of humor and became hardy predators. Viruk magic could not stop them, at least not directly. Warriors could kill them, but not easily; Fenn claws could shred their flesh as if it were smoke.

One warrior fell, then another as knots of Fenn pounced and rent them. The furred carpet of muscular bodies would have muffled any scream had the warriors time to voice one. Blood gushed and the Fenn anointed themselves before bounding off to kill more.

The Fenn advanced in a crescent with wings extending past the lead Viruk and closed slowly. The Viruk burst into a clearing. The scout plunged on through, reaching the tree line, then stumbled back with a half dozen Fenn tearing out mouthfuls of flesh. The two in the rear guard never even made it to the clearing, leaving the last two warriors warding the youth, staring out at the luminous eyes blinking from the shadows.

Though the warriors tried to restrain the youth, he stepped forward and spoke in a clear voice with no detectable fear. He described a circle with a finger and a wall of fire burst into existence around the three of them. The flames rose to the height of Talrisaal's eyes. The warriors hunkered down, waiting and watching.

The Fenn drew the scout's body into the forest.

The youth stood there, not cowering, but slowly turning to stare back at the Fenn. Fear still lurked within him, but he refused to surrender to it. He sought to project courage, and praised Wentoki's name with every breath. He wanted the Fenn to know he would not run or scream. Though they might kill him, they would never break him, and even the Fenn seemed to acknowledge that as truth.

Wentoki manifested in the clearing as a man. The Viruk stared at him. Talrisaal could not hide his astonishment at a Viruk god choosing to assume the form of a slave. The youth dropped to his knees and touched his forehead to the ground.

"It gladdens my heart, oh Wentoki, that you would come see how your gift is spent." The innocence of youth filled the words with sincerity. "I shall not dishonor your gift."

Wentoki chose to ignore the warriors who still begged for his dog-brother's intervention. "You've prayed for courage to die well, Talrisaal. You don't need it."

The Dragon god gestured and the flames vanished. Darkness fell, shot through with snarls and screams.

Then the flaming circle returned, smaller, with the youth kneeling at its heart. The blood of his companions had been splashed over him, but no other trace of them remained. The fire's renewed light did not fill the clearing, and the Fennych had encroached to shadow's edge.

"Do you test me to see if I will be unworthy of your gift?"

"You are days and weeks from home. You are alone. Have you sufficient wisdom to survive?"

The youth's mouth gaped for a moment. "I do not even have the wisdom to know how to answer you."

"Then you will pray to my sister, Tsiwen." Wentoki opened both arms and the circle of Fenn parted. "You have no need for courage, but I should not hesitate to lend it to you if you did. Go now. Tell no one of our encounter; they would not believe you."

The young Viruk got to his feet and, without looking back, began the long march to his home.

Wordlessly, Wentoki commanded the Fenn to escort him. Talrisaal traveled north in the company of forest spirits that guided him to freshwater, scared away predators, and watched over him while he slept. All of this Wentoki observed from afar.

Jorim blinked. "Talrisaal became a great sorcerer among the Viruk."

Chado nodded. "When our father thought to remake the world, he chose nine of his Viruk to replace us. They were sorcerers all, well versed in the warping of reality. He revealed to them his plan to supplant the gods, and Talrisaal revealed the plan to you. With the courage you lent him, he rebelled. While our father was distracted fighting to preserve Viruk unity, we were able to strike and kill him."

"But not destroy him completely." Jorim glanced at Grija. "He was trapped in your realm, in a place of your creation, which was why he could not escape."

"Not until your sister did."

"How did she do that?"

Tsiwen gestured and the world spun beneath them. Out in the vast Eastern Sea loomed a new continent. "She is there, in a place called Kunjiqui, in the land of Anturasixan."

Jorim stared down. "A continent named for my family. How?" He thought for a moment and pain radiated through his chest. "My grandfather, he has become a Mystic. He created this place and pulled Nirati into it instead of losing her."

"Is that so hard to understand?" Grija snarled, baring his teeth. "You created human magic, and through it this place was created. We are barred from interfering there, but you are not. Go there, destroy her, and the threat of our father's return can forever be ended."

Chapter Five

6th day, Month of the Hawk, Year of the Rat
Last Year of Imperial Prince Cyron's Court
163rd Year of the Komyr Dynasty
737th Year since the Cataclysm
Kelewan, Erumvirine

Prince Nelesquin dismounted before the walls of the Illustrated City. He would enter the capital of his empire on foot, unguarded. His new subjects might not believe he was *that* Prince Nelesquin, but as long as they knew he was both strong and fearless, that was all that mattered. Strong, because those who had conquered the city would bend their knees as he passed. Fearless, because he would walk through Kelewan's streets unarmed.

The large man strode confidently toward the Violet Gate. It was the smallest of the city's gates and only those of royal blood were allowed to pass. The massive purple doors slowly slid open and a dozen of his Durrani warriors fell crisply into ranks on either side. The dawning sun washed gold through their silver mail and lightened the blue of their flesh. The sharpened tips of ears appeared through thick, dark manes, and their amber eyes searched restlessly.

As he drew closer, the warriors dropped to a knee, hammered right fist against left shoulder, and bowed their heads. Not all at once, of course, but in sequence, so someone could always ward him. And beyond them, on the shadowed road, their commander waited, even more watchful.

Nelesquin's blue eyes tightened. "If you are here to greet me, Keerana, then I assume Gachin is dead?"

The Durrani leader nodded once before dropping to a knee and saluting his master. He held that posture until bidden to rise again. As he stood, he drew his sword and presented the hilt to Nelesquin.

"What is this?"

Keerana looked up, meeting Nelesquin's gaze without fear. "Had I not petitioned you for permission to pacify the Five Princes, I would have been the one assaulting Tsatol Deraelkun. I would be the one lying in state."

Nelesquin threw back his head and laughed. "Tsatol Deraelkun has defeated the greatest of warriors. Even I was defeated there once."

Keerana frowned. "How is that possible, my lord?"

Nelesquin beckoned his warlord to walk with him as he started through the narrow streets. The tall buildings choked off all but a bare glimpse of the sky, but it did not matter. Nelesquin only had eyes for Quunkun, the Bear Tower, and the palace that was meant to be his.

"It was not your failing, Keerana, that cost Gachin his

life. He fell to a man who once defeated me on those plains. We were brothers." Nelesquin shook his head. "Would that my blade had slipped and killed him then."

The Durrani, trailing half a step behind and to the left, kept his voice low. "The man called himself Moraven Tolo. He took Gachin's head, though he had the grace to let us recover it."

"It does not matter what he calls himself. I know who he is. I will deal with him in time." Nelesquin's voice trailed off wistfully. He studied the buildings lining the street. Kelewan had been divided into a dozen cantons of varying sizes, and the Violet canton was home to nobility minor and major, as well as embassies from the provinces. They thought of themselves as nations, but Nelesquin refused to acknowledge them as such. Their birth had been as illegitimate as that of Gachin's killer.

The colorful murals decorating the buildings earned the Illustrated City its name. He strode past one embassy—Moryth by the look of it—its layers of images celebrating historical high points. Lies and fantasies all, as near as Nelesquin could tell. He would order the walls whitewashed and repainted with more suitable work.

He would have issued an order to Keerana to begin the task, but he would not dishonor him. The Durrani had been created to be perfect warriors, and they were. Nimble, strong, fearless, and intelligent, they had spent generations fighting every challenge Nelesquin had thrust upon them. The Durrani who had sailed from Anturasixan had conquered most of Erumvirine with blinding speed, and had likewise pacified the Five Princes. That secured the southern border, so now all that remained was driving north into Nalenyr and beyond.

Soon, very soon. Nelesquin smiled, turning onto an avenue that widened on its way to the heart of the city and the palace, Quunkun. The Prince paused and the Durrani came forward. Keerana dropped a hand to the sword at his hip, but Nelesquin's grip on his shoulder restrained him.

"There is no danger, Keerana. It's just that the beauty takes my breath away."

Unlike the gaudily painted city surrounding it, Quunkun remained unadorned. The building had been clad in white marble. Nelesquin found it easy to imagine he'd been gone only a week, not seven centuries.

He glanced at his warlord. "They did not surrender the tower without a fight."

"No, Highness." Keerana looked up at him. "We rounded up masons and quarrymen and the damage was repaired as best as possible."

"Very well done. It is as I remember it." Nelesquin picked up his pace and, moving into the wide courtyard surrounding the tower, became aware of how much destruction had been visited upon Kelewan. While the Violet canton had been scoured clean, soot still stained other buildings. Empty windows stared back at him with shutters askew. People, gaunt and moving slowly, huddled in shadows or listlessly picked through middens for scraps.

"Have the people been much trouble?"

"Resistance collapsed with the military. Prince Jekusmirwyn was convinced to make a public statement which put an end to any other trouble. We control the storehouses, so people must come to us for food."

Keerana smiled wryly. "Each person is entitled to a fistful of rice a day, but our quartermasters give more to those who serve us."

"You have dealt with this wisely. Have you also assumed the post of Dost, so you may properly lead your people?"

"Not unless you deem I should, my lord."

"The position is yours, Keerana." Nelesquin ascended the broad steps to Quunkun. He entered through doors that bore no sign of the battle for the tower. His boots clicked against the rotunda's marble floor and again he paused. Beneath the dome had been placed a bier. On it lay a body, which he assumed to be that of Gachin. A tall, slender figure in an emerald-and-black hooded cloak stood beside the body, his extended hand wreathed in purple fire, which he passed forward and back over the corpse's chest and head.

Keerana stepped forward, his sword coming to hand with a hiss. He moved without hesitation; Nelesquin marveled at how easily he stalked ahead—effortless and lethal. That he faced something he had not seen before did not daunt him.

"Keerana, wait." Nelesquin smiled. "Friend, throw back your cloak so my eyes may confirm what I know in my soul."

The purple fire died as the figure reached up and unclasped the cloak. It fluttered to the ground, revealing a man wearing a jet robe with a green dragon coiled breast and back. The slender man smiled, and delight played through his hazel eyes.

He dropped to a knee and bowed his head—though

he held the bow neither as long as Keerana had nor Nelesquin liked. "Greetings, Prince Nelesquin. It has been forever."

"At least you could mark the time, Kaerinus. This is a luxury unknown in Grija's realm." Nelesquin put aside his pique with minimal difficulty, then grasped his friend by the shoulders. "This has been a long time in coming."

"As per your plans, my lord." Kaerinus stood and nodded toward Gachin's body. "He is too far gone for me to revive. His spirit and soul have fled. He is lost to you."

"No matter." Nelesquin waved the Durrani warrior forward. "This is Keerana, now Dost of the Durrani. And this, Keerana, is Kaerinus, one of my *vanyesh*. Certainly the most faithful of them. You were named in his honor."

Kaerinus smiled. "You must feel the others out there as I do, my lord. They gather to your service."

"I feel many things." Nelesquin extended a hand toward the corpse and invoked a spell. He sought to confirm what he already knew. "It *was* Virisken Soshir who killed him. How is it that he still lives?"

"I do not know, my lord." The wizard gestured vaguely toward the north. "I have spent my time in Nalenyr healing those who dare risk the touch of magic. We made it infamous. They blamed the Cataclysm on us. The *vanyesh* are seen as fell creatures whose return to the world is dreaded."

Nelesquin laughed. "It is good we are feared."

"But we were also anticipated. I felt Soshir again, dimly and distantly, last year at the healing. He did not know who he was then, but I think my magics may have helped him learn. He will be coming for you, of course."

"Of course. It was to destroy him and his ilk that I shaped the Durrani. Keerana here would kill him with ease. Is that not correct?"

The Durrani warrior dropped to a knee. "As my lord desires."

"That, and more." Nelesquin smiled. "More ships are coming, and aboard them I have many weapons to crush Soshir and his army. You will choose for me a cadre of your best warriors—yourself included—and you will rise to heights you could not have imagined."

Keerana nodded, then bowed his head. "Shall I begin now, my lord?"

"Please. My friend and I shall make ourselves at home."

The warrior gave Nelesquin a salute, then withdrew. The Prince looked at Kaerinus. "They are quite remarkable in their loyalty and ferocity. Rather like dogs in that way, only smarter."

"Not many dogs would engage Soshir at Tsatol Deraelkun."

Have you forgotten I did just that and lost to him? Nelesquin watched his companion for a moment, then shook his head. "You will see Keerana engage him there and take the fortress."

"That is a bold claim."

"He would sooner die than disappoint, and with what I have brought, he will prevail." Nelesquin sighed and glanced at Gachin again. "Their loyalty does complicate things. Imagine, allowing this one to rot here in the palace."

The Prince gestured, and violet energy trailed from his fingers. It swelled to a billowing cloud that engulfed the corpse and bier both. Lightning flashed argent within the cloud. The heat of high summer pulsed heavily enough to send Kaerinus' cloak rolling across the floor. It wrapped itself around the base of the column within the empty alcove.

A wan smile twisted Nelesquin's lips. He waved his hand toward the alcove. The cloud filled it, then fell away like Kaerinus' cloak, unveiling a statue of Nelesquin.

Kaerinus smiled. "Very well done, my lord. Your return makes things right again."

Nelesquin opened his arms, intending to rise on magical wings, but weakness washed over him. He staggered, yet before he could fall, Kaerinus caught him. He lowered the Prince to the ground, but Nelesquin refused to be prostrated before his own statue.

Nelesquin shoved him away, surprised at his own weakness. "Speeding my ship, making that statue . . . I have overtired myself."

"There is some truth to that, but it is not the whole of the matter."

"I have not felt this weakness before."

"Yes, you have. You have just forgotten."

Nelesquin shook his head, but dizziness sapped his strength. He sank back onto his elbows. "It was not like this, the time we perfected the magic. I felt some weakness, but it was transitory."

"As this will be, my lord; but you will tire."

"I don't understand."

Kaerinus crouched beside him. "When we perfected the means to sever your spirit and soul, then draw your soul from your body, we guaranteed you could not die. When your body ceased to function, Grija drew off your spirit and thought your soul had come with it. Your spirit languished in his realm until your return. Body, soul, and spirit form the eternal triangle—your spirit anchoring your soul in whichever realm it inhabits. Your spirit drew to it the materials to create a body as you emerged from the underworld, but this creation was not perfect. You feel the lack of your soul. Once we return it to you, you shall be greater than you ever were."

"As we planned." Nelesquin smiled. "I have not forgotten the bargain, Kaerinus. When I am world emperor, you shall rule many nations. Ours will be the whole of the earth. You, me, and my consort."

"Consort?"

"Nirati Anturasi. She is the one who granted me escape from the Nine Hells."

Kaerinus' eyes narrowed. "Nirati Anturasi. I know her. I have touched her with magic. I had not thought she was that powerful."

"No matter." Nelesquin sat up again, clutching his knees to his chest. "I shall husband my strength until we can undo what was done at my death."

"Do you sense where your soul lies?"

Nelesquin concentrated for a moment, then nodded. "North, distantly north. If I could feel more, I would command it to appear."

"And the effort would likely kill you."

"Ironic, no?" Nelesquin slowly rose to his feet. "I felt

something else. The Empress. She stands between me and my destiny."

Kaerinus shook his head. "That is not a place I should like to be."

Nelesquin smiled. "That is an opinion I am sure she will quickly come to share."

Chapter Six

RUNDE 8th day, Month of the Hawk, Year of the Rat
Last Year of Imperial Prince Cyron's Court
163rd Year of the Komyr Dynasty
737th Year since the Cataclysm
Tsatol Deraelkun, County of Faeut
FOLOTEL   Erumvirine

I leaned on the battlements of Tsatol Deraelkun and stared down at the battlefield. Green fields had been churned into bogs of grasses, matted with blood. The *kwajiin* had recovered their dead companions and withdrawn. My scouts had trailed them, and reported they were returning to Kelewan.

It didn't matter. We knew they would appear again, soon.

The blue-skinned warriors had abandoned the bodies of their *vhangxi*. I really couldn't blame them, as the batrachian creatures had smelled none too pleasant in life, and even less so after they had been slaughtered. The web-footed, leaping beasts were good in an open-field battle—that much I'd seen when they destroyed the Iron Bears. Laying siege to a mountain fortress, however, requires more brains than bravery. The *vhangxi* had neither.

The mud had begun to dry, freezing footprints as if they were tiny fluctuations on a calm brown sea. If I looked closely, I could have picked out tracks of scavengers, including a few of the *vhangxi* survivors hiding in the nearby woods. They would venture out to feed, and House Derael's archers placed bets, then killed them.

A small island lay at the center of the battlefield, with a stone circle upon it. I'd come close to dying there. Gachin *had* died there, and his assault with him. Had he killed me and left anyone alive to remember the fight, I might have had a small shrine erected in my memory.

Instead I just had a story destined to become legend.

As with other Mystics, though, I was healing quite nicely, and far more quickly than a man of my years should. My right ear still itched from where the Soth Gloon, Urardsa, had sewed it back on. The wound in my chest had closed, but it still hurt when I coughed. One more scar in a lifetime of them. But the good thing about scars is they mean you survived.

"Master Tolo, are you going to die?"

Smiling, I turned toward the boy who had climbed up to share the tower with me. I'd met him when he was only nine, on the road with his father and grandfather, bound for Moriande and the Harvest Festival. Barely six months later, it was hard to recognize him. Dunos had been small for his nine years, but bright-eyed and happy. He weathered his withered left arm well: his greatest desire at the time had been to become a swordsman, though he would have been happy to help in the family mill.

Even now, despite the horrors he'd witnessed, he still possessed a touch of innocence. His lower lip trembled and his green eyes glistened. "They said you were going to die."

I slowly shook my head. "They misunderstood."

"They said the Gloon saw it. They can see the future."

"Not always, Dunos." I removed the twin swords from my robe's sash and sat at the base of the wall. Dunos sat at my feet, his withered arm looking close to normal sheathed in ring mail. He'd been given a red robe once worn by Pasuram Derael, resplendent with the family's wounded-bear crest embroidered in yellow. In spirit, he was one of them.

I made sure my voice was warm. "Do you remember when we were in Moriande and went to the healing Kaerinus performed?"

"We were there with that lady, Nirati."

"Yes, we were. You saw that big scar on my chest, re-member?"

He nodded. "It looked like someone tried to cut you in half."

"They did a better job of it than the *kwajiin*. I went to the healing in hopes that it would be healed. It wasn't." I tapped a finger against my temple. "There was some-thing else I needed healed and, over time, it has been. The scar...well, I remember little about it. It's much like you and your arm."

"I was out playing and found a glowing stone in a riverbank. I grabbed it and don't remember anything un-til my father fished me out of the mill stream." Dunos lifted his left arm and let it drop. "When I woke up, my arm was like this."

"I remember you telling me. You were a mile or more downstream, but you survived. I survived, too, and woke up in my master's home. They took care of me. They nursed me back to health. My master trained me to be a great swordsman. He passed on all the lessons he'd learned from *his* swordmaster, Virisken Soshir."

I handed him one of the two swords I carried. "Take a good look. The cords wrapping the hilt are orange and black in a tiger-stripe pattern. The man who carried them came from Moryth."

He peered closely at the cords. "Yes, I see the little bronze tiger charm under there."

"That's Chado, the tiger of heaven. Look at the hand-guard. You see the dragon at the top of the disk? That means the swords were manufactured before the fall of civilization. They also mean the swords belonged to a member of the Emperor's Bodyguards."

Dunos nodded. "Virisken Soshir."

"You're absolutely right."

He looked up. "Why did Count Derael give these swords to you?"

"He didn't give them to me, Dunos." I met his wondering stare openly. "He *returned* them to me."

Dunos' brows arrowed together.

"The thing Kaerinus healed was not the scar, but the memories I'd lost when I was so badly hurt. I'm not Moraven Tolo, not really. I'm Virisken Soshir."

The boy blinked, not comprehending.

I couldn't blame him. I'd found that realization completely alien, and yet I'd also known it was true. Somehow, over five hundred years had passed between the time I rode with Empress Cyrsa to Ixyll and found myself at *Serrian* Jatan. My former apprentice became my master, never revealing to me who I really was. In retrospect it was easy to see he'd known all along but had never seen fit to tell me.

Dunos pushed through his confusion and focused again. "Didn't the Gloon say you were going to die?"

"No. He said because I now know who I truly am, I'm *free* to die. But I've been close a number of times, and I really have no taste for it."

"Me, neither."

I reached out and tousled his brown hair. "That's good. I don't want you dying. You have a long life ahead of you."

He shrugged. "I'm pretty good at avoiding the *vhangxi*. They've hit me a couple times, but it hasn't hurt."

"Excellent."

"So, you were a warrior a long time ago?"

"I was the last Emperor's bodyguard. I was one of his sons—not a prince like Nelesquin, but I was trusted nonetheless. Then the Turasynd came."

"That was a long time ago. You're alive because you're a Mystic, right?"

That *was* the obvious answer. I was alive, in part, due to being a Mystic. But Phoyn Jatan, who had been younger than me, was now far older. It should have been impossible that I had somehow skipped several hundred years of aging, but I'd met Ryn Anturasi. Count Derael said Ryn had given my swords to his ancestor, and yet he was hale and hearty when I met him. Moreover, he had some odd conveyance that had transported me from the heart of Ixyll to Erumvirine in the blink of an eye. Given evidence that he could instantly travel vast distances and perhaps even through time, I had to assume that he found me and brought me forward to be healed and re-trained as Moraven Tolo.

"I think you're right, Dunos." I frowned. "You've seen the scar, though. Someone wanted me dead, and I don't know why."

The boy shrugged with the confident carelessness of a child. "It had to have been Prince Nelesquin. He was your enemy."

"Life is never as clear-cut as bards' tales." I wanted to elaborate, but a thought occurred to me. The Time of Black Ice and the war against the Turasynd had created two key figures: the Empress Cyrsa and Prince Nelesquin. She waited, sleeping, to save the former Empire. He was evil incarnate and the source of all the hardships that had befallen the world. His *vanyesh* were demonized. And various other heroes, like Amenis Dukao, had their cycle of stories, which never let common citizens forget the great sacrifices made to stop the Turasynd.

But Virisken Soshir remained virtually unknown. I'd learned a great deal about him, but only from Phoyn. The stories about Cyrsa seldom included anyone even close to me, and even when they did, my name was man-gled beyond recognition. Granted, some of the stories Phoyn told me were unpleasant, I had clearly not been an easy taskmaster. But I'm sure the people I'd led from Kelewan would agree with that assessment.

Ranai Ameryne would. In our escape from Kelewan, I'd used a crowd of hopeless souls to distract the enemy so we could break through their siege lines. Though memories of my life as Virisken were distant, disorganized, and fragmented, at the time I felt no difficulty with what I had done. Virisken, an Imperial bastard, had no qualms about using his inferiors. I had been ambitious—easily the equal of my half brother—so a conflict between us was inevitable.

Thinking on it now, however, I did feel remorse. I'd told Ranai that the people were destined to die anyway, and that some of them *might* escape. I didn't believe it, but I also did nothing to help them. If I had turned my force and attacked, more of them might have gotten away. We surely could have pulled some out with us.

But would one or two, or even a dozen, have made any difference? Virisken would have said no because they were homeless peasants being driven before the invaders. People like them always fell to advancing warriors, just as mice fell prey to hawks. It was the way of the world.

But that was the attitude of a bastard child who believed himself better than his legitimate kin. He should have been in line for the throne. He would rule more efficiently and better than they had. However, the chances of his attaining that throne were nonexistent.

Unless there was a revolt and a new dynasty replaced the old.

I shivered, because the person I had once been felt no qualms about that idea either. In fact, he found it attractive.

But I was no longer that person. *That* was the reason Phoyn had trained me as he had. It was not to hone my skill with a sword, but to remake me as a man. The trauma of my wounding had cost me my memory, and

Phoyn made me over into the man he had perceived me to be. He saved me in more ways than one.

I blinked. "Forgive me, Dunos, I was lost in thought."

"My grandfather used to . . ." The boy's voice trailed off. He pursed his lips and turned his face from me.

I reached out and turned it back as a big tear carved a track through dirt. The boy sniffed then smeared the tear across his cheek. "I'm sorry, Master."

"Don't be, Dunos. I met your grandfather, remember? He was worthy of tears. Your father as well—your whole family. You're right to mourn."

"I hate the *vhangxi*."

"You're not alone."

Dunos pressed his lips into a tight line. "Why didn't I die?"

I shook my head. "I do not know, Dunos. I know you wish your family was alive. Why Grija takes one person and not another is a mystery only the gods can answer."

"A witch in our village said I was Grija's pet." Dunos spat to his left. "I hate him, too."

I smiled. "I expect you're his worst nightmare, young man."

"Why do you say that?"

"You're young, you're brave, you're certainly not afraid of him, and others can learn from your example." I narrowed my eyes. "He's never been my favorite god."

"Why not?"

"He may be the god of Death, but what does he do? He takes the weak and defenseless. He skulks." I touched the hunting tiger emblazoned on my robe. "Chado is a true hunter. Wentoki the Dragon is courageous. Even the Virine bear is steadfast and strong, and Kojai is the dog of War. He's worthy of worship, but not Grija."

Dunos shivered. "But Grija can trap you in any of the Nine Hells."

"After what we've seen? How scary will that be?" I shrugged. "Besides, we will have other gods to help us into Kianmang. That's where warriors are supposed to go."

Dunos smiled. "And I can get in there even with my arm?"

"I will guarantee it." I winked at him. "I'll tell the gods you were so great a warrior you only needed one arm."

He laughed and I joined him. It felt good to be laughing. The sound banished the last lingering bits of malevolence left over from the battle.

"One thing is very important, Dunos."

The boy nodded. "What, Master?"

"You have to keep hoping. The *vhangxi* killed your parents, but we don't know that they got Matut. He may be out there looking for you."

The boy considered, then nodded. "And that's why we kill the monsters. To keep him safe."

"Him and everyone like him."

Dunos stood and hauled himself up to look over the battlements. "They'll be coming again, won't they?"

"And they will be ready to destroy us."

"Will they?" He lowered himself and stared at me.

"Tsatol Deraelkun was meant to *discourage* invaders, but no one ever imagined it would stop them. The *kwajiin* have taken Kelewan and who knows how much more. If they bring their full force to bear, this fortress will fall."

The boy frowned for a moment, then looked up at me. "Now that you have these swords, you have no use for your others, right?"

"Right."

"I'll get them. You can start teaching me." He nodded solemnly. "Teach me well. If I'm going to Kianmang, I'm going as a swordsman."

Chapter Seven

22nd day, Month of the Hawk, Year of the Rat
Last Year of Imperial Prince Cyron's Court
163rd Year of the Komyr Dynasty
737th Year since the Cataclysm
Tolwreen, Ixyll

Ciras Dejote wished he had stuck to his principles and refused to ride one of the *gyanrigot* mounts. Borosan had been correct. The constructs could go further and faster than horses. A virtue, certainly, but training ate up time that would have better been spent on the road home.

The problem lay in figuring out how the things actually worked. Borosan started from the assumption that they were similar to his *thanatons*. He created control-slates to command them, which they dutifully obeyed. Still, the devices did nothing to provide for interaction with a rider.

Thus began a second phase of testing and instruction that revealed the variety of hidden abilities the mounts possessed. When a rider swung into the saddle, for example, armored plates fanned out from the mount's shoulders to protect his legs. This led Borosan to examine the creations even more closely. He modified control-slates so the mounts would respond to pressure on switches: if a rider pressed in with a left knee, the mount would turn right—and the amount of pressure would determine how tight the turn would be.

And they could be quite tight. Ciras shifted his shoulders. The bruising was almost gone, but some of the stiffness remained. He'd decided to see how sharply one of the mounts could turn midgallop. He dug his right knee in hard. The *gyanrigot* pivoted on its left forehoof and came about immediately, launching Ciras into the air. He hit hard on his back and bounced, then found the mount standing there, stock-still.

Borosan had helped him to his feet. "It would seem, Master Dejote, the *gyanrigot* are capable of things humans cannot withstand. I will make sure that will not happen again."

"No. Make no changes to hobble the mounts."

The inventor looked askance at him. "I thought you did not like these things."

"I do not. But I would not ask a swordsmith to dull a blade because a clumsy student might cut himself."

So as much as he disliked the metal mounts, he forced himself to master riding one. He pushed himself to become the expert, and then helped instruct others. He even made suggestions to Borosan that further refined the mounts' capabilities.

He enjoyed training the others; it made him feel worthy. He turned in the saddle as they rode through a glass valley in Ixyll and studied the twisted reflections of the heroes. Three companies of warriors, Mystics all, who had survived the battle with the Turasynd and the Cataclysm. These were people who had been legends in the Empire. They had kept faith with their leader, and over seven hundred years later answered the call to duty once again.

Vlay Laedhze rode up beside him, his shaved head protected by a leather helmet. "You seem amused, Master Dejote."

Ciras shook his head. "More amazed. I have long dreamed of being a hero. I wanted to be worthy to have served with you. Even so, I cannot imagine doing what you have done."

"Surviving? Remaining faithful?" The elder warrior shrugged. "These are really little things. Survival, well . . . is there another choice? Survival depends so much on chance. Why would an arrow take a man standing beside me and not me? Arrows do not target the virtuous or the malign; and those shot in volleys fall without the true intent of the archer."

The man smiled slightly. "And faith, how difficult is that? You make a decision and you choose not to question it. You honor the wisdom you exhibited when you made the choice."

"And what if it was a mistake?"

"Then you must honor the wisdom that has shown you the mistake. You rectify it."

"That is not always easy."

"Do you think you have made a mistake, Master Dejote?"

Ciras spat disgustedly, then patted the neck of the mount he rode. "I am astride one of these."

Vlay laughed. "It's been a long while since I have been in the saddle, but I have no complaints. This is as fine a horse as I have ever ridden."

"But, Master, it is not a horse. It is a machine. A monster."

"And you find you like it."

"Yes." Ciras shook his head. "These *gyanrigot,* they are evil, they truly are. They put magic in the hands of those who do not have the discipline to control it. They are a danger."

"A danger to whom, Ciras?"

"To the world. To peace. Things like this mount, or a *gyanrigot* sword, or one of Borosan's *thanatons,* can convince anyone that he is a warrior. Armies can be raised and equipped and nations can be destroyed."

"And how is this different from the magic you possess?"

"I have spent years perfecting my skills. I am aware of what I can do, how badly I can hurt others."

"And have you ever attacked anyone without just cause?"

Ciras shook his head. "Of course not."

"Then you are a very fortunate man." Vlay gestured toward the east. "You were raised to see us as heroes, but we were—and still are—humans like you. We have made mistakes. Take the Turasynd war, for example. The Turasynd invaded, but why? Are they just evil, raiding for the sake of plunder?"

"That is what I learned." Ciras studied the man's distant expression. "Is that not what happened?"

"I believe it is, but I have heard many things. I've heard that a company of Imperial Dragons went raiding in the Wastes. Perhaps they wanted plunder. Perhaps they were out to punish the Turasynd for raiding in Deseirion. I do not know the truth of it, but I am confident there is a truth somewhere."

Vlay looked at him and smiled. "The reason I point this out is simple—the Imperial Dragons had the same sort of training as you, yet it did not prevent their commander from giving orders to kill women and children. Training and discipline are no brake on ambition—nor is a lack of training a license to revert to barbarism."

"But is it not true, Master, that a man who is aware of his responsibilities will be less likely to abandon them?"

"True, but let us examine two situations. The first is one in which a leader you trust gives you an order to kill. He tells you the target is evil and must die for the good of the world. You do as you are bidden and, it turns out, you have just slain a poet whose only crime was to write a satire about your leader. You have acted responsibly, but you have been made into a tool for evil despite your discipline."

Ciras nodded. "I would be bound by honor to pursue justice and make amends."

"Honorable as that is, it won't bring the poet back to life. The second case is simpler still. If discipline is the brake on ambition, then the only way to prevent war is to train everyone to wage it. If everyone was a warrior such as yourself, do you foresee a time of eternal peace?"

Ciras started to answer, then stopped. All the training in the world might not blunt ambition. In fact, ambition could motivate training. His own ambition to become a

hero was what kept him training when he might well
have quit. *Another's ambition to become emperor could drive
him as I was driven.*

"You are correct. Discipline may not counter ambition. But this is no reason to put lethal weapons in the
hands of those who have no understanding of what may-
hem they will cause."

"I agree, Master Dejote. Your solution, however, is to
label the tool *evil.*" The elder warrior shrugged simply. "I
reserve my judgment for the means in which the tool is
employed. You have trained with the sword. Now you
will train with this metal horse. Master it. Justice will
curb ambition, and, through you, a sword and a mount
may serve justice well."

The Voraxani expedition headed southeast as quickly
as possible. Because it was home to the *vanyesh,* Tolwreen
became a target. Empress Cyrsa might not have called
them forth to destroy the *vanyesh,* but allowing them to
live would not be serving her.

Ciras had feared the path to Tolwreen would be hidden. He and Borosan assumed the *vanyesh* would be
watching for them, so the expedition remained alert as
they approached.

But the way to Tolwreen had neither been hidden, nor
had it been guarded. They found the mountain strong-
hold without difficulty and even spotted their own
tracks from three weeks previous. The preservation of
the tracks unnerved Ciras. It was as if no time had
passed, and he found it easy to imagine he would somehow see himself and Borosan escaping again.

The tunnel at the mountain's base gaped open like a mouth waiting to swallow them. Borosan sent two of his spider-legged *thanatons* in, and they returned without incident. One even brought with it a small *gyanrigot* mouser that was still in full working order.

Borosan held it up. "This was the one you gave to Pravak."

"Did he abandon it because he knew we used it to track him, or is it bait for a trap?"

Vlay took the mechanical kitten from Borosan. "Pravak was never terribly subtle. If he was present, he'd challenge us immediately. Shall we ride in?"

He kicked his heels back, prompting the mount to trot forward. Ciras fell in line behind him, taking heart from the fact that the giant statues that had guarded the entrance were no longer present. Metallic hoofbeats echoed through the short tunnel, then the riders entered the heart of the mountain and spread out.

"They've gone." Borosan pointed to the remains of the citadel that had once stood tall and proud. "And they've taken their weapons with them."

Ciras nodded. The citadel had been pieced together with swords and shields, armor and spears. It had been a martial masterpiece. Now the wires that once suspended it hung slack and what remained lay scattered like gold coins spilled from a cut purse.

Wildmen emerged from the distant shadows. Some brandished weapons as if they were talismans. A few had pulled on armor. Greaves hung awkwardly from shoulders, and bracers pinched calves too tightly. Helmets had been put on backward, then tipped up to let the wearer see his feet.

Vlay clapped his hands commandingly and the wild-men scattered, hooting and screaming. He turned in his saddle and looked at Ciras. "There is discipline for you."

"Where have the *vanyesh* gotten to?"

Borosan pulled a small, boxy device from a saddlebag. "There are several mousers below the Prince's Hall. Let's see what they're doing down there."

It took some hunting, but they found a series of tunnels that carried them deep beneath the mountain. Using Borosan's device to guide them, they entered a series of natural caverns that opened into one huge cave that had been extensively altered. At first glance, it reminded Ciras of the workshop where the mounts had been created in Voraxan, only much bigger.

Borosan dismounted immediately. He attached blue *gyanrigot* lights to his *thanatons* and explored. The ghostly light revealed massive forges with huge hammers and tongs, supported by geared circles that allowed them to rotate freely. Further a device with smaller hammers could be seen; and beyond it were other machines with arms ending in even smaller hammers for fine work.

Borosan paused near the large device and held up one of the command-slates. "The *vanyesh* used these forges to create the bodies they wore. I cannot tell what else they might have made, but there is a pile of command-slates here. They probably have mounts just like ours. They might even have created enough for the Turasynd Black Eagles."

Ciras shivered. "Would they be that insane?"

Borosan shrugged. "You saw them. Most had left

humanity behind a long time ago. They were talking to the Turasynd. Why would they hesitate to arm the barbarians?"

"I can't imagine." Ciras sighed. "Can you make sense of those slates?"

"Probably. If we fire up the forges again, we can see what they were making. I can make more parts for our horses. I've had some ideas since we rode out . . ."

"Figure out what they were doing first." Ciras looked at Vlay. "What are your thoughts?"

"The *vanyesh* clearly believed Nelesquin was calling them to arms. I don't know why; Nelesquin is dead. His head was struck from his body and both were buried in a tomb built to the Empress' specifications. The tomb was disturbed, however. We can assume the *vanyesh* violated it. You said his skeleton is housed in a chamber above us."

Ciras nodded. "Gilded, every inch of it, save for the skull, which was missing."

"Show me, please."

Vlay and a handful of warriors accompanied Ciras up to the Prince's Hall. Tall, narrow, and deep, the chamber seemed even more forbidding because it lacked the reflected light from the *vanyesh*'s golden robes. Tiered seating rose on either side. Entering, the hall appeared as if it had been abandoned for eons.

Three weeks, and already decay has set in.

Hand on sword hilt, Ciras marched beside Vlay. They stopped just shy of the purple strip of carpet leading to a massive stone throne.

Vlay nodded. "It's the Celestial Throne, the one Nelesquin coveted."

Ciras drew his sword and pointed at the purple garment discarded across the throne's arms. "The skeleton had been wearing that robe."

"It looks like the one we buried Nelesquin in." The ancient warrior shook his head. "We'd placed his tomb at a crossroads so he'd not know which way was home. That precaution, apparently, was insufficient."

Chapter Eight

23rd day, Month of the Hawk, Year of the Rat
Last Year of Imperial Prince Cyron's Court
163rd Year of the Komyr Dynasty
737th Year since the Cataclysm
Helosunde

Keles dropped to a knee on the forest trail. He could sense the others behind him, but they had learned to keep quiet when he raised a hand. He pressed his right hand to the damp loam, rubbed a bit between finger and thumb, and concentrated.

The world flowed away from his consciousness. He focused on the cool, wet soil staining his fingers. He caught an immediate sense of decayed leaves and dirt churned by deer hooves. Men had passed this way, too. But that impression was fleeting and unreliable; it could have been yesterday or two hundred years before.

His sense spread out from the soil and sped across the surface of the earth. The world unfolded in his mind, spreading out like thick oil. Awareness surged over hills and down through ravines. It poured over rocks and flowed into streambeds. It grew thin at fords, and eddied where water curled around smooth stones.

Experience helped him read the land. He knew woodlands well. They were heading south across rising land, so the ravines tended to run to the north and east. Their runoff would eventually trickle into the Black River.

He pushed his senses further into the land and felt a tingle at the base of his scalp. There, off to the east, up and around a steep-sided ravine, lay a forest clearing. It was big enough for the refugees to camp. A bit further east was a stream from which they could draw water, and the forest had enough windfall to provide firewood.

Keles opened his eyes and smiled as Rekarafi appeared in front of him. "Over there, about a quarter mile. A clearing?"

The Viruk nodded. "There was a small one. Will it be bigger when I scout it out again?"

"It's big enough." Keles rubbed a hand over his forehead, smearing it with dirt. "You seem to think that I make a decision and the world changes. It's not like that."

"I have seen the changes you have wrought. I have *felt* the magic." The Viruk squatted and carved a symbol in the ground with a talon. "You must understand what you do so you may claim it as power."

"Perhaps it is a power I don't want. And yet, if I do not master it, my grandfather can destroy the world."

"Think, Keles. Tell me how the power works."

Keles closed his eyes. "I don't impose my will on the land. I simply see things the way they are supposed to be.

At least that's what it feels like. I just see what is meant to be there."

"Meant by whom?"

The cartographer opened his eyes. "I don't know. Me? My grandfather? The gods? Maybe the land itself. All I know is that I see what feels right. Do you suppose that is possible?"

"*Possible?*" The Viruk rose and pointed off toward the clearing. The group's scouts led the people past in a serpentine procession that disappeared into the growing dusk. "Did it feel right to remake the people?"

"Maybe, in a way. The children became the adults they would have been, and the elders regressed to the people they had been. The minister and his guards became idealized versions of themselves—every bit the heroes they imagined themselves. Only you, Tyressa, and Jasai remained unchanged, because you are the people you were meant to be.

"The land, though, I wonder . . . In Ixyll, the magic changed the land in many ways, but there were basics that did not change. A valley might grow living metal flesh, but it was still a valley. Rocks might have been transformed into giant fruits, but they still rolled downhill. Is it possible that the world itself has a magic that can resist magic? Is reality too difficult to change on so vast a scale?"

Rekarafi's ivory teeth glowed in the twilight. "I have lived for many years, Keles Anturasi. I saw the Viruk Empire collapse. I saw the empire of Men collapse. There are constants. This idea of the land possessing its own magic is not without merit. Perhaps you need to concentrate on finding what exists and perfecting it."

Keles smiled. "Flow with the river, not against it?"

"It makes it less likely that you will be destroyed by the current." The Viruk waved him on. "Let us see if what you thought matches what I remember seeing."

The refugees had already begun to make camp and establish guard positions by the time they arrived. They organized on a standard plan, with the warriors occupying an outer ring and Princess Jasai's shelter constructed in the middle. The guard stations pushed out into the woods. Given the nature of the Eyeless Ones and how they hunted, the company would need ample warning of their approach.

Fortunately, the sour weather that had kept them soaked for much of their trek south had also limited their pursuit. Rekarafi had estimated that they had gained a day over the Eyeless Ones, and their monkeylike companions had not been seen for a week.

Keles smiled at the Viruk. "Is it what you remember?"

"You only changed it a little. Bigger. Better drainage." The Viruk shrugged off the baggage he'd been carrying. "Next time, bring the deer yard closer."

As Rekarafi dashed off to hunt, Keles picked up his gear and carried it over to where Jasai sat before a small fire. He pulled off his own pack, then sat. He rolled his shoulders around and felt a series of pops ripple up his spine. He groaned, and she smiled as she fed a small stick into the fire.

"Keles, you really must let me carry something when we head out again."

"You are carrying enough, Princess."

The blond woman stroked a hand over her stomach.

"Yes, I know, the future of Helosunde—a child to unite my nation with Deseirion."

"It doesn't matter whose child it is. It's enough that you're carrying a child." Keles looked around at the others preparing their shelters and lowered his voice. "And you are the leader of our expedition. These people are loyal to you, not to Deseirion."

Golden firelight could not melt the ice of her blue eyes. "They are my husband's subjects. He had them so cowed they would follow me to the Mountains of Ice and through the Gate to the Underworld. They are suspicious of everything here. They see themselves as enemies in a foreign land."

"Is that how you see yourself?"

She snorted, anger tightening her eyes. "I should. The Council of Ministers chose my brother to be Prince, then convinced him to attack Meleswin. They abandoned him there, and Pyrust took me to wife and to bed. The only reason they will be happy to see me is to use me as leverage over Pyrust."

Keles laughed and she turned her cold stare on him. "You are amused by something?"

"Just by how wrong they are. Anyone thinking you're a means to an end is a fool—and that includes Prince Pyrust."

She looked a bit mollified by that, but Keles had already learned not to take too much comfort in appearances. Jasai had told him that, for her, he was also a means to an end. She had meant to use him to enable her escape from Deseirion. But her aunt had suggested that Jasai had grown to love him.

I wonder what the reality is. He had no way of knowing,

and no mind to trust any assumptions. In fact, he didn't want to make assumptions because he was in love with Tyressa. Though he found Jasai desirable, Tyressa was even more so. But if Tyressa did not exist, if Jasai was not married to the Desei Prince and carrying his child . . .

Too many ifs, and none of them real.

For a heartbeat he wondered if he could change such things—make *if* into *is*. That would greatly reduce the complications in his life. But what shone gloriously for a moment became dark and twisted a second later. In many ways, his grandfather had used his will and influence to change the lives of those around him. He had even swapped Jorim's fate with Keles'. In a fit of pique he'd exchanged their missions. Had his grandfather possessed true magic then, there was no doubt he would have used it to do that and worse.

Keles frowned. Perhaps that was the problem with magic. When it came easily, the magician had no sense of consequence for his actions. Rekarafi said he'd improved the drainage in the clearing, yet the plants in the center preferred swampier soils.

To dry the clearing I shifted a thousand cubic feet of water.

From the lay of the land, it had drained off to the west and into a ravine. The trickle there would have become a small flood. The swollen stream would have boiled through the forest.

Keles stopped imagining and began *seeing*. Further downstream the water undermined the support of a small stone bridge. The bridge began to crumble. Stones shifted and mortar cracked. The children playing on it froze. Angry water splashed high. One of them screamed . . .

"No!" Keles thrust his hand into the water. He lifted the bridge, held it together. The children shrieked, but leaped to safety. The bridge's stones tumbled into the raging stream, trickling like gravel through his unseen fingers.

"Keles!"

His eyes jerked open as Jasai slapped his hand aside. A shower of hot coals arced out and hissed against the moist ground. He shook his hand, then slapped at his smoldering bandages.

"What were you doing?"

"Um . . ." He glanced off into the distance. "I think I stopped a small flood from killing two children."

"By digging your hand into the coals?" She reached out and took his hand into hers. She brushed away the ashes. "Are you hurt?"

He slowly shook his head. "No, I don't think so. It doesn't hurt at all."

"You have to be careful."

"I'll try." He exhaled and weariness pounded him. "I don't know if I imagined things or . . ."

"It doesn't matter." She kissed his palm gently, then released his hand. "No harm done."

A day later, as they followed the trace of the flooded stream, they came across the ruined bridge. They forded there, and following Keles' instruction, found the house where the children lived. Their father happily guided the refugees to a nearby village, and from there riders were sent to a larger town to summon help.

The refugees nearly outnumbered the villagers, but

they did not seem concerned. They immediately put Princess Jasai up in the Headman's home and began preparations for a celebration. The refugees were divided up into small groups to be housed in the village, where they chopped wood, hauled water, and otherwise traded sweat for hospitality.

Yet as much as the villagers revered Princess Jasai, they stood in awe of her aunt. The Keru were legendary for their courage, and since they served Prince Cyron of Nalenyr, they'd not often been seen far from the court at Moriande. Tyressa constantly had a gaggle of young girls following her, spying on her from behind buildings or beneath wagons. Tyressa bore her semidivine status with good humor and even devoted an hour to drilling the girls in the fine art of marching.

All was proceeding well, with food being prepared and tables gathered in the village square, when one of the riders returned from the trek to town. He reported that authorities would arrive in a day or two to help the refugees. He also reported that Prince Eiran had been slain.

The news of her brother's death crushed Jasai. Keles found her hugging a homespun blanket around herself, weeping quietly. What had been planned as a raucous celebration became a muted memorial.

Keles sat with her, holding her hands while she told him about her brother. "I was so angry with him. He hadn't the courage to stand up to Prince Pyrust. He let Pyrust take me away—and what made it worse was the look in his eyes. He wanted to act, but he couldn't. He was too afraid, too unsure. In that one moment, he realized he'd been used by the Council of Ministers and, because of that, I had been put in jeopardy."

She sniffed. "I'd vowed I'd never forgive him but . . ." She shrugged and Keles brushed a tear from her cheek. "In recent months, I had softened my stance. I wanted my child to have an uncle. Pyrust had killed his brother, so Eiran was my only choice."

Keles smiled weakly, happy his face was hidden in shadow. "I'd be happy to stand in as an uncle. My brother, too, I'm sure."

She closed her eyes and pressed her cheek against his hand. "Thank you. Please do me a favor?"

"Anything."

"Stay here this evening. Just . . . sitting here. I don't want to be alone."

"Of course, as you desire, Princess."

Help from the outside came faster than predicted. By the next noon a local militia battalion arrived. A few had arms and armor, but most had flails, pitchforks, and other tools. They asked the refugees to lay down their arms, and seeing the wisdom of that request, Jasai gave the order. What tension had been in the air evaporated, and the village again began preparations for a celebration.

By midafternoon, a tall, well-muscled man in ministry robes wearing a sword rode up on a well-lathered horse. He dismounted and spoke to the militia's leader. The captain gave orders and his men began to form up. The minister then approached Princess Jasai and bowed to her—but not too deeply and for none too long.

Jasai regarded him warily. "You are Ieral Scoan. I remember you as the one who brought the crown to my brother."

The man produced a handkerchief and wiped his upper lip. "I am flattered, Duchess."

"You needn't be. I do not remember you fondly." Jasai raised her chin. "Duchess was the rank I was given by the Council of Ministers. I am a princess now."

"Yes, of Deseirion." He smiled graciously, but contempt crept through his words. "But we are in Helosunde. Here you are a duchess, nothing more."

Keles took a step forward. "But nothing less."

Scoan laughed quickly. "Actually, much less." He produced a small square of folded paper, sealed in red wax. "You are requested to report to Vallitsi and appear before the Council of Ministers."

Jasai stared down at the paper, then back up at him. "And if I choose to ignore that *request*?"

"Forgive me. I never meant to imply you had a choice. You're under arrest." The minister gave her a predatory grin. "You've been consorting with the enemy, Duchess. You'll be tried for treason and hanged by the neck until dead."

Chapter Nine

23rd day, Month of the Hawk, Year of the Rat
Last Year of Imperial Prince Cyron's Court
163rd Year of the Komyr Dynasty
737th Year since the Cataclysm
Wentokikun, Moriande
Nalenyr

Save for decades of practice, the Naleni Grand Minister could not have kept surprise and outrage from his face. He had served the Komyr court perhaps not always enthusiastically, but diligently and certainly above the level the Princes deserved. The Komyr Princes had never fully appreciated the role the bureaucracy played in stabilizing the world.

But this—this outrage—showed how far Prince Cyron's mind was gone. *And Prince Pyrust has joined him.*

Pelut Vniel stood in the doorway to the Naleni throne room, with a phalanx of lesser ministers behind him. Wooden columns split the room in three. A red carpet edged with purple occupied the center and ran right to the door. Had Vniel stepped through incautiously, he would have trod where only nobility walks, and his life could have been forfeit.

To the left of the throne stood Prince Cyron. He wore a purple robe emblazoned with a golden dragon. Pelut had never seen the robe before, and the way the dragon coiled around a golden crown certainly had not been seen since before the Empire had been sundered. The crown's nine points each bore a sign of the Zodiac, the foremost pair being those of the Naleni dragon and the Desei hawk.

Pyrust aided and abetted Cyron in this lunacy. He wore a deep blue robe with a flying hawk emblazoned on it. The left wing had two feathers clipped, marking the Prince's half hand. The hawk was poised to land on an Imperial crown, within which nested two fledglings. The image again had not been seen since before the Cataclysm.

But it was the third person, the woman seated on the Dragon Throne, he focused upon. She was Prince Cyron's whore—uncommonly beautiful and rumored to have been a bed companion to previous Komyr princes. Her imposture was an absurd satire, worthy of Jaor Dirxi or other artists of his ilk.

The ministers behind him gasped.

The woman on the throne snapped open a fan as if to shield herself from the sound. The fan was emblazoned with a purple crown, as was her antique golden robe. The woman sat the throne as if it truly belonged to her, and her calm shocked Pelut so much that he finally began to assess what he was seeing.

The way she deployed the fan and used it to shield her

face meant the ministers were to take no notice of her. She clearly understood the games played at court, but she was not alone in being able to invoke symbols.

Pelut bowed deeply to her and held the bow for only as long as appropriate to honor the throne had it been empty. He then straightened and bowed first to Prince Cyron, holding it for as long as was appropriate for the ruling Prince. He waited for Cyron to acknowledge his gesture, but the half-armed Prince graced him with nothing more than a nod. When he bowed to Prince Pyrust, Pelut only got a grunt, but he covered his reaction to this affront passively.

Entering the room, Pelut had a choice. As Grand Minister, he could take a place at the throne's right hand, but doing so would place him before Prince Cyron. Alternately, he could position himself on the left. Since both men's left arms were crippled, through this choice he could signal his willingness to serve the throne more ably than they could.

He chose this latter course, skirting the edge of the carpet and making certain the hem of his robe did not touch it. He moved forward with tiny steps. The gait was appropriate to the occasion, and it allowed Pyrust's impatience to simmer nicely. Pelut reached his appointed place and bowed low to the throne again as his ministers filed into the room behind him.

Once their shuffling had ceased, he came upright again. "It is my pleasure to see both of you well, my Princes."

Cyron nodded dismissively. "I am feeling more hearty, thank you."

Too hearty. The last time Vniel had seen him, Cyron

had been three-quarters dead and appeared to be losing ground. Pyrust's invasion of Nalenyr had brought a foreign army to the edge of the city. Traitorous westron nobles had thrown open the city's gates, confident Pyrust would murder Cyron. While Cyron did not look fully recovered, Pelut inwardly despaired at the rosy hue of his cheeks.

Cyron stepped down from the dais and dropped to his knees opposite the Grand Minister. He bowed to the throne but was summoned back upright by a flick of the fan. He sat back on his heels, then waved the stump of his arm in the throne's direction. "It is my distinct honor to present to you Empress Cyrsa. She has come to reclaim her empire."

"What manner of game is this, Prince Cyron? A joke, now, in these dire times?" Pelut looked up at Prince Pyrust. "Have you not seen his army swelling on the plains around Moriande? Have you not heard their measured steps as they cross the bridges and form up to the south? Your nation is no more."

Pyrust laughed. "There *are* no nations anymore, Minister, only Imperial provinces. Can you not read the crests we wear? Have not your spies told you of the flags our troops gather beneath?"

"Yes, but . . ." Pelut had seen the banners and had reports of their commissioning. He had assumed they signaled the Desei Empire rising.

Cyron looked at him inquiringly. "Had you not wondered at all the reports I demanded in the past weeks?"

Pelut's head came up. "If I may be frank, Highness, I had assumed you traded cooperation with the enemy for your life. All those reports told Prince Pyrust about our supplies and capabilities. They would facilitate his conquest of Erumvirine."

"You mean to say Erumvirine's liberation." Cyron's blue eyes slitted. "It may seem a semantic difference, but I have learned—from you—that the precise use of words is valuable."

"You should have learned as well, Highness, that my ministers and I live to serve the state. We would serve Prince Pyrust as well as we have served you."

Pyrust growled. "I hope better than you served him."

Pelut looked down, furious at the hint of a blush coming to his cheeks. Cyron had lost half his arm in a bungled assassination attempt Pelut had sanctioned. The man who had acted as Pelut's agent had gone missing. Had either Prince found him and extracted evidence of the minister's complicity, the red carpet would be drinking Pelut's blood.

"You will forgive me, my Princes, if I point out that the charade of making the Lady of Jet and Jade into the Empress is unnecessary. If you rule as a coalition, we shall serve you faithfully. You need not create a figurehead, unless you believe the people need such a symbol to hearten them in such dire times."

Neither Prince replied. Silence fell for a handful of heartbeats, then measured clicking broke it. Panel by panel the fan closed, delicate fingers slowly and precisely making the crown disappear.

The Lady of Jet and Jade looked down from the throne. Pelut felt panic rise. Behind him ministers instinctively bowed, hiding their faces. Pelut started to bow, too, but caught himself as his hands pressed flat against the cool wooden floor.

"You have no reason to believe I am the Empress Cyrsa, returned from the Wastes. You know me as the Lady of Jet and Jade. You know I have trained countless women in the pleasures of the flesh. Your wife is not among them, but your mistress is."

"All true, but none of it makes you the Empress Cyrsa." A bit more confident, Pelut sat back on his heels. "There is nothing you could do or say that would convince me you were anything but an impostor."

"Which is exactly why you lack the imagination to be the Grand Minister of my Empire." She pointed the closed fan at Prince Cyron. "Prince Cyron is your master now, and you shall obey him in all things, lest I choose to become angry with you."

"*What?*"

Cyron smiled. "It matters not if you believe that she is the Empress. Prince Pyrust and I *do* and we're acting in accord with her commands. Through you and your ministers, I shall coordinate the resources of Nalenyr, Helosunde, and Deseirion so we may crush the invaders."

Pelut looked up at the half-handed Desei Prince. "You would give him command of your nation's resources?"

"He has given me command of his nation's armies. Is this not a fair bargain?"

The woman on the throne flipped the fan around to point to Prince Pyrust. "Behold my warlord. He shall lead the defense of my Empire."

This is not happening. Pelut opened his arms. "My Princes, if there is a point to this game, please, reveal it now. If you have reached an accommodation, share it with us. If you require us to join with our counterparts in

Helosunde and Deseirion, we shall be pleased to do so. We will help you draft laws of succession. We can help you apportion the nations. But do not dishonor yourselves by elevating this woman."

Cyron's face hardened into a mask. "The point is that this is *not* a game—it never has been. Yet, for too long, you've treated it as such. You believe you know more and better than the rulers of a nation. Often you *do* because you choose the information we are given. You create an impression, then tailor our responses to fit the reality you shield us from.

"That approach no longer works, Minister Vniel. There is no more tailoring the dire news from the south. You hid things until well past the time I realistically could have done anything about it. This alliance you believe exists between Prince Pyrust and myself might, at one time, have been possible. But because of your scheming, I could not meet him on equal footing, so I was forced to deceive him; and here we are at this state of affairs."

"You make it sound, Highness, as if I give your words and wishes no regard."

Cyron laughed. "I point out a single instance and you turn it into an indictment of your performance since you entered the bureaucracy. Your rhetorical trick may have other princes retreating and praising your efforts. They miss the truth your trickery confirms: there *are* instances where you utterly disregard my orders. It is those instances in which you presume to place your judgment above mine. In doing so, you fail to serve the nation and, instead, serve only the bureaucracy."

Pelut let shock rise on his face.

Pyrust dropped a hand to his sword. "Empress, allow me to take his head now. I will take all their heads, and we will replace them."

The Lady of Jet and Jade waved that suggestion away. "Their heads are not gourds to be harvested. Each of these men is a spider who has spun a web. Their webs run together, and that network has value."

She looked straight at Pelut. "Unlike the Princes, Minister, I have ample evidence of how you work. I have my own network of agents, and what you deny, here, to Prince Cyron, you gloat about in the safety of a trysting bed. So let it be understood that if you deal with this as a game, it is a game you will lose."

Pelut pressed his hands together. "I am judged harshly. I fear those who serve me are judged harshly as well. It has been our duty, since the Empire was first established, to preserve order and maintain stability. If this is a vice, then I shall gladly be a criminal. Perhaps it should be best, in that regard, if Prince Pyrust were to harvest my head."

"No, that shall not be necessary." She snapped the fan open again.

"What is necessary, then, is the following." Prince Cyron began reciting his wants and needs in an even voice. Various junior ministers scribbled notes. The rustle of rice-paper sheets reminded Pelut of autumn leaves scuttling over cobblestoned streets.

He did not listen. He could not. The words were blasphemy. Everything Cyron wanted would have to be gathered in haste, and haste bred incomplete and unreliable information. Acting on bad information bred disaster.

Only a fool would deny that the situation in

Erumvirine required urgent action; but so much remained unknown about the invaders that it would be impossible to field a force to oppose them. Some tales suggested they were inhuman monsters. Others suggested they were superior beings who would drive Men from their Empire as Men had driven the Viruk from theirs. No one knew if they could be negotiated with, or even if they intended to head north. And what good would racing troops to the south do when so much coastline remained vulnerable to attack?

Too little was known. Cyron and Pyrust could play their game, but it would destroy them and their nations. It would leave the people without leaders or a means to survive. It would be worse than the Time of Black Ice.

And I cannot permit that. Pelut kept his face frozen. He would comply with Cyron's wishes and give him what he wanted. All of it. He would overwhelm the Prince with details too vast and trivial to be of use. Once Cyron had been overwhelmed, he would leave the working of the world to those trained for it.

Then the game would end and the losers would be very sorry indeed.

Chapter Ten

23rd day, Month of the Hawk, Year of the Rat
Last Year of Imperial Prince Cyron's Court
163rd Year of the Komyr Dynasty
737th Year since the Cataclysm
Jaidanxan (The Ninth Heaven)

"You are perplexed, my brother."

Jorim had sensed Tsiwen's presence, but had chosen not to acknowledge it until she spoke. He turned from the edge of his palace's courtyard and leaned back. A balustrade materialized, preventing him from tumbling to the earth. He was not sure which of them had manifested it, but he let it accept his weight.

"I am, sister." He folded his arms over his chest. "I have stood here and watched since my brothers left. It seems as if no time at all has passed, but nights and days have blinked over the face of the world. It hardly seems enough time to consider all I have been told—and certainly not to reach a decision about Nirati and her death."

The goddess laughed lightly, the sound coming as gently to his ears as a warm spring breeze. "Our brother believes death is the solution to everything because he is the Master of it. Because of the magic you gave Men, he cannot touch your mortal sister.

"I do not believe I can, either."

Tsiwen raised an eyebrow. "Dire news if true."

Jorim waved her to the courtyard's edge and the balustrade obligingly evaporated. "See, down there: Anturasixan. My grandfather used magic to create it."

"Yes, I can feel the power in it and him."

"My brother and I used to debate about whether or not a cartographer could become a Mystic. What would magic enable us to do? Draw maps without brush and ink? Would we be able to make one master map, and all maps drawn from it would change as the master changed? These were the lines along which we were thinking, but Qiro seems to be able to create lands by whim. He used to say that no place existed until he put it on a map, and now places seem to exist *because* he places them on a map."

"So it would appear."

Jorim scratched his throat with a gold talon. "But now he has created his own world. And wittingly or not, he has defied the gods and denied them access to his creation."

Tsiwen hugged her arms tightly around her middle. "So even if Grija's solution were the key, you could not simply appear there and destroy Nirati."

"No. Nothing lacking a blood tie with my grandfather can set foot there. Nirati is allowed. The things he makes—some of them creatures plucked from nightmares I confided to him—are free to leave. I think he had created those things before he even made his continent, and they had ventured out to attack the Amentzutl. The Mozoyan became more complex over time as he unconsciously redesigned them, making them better."

"If what you say is true, then nothing can reach your sister."

"No. She is there because she is his flesh through my father. Likewise my brother. He could get there."

A cloud passed beneath the palace, momentarily eclipsing the world. Tsiwen turned and looked up into his golden eyes. "How does he prevent someone from going there?"

"He's crafty. He always has been." Jorim waved a hand toward the continent. "You are Wisdom incarnate, sister. Perhaps you can find a way to outwit my grandfather."

Tsiwen smiled impishly, then stepped off the courtyard's edge and streaked earthward. Her silken gown snapped as the wind plucked at it, then the flailing sleeves grew into bat's wings as she dove, flittering out of his sight. She looked to be having so much fun that Jorim almost sprouted wings of his own to join her.

But he had already failed in the mission she was attempting. He had no desire to be frustrated again. It was less anger at being thwarted by a mortal than being unable to best his grandfather. He'd never been able to outfox Qiro when he was human, and divinity hadn't made much of a difference.

But isn't Qiro a god of sorts himself? Because Qiro had become a Mystic, he had access to the fabric of reality. He might not have as much power as a god, but he had enough. Unlike other Mystics, Qiro did not seem to release a lot of chaotic magic as a by-product of his talent—he appeared to use all of it.

I wonder if that is because he is creating *something, not just performing a task*. Could it be that Mystics tapped into far more magical energy than their task could accommodate, hence the release of the excess? *The release of excess magic should have warned people against profligate use.*

The flapping of Tsiwen's wings revealed her irritation as she returned. She landed, then blossomed upward with a venomous expression on her face. "You could have warned me, brother."

"I did. I told you he was being clever."

"And you knew I would take that as a challenge. You are correct, however. I can see the continent, but I cannot find a path to it."

"Exactly. Unless he grants us a map or wills us to approach, we cannot *reach* Anturasixan."

Tsiwen looked at him closely, then her eyes widened. "Your grandfather is not the only clever one. *You* could get there, if you reanimated your body."

"I'm certain of it." Jorim pointed and the world spun. Beneath them now lay a continent far to the east of where Jorim had been born. With another gesture the world drew closer, providing a clear view of the Amentzutl capital, Nemehyan. Almost a dozen ships bobbed in the bay—the largest being the *Stormwolf.* People moved along a floating quay, bringing supplies to the ship.

"They bound my body tightly in rags and sank it in a cask of oil to preserve it. They are bringing me home for a funeral." He smiled. "I could enter that body again and reanimate it."

"That would cause something of a commotion." Tsiwen shook her head. "This is not a course I would recommend."

"If there were another, I would choose it." Jorim frowned. "I have seen my sister and I have searched for my brother. I found him in Helosunde. He is distant and unapproachable."

"How so?"

"Keles does not seem to know who he is. Since he is lost, there is no way to find him." Jorim shrugged. "The point is moot, however, since getting him to Anturasixan would take a long time and then . . . They are twins. He could never kill her."

"Could you?"

Jorim slowly shook his head. "I do not know. Grija and Chado tell me that Nessagafel wishes to scrape away all creation save for his Viruk, and start over. That would destroy everyone I know and love. I can't let that happen. At the same time, can I kill my sister to save everyone else?"

"Could you kill me to save everyone?" As she spoke, Tsiwen took on Nirati's form and stole her voice. "Which do you love more? A small piece of creation, or the larger part of it?"

"Don't do that, please." Jorim turned from her and stared down at Nemehyan. There, on the *Stormwolf*'s deck, Anaeda Gryst shouted orders to sailors. A portion of the crew looked to be made up of Amentzutl, which surprised Jorim. The Amentzutl had no maritime tradition to speak of, but it looked as if they'd taken to their training rather quickly.

From belowdecks emerged a tall, slender Amentzutl woman—Nauana. She possessed a serenity out of place with the beehive of activity around her. What struck Jorim most about her was the black silk robe she wore with gold at the cuffs and lapels. It had been embroidered in gold with an image of Tetcomchoa, the feathered serpent. Jorim had been recognized as the incarnation of that Amentzutl god. The robe, clearly manufactured from Naleni material, had been decorated with Amentzutl designs, demonstrating cooperation between the two peoples.

Jorim watched her as the sea breeze caught a lock of long, black hair and brushed it over her cheek. He wished he was there to sweep it back, to kiss that cheek and enfold her in his arms. As a god, he would have the ability to crush her, but as a man he could have held her tight and shaped a new reality with her. Though her face betrayed none of it, he felt the ache born of his death lodged deep in her heart.

He would have sunk into glumness, but Shimik bounced and rolled after Nauana. His fur had become midnight black, save for gold over his throat, chest, palms, and soles. His eyes had even become golden, completing a transformation that marked him with Jorim's colors. The Fennych darted between sailors, scaled one of the ship's nine masts, ran along a yardarm, then leaped to the deck right in front of Nauana with a shriek.

She caught him up off the bounce and laughed. That laughter spread through the crew, and even Anaeda Gryst cracked a smile at the creature's antics.

Tsiwen rubbed his shoulder. "I know the pain you feel;

the pain they feel. You mustn't think of returning, however."

"Why not?"

Grija growled and materialized in a grey, furry lump. "Because I simply will not allow it. You've passed through the gates of my realm and they have closed behind you. If I let you back out again, who knows what havoc you could wreak? You might release the demons of the Fifth Hell, or the wizards in Tolwreen. They could cause more trouble than Nessagafel."

Jorim's golden eyes narrowed. "How is it, brother, that you have such poor control over your realm? Are you not the god of Death?"

"I am." Grija drew himself up to his full height and manifested as a black wolf with fiery eyes. "I have claimed you, have I not?"

"You have. Many times. I was trapped below because of you."

"Then you know my power. Do not trifle with me." He glanced toward the mortal world. "Have you determined how to get rid of the woman?"

Jorim said nothing because Grija's protestations of power seemed paper-thin. Either he could control his realm or he could not. If he could not—and Qiro's defiance suggested weakness—then could Grija's solution be the only one?

Or would it be the most expedient and beneficial only to Grija?

Something else struck Jorim as odd. While the Naleni had nine gods, the Amentzutl only had six. In their cosmology, Omchoa had consumed the god of death, Zoloa. To the Amentzutl, Grija existed, but only as an aspect of the Jaguar god of Shadows. Jorim did not know how the gods had become consolidated, but he wondered if that somehow reduced Grija's grip on power. Was his ability to manipulate reality limited by the number of people who believed in him?

"I have tried to reach Nirati on Anturasixan. You know she cannot be touched. And as I am now, I am not part of Qiro Anturasi's creation, so I am barred from interfering with it. The only way I know to reach her is if I reanimate my mortal remains. That is the key—much as I was the key to unlocking the divine aspect of myself to recover my power. Let me do that, and this can be over."

"No. Impossible."

"Why? You allowed me to reincarnate time and time again."

"Yes, but always in a new body, a new place. That is the way it is done." The wolf flashed fangs. "Bodily resurrection, never."

" 'Never' is a strong word."

The wolf glanced at the goddess of Wisdom. "You should lend him your intelligence, dear sister, for he is in sore need of it."

Jorim looked at his sister. "What is he talking about?"

"When Nessagafel created us, we did not have our aspects. There was no god of Death nor goddess of Wisdom. But when we created Men, we also shaped these aspects for ourselves. They allowed us to concentrate power—much as your Mystics do in perfecting a skill. Yet while death was a reality, none of us chose to become the guardian of it, except that it proved necessary."

Grija growled from deep in his throat. "Our father

made the Viruk long-lived. Our creation was flawed, so Men died in an eyeblink. Their souls reincarnated and Men *remembered* their previous lives. This became messy, so the underworld was created. We shaped the Nine Hells, then matched them with Nine Heavens. I kept spirits and souls for as long as it took them to forget who they were, then I would release them to be born again. Some I keep longer, like the wizards, for they cling to their memories and power, but most return shortly."

"And if I were to reanimate my mortal body, some balance would be upset?"

"You are a god, Wentoki." The wolf sniffed. "Your mortal body could not contain what you are. And the essence that could not fit would be loosed in my realm to cause havoc."

Jorim frowned. "But a vast chunk of my divine nature was severed from me before. Could that not be done again, allowing me to return to deal with Nirati and Nessagafel?"

"If you would fully embrace your divinity, you would recall how painful that was." The wolf's hackles rose. "The scream of a god is not pleasant."

"But it would work?"

"It might. But, no, I cannot allow it."

"I think you must." Jorim's form swelled into that of a dragon. He curled around the wolf and looked down upon him. "It is our only choice, brother."

The wolf leaped from within the circle of Jorim's tail. "Do not think to threaten me. This is not an action to be taken lightly. I will consider it, but it *must* be the only way."

Jorim returned to his mortal form. "I do not threaten

and I will seek an alternative. Understand this, however. The pain is of no consequence if all we know is to be saved. I suspect the discomfort will be as nothing compared to the loss of never having existed. Deliberate with haste, brother, lest we find out my fear is true."

Chapter Eleven

23rd day, Month of the Hawk, Year of the Rat
Last Year of Imperial Prince Cyron's Court
163rd Year of the Komyr Dynasty
737th Year since the Cataclysm
Wangaxan (The Ninth Hell)

He always wondered why Grija made a light when coming to torture him. Nessagafel saw no need for it. The Underworld existed, but its shape and form was an illusion agreed upon when Grija accepted the role as its sovereign. The Underworld was dark because it was dark, but no god needed light there.

Grija's movement and hunger drew Nessagafel back from infinity. If Nessagafel had actually given it any significant amount of consideration at the time he had created everything, he would have made himself omniscient. But as he created things, especially his children, he found bits and pieces of his creation shut off to him. At first this was intriguing, since he found his children's surprises a challenge. He could always discover and destroy their little plots, but he allowed them to plot because he found the challenges so entertaining.

Grija, being the first of his children, was conceived in haste and therefore lacking in imagination. Grija latched on to death as his aspect without thought, while the others choose more carefully. While all of his children hid things from him, Grija had the least amount to hide. Over the eons, Nessagafel had come to know him very well.

Almost completely.

Grija grew closer—though distance was again a concept without meaning in the Underworld—so Nessagafel gave himself form and substance. He had not yet escaped the heavy shackles and slender ring his children had fashioned for him. An eternity of imprisonment would soon end, however, as well-laid plans slowly coalesced.

Grija came to him as a wolf, so Nessagafel became a wolf's carcass, rotted and bloated, flesh black where his fur had fallen out. One eye hung against a blood-caked cheek. His lips had been eaten away, giving him a perpetual snarl.

"Very nice, Father. A vision of my future?"

"Not one you would ever see, my child."

Grija recoiled from the comment. "I shall never end up thus. Things progress as I have planned. Soon, very soon, I shall set you free. As my agent, you may again raise your Viruk to the heights they once enjoyed. You may rid the world of Men."

Nessagafel allowed the flesh to slough from a forearm. "And you will then bring your Ansatl to full flower? Men defeated them when you sought to make them ascendant."

"Wentoki followed in your footsteps and became a man. He gave Men magic. Without him leading them, my Ansatl would have crushed Men."

And then would they have come to oppose my Viruk—what remained of them? He would have laughed had he not found Grija's transparency so tedious. When Grija and the others conspired to create Men, Grija chose an aspect which Men would never respect or truly worship. They might pay Death attention and deference, but revere it? Impossible. And then Wentoki, the clever one, had created the Fennych and Tsiwen had created the Soth. Grija attempted to make his own creatures, the Ansatl, but the lizard-men were, like Grija, shallow and ill-suited to conquest. Their appetite for killing meant they always overgrazed their home and Men were forced to destroy them. Even now, the remaining populations remained on a scattered archipelago where they had split into factions and waged cannibalistic raids on each other.

Grija bared his fangs. "There need be no conflict between us, Father. The Ansatl and Viruk will rule the world between them. We shall destroy those who oppose us, then we shall balance each other. Twin powers, night and day, light and dark."

"Creation and the absence thereof."

"Reality and the void from which it was sprung." Grija looked up toward the heavens—another unnecessary gesture. "You were correct when you decided to unmake things, but you wanted to go too far. You had to be stopped."

"Of course. Much consideration of my errors has convinced me of this. But your brothers and sisters must be destroyed. They are too unpredictable and too difficult to control. If they did not fear you, Grija, they would have long since destroyed you."

"Speak plainly."

Nessagafel opened his jaw in a smile, then let the bone hang loose from one side of his head. "They think you weak. They have accepted that Wentoki is the key to keeping me locked away here in the Ninth Hell. They have no idea that when you agree to strip divinity from him, you will assume his power. Then, using it to control me, you will destroy them. They think you incapable of such subterfuge."

Grija growled defiantly, yet both of them knew it would become a whimper if Chado, Quun, or Wentoki were to appear. "They have forever underestimated me. They assume I care only to harvest souls and keep them here to draw sustenance from them. The prayers of the dead are thin broth compared to the devotion of the living. They think I am weak because of it."

"But you *are* weak, Grija."

Grija's dark eyes became molten hatred. He lashed out and the collar around Nessagafel's throat tightened. Pure fury flowed through it, constricting it. Agony pulsed into the elder god. It turned Nessagafel inside out. It melted his bones into ivory plasma which Grija carved into an intricately decorated sphere, trapping the rest of his father's essence.

Pain rose through Nessagafel as bubbles through boiling water. He could not speak and would not scream. He could barely twitch. Pain played over him as argent lightning arcs, then sank deep like fangs into flesh. It melted him from the inside out, churning him into a roiling lump of unrecognizable existence.

"Weak? *Weak?* Is *that* weak?" Grija assumed human form to more properly strut his outrage. "You are in *my power.* Do not forget that, Father. You *will* obey me. I do not *need* you to succeed. I wish to return to you the freedom you have long been denied because my brothers have wronged you. Their oppression wearies me."

Nessagafel allowed himself to gasp weakly, feeding Grija's ego. As quickly as he could, the elder god hardened the lines pain made in his essence. He clung to that lattice, pouring himself into it. Through it he could read every outrage Grija had known since the moment he burst into existence. As with every other instance of torture, Grija used his own pain as a model for that which he visited upon his father. Instance by instance, he gave Nessagafel what a lack of omniscience denied him.

One does not escape a prison, one escapes the warden.

Grija paced and prated. "You alone are capable of understanding what I put up with, for we are both trapped here. They think they tricked me into accepting the Underworld as my realm, but I knew what I was doing. I will have all the power eventually."

"But you were not content to wait."

"Impatience is only a vice to those who lack the intellect to see the inevitability of the future." Grija closed a hand into a fist. "All is to be mine, so why wait?"

"Why, indeed?"

Grija narrowed his eyes. "Why do you say that? What do you know?"

Had Nessagafel felt the need, he would have shrugged.

"Is it not curious that you are the god of Death and, yet, you have not died?"

"Curious, but immaterial. Were I to die, I would simply bring myself back into existence."

"Create something from nothing? That is quite a difficult task."

"But you did it."

"So how hard can it be?"

Grija laughed. "Exactly."

"Not hard at all." Nessagafel chose to smile, but Grija could not recognize it as such. "I made death from nothing. I made all of you from nothing."

"And yet, here we are." Grija shook his head. "But you shall be freed soon, to be my vassal."

"I prefer *agent*."

Grija's eyes sparked and pain drilled through Nessagafel. "Be pleased I do not make it *slave*."

Nessagafel grunted and became quiescent.

"I am not fooled, Father." The god of Death shook his head. "Do not think I have not considered treachery on your part. I have taken precautions."

I am certain you have. Nessagafel formed an eye and stared at Grija. *I do not choose to believe they will be effective.*

"Soon, Father." Grija waved a hand and the glow surrounding him blinked out of existence. "Gods will tremble and gods will die."

Chapter Twelve

24th day, Month of the Hawk, Year of the Rat
Last Year of Imperial Prince Cyron's Court
163rd Year of the Komyr Dynasty
737th Year since the Cataclysm
Kelewan, Erumvirine

The trio of ships stood out, in part because of their enormous size. The hulls had been made of a black wood and the ships were so broad abeam that little of the deckhouse could be seen from the riverside. Six tall masts rose from the center of the ships, but none bore any canvas. They drifted upriver slowly, and had they been found floating in a bay, they would easily have been taken for derelicts.

Though clearly designed for traveling the ocean, the ships moved up the river steadily. As with much other river traffic moving against the current, the ships had a line out which had been fastened to the harnesses of draft beasts. But where a buffalo or ox might have drawn a raft along, a dozen of them could not have even held the ship in place against the current. Yet the lines did go out, and draft beasts did draw them along, step after plodding step, closer and closer to Kelewan.

Nelesquin read the disbelief on Keerana's face as the first of the black ships came around a bend in the river. The warrior's expression had begun to change earlier, into one of puzzlement, as the ground shook with the beasts' footfalls. Nelesquin had known what to look for, so he'd seen the first beast's head rising just past the tallest trees. The creature, easily a hundred feet long and half again as tall, had a long neck which made nipping tender leaves from the tallest branches easy.

The Durrani stared, dumbfounded. "Such a beast I have never seen."

"They were created after you departed." Nelesquin waved casually toward the dark green creature pulling the ship upriver. "I remembered, belatedly, how difficult Tsatol Deraelkun could be to destroy. I created a few things to aid you, and I shipped them here."

"But how?" The warrior's amber eyes slitted. "You could not carry more than one or two of those creatures on the ship. Its appetite must be enormous."

The ground shook more violently as the creature came closer. Nelesquin's mount shied, and the Prince roughly reined it back under control. "We fattened them up in Anturasixan, then laced their food with Bloodstar orchid blossoms. The creatures slept, and the three you see here were wakened at the coast. They are docile and easily controlled."

Nelesquin pointed to the creature's long back. Between the creature's shoulder blades sat a Durrani warrior. He manipulated two golden rods that looked to be the size of broom handles. "Those rods are driven down into slots in the vertebrae. The driver controls the beasts that way."

Keerana nodded, watching, his hands imitating the motions of the driver.

Nelesquin smiled. *From curiosity to shock to cunning. He measures the beast for combat.* "Magnificent, no?"

"Yes, Master, incredible. I can have my men shape a platform for the back. Archers can shoot from it. Depending upon the fortification, the creature could smash walls, or we can step from its back to the top of a palisade."

"Oh, no, no, no, Keerana, nothing of the sort. These creatures—which your people have dubbed *kasphana*—are for pulling wagons and ships. I have others for toppling walls. You shall be amazed."

"Yes, Master." Keerana smiled. "Please thank your lady, Nirati, for her part in this. I can see her gentle hand in its shaping."

"Then your eyes deceive you, Keerana, for Nirati had nothing to do with the *kasphana,* nor any of the others I have brought. Certainly some of the failures reside in her realm, but not these. They were bred for war and, mercifully, she knows little of that."

"She is too gentle a creature for war."

"How very true." Nelesquin frowned, thinking back to his reincarnation. He had emerged from nothing and had met the most beautiful woman he'd ever seen. At least, that is the way he'd felt. There was something about her which seemed to answer his every need. She had been his perfect match.

At least such had been true at that moment.

Then he had met her grandfather, Qiro Anturasi, and recognized in the man's hatred for the Nine Principalities a commonality. In no time, Nelesquin's imperial designs and ambitions had been reborn. With Qiro as an ally, shaping an army to fulfill their mutual desire for revenge and justice had been child's play.

Nelesquin labored under no illusions that he would have to destroy Qiro. He'd known that from the first, of course. Qiro wanted to destroy the nations so he could be raised above all others. Nelesquin knew he *was* above all others, and a rival was not something the Prince would tolerate.

But Nirati would not take her grandfather's death well. That was the difference between them, for Nelesquin had helped *plot* his grandfather's death.

A light burned in Keerana's eyes when he mentioned Nirati. The Durrani worshipped her quietly, seeing her as a goddess of peace between battles. Keerana was blessed among his compatriots, for she had smiled upon him. He likely even loved her.

As I do. But Nelesquin hesitated, wondering if he did love her. He certainly *had* loved her—he remembered that much. The memory of her, her soft body, her bright green eyes, the scent of her perspiration after they had made love; all of these things brought a smile to his face. She was his Queen, no doubt of it, but did he actually love her?

Nelesquin reined his horse around and began to pace the black ships. Nirati had been everything he desired in Anturasixan, but since his return, things had changed. Here he was, on the cusp of victory, reclaiming that which was his by blood and right, and where was she? She had remained with her grandfather, blocked from joining him, no doubt by the old man himself.

And why was it that she would take the detritus of his experiments? What did she do with them? What did she want with them? They were dead ends, much as the Principalities were.

A new thought occurred to him, one he did not much like. She had brothers she loved dearly. And her grandfather was arguably the most powerful man in the world. Were he not so focused on revenge, he might seek to become a god or at least challenge the gods. What if Nirati had meant for Nelesquin to fall in love with her so he would go out, reconquer the Empire, then she would usurp him and establish the Anturasi family as the Imperial line?

That is not possible, is it? But Cyrsa had killed her husband to usurp his throne. It had been done before.

Nelesquin turned in the saddle. "How freely do you trust, Keerana?"

The Durrani's eyes widened. "You, Master, utterly and completely. You are father to my race. We owe you everything and live to serve."

"Your fidelity is most appreciated." Nelesquin gestured and the warrior rode up on his right side. "But among your people, how easily do you trust?"

"Within my clan, Master, trust is complete. There may be rivalries, but this is only the way that we improve ourselves, as per your wishes. Outside of my clan, trust must be earned."

"If you were given a wife from another clan, would you trust her?"

Keerana frowned. "She becomes one of my clan then, so I must trust her. If she betrayed me, it would benefit neither her nor her clan, for you would punish such treachery, would you not, Master?"

"I would indeed." Nelesquin smiled. In creating the Durrani he had fashioned the greatest of warriors. Fierce, implacable, arrogant in combat, respectful in repose, they were everything a leader would want. Intelligent, too, for Keerana's face already betrayed he was thinking more about the question he'd been asked.

"What do you expect of the enemy, Keerana?"

"They will be resourceful, but this will avail them nothing against us."

"Well said, but Gachin was slain and his army thrown back from Tsatol Deraelkun."

The warrior's expression sharpened. "Gachin dismissed the clues to what awaited him as aberrations. The force that broke out from Kelewan later ambushed our troops in the forests, and stood against him at Tsatol Deraelkun. Because they struck from hiding and ran from the siege, he perceived them to be cowards."

"But you do not?"

"I expect a viper to coil and strike. That it does not fight claw with claw surprises me not at all." Keerana pointed off to the northwest. "Tsatol Deraelkun is well positioned for defense, and having an able warrior leading troops makes it still more effective. It is an interesting puzzle to be solved."

Nelesquin smiled as a large, leather-winged, short-legged creature hopped up on the lead ship's wales. A warrior sat in a saddle fastened where long neck met body, and gold control rods had been inserted into the creature's spine. The beast threw its triangular head back and shrieked, then launched itself. It swooped low over the river to pick up speed, then beat its wings and rose easily to where it could float on the air currents above the land.

Nelesquin pointed to the flying beast. "That is a *jaran-daki,* and I mean it for use in scouting. I supposed a couple of archers could be put in a saddle on its back, but they would have to master shooting while in a swoop."

Keerana recovered himself and nodded. "It would not do for them to shoot the *jarandaki* in the wing."

"No, not at all. The nice thing about them is that they will provide perspective on a battle. Had Gachin had a scout up on one, he would have known of the ambush that took his troops."

"It is possible, Master, but even with that knowledge, he might not have reacted correctly." Keerana bowed his head. "Those who fight beneath the Ram Crest are often given to vainglorious displays. Gachin might have dismissed the threat, or assigned a subordinate to deal with it."

Nelesquin regarded his warlord closely. "You would not make such a mistake?"

"I could not, Master. I do not serve myself; I serve you. To fall prey to such an ambush would be an abrogation of my duty. My service to you is paramount."

"Have you determined your strategy for taking Tsatol Deraelkun?"

"My plans shall be revised to account for the wonders aboard the ships, Master, but I have studied the matter and have worked out a strategy." His eyes became keen.

"To win Tsatol Deraelkun's wall one must attack strongly at a single point. Relentless pounding will win through at least the first set of walls."

"But if you attack that way, you allow your enemy to slip a force out to harass your flanks."

"So I cannot allow myself to be flanked." The warrior gestured toward the black ships on the river. "I will deploy my forces in depth. An attack against my flank will be repulsed by an attack against the enemy's flank. With the *jarandaki,* signaling between units will be much easier and more direct. If the rider carries a flag aloft, he will be able to communicate information between the units."

Nelesquin clapped his hands. "Brilliant. Your attack must be relentless and swift."

"I beg your pardon, Master, but it is likely to be one or the other."

The Prince frowned. "Enlighten me."

"The line between swift and haste is thin. So is the line between relentless and obdurate. To move fast is to surrender flexibility. Relentlessness can become stubborn support for strategies that are not effective. I would not waste your troops, Master, in an effort unworthy of you and incapable of victory."

"Yet is there not a chance that by remaining too flexible you will refuse to push at a time when one more effort would carry the day?"

Keerana's expression hardened. "A coward might, Master."

Nelesquin nodded approvingly. "And you are no coward. Good. And flexibility means you will employ my gift to you in the proper way."

"Have no fear, Master, Tsatol Deraelkun shall fall. It is your will, and I am the instrument of your will."

"Exactly."

The two horsemen headed off into the forest, letting the *kasphani* draw the ships toward Kelewan. They passed through a vale and crested a low hill. Nelesquin reined back quickly, while the Durrani rode forward and interposed himself between the cloaked figure which revealed itself on the road and the Prince.

Nelesquin snarled. "Why do you play at this game, Kaerinus? I find you lurking, and Keerana is again prepared to kill you."

The sorcerer smiled and turned toward them, holding out a hand. A black-and-emerald butterfly clung to one finger. Kaerinus smiled, then puffed breath at it. The insect took flight and quickly vanished in the branches above.

"It is not out of disrespect, Prince Nelesquin, but urgency." The *vanyesh* shrugged. "I have spent so much time away that I sometimes forget Imperial manners. Wonderful creatures you have there. I pray the winged ones do not eat my butterflies."

"They prefer somewhat bigger prey." Nelesquin rode around Keerana. "What is so urgent?"

"Do you recall, my Prince, Mount Shanfa in Moryth?"

"You know I do." Nelesquin glanced back at Keerana. "It was a nasty place, dark and dismal, a stone thorn shoved up through the world's flesh. Virisken Soshir spent much time there."

"I recall the place from my brief campaign in the Five Princes." Keerana nodded slowly. "This tells me much of value."

"Good." Nelesquin returned his attention to Kaerinus. "What of that place? I'd sooner forget it than remember."

"Then you are in luck, my Prince." Kaerinus pointed to the south. "There have been reports. The mountain is *gone*."

Chapter Thirteen

30th day, Month of the Hawk, Year of the Rat
Last Year of Imperial Prince Cyron's Court
163rd Year of the Komyr Dynasty
737th Year since the Cataclysm
Tsatol Deraelkun, County of Faeut
Erumvirine

The army that came to destroy Tsatol Deraelkun was not what I had expected. I was not foolish enough to imagine that my half brother would bring the same army he had led ages ago when we fought a mock battle for our father's pleasure. Of course, our father had not bothered to watch. Even if he had, he'd not have noticed how Nelesquin and I strove against each other.

We'd not come to hate one another yet.

I stood at a tower window with Count Derael seated in his wheeled chair beside me. "I believe you are right, my lord—the hammer-headed ape creatures are meant to hurl stones as a catapult might. The other long-armed ones are climbers. The bony shield around their necks covers their shoulders as they scale the walls."

His voice did not waver despite the tremor running through his limbs. "They're very pale and have no eyes to speak of. They must operate by scent. We can deal with that."

I glanced down at him. "I imagine they will scent-mark the walls. Something hurled."

He turned his face up at me, surprise flashing there for a heartbeat before his general fatigue returned his face to impassiveness. "Did you not notice the little white things, over there, on the left in the shadow of the woods?"

I looked. "I'd taken them for sheep, my lord, though they have the body of spiders."

"Yes, and their wool is spun webbing, ready for deployment. Given how the climbers are segregated from the woolspiders, but keep sniffing when the breeze blows across, I suspect the climbers eat them." Count Derael inhaled laboriously. "The woolspiders will be sent against us. When we kill them, their ichor will mark the battlements and perhaps even drive the climbers into a frenzy."

"And then the *kwajiin* come." I slowly shook my head. The invaders had assembled nine thousand warriors and had their entire force arrayed against the southeastern corner of the fortress. A conventional army would have found that approach difficult. The only suitable staging area for siege machines was at the edge of their range and below the castle's ground level. While they could still hit the walls, it would take a long time to bring them down, and then the troops would have to race uphill to engage the defenders.

"Do you see any tunneling beasts, Master Soshir?"

"No, but that does not surprise me, either." I crossed my arms. "Nelesquin had no great love of tunnels after we scoured a Viruk labyrinth of pirates. He was lost for a time, and once we had destroyed the pirates, he wanted nothing more to do with tunnels."

"And yet, because this prejudice is known to you, I must assume he has worked against it." The man's eyes burned intensely. "This complicates the defense of our home."

"It cannot stand."

"This I know, Master Soshir." He twitched a hand to the right, and the gesture seemed to exhaust him. "If you could turn me to the maps."

I dutifully turned the chair and rolled him across the round room to where maps had been hung on the opposite wall. Diagrams of every level had been drawn in great details and marked with sigils and signs I could not decipher.

"I have my engineers opening the false columns below. We will light fires in them. They will bring fire to key stones. You know what happens to granite when it is heated, yes?"

"It can powder."

"Exactly. Within an hour or two this fortress will collapse. With any luck, it will take the bulk of the invaders with it."

I nodded. "A couple of hours is enough to get everyone clear. We've already stationed the First Naleni Dragons and the Keru in the mountains to hold the gaps as we evacuate. The messages we've sent to Moriande should bring more troops. We'll live to fight another day."

"You may, Master Soshir, but this is my last battle."

I crouched and laid a hand on his. His flesh was cold, but I still felt life in him. "This is not your final battle. The previous times the walls have fallen did not signal the end of the Derael family. You might think, had you not become ill, this place would never fall. You could have held it—through the first assault and the second. Perhaps a third. But all the Mystics Empress Cyrsa led into the Wastes could not stop Nelesquin from taking this fortress. Just as he brought his invaders and his living siege machines, he would bring more and more terrible creatures. Losing this fortress is not defeat, but surrendering because of its loss *is*."

The man hung his head for a moment. "You do not understand how it is, Master Soshir. I *am* Fortress Derael. My weakness is its weakness. We die together. There is no dissuading me from this."

Another voice, a young man's voice, broke in from the doorway. "I shall not dissuade you, Count Derael. I *order* you to evacuate."

The count did not look up. "You honor me, Prince Iekariwynal, but that is an order with which I cannot comply."

The young Virine prince strode into the room in white armor with a red bear rampant crest on the breastplate. "You are my champion, Count Derael, and I need you. I will not have you die here."

"But I am useless in your service."

"No. I heard Master Tolo lecture his troops on the

way about how it was more important to make the enemy worry about death than it was to kill them. These *kwajiin* know no fear, but they can learn it. Your very survival will inspire fear. Your knowledge will be the seed of their defeat."

"Better the two of you conspire to defeat the enemy than convincing me of my worth."

But before either of us could comment, a horn blew from the battlements outside. I ran to the window and the Prince wheeled his champion forward. There, in the distance, came a massive beast with a pavilion on its back. The creature plodded along slowly, but such was its size that it closed the distance swiftly. This made it easy for me to read the pennants flying above the pavilion.

"Nelesquin has arrived."

The Prince pointed. "Look there."

Evil looking bat-birds drifted along over the treetops, then climbed and began to circle like vultures. "They have archers on their backs."

"So they do, Highness." The count's eyes narrowed. "This changes things. He will begin the assault now."

"I know. Perhaps I can slow him down."

The count caught the hem of my sleeve. "You will not commit the foolishness you accuse me of, will you?"

"We'll both live to continue this discussion later, my lord." I squeezed his shoulder then left the tower. I crossed the inner courtyard, passed through a sally port which was closed behind me, then mounted the battlements on the outer wall. Though I wore no armor, the tiger-hunting crest in orange on a black robe would be easy enough for my brother to spot.

The creature bearing the pavilion stopped and lowered its head to the ground. Two figures emerged from the tent, walked past the driver, and along the beast's neck. Nelesquin leaped to the ground from the snout while his companion floated down. As they came forward, a company of the Steel Bear archers mounted the battlements to either side of me.

I waved their bows down. "We'll trade words, not arrows."

Nelesquin strode forward casually. He picked his way carefully across the battlefield. New grasses had sprung up, but there was no mistaking the white of bones and the black of blood-fed earth. The confidence on his face brought back fleeting glimpses of our previous meeting at Tsatol Deraelkun, back before we had become mortal enemies.

He opened his arms wide in welcome. "I had been told you lived, brother, though I already knew it in my heart."

"I would not know who I am, brother, save for your companion's healing arts." I bowed in the direction of Kaerinus. "For the first time ever, I am grateful for the *vanyesh*."

"Had you come to be healed sooner, Soshir, we could have finished this game much more quickly."

I shook my head. "This game is played on a schedule none of us have made."

A peevish expression flashed over Nelesquin's face, then a false smile conquered it. "A call for the surrender of Tsatol Deraelkun will be rebuffed, yes?"

"As quickly as my suggestion that we duel again for possession of the fortress."

"Gambit offered and declined; very good." Nelesquin

looked around at his army. "You cannot win. You know that."

"But I can cost you a victory." I pointed to the north. "You know the might of Nalenyr is coming."

"You always did find the Naleni daunting. But me, never." He posted fists on his hips, drawing attention to the fact he wore no swords. "Do not take it as any sign of insincerity that I do not kill you myself."

"Not that. Perhaps cowardice."

"I expected that." He pointed toward his troops, and one of the hammer-headed apes, easily thirty feet tall with heavily muscled arms almost as long, lifted a huge stone. He drew it back over his head and I thought for a moment he meant to knock me from the wall. Instead the creature—responding to the driver's jerking of gold rods—pounded the stone into the ground. It bounced, and I felt both that initial impact and the second.

Before I could puzzle out the reason for that action, another tremor ran through the ground. The wall shifted. Cracks appeared in the mortar, and support for the catwalk snapped. Archers fell, some over the wall but most into the courtyard. I dropped to a knee, then leaped free as my section of the battlement collapsed.

The roadway between the castle's walls exploded upward. Cobblestones rose to meet me, propelled by the star-shaped nose of a mole the size of an elephant. Its stubby claws raked dirt into the hole, then it sprang out. Once the mole uncorked the hole, *kwajiin* warriors swarmed from it.

Arrows sleeted down, spinning blue-skinned warriors away. I landed in a crouch, drawing both my swords.

Draw-cuts swept an arm from one *kwajiin* and blinded another. An arrow-stuck soldier stumbled into a lunging warrior. I parried with one blade and stabbed the other through his throat.

Beyond that hole another opened, and another. Then rocks flew, shattering crenels. Stone shards rained down into the space between the walls, ricocheting indiscriminately. Men screamed as they pitched from the walls. At such close range, the Steel Bears could speed shafts into gaps in *kwajiin* armor. One arrow punched clean through a helmet, emerging below the warrior's jaw, dropping him at my feet.

No time for rally cries or bold boasts; it was Grija's harvest. Reap or be reaped, mercy a mere fancy that would find no champions. Blood sprayed over walls, glistening wetly long after the heart stopped pumping. Cleaved limbs fell heavily to the ground and hands clutched convulsively. Men sat against walls, futilely stuffing entrails back into their abdomens. Others shrieked silently, their words emerging as black blood from deep within.

I was at once unconscious and hyperaware. In the chaos I noticed everything. Without thought I labeled the enemy in terms of threat, then dealt with the most deadly. I flowed forward with purpose, not trying to escape. My intent was to kill as many of the *kwajiin* as I could.

More stones flew and the walls began to crumble. The woolspiders gained the battlements, looking not at all like sheep with their webbing played out. They affixed it to the crenels, then leaped away into the fight. The web lines tightened and whole sections of the walls flew outward. The woolspiders attacked anything that moved, proving an equal annoyance to the *kwajiin* as to us.

At one point, in fact, a *kwajiin* and I broke off our swordplay to each dispatch one of the spiders. He killed his with a quick thrust through the carapace. Armed with two swords, I scissored its head off. The *kwajiin* and I shared a smile, united in our joint efforts—an omen of how our collaboration could have been.

Then with a casual cut, I matched a slash on his throat to his thin gash of a smile.

"Master Soshir, this way!" Dunos stood in a small sally port, a dead spider before him. His eyes blazed and though his lame arm held one of my old swords weakly, the other blade dripped with dark fluid.

I cut down two of the *kwajiin* as I dashed for the opening. "Get back, Dunos! Close the gate." I turned my back to it, ready to deny the *kwajiin* access. A firm hand on my sash yanked me backward. I stumbled over Dunos and went down, thinking all was lost.

Then bows sang and arrows filled that gap. The first *kwajiin* fell well shy of the gate, and at least a half dozen fell behind him. Then a giant warrior in the armor of the Virine Jade Bears slammed the gate shut and secured it with a stout bar.

Captain Lumel hauled me to my feet. "There is no holding this place. We're withdrawing. Come on."

I sped away with his men and Dunos. Deep in the fortress' bowels I caught up with Deshiel Tolo, Ranai Ameryne, and other of the *xidantzu* that had fought by my side. With them waited Count Derael, his wife, son, and Prince Iekariwynal.

The count nodded as best he was able. "The fires have been started. Nothing can stop the destruction."

"Then get clear. Captain Lumel, you see them out. Dunos, you guard the Prince." I looked at the rest of the *xidantzu*. "You have seen the plans. You know the bottle-necks. We hold them as best we can, and when the fortress comes down, we kill the survivors."

Fighting in the tunnels was not as fierce as I had ex-pected. Nelesquin, happy that his ruse had worked, did not press us. While we killed more than a few *kwajiin*, they didn't pursue. We withdrew back through the moun-tains. I emerged at an overlook above Tsatol Deraelkun.

Fire engulfed the fortress. Its blackened towers vom-ited fire and smoke like distant volcanoes. Then, one by one, they sank into the inferno. Sparks rose and hot wind issued from the tunnel through which we had escaped. Down below the *kwajiin* cheered the fortress' death, but it sounded hollow.

I resheathed my swords and set my feet on the path north. I had beaten Nelesquin at Deraelkun once, and now he had defeated me. I tried to tell myself that this did not worry me, but there was no sense in lying.

Nelesquin had come back from the grave. That vic-tory, and the taking of Tsatol Deraelkun, started a nice string of conquests. That might have been enough to sat-isfy anyone but Nelesquin. His ambition had been strong enough to return him to life, and I was uncertain if there was much I could do to stop him.

Chapter Fourteen

RUND 32nd day, Month of the Hawk, Year of the Rat
Last Year of Imperial Prince Cyron's Court
163rd Year of the Komyr Dynasty
737th Year since the Cataclysm
Ixyll

Though all of the warriors in the Voraxan expedition wished to answer Empress Cyrsa's call as quickly as possible, they agreed with Borosan that a delay, so he could make their mounts faster, would be a benefit in the long run. The inventor made changes to gearing and other aspects of the mounts, then produced brand-new mounts in the Tolwreen factory. The old ones would be used as pack animals—an idea that saddened Ciras, despite his continued ambivalence about the mechanical beasts.

Vlay found that idea rather amusing. "You are very like Jogot Yirxan, whose blade you bear."

Ciras swung from the saddle of his new mount, which was bigger, wider, and stronger than the previous one, decorated with a silver filigree of flames and sleeping tigers. "You knew him?"

"Not well. I knew him before he joined the *vanyesh*." The swordsman passed a hand over his shaven pate. "He came to *jaedun* through the sword, then his curiosity got the better of him. He learned much from Nelesquin and Kaerinus."

Ciras slid his sword from the scabbard. Black sigils writhed over it. "He created this sword and the changing words?"

Vlay smiled. "He did. He was quite proud of it. He said the sword would be the bard to tell his tale."

Ciras frowned. "I have been given to understand that Prince Nelesquin and the Turasynd struck a bargain."

"True. Empress Cyrsa sent Virisken Soshir forth with a contingent to destroy the *vanyesh*." He looked around at Tolwreen. "Apparently they did not succeed, but hurt them significantly."

"When they showed us Nelesquin's skeleton, there were no more than eighty-one remaining." Ciras returned the blade to the scabbard. "I had an unusual experience the first time I used that blade. It was here, in Ixyll. I was working through the forms and as I imagined foes, they came at me. Turasynd, all of them save one. Why would Yirxan fight with the Turasynd if he was of the *vanyesh* and they were allies?"

Vlay's eyes tightened. "As I said, I did not know him well, but I heard things of him even after he joined the *vanyesh*. I was told he retained his loyalties to the Empress. He was her agent among them. Through him, we learned of the alliance. No doubt the Turasynd would have taken a disliking to his show of allegiance."

"And the Turasynd could not have reported back if they were all slaughtered." Ciras nodded, thinking back to the exhilaration he recalled from that exercise. Jogot Yirxan had been exultant in his destruction of the Turasynd. He had likewise been magnificent, facing them fairly, striking them down.

"If this is true, I have to wonder at another thing I saw."

"What was that?"

"Yirxan struck down a swordsman. He attacked him from behind, wounding him terribly." Ciras closed his eyes. "I did not see the face of the man he struck, but the crest, it was of a black tiger hunting."

"A black tiger hunting?"

The surprise in Vlay's voice prompted Ciras to open his eyes, but he caught no emotion on the man's face. "You know who that was? I ask because my master, Moraven Tolo, wore that crest. He also had a scar on his chest that corresponded to that cut."

"You're certain?"

"As best I can be."

Vlay pursed his lips for a moment. "The black tiger hunting was worn by the Empress' lover, the leader of the Imperial Bodyguards. You say his name is Moraven Tolo?"

"I can describe him for you, if you wish."

The other man shook his head. "No need. If Nelesquin has survived, it stands to reason Virisken Soshir has as well. They were both men of great ambitions—the sort which you are wise to fear, Master Dejote."

"But that makes no sense." Ciras frowned. "My master was anything *but* ambitious. He was *xidantzu,* and though he was known to Princes, he had no pretensions or wild desires. He did not even want me as an apprentice, but his master insisted."

"Perhaps I am mistaken, and the matter of crests is merely a coincidence."

"But the mystery remains. If, as you say, Yirxan was loyal to the Empress, what reason would he have to attack her lover?"

Vlay smiled. "No mystery at all. Soshir was ambitious. The Empress was a means to destroy Nelesquin, his rival. If she made him Prince-consort, Soshir could become the Emperor in all but name. To rise to such heights from so lowly a start would have been remarkable. And yet, he could have risen higher. She ascended, after all, when she killed her own husband. Soshir could kill her, setting to rights the balance, restoring royal blood to the Celestial Throne. That was how Soshir would think."

"So she sent him out on a mission against Nelesquin that should have killed them both, and when Soshir failed to die . . ."

". . . She had him killed by a man she knew could be trusted." Vlay shook his head. "Ambition can often counteract ambition, but to be caught in the middle of such a struggle is a lethal proposition."

"So it appears."

"Do not dwell on it, Master Dejote." Vlay smiled and headed off to finish loading the wagons. "Just find a way to avoid it."

Ciras nodded, but his thoughts were already racing. If his master was indeed Virisken Soshir, then would he be as much of a danger now as he had been? And if he *was,* could Ciras kill him? He would never strike his master from behind, and he was not sure he could defeat him in an even fight.

More important, his loyalty was for Moraven Tolo, not an Empress he'd never met. He'd known of her as a courtesan. She and his master knew each other, but did Moraven know who she was? Did Moraven know who *he* was? Was his choice of names a window on his intentions, or a blind meant to hide them?

Many warriors changed their names. Some did so on a whim. Others did so to honor a master or a patron. Often a warrior did so to commemorate a great deed. Ciras had not because he was proud of his name and wished to honor his family.

Moraven Tolo, when written out, could be read one of several ways. *Sleeping dragon* would be the most common reading. Another would be *courage unfolding.* The darkest reading, however, was *victory of desire,* which did not seem in keeping with his master, as it hinted at hidden ambitions.

Ciras growled to himself. "You're playing children's games. You know your master. You know his character. His ambition is to keep his sword in the scabbard."

But his mind would not be turned from consideration so easily. Jogot Yirxan likewise could be read many ways. *Steadfastly loyal* came easiest, and yet what Vlay had said about Yirxan put the lie to that from the *vanyesh* point of view. *Midnight justice* also worked. As Vlay had said, justice can oppose ambition, and Yirxan must have done just that.

Perhaps I can do both things. Ciras rested a hand on the hilt of his sword. "I am heir to a sword, but not the circumstances that drove it through my master."

* * *

With the last of the wagons loaded and groaning under the weight of Borosan's loot from Tolwreen, the Voraxan expedition headed out again. And Ciras admitted that the new mounts could appear almost lifelike—but he refrained from calling them beasts or horses. They carried the riders smoothly along, almost as if they were floating on a river.

They passed swiftly through a series of valleys. Ciras recognized none of them. Forests of silver trees sprouted leaves that tarnished into dust before they could spiral to the ground. A carpet of red flowers looked innocent enough, but when one of the *thanatons* scurried into the valley ahead of the riders, serpentine warriors slithered from the ground, each with red blossoms atop antennae. They sought to wrestle the *thanaton* to a stop, but the *gyanrigot* pulled away and Voraxani arrows cut down the pursuit.

They skirted that valley, which made their journey longer. The valley curled around to the south and extended across their line of march. The riders increased their speed because the serpent-men didn't move very quickly, but in doing so almost raced into disaster.

They crested a line of hills and started down into a wide and dusty bowl. Ciras rode in the lead and found the place refreshingly benign until, up ahead, he saw riders riding hard toward them. Before he could suggest they slow down, he recognized the lead rider as himself, growing larger as if he were riding into a mirror. Uncertain if it was a mirage or something more malevolent, Ciras drew his sword and touched a switch on his mount's neck, snapping armor and spikes into place.

A heartbeat before the Voraxani ran into the mirror, Turasynd horsemen burst through the illusory curtain. They let fly with a volley of arrows. The missiles sped across the narrowing divide, intended to sweep the Empress' riders from their mounts.

Arrows bounced from Ciras' mount. Curved metal plates had slid out to protect his shins and thighs. The mount's mane stiffened into a coarse line that then split like butterfly wings to either side of the neck. Missiles glanced from the mane or snapped harmlessly against the mount's broad breast.

Blades and spikes bristled from the mount's shoulders and flanks. Ciras crashed straight into the Turasynd riders. The shock of the collision shook him, but he remained firmly in the saddle. Blood spattered and horses reared. Crippled horses went down squealing and kicking, crushing hapless riders beneath them.

Ciras lashed out, stroking his sword through an armpit. Dark feathers flew, for these were Black Eagles. Hot red blood splashed against the sword's guard, then sprayed as he cut at another Black Eagle. The scent of copper filled the air. Guiding his mount with pressure from his knees, Ciras parried, then stabbed and cut. Riders fell, and mechanical mounts stamped the remaining life from them.

He burst through the Turasynd line, and through the magic curtain beyond it. No more Turasynd lurked there, giving him some hope. Reining his mount about, he plunged back into the fray. There were more than enough Turasynd to kill—*perhaps even too many*.

The Turasynd had attacked in a slender line. Their formation flanked the Voraxani on both sides, reaching as far back as the wagons. The Empress' warriors fought hard, but the Turasynd outnumbered them four to one. Turasynd cheered triumphantly as one of the wagons tipped, rolling over twice, casting its load all over the battlefield.

Ciras purposefully drove his mount in close grazing runs that carved up Turasynd and horse alike. He hated hurting the animals, but sowing havoc in the Turasynd ranks was more effective than simply killing them. The screams of a dying horse and the pleas of gutted comrades could take the fight out of even the most dedicated warrior.

A huge Turasynd Black Eagle, sunlight flashing silver from the feathers covering his shoulders and arms, engaged Ciras. There was none of the nicety of civilized fighting. No challenges formal or otherwise, just a wild scream and a sword raised in fury.

Ciras parried a blade high, then slashed down. His cut split ring mail and opened the inside of a man's thigh. Bright blood splashed against the horse's neck, then another Turasynd was upon him. Ciras leaned away from that cut and felt the sting of a flesh wound, then spitted the man. He ripped his blade free and the dying man spun from the saddle.

One or two Black Eagles gave off traces of *jaedun,* but their lack of discipline doomed them. Ciras had practiced countering such assaults. Jogot Yirxan's blade seemed eager to gorge on Turasynd blood, and Ciras allowed it to drink deeply.

Ciras raced along the Turasynd flank toward the overturned wagon. The barbarians had gathered there, intent on plunder despite the battle continuing to rage. A number of the Voraxani put up a spirited defense, but it was only a matter of time before they were overwhelmed.

Borosan pulled another wagon out of line as if to block the Turasynd advance. Wide-eyed, he leaped from the driver's seat and into the back, quickly taking refuge behind the ancient shields that had been mounted on the wagon's sides. Arrows rattled off them, and a half dozen Turasynd charged the wagon.

One by one, a handful of the *thanatons* popped up from behind the shields on their spider legs. Panels slid back and crossbow bolts sped out. The volley swept Turasynd from their saddles, killing several.

A wounded Black Eagle limped behind the overturned wagon. He sought sanctuary, hunkering down amid rectangular metal boxes. Small *thanatons*—the ones Borosan considered mousers—sprang away in response to the man's guttural growl. His laughter followed the *gyanrigot* as they scuttled along the ground, but died abruptly as the first of the metal boxes unfolded itself. Legs unfurled and arms thrust, raising skeletal, gearwork warriors which towered over the Black Eagle. Before his expression could shift from triumph to terror, the nearest *gyanrigot* brought a clawed hand up. It closed around the man's throat.

He struggled, tearing at the metal hand, kicking at the body as the machine jerked him upright. He gurgled and his face purpled as booted toes scraped in the dust as the *gyanrigot*'s claw shifted and snapped his neck cleanly.

More *thanatons*' missiles dropped riders. Something metallic clicked behind Ciras. One of the mousers had leaped onto his mount's rump and snapped its legs into little holes astride the tail. The upper half of the mouser's dome twisted and a small dart shot out, glancing off a Turasynd's nose guard.

Ciras spun and cut the man from the saddle. Two more of the barbarians charged at him. The mouser shot one in the throat. While hardly lethal, the dart distracted the warrior enough that Ciras dispatched him with ease. The swordsman then turned in the saddle and parried the second man's slash as they passed.

He turned to engage the man again, but one of Borosan's *gyanrigot* warriors had already struck. Barely modified from the blacksmith it had been in Tolwreen, its first hammerblow crushed the horse's skull. The beast went down, pitching its rider headlong. The barbarian struggled drunkenly to his feet and was knocked aside by another Voraxani.

He went down again, his face slashed open. The *gyanrigot* blacksmith finished the job, driving most of the man's helmet deep into his skull. The Turasynd crumpled, blood and brains dripping from his killer's hammer.

The *thanatons* moved forward in concert, rolling up the Turasynd flank. Ciras and others ranged wider, cutting off retreat. They killed as many of the Black Eagles as they could.

The rest they drove into the valley of the serpent-men. Whether it was better to die there, or be killed by a *gyanrigot,* Ciras could not be certain. In the end he decided it didn't matter. But if forced to, he'd have chosen the serpents.

Chapter Fifteen

32nd day, Month of the Hawk, Year of the Rat
Last Year of Imperial Prince Cyron's Court
163rd Year of the Komyr Dynasty
737th Year since the Cataclysm
Vallitsi, Helosunde

Keles bounced once, then rolled to a stop in the small stone cell. Naked and aching, he braced for what he knew would come next. He pulled his knees up as the bucket of cold water hit him. He coughed and sputtered, refusing to relax until the door to his dungeon closed.

The guardsmen, both wearing circular amulets, spat on him from the doorway. "We know how to deal with your type. We'd have done for you already, but we have orders. That'll change soon, though. The night's young, and your fate will be decided well before dawn."

The two men laughed gruffly, then slammed the door shut and locked it with a grinding click.

Keles remained huddled on the floor, shivering. The

cloak of darkness gave him some fleeting pleasure. He couldn't see the burns and bruises covering him. Every day—*twice today*—his captors pulled him from his cell. They beat on him with split sticks and knotted cords. They hung him by his wrists until his arms had all but been pulled from their sockets. They hammered his kidneys with heavy fists.

He couldn't see it, but he had to be pissing blood.

At first he didn't understand why his captors were abusing him. He was from Nalenyr, and Nalenyr had long been Helosunde's ally. Princess Jasai's arrest suggested a shift in politics, but Helosundian politics should have had little bearing on his situation. He was an Anturasi, and that fact alone should have kept him safe.

But Anturasi or not, his captors quickly learned what had happened at Tsatol Pelyn. Keles had worked magic there, and it did not matter that his magic had saved lives. It warped people. It was *evil*. He was a *xingnadin*, and perhaps *more* than just a practitioner of magic. He had to be a master of it—a *xingnacai* or even *jaecaixingna*: a Grandmaster. That made him the equal of the *vanyesh* and everyone knew the horrors that they spawned.

Fear of magic prompted his captors to be creative, lest he strike at them. Because he *was* an Anturasi, they feared killing him outright; torturing him was simply erring on the side of caution. They also drugged the meager rations they gave him, hoping that between the beatings and narcotics, he would be unable to work his foul arts.

If they only knew.

Lying there on the cold stone floor, Keles drew his consciousness inward. He retreated from the pain and the cold. His teeth chattered. Cold water dripped from his nose. Hunger gnawed at his belly. Gooseflesh covered him, but all these seemed abstractions. They were part of his physical nature, but that was all.

You have figured it out. You must do this now, while you still have some strength.

He focused on the water and sought its true nature. It wanted to flow to the lowest point in the cell. He encouraged it. He gave it a little push, and then another, registering the tingle at the base of his brain. He was touching magic very lightly, but it was enough. The water that had puddled around him slowly flowed away.

He next turned his attention to the stone under his cheek. It was just a slab of stone, hardly remarkable, but he sought inside it. He'd made this journey before and found the path easier with each repetition. He pushed into the stone's past to a time when it rested in a dry riverbed, soaking up sunlight. Keles caught it at the moment of its greatest heat, and tickled that energy into the present.

The stone warmed beneath his cheek.

He lifted his head and pushed himself back as steam began to rise. The stone began to glow softly. He stared at his battered hands for a moment, then began to laugh.

The laughter came softly. Though not yet that of a madman, it still carried enough menace that rats squealed and sought sanctuary in the walls. If his captors were listening they likely thought him unhinged—and their work completed.

Keles could have healed his hands. It would have been a simple matter of returning them to their true nature. He had enough knowledge of anatomy to know how they should be, but that was not enough for him to invoke magic. To make a change, he needed to know his own true nature. And as much as he tried to identify it, he could not. Perhaps it was because he was changing.

"It's not healed hands I need." He levered himself into a sitting position and shifted his shoulders. Stiffness had already begun to set in. Combating that problem didn't require magic, so he didn't even consider using it. He focused on the larger problem and sought solutions to win his freedom.

After their capture they'd been transported to Vallitsi to await the pleasure of the Helosundian Council of Ministers. The Desei he'd transformed had willingly set their arms aside, but each morning they rose, clad again in their armor, weapons at hand. The Helosundians didn't know what to make of that. The Desei weren't hostile, so the Helosundians decided not to slaughter them.

Tyressa and Rekarafi had remained with the column for three days, then disappeared just as they reached the capital. Neither of them had surrendered their weapons, so Keles had little fear for their safety. *Even unarmed, they would be in no danger.*

At Vallitsi the beatings had begun, no doubt at the behest of Ieral Scoan. Keles was fairly certain the man was trying to reach an accommodation with Jasai that would give his patron an advantage over the other ministers. He tortured her with the idea that Keles was being beaten and offered to stop the beatings in exchange for her cooperation.

Keles took the beatings simply because he had no realistic alternative. He tried to use magic to escape earlier, but it wasn't working. When rats refused scraps, he guessed he was being drugged. Once he stopped eating, he could work magic again, and slowly set out to escape.

And it has to be now.

Overhearing a chance comment by one of his torturers made things urgent. The man admonished another not to strike Keles in the face and to refrain from breaking a leg. "He has to be presentable to the full Council."

While the other torturer had agreed, he'd countered with, "They'll have their hands full trying Pyrust's whore."

The guard's remark meant the full Council had gathered in Vallitsi. Jasai was in serious trouble. Keles—tired, aching, and starving—had to act.

Part of him remained detached and distant as he invoked magic. He used it to draw himself to his feet and steady his limbs. Taking a deep breath, he glanced back and slowly nodded. *Now it begins.*

He touched the water and shifted its nature from fluid to vapor. The steam drifted through the dungeon and poured into the iron lock. Once vapor touched metal, the water condensed.

Keles pushed his sense into the lock. He could have touched the iron and, as he had with the stone, recalled it to a time when it was very hot, but that would take too much of his strength. Instead he concentrated on the water, making it eat into the metal. The water coursed through worn spots and tiny fissures, spreading like rusty ivy through the bolt. In no time at all, the bolt parted.

The door sagged, then the hinges, which had also rusted through, snapped. The dungeon door fell inward, then burst apart on impact. The door's nails disintegrated into rusty stains. The din of planks rattling against the dungeon's stone steps echoed loudly.

A wave of exhaustion staggered him. *Too sloppy. I have to be more careful. I don't have that much strength.*

The door's collapse brought shouts. Feet pounded along the corridor. The guardsmen's shadows fell across Keles, eclipsing him. "What deviltry's this?"

One guard dropped a hand to his sword. Keles touched magic and caressed more of the water. A fluid stream stabbed up into the man's nostrils. He sputtered and choked, his hands flailing. He tried to scream, but more water choked him. Eyes bulging, he shoved himself back, slamming the other guard into the wall, then dropped to his knees. His face darkened as he noisily tried to suck in air, then fainted.

The other guard rebounded and went for his sword. Keles forced water into the wooden scabbard. The wood swelled, holding the sword fast. Confusion knotted the man's brow, then gave way to rage. The guard pulled sword and scabbard free, then charged.

Keles took one step forward and stamped down. An oaken plank levered up, smashing the guard in the knee. Screaming, the man crashed face-first into the floor. His sword bounced from nerveless fingers. It rolled to a rest in the puddle and slowly dissolved into an orange stain.

Fatigue wrapped Keles in a leaden cloak. He wavered and caught himself with a hand. Pain arced up his arm, shocking him to clarity. He rested for a moment, then staggered forward, slowly picking his way up the steps. He stepped over the other guardsman and continued up the corridor.

At the guard's station he stripped a rough woolen

blanket from a pallet. He pulled it tight around himself, scratching his raw flesh. Shivering, he worked his way up the next flight of stone steps.

He stopped near ground level, peering through the narrow, barred window in the door. The guardroom doubled as a barracks. He couldn't see any soldiers sleeping or sitting around the lone table. A fire still burned in a central pit, and a pot of broth bubbled there. Four bowls of steaming rice sat on the table. Whoever had been on duty had been recently called away.

Probably to attend the Council. Lucky me.

But why they had left did not matter. A key ring hung on a peg set in the wall. His freedom depended upon getting his hands on those keys.

But how?

Then he smiled. A leaky bucket of water sat by the fire pit. He concentrated and pushed. A stave cracked. The bucket emptied, and Keles channeled the water to the wall beneath the keys.

Once the puddle had grown large enough, he shifted the water from fluid to solid. An icicle stabbed up and lifted the key ring from the peg. Caught at the pinnacle, the keys jangled discordantly.

Another push and the ice cracked at the base. It fell toward the door. Two more times the water melted and froze, raising the keys, then dumped them in a jangle. Finally, the ice lifted them to the tiny window and Keles unlocked the door.

Then, just as he emerged from the dungeon, the guardroom door opened.

Water flowed into Keles' outstretched hand and froze into a short dagger.

The woman coming through the door glanced at him and smiled. "Your weapon is melting."

"Tyressa?" Keles' weapon shattered against the floor. "What are you doing here?"

"Have you forgotten Prince Cyron made your safety my responsibility?"

"No." He leaned heavily against the doorjamb. "We have to find Jasai and save her."

"Already done." She crossed to him and scooped him up in her arms. "I'm getting you out of here."

"Put me down. I can walk."

"We need to run." Tyressa toed the door open and slipped into the night. She cut down an alley heading east. Other shadows detached themselves from buildings and moved with her. A sliver of light revealed Grand Minister Rislet Peyt—an ally. Keles relaxed and Tyressa laughed gently.

"My job was to find you after we'd freed our companions."

"Now you go back for Jasai, yes? I can help."

"No need."

Tyressa slowed, then set Keles down in a small courtyard near one of the city's eastern gates. It stood open, and several wagons waited near it. The Desei from Tsatol Pelyn held the gate and, at Tyressa's signal, headed out.

"I don't understand. Wagons? Supplies? How did you accomplish this?" Keles sagged against Tyressa's shoulder.

The clatter of hooves on cobblestones echoed through the night. Riders were coming fast. Tyressa lifted Keles into the back of a wagon, then turned and drew her sword. The Desei warriors spread out, sinking back into shadows, ready to attack if required.

Riders came into view and Tyressa's triumphant laugh signaled that no fighting would be necessary. Most of the riders swept past and out the gate, but one drew rein at the wagon. Tyressa plucked the woman from behind the rider and deposited her beside Keles.

"Jasai?" Keles wanted to say more, but the lump in his throat choked him.

"Yes, Keles." The Princess leaned over and gave him a firm kiss.

That brought a laugh from the rider. "You're the Anturasi she was on about."

Jasai fell back as the wagon jerked and started through the gate. "He saved us at Tsatol Pelyn."

"You have my thanks, then."

"You're welcome." Keles peered hard at the rider. "Who are you?"

"Prince Eiran, at your service."

"But you're dead!"

"The Council of Ministers certainly intended me to be." The Prince laughed. "While they're all having a banquet to celebrate my sister's capture, we've gone and stolen her away. I doubt that will help their digestion."

Keles arched an eyebrow. "Somehow I doubt that concerns you terribly."

"You're right." The Prince glanced back at the city and the open gate. "I'm more concerned about what they'll do to get her back. I'm hoping we'll get far enough away that we'll never have to deal with the consequences."

Chapter Sixteen

32nd day, Month of the Hawk, Year of the Rat
Last Year of Imperial Prince Cyron's Court
163rd Year of the Komyr Dynasty
737th Year since the Cataclysm
Plains of Tsengui, Nalenyr

Prince Pyrust recognized Virisken Soshir as a kindred spirit the very moment he laid eyes on the man. Though Soshir appeared unkempt and harried, having retreated from the fall of Tsatol Deraelkun accounted for his condition. Rumors casting him as an ancient Mystic returned to help the Empress destroy her enemy intrigued the Prince—as any military experience was quite welcome.

What Pyrust found most agreeable was the way others reacted. The core of his cadre were all *xidantzu*—independent, strong, and talented individuals. Despite that, they were clearly ready to die for him. Even the boy with the withered arm looked as if prepared to cut Pyrust down at the flick of Soshir's finger.

Pyrust had come south to the Plains of Tsengui with most of the troops he'd brought into Nalenyr. He'd deployed on the plains with two armies of his best-trained Desei troops in the center. An equivalent force made up of Naleni troops occupied the left flank. Count Linel Vroan took up the right flank with an army of troops drawn from Nalenyr's rebellious western provinces. The Prince held two armies of Desei militia in reserve, ready to reinforce as needed.

As the Prince stood with Soshir and Vroan on a hill in twilight, the *xidantzu*'s displeasure with the arrangement became evident.

"What is it you disapprove of, Master Soshir?"

"The position won't hold."

Linel Vroan, tall and arrogant, snorted with disgust. "The Plains of Tsengui have seen many battles. The Prince has stationed our troops upslope of the stream running through the center. We've dammed it at the eastern edge to flood the lands near the escarpment. This doubly wards our flank. It also allows us to concentrate our troops here, astride the road, to block the passage."

Soshir looked up at the Prince. "Your placement of troops is flawless. Turning the battlefield's edge into a marsh is likewise good. Were you fighting a conventional force, they would think twice before engaging you. The *kwajiin* will not. They will break through your lines."

Disgust filled Vroan's words. "Do not think our men cowards simply because *your* troops broke and lost Tsatol Deraelkun."

Soshir slowly turned his attention on the Naleni lord. "You assume many things, my lord. You are a fool. You believe Tsatol Deraelkun was unassailable. For it to be lost, therefore, betokens a failure of the troops defending it."

Vroan's eyes narrowed. "You deny this is what happened? You had defeated a force twice the size of that which broke the fortress. How else does one interpret what happened?"

Pyrust raised his half hand. "I believe, Count Vroan, Master Soshir wishes us to consider the possibility that the enemy we face was able to accomplish with an army and a half that which had never been accomplished before. These are some remarkable circumstances, after all."

Vroan laughed. "Yes, war-moles and giant, stone-throwing apes. Nightmare creatures to explain away cowardice."

Soshir pointed off to the right flank. "If that is what you believe, Count Vroan, then you should move your troops. It's the Virine forces that retreated from Tsatol Deraelkun which hold your flank."

"I don't need them." Vroan spat. "Let them go north with Count Derael and the Virine princeling. They can all cower in Moriande."

Where you would no doubt be happy, Count Vroan, had you supplanted Prince Cyron. Pyrust extended his hand. "Please, my lord, calm yourself. I believe, Master Soshir, you can understand Vroan's discomfort. We were hoping to invest our forces in Tsatol Deraelkun to stop the invasion. Instead, when we met your scouts, we stopped here and made the best of our situation. Historically this has been a good position."

"I do not argue that point, Highness. It is just that,

historically, no one has ever faced a force like this." Soshir shook his head. "You should pull the main bulk of troops back to Moriande."

"And surrender half the nation?" Vroan threw his arms wide. "We cannot concede that much territory to them."

Soshir ignored his protest. "You will force them to lay siege to the city and stretch their supply lines. You can keep forces in the field to attack their supplies. Laying siege to a city like Moriande will require an incredible force, and even if they field it, they have to feed it. You can bleed them. You can raid into Erumvirine. You can force them to focus elsewhere. Nelesquin will tire of his war when things slow down."

Pyrust frowned. "You truly believe Prince Nelesquin—*the* Prince Nelesquin—has returned from the grave to lead this force of *kwajiin?*"

"I have seen him with my own eyes. I've spoken with him. Yes, Count Vroan, you can mock me if you wish. I shall not challenge you since this force needs your troops. But I pray Grija does not take you, because I shall demand an accounting of your affronts later."

Vroan sneered. "Your flesh will be more easily pinked than your vanity."

"No, that is where you confuse my motivations with your own, my lord." Soshir gestured off to the south. "I don't care what your opinion of me or my troops is. We've shed enough blood; for good or ill, your opinion is of no consequence. What makes me angry is the appalling stupidity that locks you into believing you know your enemy, your battlefield, and history well enough to decide this is the place where you will be the victor.

"You say battles on these plains have brought victories

to Naleni forces, but you do not ask yourself *who* actually fought here. A hundred and twenty years go, *I* was here and fought to defend Nalenyr. Before the Cataclysm, I was here again and so was Nelesquin. We fought together here and won a great victory. I know this ground better than you, and so does he. Just as he shaped a plan to take Tsatol Deraelkun, so he has a plan for defeating an army here."

Pyrust stroked his half hand over his chin. "What do you think it is?"

"I would be lying if I told you I knew. Come." Soshir turned and entered the tent that served as Pyrust's command center. He crossed to the table, where a map of Nalenyr had been laid out. He tapped a finger against their current position.

"He knows there will be a force waiting for him here. It makes sense. So, he sends a force in that will engage your troops. He can take his time coming up through the mountains because your supply lines are stretched as thin as his."

Soshir pointed to the mountains on either side of the pass through which the Imperial Road ran. "There are other passes through the mountains. They're small and scattered. Normally getting troops through them is ill-advised because linking back up to a larger force is difficult. Nelesquin, however, has flying creatures that can carry several men. He can use them to coordinate troop movements."

Pyrust nodded. "You're saying he could infiltrate units all along the border? Do you think he would use them to disrupt our supply lines?"

"I don't know. I thought his loathing for tunnels

would preclude anything like his giant moles. But perhaps he's learned."

"Perhaps he's not Nelesquin."

Soshir's head snapped around. "If that is true, Count Vroan, we have an even bigger problem. You see, if it *is* Nelesquin, then we know he's trying to consolidate the Empire. If it isn't—if it is just someone pretending to be him, who has somehow garnered the power to create the *kwajiin*—then we have no clue as to his motivation. As nearly as we can tell, his troops slaughtered everything in the eastern half of Erumvirine. He has a foothold there. Could be he has colonized it and that's where he gets new troops."

Pyrust shook his head. "It would take fifteen years at least to raise a new crop of warriors. Twenty would be better."

"I hope you're right, but the fact is that we've no idea how many troops he's fielded. His *vhangxi* are animals, but they've torn apart troops the equal of any we have in the field. The *kwajiin* are as fierce fighters as I have ever seen." Soshir glanced at Vroan. "And you'd best not make any comments about my experience. I am *jaecaiserr,* and *kwajiin* swords have cut me more than once."

Vroan chewed his lower lip and said nothing.

Pyrust traced a finger over the map. "If he did slip troops through the mountains, he could use them to harass our lines. Were I he, I might push a larger force through and go raiding through the western Naleni marches, into Ixun."

"I don't disagree, but then we know more of Naleni politics than he is likely to." Soshir folded his arms. "I would not blame you, Count Vroan, if you returned to Ixun to safeguard your home."

The slender man's chin came up. "If Nalenyr falls, Ixun will go with it. The battle will be decided here."

Soshir shook his head. "You're still not listening to me. Nelesquin knows how to fight this ground. It may not look it to you, but this is a trap. Withdraw. Strike at his flanks. Raid his supplies. Send troops into Erumvirine."

Pyrust listened. The urgency in Soshir's voice underscored the wisdom of his words. They were facing a foe they did not know, who might well have superior troops—thousands of them. To take up a position and adopt a strategy in the face of so many unknowns was foolishness.

"Understand something, Master Soshir. Your assessment of the enemy may be accurate—and I base this on your experience in Erumvirine alone, not your history with Prince Nelesquin. I shall even break one of my reserves down into regiments and send them east and west to find any troops Nelesquin has sent through the mountains. That said, I feel I must make a stand here. You may be correct that Nelesquin knows this site, but we both know there is no better spot between here and Moriande to oppose an army."

The *xidantzu* nodded reluctantly. "There is no arguing that point."

"I find myself, therefore, on the horns of a dilemma. If I act on what you have told me and it turns out that you have erred on the side of caution, withdrawal could jeopardize the whole of Nalenyr. While Moriande can doubtless hold out against the army for a while, if we are bottled up there, Nelesquin could pour past, take Helosunde and Deseirion, and then return for Moriande."

"If he shatters your force here, he'll do that anyway."

"Yes, but he will have fewer troops with which to do it." Pyrust shrugged. "There is another problem, of course."

"Which is?"

"The Empress Cyrsa has commanded me to stop Nelesquin here."

Soshir blinked. "Then the Imperial crown on the unit banners was not to annoy Nelesquin? The Empress *has* returned?"

Pyrust nodded solemnly. "She has."

Soshir looked toward the tent flap. "I saw none of the troops that have been waiting in Ixyll."

"I don't know if those troops are myth or not." The Prince rubbed his half hand over his jaw. "She said nothing about them."

The *xidantzu* frowned. "I had an apprentice who was traveling through Ixyll to awaken her. Did he succeed?"

Pyrust shook his head. "I do not know. The Empress had long since left her sanctuary. She's been here for eons, waiting and watching, creating her own intelligence network. You certainly knew of her: the Lady of Jet and Jade."

Soshir blinked with disbelief. "That cannot be."

Vroan nodded. "I confirm it. I met her before I left Moriande. She was the Lady of Jet and Jade. My first wife was once a student of hers."

Soshir rubbed a hand over his forehead. "How could I not have seen it? She was Paryssa."

Vroan nodded slightly. "You called her Paryssa, after the flower?"

Soshir looked up, his expression open and unguarded. "It was after a scent she favored before she became Empress. When I later met the Lady of Jet and Jade, she burned paryssa incense. I called her that. Part of me may have remembered, but . . ."

The man's reaction to the news fascinated Pyrust, primarily because it revealed an unexpected side of him. Virisken Soshir, if camp gossip was to be credited at all, had a soul of iron armored in steel, and the combat skills to keep that armor untouched.

And yet, at the mention of a woman, he has softened abruptly. Is that love? Pyrust thought fleetingly of his wife, Jasai, seeking a similar reaction. He certainly had felt something for her. Pride. Anticipation for the child she was carrying. He might have even labeled what he felt *love,* but it burned so much more coldly in him than it did in Soshir.

"She's in Moriande now. She stopped me from killing Cyron."

"And ordered you down here to destroy her enemy." Soshir nodded. "Did she . . . ?"

"There doubtless would have been orders for you, had she known you were here." Pyrust shrugged. "She likely thinks you in Ixyll with your apprentice."

"Of course. You're right." Soshir nodded. "Will you have your dispatch rider convey a message for me?"

Pyrust nodded. "A rider will leave at dawn. A reply could come as early as the next day."

"Thank you, Highness."

Pyrust bowed his head. "Of course, your troops are

welcome here. I trust they are eager to kill more of the *kwajiin*."

"As many as we are able, Highness." Soshir's eyes tightened. "This is not the place I would choose to die, but for killing, it will suffice."

Chapter Seventeen

32nd day, Month of the Hawk, Year of the Rat
Last Year of Imperial Prince Cyron's Court
163rd Year of the Komyr Dynasty
737th Year since the Cataclysm
Jaidanxan (The Ninth Heaven)

Jorim gave Tsiwen as brave a smile as he could muster. "This will be for the best, sister. Thank you for convincing Grija."

She gave him a dark-eyed look. "This will get you back to the mortal realm, but it does not settle how you shall deal with your sister. What will you do?"

He began pacing along his balcony, relishing the feel of cool stone. It didn't matter that it was an illusion. "I do not know. Nirati might be convinced to go willingly into the Underworld to save reality."

Tsiwen frowned. "That would solve the immediate problem but leave Grija with another. Having a mortal in the Underworld—someone with her physical form intact—is trouble."

Jorim cocked an eyebrow. "This has happened before?"

"Several times. Human heroes seeking to free a loved one from our brother's clutches. They generally beat Grija into submission or trick him, and he lets the soul loose."

Jorim stopped and faced her. "A mortal has beaten Grija?"

"It happened with some frequency until we hid the gates to the Underworld. Our brother accepted dominion over the dead because the dead are not likely to out-think or overpower him."

"But a mortal?"

The goddess of Wisdom smiled. "Mortal life is a power unto itself. Mortals will often appeal to you or me for divine aid, but you have seen how swiftly time passes down there. By the time I might notice an entreaty, the time to intervene is long past. And yet, somehow, those mortals figure out a solution, or find courage in themselves. They attribute it to us and give us thanks and praise, but we did nothing. If they knew their power, they might mount a campaign to unseat us, just as we threw down our father."

Jorim rubbed a hand over his jaw. "You suggest that life itself is magic."

"No suggestion. It is the way of things. The birth of a child is as much creation as making a world. Shaping a bow or mastering a sword cut, all of these things are creations." Tsiwen's smile grew. "Every act of creation, no matter how big or small, changes reality. The consequences of a change are all but impossible to calculate, which makes our position a precarious one. Once someone decides the gods do not exist, we may, in fact, cease to exist."

The dragon god slowly nodded. "Those who create instead of destroy get used to expanding reality. There comes a time when their access to it expands. They gain control over it."

"True, but too many see themselves as limited. You and your brother may have wondered what it would mean to become a Mystic cartographer, but that was to study a cup of water when you were submerged in an ocean."

"So developing a skill is a means to an end, not an end in itself?"

"Not if one is capable of pushing beyond." Tsiwen walked to him and enfolded him in a hug. "Our brother comes to strip you of all I love. I recall only too well the pain of the last time, so I shall not stay."

Jorim lowered his head and kissed her brow. "Wait for me on the *Stormwolf.* I may need help navigating to Anturasixan."

"I shall be glad to be of service." In the blink of an eye she shrank into the form of a bat. She flapped hard and circled him twice before diving from his heavenly palace to the mortal plain below.

Jorim watched her go, only to turn and face Grija. Something looked different about him. He appeared less craven, more bold, but the difference was subtle and made Jorim wary.

"We have agreed, have we not, brother, that I shall

remain in my physical body for a normal span of years, then return here?"

The god of Death nodded solemnly. "We have, brother. I will not cheat you of years, even though I know it is your intent to waste them in dalliance with the woman from the east."

"You almost sound jealous."

"Of the pleasures of the flesh? Never. Too fleeting." Grija opened his hands. "Shall we begin?"

"Please." Jorim let his brother precede him up the broad ivory stairs to a bedchamber. "We have agreed my essence shall remain here until my return?"

"I have already sworn there would be no trickery."

"I wish I could remember if you made that same oath last time." Jorim lay down on the bed and shifted until he felt comfortable. He knew he needn't do that, since his discomfort was also an illusion, but the shifting was something he had done as Jorim. "I am ready."

"Good." Grija raised a finger and a long talon grew out of it. Light glinted from the edge. "Death is change. What I shall do is slice away all that is not Jorim Anturasi."

"I will remember nothing of being a god?"

"You may retain some memories, but they will gradually fade. Once I've severed your divine essence, you will be unanchored. That piece of your soul which was shaped during your time in that identity will return to his physical form."

"*My* physical form, you mean."

"Meat, skin, and bones, yes, yours." Grija's eyes hardened. "Shall we begin?"

Jorim nodded and closed his eyes. He willed himself

to melt all the illusions. Gone was his sense of the physical, of heat and cold, of light. These things still existed, but they meant nothing to him. He sank into a dim void, then a rainbow of images danced before his eyes. One was a dragon, another was a Fennych. He saw himself as Jorim, and again as Tetcomchoa and the first Emperor, Taichun. All of the images floated around, connected by ethereal tendrils.

Then a claw swept through, severing his connection to the dragon. Pain such as he had never known ripped through him. Part of him remembered that it was all illusion, but even that knowledge was drifting away. A key piece of his essence grew dim, losing itself in the void.

The talon made another circuit and Jorim screamed. He could feel his throat ripping itself to pieces as Taichun vanished. More pain, molten and surging, pummeled him as Tetcomchoa disappeared. His blood burned like acid. His body shivered.

His mortal form, stiff and cold, was pulling him in.

Grija's claw raked through his essence again and again. Each tendril parted with the twang of a tendon ripping free. Light exploded before Jorim's eyes. Panic pounded through him. He'd lost who he was, what he was. He did not know himself anymore.

The part of him that was a god had vanished.

And his body accepted him again. Spasms wracked him and bowed his back. His arms fought. Fabric tore. His arms flailed, his legs kicked, then he landed hard on a solid surface. Sparks exploded before his eyes as his head hit. He struggled to suck in breath and finally succeeded in one grand wheeze.

He rolled onto his side and coughed. He tore at the

cloth over his face. It ripped, freeing him. He inhaled again, hot air filling his lungs. He coughed explosively, tasting brimstone. Then he felt the heat of the stone and remembered that his body had been preserved in a barrel of oil. The rags binding him still reeked of it, but of the barrel there was no sign.

A low wail sounded from behind him. "Oh no, what have you done?"

Jorim rolled over and sat up. "Who? Grija?"

The god of Death looked every inch a starved cur. A thick black collar circled his neck, and a pair of black chains ran from it into infinity. The chains weighed him down, keeping his head low.

"What have you done?"

"I've done what you helped me do." Jorim tore away the rags binding his legs. "I've returned to my body."

"No, no, no, say you have not. I told you not to."

"You did nothing of the sort." Jorim stood over him and raised a fist. "You agreed to let me return."

Grija cowered. "That was not *me*. That was Nessagafel in my place."

"What? How is that possible?"

Grija wailed like an orphaned child.

Jorim almost slapped him. He dropped to a knee and lifted the chains. They didn't seem heavy at all, but Grija was barely able to move. "You have to tell me what happened."

"It was all your fault, you and the others." Grija curled a lip back in a snarl, but it had no power or menace. "You all mocked me. You defied me worst of all. I punished you, but you did not care. The others laughed at me for it. I couldn't abide that, you know, I couldn't. No one admired me. No poems praised me. No songs favored me. All I got was fear. You cannot live on fear, Wentoki, you cannot."

Jorim shook the chains and Grija yelped. "I need to know what you did."

The god of Death looked through him. "You had all given Nessagafel to me and here he slept. You helped bind him and once he was gone, you chose to follow him, to become mortal, to live as he had lived. The others watched you, watched Men, enjoyed their antics, but could I? No. All I got was the shrieking souls coming here after they died. The dead are not peaceful. I do not visit torments upon them out of need. To torture one, all I need do is catch him in a mirrored sphere so he can watch the failures that shaped his life. Then, eventually, I release them so they live again. If they succeed, they dwell with you in the heavens. If they fail, they are mine again."

Grija's eyes focused. "But you know who did not scream or complain? Nessagafel. He knew peace, so I would steal here, to the Ninth Hell, the one we reserved for him and him alone. I would stay here, bask in his peace, and he began to speak to me. I talked back. He said we were wrong to kill him. He was not going to un-make everything. He wasn't going to destroy us, not all of us anyway. Just some. Chado and Quun. They killed him. I convinced him that we were innocent, brother, you and I. We would have been fine."

Jorim sensed the lies, but it really didn't matter. He had sought to reenter his body so he could lead the way to Anturasixan and trap Nessagafel forever. Grija had re-sisted that plan—knowing Wentoki would insist on it.

Whatever Grija had been planning had failed, and Jorim needed to know what his brother had intended.

"You meant for me to be trapped in my mortal form again, didn't you? Why?"

"No, I didn't."

Jorim threw the chains down. Their weight choked Grija and forced him to the ground.

"Don't lie to me. You wanted me to be mortal again. Why?"

Grija flashed fang. "I needed your essence. I needed the strength."

"Then this thing with Nirati was a lie?"

"Yes, a ruse, and you fell for it. And Tsiwen, too. Not so wise, is she?"

Jorim stomped on the chains, again smashing Grija's face against the ground.

The death god raised his muzzle, black blood oozing from his nose. "With your essence, brother, I could have controlled our father. He could have unmade some things and remade others. I would have been first among the gods. Then you would have feared me."

"What use has Nessagafel for my essence?"

Grija laughed madly. "You helped imprison him here. Your essence was the key to his restraints. With it he regains his freedom. To acquire it, he replaced me."

"But he wasn't quite you." There *had* been something off about Grija. "There was no simpering, no fear."

"I do not simper."

Jorim growled and Grija shrank back. "If our father could replace you, why hadn't he done that earlier?"

"He had plans, brother, and they have come to fruition. He was never strong enough to rip your essence from you. You gave it freely."

Did I? His memories of being a god weren't fading. In sensing the changes in Grija, had he clung to them more tightly?

Grija peered at him closely. "You're more than mortal, aren't you?"

Jorim looked down over his body. It showed no sign of decay or the traumas he'd suffered before death. "I'm not sure what I am. Not a god. Perhaps a user of magic—unless Nessagafel healed me. Why would he do that?"

The craven god whimpered. "For his own terrible reasons."

Jorim stood. "We're in the Ninth Hell, you said. Wangaxan?"

"Yes, and there is no escaping it."

"Ha!" Jorim looked around. Aside from his brother there was nothing. "Nessagafel escaped. If he can do it, so can I."

"You will have cause to reconsider that statement, Jorim Anturasi." Nessagafel materialized as a Viruk. "After all, this place was meant to imprison gods. What chance has a mortal of escaping it? Especially when I have no intention of letting you get away."

Chapter Eighteen

33rd day, Month of the Hawk, Year of the Rat
Last Year of Imperial Prince Cyron's Court
163rd Year of the Komyr Dynasty
737th Year since the Cataclysm
Wentokikun, Moriande
Nalenyr

Though the stump of his arm itched fiercely, Prince Cyron had no time to scratch it. It had been itching for a while, but he'd not really noticed...which surprised him. Less than a month previous, the way that arm had been sucking the life from him had been the center of his existence.

The unhealed wound was a metaphor for the world. The invasion from the south, the invasion from the north, Qiro Anturasi's disappearance, and the revolt of his western provinces had torn him apart. They had distracted him, made him incapable of anything but surrender. He had been as dead as the flesh the maggots devoured in his wound.

But now ... Cyron laughed as a junior minister handed him a sheaf of figures detailing the inventory of arrows, bows, and bowstrings in Moriande's nine armories. He had thousands of bows, and hundreds of thousands of arrows, but fewer than two thousand bowstrings.

He raised the papers in his right hand. "What's more likely to break? A bow or a bowstring? What is worse, a wet bow or wet bowstring?"

The clerks and minor ministers remained hunched at their tables, nodding to acknowledge his question. They'd become used to the outbursts but, at first, they had been completely disturbed by them. None dared answer.

But circumstances had changed.

A clerk turned. "Strings, Highness. How many do we need?"

"Two per bow."

"I shall arrange for three, Highness, and settle for two and a half."

Cyron gave the man a curt nod. The clerk wrote out an order and a runner—wearing a broad, bright red sash around his middle—took it and sped from what had once been Cyron's private receiving room. He would carry the order to another room in the Dragon Tower, where it would be duplicated and distributed to every bowyer in the city and beyond. They'd sell him everything they had and produce more, quickly.

Cyron set the archery inventory on a table and another clerk removed it to be sorted and filed for immediate retrieval. Yet other clerks would pore through the files, reading everything, noting anomalies and similarities, and they would be brought up to him. He'd make a quick decision, more orders and reports would be written, and the process would cycle on.

The standing bureaucracy hated Cyron from the first. Some of it was a holdover from before, but his appointment as the Imperial Grand Minister made things worse. He compounded them. Instead of passing orders down through Pelut Vniel and the other high ministers, Cyron had demanded a staff of low-ranking clerks. He wanted men and women who had not yet become entirely beholden to their superiors. This meant he raised up many clerks who had not formally been recognized by their ministries. Cyron catapulted them ahead of others who had labored far longer.

Thirty clerks filled the room; their counterparts were scattered in a half dozen rooms throughout the castle. When a project demanded more resources than immediately available, a clerk would leave to handle that problem and another would replace him. While waiting to be called into the First Chamber, the others would engage in the review process.

This turned the bureaucracy completely on its head. Previously, it had acted as a filter. It distilled information so that the Prince only learned what the bureaucracy felt he should know. Ministers hoarded information, concealing it from their fellows and superiors. Because information was power, it flowed none-too-freely.

Cyron shook his head. The bureaucracy had enshrined inefficiency by stifling the creative power of those working in it. Innovations died at roadblocks. Problems were sequestered and buried so no shame could come to the minister whose responsibility it was to find a solution. This allowed problems to fester—even simple ones.

Cyron expanded distribution of information and encouraged solutions. With every fact passed up to him, he demanded analysis and solutions. The bureaucracy would have previously made decisions on their own, but Cyron relished having options. If he chose to ignore them, so be it; but he had hundreds of people concocting solutions that might never occur to him.

Pelut Vniel tried to stop Cyron. The Prince had gotten everything he asked for and more. Ministers buried him beneath an avalanche of information. It came in jumbled and confusing—the mess begged for ministers to sort it all out. Vniel magnanimously allowed Cyron to take as many clerks as he wanted—especially those with no experience—to deal with the information.

Cyron had turned the tables on them. He'd started by drafting plans based on the data he'd been given, then forwarded them to the ministers for their opinions. They'd taken their time getting back to him, but he'd anticipated that. He'd acted without their advice, tweaking things when they did respond, but mostly moving ahead with his plans. When they protested that he had ignored their input, he noted that their belated comments agreed with his actions.

Then he turned around and buried them with reports, requests, and other make-work. Those ministers who complained he was not giving them anything substantive to do were rewarded with serious tasks. If they delivered solid product, he continued to use them. If they did not, he neutered them with flattery and marginalized them.

Pity stupidity isn't lethal. The bureaucracy had practiced stupidity in a manner calculated to harm the nation. Primarily they neglected *maintenance*. The armories were a prime example. The first inventory had indicated there were twice as many arrows, but there had been no physical inventory—the number had been derived from adding up old records, some of which came from Imperial days. Weapons disbursed in time of emergency weren't counted as they went out, and few enough came back. As a result, a prince could look at the numbers and feel secure about his nation's preparedness.

But when an enemy came to call, he would be in serious trouble.

That worked in the bureaucracy's favor and Cyron understood that. A secure prince promoted stability. An aggressive prince might consider going to war, but his ambitions would be blunted when the true numbers were produced. The bureaucracy would promise him weapons, and would procure them; but their counterparts in other nations would then prepare for war themselves. A stalemate would ensue and stability would be preserved.

The Prince did not doubt that there were other benefits to the bureaucracy. When arrows had to be produced in haste, prices rose. Bowyers who wanted part of a government contract would willingly reward bureaucrats for favoring them. Likewise for those paid to transport the arrows and those whose warehouses stored them. The wastage inherent in that system could easily enrich bureaucrats, so motivation to change it didn't exist.

On top of that, he had other clerks going out to see if bribes were still being paid. Those who pointed out corrupt officials were given rewards and the officials were fined. Cyron functioned under no illusions that his system would eliminate corruption—he just wanted to make it less profitable.

It was too early to determine if his efforts would pay off. Senior ministers complained as if they were feeling pinched. Most feared substantial punishments if past corruption was revealed. While reports of the same had come in, Cyron did not act on them. He didn't promise that he would *not* act on them, however; he would wield that club when necessary.

And it would be. The only minister unsullied by corruption was Pelut Vniel. Rumors abounded, of course. The assassination attempt that had cost Cyron half his arm *must* have been sanctioned by Vniel. Count Nerot Scior had been identified as the man behind the plot, and there seemed little doubt that the assassin's wage had come from *his* purse. The man had fled Moriande for the westron counties, but he never would have dared try to usurp the Dragon Throne if some sort of accommodation with the Grand Minister had not been reached.

So far, Cyron's only effort against Vniel had been his general assault on the bureaucracy. Fractures were already beginning to appear as the ministers, one by one, began to cooperate with Cyron. Copies of all missives flowed to Vniel's office, but unofficial transcriptions of consultations did not. Cyron assumed that simple knowledge of these consultations would annoy Vniel. With any luck, Vniel's quest for knowledge would distract him and keep him from causing trouble.

A runner bowed before the Prince. "Highness, the Empress suggested that within the hour she would be prepared to hear your report on preparations for attack."

"Tell her I shall be with her shortly." The Prince nodded to the man, then glanced at the shaft of sunlight pouring through the doorway overlooking his animal sanctuary. It fell on the backs of two clerks who both set their brushes down simultaneously. The man handed a sheaf of pages to the woman, who gathered them into a folio. She stood and presented them to Cyron.

"The latest reports, Highness, including lists of matériel on its way south and the readiness of the troops gathering here at Moriande."

He did not take the folio from her. "You will come with me, Minister Tamirsai. You will hold the papers so I may consult them."

"As you wish, Highness." The woman smiled. It was, of course, a great honor to be presented to the Empress. Cyron regularly rewarded clerks for good work by having them take papers to the Empress. Tamirsai worked diligently and was well deserving of the reward.

Tamirsai had also received training from the Lady of Jet and Jade, though none of her fellow clerks were aware of this. She acted as the Empress' eyes and ears—one of many such agents in a cadre about which Cyron knew very little—and probably less than he thought he did. While the information she bore would be of great value to the Empress, awareness of any subterfuges among Cyron's staff would be more so.

"Very well, let us proceed." Cyron waited for her to pass in front of him. "We shall return as quickly as possible, doubtless with new orders. I shall need the figures for stored grain and a survey of wells by the time I get back. Do your work well, and you, too, shall soon know the Empress' favor."

Chapter Nineteen

34th day, Month of the Hawk, Year of the Rat
Last Year of Imperial Prince Cyron's Court
163rd Year of the Komyr Dynasty
737th Year since the Cataclysm
Plains of Tsengui. Nalenyr

We took heart in the way the skies opened up and rain poured. Water flowed into the battlefield, expanding the swamps. The clouds came in, dark and ominous, hiding the Virine mountains. They also kept Nelesquin's fliers close to the ground. Prince Pyrust ordered a watch kept and, save for grazing runs the hellbats made over the swamps, or the occasional arrow launched from on wing, they did nothing.

The marsh's expansion caused us to shift our battle formation. Count Vroan took the opportunity to initiate a realignment of our positions. One of the Desei militias shifted to the left flank to cover the swamp. The Desei Hawks came next, occupying the center, but the Naleni troops moved to the right. Vroan's westrons still held the right flank, but our lines had shifted from an east–west axis to a northeast–southwest position. This actually put Vroan's troops closest to the enemy, but he still had the stream to guard his flank.

Vroan demanded, and Pyrust agreed, to pull my half army of *xidantzu* and Virine troops back into a reserve position. Faulting his logic was difficult. The new positions had Naleni troops supporting each other on the right, and Desei troops supporting each other on the left. Where Naleni and Desei mixed in the center, Pyrust would be able to command directly. The regiments within the armies had been staggered so Naleni and Desei troops overlapped in the center.

Nelesquin's troops had come up in good order and arrayed themselves in a tighter formation than ours. We had forty-four thousand troops on our side—seven of those in reserve. The *kwajiin* numbered roughly half that. They brought with them a number of the monsters we'd seen at Tsatol Deraelkun. Their appearance shocked our troops, but the way their feet sank into the mud heartened us. While the hammer-headed apes— Dunos decided they should be called *xonarchii,* meaning "stick brains"—might be able to hurl stones into our lines, their missiles would likely get stuck instead of bouncing on through formations.

On the eve of battle, Prince Pyrust invited me to his tent. We stood beneath an awning. Rain pattered heavily against the canvas and dripped through a couple of seams. Neither of us wore armor, but we did bear our swords. I took it as a sign of respect that he allowed me to retain mine.

Pyrust studied the enemy lines. "They have no cavalry."

"In the mud they will not be terribly effective."

"That's why I'll keep mine out of the mud."

I nodded. "Good idea. Nelesquin cut his teeth fighting against bandits and pirates. He never developed a feel for the use of cavalry. When I was learning cavalry tactics, he was devoting himself to magic."

"But wouldn't his commander see the value in cavalry?" Pyrust pointed to a large pavilion across the battlefield from us. "I am assuming he's not there, your Nelesquin. He doesn't fight under the tiger-tail banner."

"No." I shrugged. "I imagine he's returned to Kelewan. He's already divined the battle's outcome with his Viruk scrying stones."

The Prince arched an eyebrow. "Does he believe such oracles?"

"It was an affectation he picked up later in life. He used to say the stones never led him astray, but the Turasynd invasion did not turn out well for him."

"Let us hope they fail him again here." Pyrust's chin came up. "Have you seen his general fight?"

"No. The battle at Tsatol Deraelkun revealed little about how he will fight here."

"But you are still of the opinion we should pull back, disperse, and bleed them?"

"Yes." I narrowed my eyes. "Is that why you agreed with Vroan's suggestion that my troops get pulled back into our reserve? Do you think I would pull my troops out too soon?"

"If I thought that, I'd have sent you to Moriande days ago." Pyrust clasped his hands behind his back. "I am confident we will fight as best we are able, but that does not guarantee victory. I do not know how this general will conduct this battle. While you and your people have provided me with some insight, it doesn't mean we might not lose."

He looked up at the Imperial banner swaying in the breeze. "There's not been a prince since the creation of the Nine who has not dreamed of fighting beneath an Imperial banner. Well, perhaps Cyron is an exception, but I certainly was not. When I came to Moriande, I was a step from killing Cyron, but he asked a curious thing of me. He asked me not to destroy so much that I could not build again. I saw empire as a political entity, but he saw it as the lives of the people."

Pyrust glanced down, the hint of a smile on his face, clearly remembering Cyron's words clearly. "My mortal enemy gave me that vision, and now it is my responsibility. I will fight here because it is my duty to do so. I would fail in my responsibility if I did not think about what might happen if I fail."

I watched him closely. "Are you going to tell me to pull my people back and not fight them?"

He turned and poked his half hand against my breastbone. "What I will ask you is to follow orders, *my* orders, no matter what they are. Count Vroan will not. He will obey until he sees a way to cover himself with glory, then my orders be damned. I will see to it he has his glory."

"Posthumously."

"It is for the best." Pyrust held his maimed hand up. "I know war well. If there is a point where things are hopeless, I will need you to organize a fighting retreat. If we fail here, the *kwajiin* will reach Moriande unopposed. If they can break our force, then the defense of Moriande will require wise leadership."

"Perhaps, then, we should change places, Highness."

"No. My people will fight for you, but they will never *stop fighting* for me. It is a difference that will mean much tomorrow."

I bowed deeply to him. "I shall abide by your orders, Highness."

"Thank you. And soon we shall laugh about my caution in the Empress' court."

"Better we do it in the Illustrated City. We'll share wine from a cup fashioned of Nelesquin's skull."

Pyrust smiled. "This we shall do, Master Soshir, this we shall do."

No one in my command appreciated the bargain I'd struck, but I understood their feelings. Captain Lumel and the Virine wanted revenge for their nation. My *xidantzu* lived to protect others through their skill at arms. Being held back grated on their souls. I reminded them that reserves would win the battle and this mollified them somewhat.

Morning dawned dim and cold. The rain had slackened into a chill drizzle. The clouds remained low, so the leather-wings did not venture high in the sky. The archers mounted on them did little damage, though our archers were not terribly effective either, save one. Penxir Aerant, a *xidantzu* archer and giant of a man who used a bow longer than I was tall, shot an arrow at a retreating leather-wing. The shaft hit its target on the downside of an arc. It passed through the driver's back and into the beast's neck. The broadhead must have severed a nerve. The right wing spasmed and folded in. The hellbat splashed down, spilling the dozen *kwajiin* archers riding it. The Desei militia sent several volleys after the survivors, killing half of them.

Our side took this to be a great victory. I thought their celebration premature. Though stuck through with arrows, the other half of the *kwajiin* made their way out of the swamp by themselves. At least one man yanked an arrow from his leg and took his place in the ranks again.

In war, the object is to destroy those you face. An enemy that does not die easily is to be feared. The *kwajiin* formations were full of such men, all of whom carried swords and long spears and woven wicker shields that had been covered with cloth. Clan badges covered the shields. The warriors had gathered tightly together, so that their formation became a wall bristling with spears.

The *kwajiin* leader had split his force into three, each corresponding to the three wings in our force. He allowed gaps between his wings, but filled those with his beasts. The *xonarchii* hauled stones forward and tossed them out into the marsh. We laughed at first, then realized the creatures could wade out to them and throw them again.

I didn't see any of the woolspiders or wall-climbers, but their use in such an open field was questionable. I likewise saw none of the flying, poison-spitting toads that had been used with some success during the siege of Kelewan. Nor did I see any of the *vhangxi,* and that was just as well. Those toad-men had a mouthful of teeth that would make a shark flee.

Pyrust's strategy was simple enough: make the *kwajiin*

pay for every inch of ground with blood. Forcing them to march over muddy ground and attack uphill would be costly. If Pyrust could bring his cavalry into play, to encircle the enemy and flank him on the right, the whole formation might collapse. That seemed like the most viable strategy, and I would have expected it to work save for one small detail.

Ranai Ameryne saw it and pointed. "This is not how the *kwajiin* arrayed themselves at Kelewan or when they killed the Iron Bears."

"They've shifted strategy. Concentrated like that, they are more likely to punch through our infantry. We have a looser formation so we can use swords."

"And that tight formation will make it tougher for horses to charge." She nodded at the marsh. "That will be a lake of blood before noon."

Below us, Pyrust emerged from his tent. He raised his right hand and snapped a white fan open. Down within the troop formations, drums began to pound. Archers ran forward through the infantry position, nocked arrows, and let fly. Though none of them had the skill of Penxir Aerant, the arrows arced into the enemy formation. The rear ranks raised their shields, forming a roof. Arrows hit, quivering in the shields. In a couple of places men fell, but the ranks closed quickly enough.

On the other side, the *kwajiin* general exited his tent and climbed up onto the back of one of the long-necked draft beasts. Its back was broad enough to have held the man's command tent, but he stood there alone on a small platform. The driver moved the creature forward. Even as far away as we were, we could easily hear the sucking sound of its feet being pulled from the mud.

As his beast came forward, the *kwajiin* executed a complex maneuver. Both wings contracted, closing the gaps. The wings then faced the rear and marched back in unison. Their formation went from a curved line, to a three-sided box open at the far side, gathering the larger creatures in the center. Once they'd gotten into position, they faced outward again, setting their spears and shields.

For Pyrust's militia to attack, they'd have to move forward into the swamp. Vroan's troops had an easier approach over more solid ground, but they'd still have to ford the swollen stream.

Once the *kwajiin* had reordered their position, they marched at us. I marveled at their precision. Spearpoints did not waver. The flanking units kept pace even though they were marching laterally. Plunging into the edges of the marsh did slow them; they came on as a unit with the *xonarchii* and draft beasts in their midst.

Pyrust exchanged his white fan for a red one. The drum cadence changed. Our arrows filled the air. *Kwajiin* fell, and their blood ran into the swamp—though not nearly enough for my taste. Within our lines, the cavalry began to maneuver, with three regiments pulling out of the center and starting around the right flank.

The cavalry would sweep around and get behind the *kwajiin* force. They would strike from behind, forcing them to flee into the swamp or onto our swords. Given our superior numbers and position, it was a flawless piece of strategy. Had I been in Pyrust's place, I might well have given the same orders.

As the cavalry thundered around in their flanking maneuver, Vroan pushed his wing forward. They moved out of pace with the other Naleni troops, who were still awaiting an order to advance. This created a gap. Pyrust flashed a signal with a fan and half his militia reserve trotted over to reinforce the breach.

On the left, his other militia unit heard the drums and mirrored Vroan's advance. They came on a bit more raggedly, but not disastrously so. But Pyrust saw their error, and signaled to them to halt. Their leaders shouted orders and the troops straightened out their lines.

Archers shot again, this time aiming. The *kwajiin* front rank went down as if scythed grass. Their spears fell, but the next rank replaced them. The *kwajiin* kept coming, spears thrusting, and finally hit our front line.

The *xonarchii* hurled stones, which struck with incredible force. One moment a man would be standing in place, and in the next his legs would be thrashing from beneath a blood-washed rock. Others would reel away, spattered with blood, arms broken, ribs crushed. Had the ground been dry, the stones would have careened further, but this was horrible enough.

The cavalry gathered on the other side of the stream, lowered spears, and prepared to charge. The creature ferrying the *kwajiin* general let out a bellow. At first, I thought it might have signaled panic because of the immediate *kwajiin* reaction. Chaos reigned for a moment, then the enemy executed a maneuver of such precision and elegance that I never would have thought possible on parade, much less in the midst of battle.

With troops like these, the world might well be yours, Nelesquin.

The back three ranks of each wing sprinted south to the formation's rear, effectively closing the box. They set themselves immediately, spears outward. Even before the cavalry began its charge, it faced a square formation that provided no opening for attack.

Pyrust signaled again and the drums boomed. His Hawks pressed forward and the Naleni wing came around. Vroan's people rushed forward, so our formation wrapped the *kwajiin* square's north and west sides. The press of soldiers stopped the enemy advance. Spears did kill some of our men, but we got into their lines and began hewing through shields.

The weight of our forces proved too great. Because it had sacrificed a third of its depth to reinforce the rear, the *kwajiin* west wing started to buckle. The cavalry waited for that wing to break or for the *kwajiin* to reinforce from the east wing. In anticipation, Pyrust waved his fan and the militia on the left flank surged forward.

That's when the *kwajiin* plan revealed itself. The swamp boiled with activity. Heads and shoulders emerged from the watery depths, rising like bubbles. Hundreds of *vhangxi*—thousands—waded from the shallow water and attacked.

I wanted to believe the *vhangxi* had been waiting in the depths of the marsh the whole time and we had somehow missed them. I needed to believe that we could have prevented the disaster that resulted. I wanted to believe there was a chance, however slender, that we could have been victorious that day. But with each passing moment, the terrible reality of the battle set in.

I think Ranai's words had been prophetic. I imagine the *vhangxi* had been sown in the water as eggs or tadpoles. They remained there until blood tainted the water. They grew quickly—with a speed somehow aug-

THE NEW WORLD 179

mented by Nelesquin's sorceries—and it was this newly spawned horde that emerged to feast on the militiamen.

The *vhangxi* erupted in the midst of our militia. They burst up out of the water, taking off legs and arms. They slashed with claws, raking off faces, then appropriated weapons from the fallen. They never paused in the attack that crushed our left flank.

Only idiots and tavern-bench generals would fault the militia for breaking. They were merely conscripts who had marched nearly four hundred and fifty miles in under a month's time. They'd had no real training. Their rations were barely enough to keep them alive. Some in the rearmost ranks did not even have weapons, and the *vhangxi* were far better at scavenging than they were.

The militia broke. While the *vhangxi* hit them in the flank, the *xonarchii* hurled stones toward where the militia linked up with the Hawks. Death lurked at either side of their formation, so their only escape was to the rear. Those too slow were trampled or cut down. Fleeing men churned the swamp into a muddy froth.

Far too many died there.

The *kwajiin* surged forward into the gap and hammered the Desei Hawks' flank. Pyrust's warriors fell back, but set themselves and repulsed the first drive. The *kwajiin* pressed hard, forcing the Hawks to give ground. The Desei held the line, every one of them knowing that once the *vhangxi* left the swamp, they would be overwhelmed.

Their only chance at survival came with reinforcements. Unfortunately, the fleeing militia headed straight for the militia reserve. The retreating troops infected the others with panic. The reserves' ranks evaporated.

They flung down their arms and raced north toward Moriande. The way they were going, I expected some would not stop until they'd reached Felarati again.

Had the cavalry been back on our side of the stream, they could have stopped the *kwajiin* advance. But out of position as they were on the far side of things, they could do nothing. The advantage they hoped to exploit never materialized.

Fans flashed and I waited to read orders to advance. None came. Drums called for retreat. The Hawks and the Naleni Dragons withdrew, but Vroan's Ixunites never managed to disengage. The *kwajiin* punched into that gap. The cavalry had come around and tried to plug it, but neither they nor the handful of militia regiments on that wing could stem the *kwajiin* advance.

The Naleni troops, hard-pressed, broke next and ran. The *kwajiin* overwhelmed the westrons. With the Ixunites laying their arms down, the *kwajiin* pressed on and slowly surrounded the Desei Hawks.

The last I saw of Pyrust, he had drawn his sword. He waved it at me—my signal to go—then he saddled up and rode down to be with his troops.

Ranai had been right. Before noon the swamp had become a lake of blood.

Too much of it belonged to the troops who might have been able to save Moriande.

Chapter Twenty

2nd day, Month of the Eagle, Year of the Rat
Last Year of Imperial Prince Cyron's Court
163rd Year of the Komyr Dynasty
737th Year since the Cataclysm
Zyarat Hills, Helosunde

Keles hunched forward and coughed as quietly as he could. His stint in the damp Vallitsi dungeon had done him no good. In the two days since his rescue, his bruises had gone from a livid purple to a slightly softer brown, with a curdled yellow at the edges. The burns had scabbed over, but the wounds remained red despite the variety of poultices he applied to them. Worst of all, his lungs had become congested and his ribs ached from coughing.

It didn't matter that he was surrounded by plants that could produce a tea that would soothe him; the refugees had little time to rest and no chance of making a fire to boil water. He did manage to chew up some leaves and roots and pack them inside his cheek. The bitter taste sent shivers through him. He managed to keep water down, but even thinking about food turned his stomach.

Prince Eiran's rescue had infuriated the Council of Ministers. They'd immediately sent messengers out to gather what forces they could to pursue Eiran and his sister. While there were those Helosundians who were more than happy to defy the Council and give the refugees aid, the band was too big for anyone to hide. The fact that over half of them wore Desei arms and had the look of battle-hardened veterans put off many sympathizers.

Though Prince Eiran claimed that he never intended to make for the Dark Sea coast, the ministers cut that avenue of escape off very quickly. That started the refugees angling southeast into the heavily wooded Zyarat Hills district in which Eiran and Jasai had grown up.

Jasai's pleasure at being home again mocked the danger of pursuit. She traveled close to Keles, ignoring warning that a pregnant woman should shy away from magic. She told folktales rich with the region's traditions. For the first time in their long association, she was truly happy.

That came as no surprise. She'd been reunited with her brother after believing him dead. The Council, working in accord with Prince Pyrust, had ordered his execution, but they'd given the job to a man whose sympathies lay with Eiran. Jasai's brother decided that disappearing would be a good way to grant him time to figure out the political landscape. He'd already gathered a small force of loyalists when he'd learned of Jasai's capture and decided to save her.

The Prince rode up on Keles' left side. "The sun will be down soon. We'll find a spot to rest, then push on."

Keles peered off to the south. "Is it me, or do the Helos Mountains appear further away?"

"Trick of the light, Keles." Jasai gave his arm a squeeze. "Eiran, can we make it to the Valley of Rubies?"

"That's where I'd like to go, but I'm not sure we'll make it. We have to cut west again. Rekarafi and Tyressa are scouting ahead, but I'm not sure that way will be open."

Keles coughed again. "I wish I felt better. If I could concentrate I could tell you where our enemies are."

Eiran laughed and the road led down into a small, bowl-shaped valley. "Don't worry, Master Cartographer, we know this area well enough. We used to drive cattle through the Valley of Rubies on our way to higher pastures. Steep, but good water; we could hold off an army there."

Jasai snorted. "You always dreamed about holding off an army there, but the only thing that invaded were our cattle."

"I'd think a valley of rubies would be invaded constantly."

"No, Keles, you're thinking of a place where the wild magic changes flowers into rubies. But this isn't Ixyll."

The Prince grinned. "You forget, sister, that stories are told of the year when all the red flowers did have ruby petals — real rubies."

"That's a silly story, and you know it." Jasai shook her head. "People tell how, that year, the flowers blossomed with gems. People ran to the valley, trampled the plants and each other. There were fights and murders. Then the plants died and the cattle had no fodder, so they died."

She gave her brother an exasperated glance. "It's all just a story to remind people that all the wealth in the world doesn't matter when money isn't what you need."

"Well, it is a very pretty place." Eiran smiled.

"I'm sure it is." Keles returned the smile. "Everything I have seen of Helosunde is beautiful. I understand why you continue the fight to win it back."

"It's more than just the land." Jasai pointed toward the mountains. "The land and our experience here has shaped us, but people must be connected to the land. It's like the story of the Valley of Rubies. How do children learn the true value of things if they don't have stories and traditions? A tree cannot become mighty if it has nothing to be rooted in."

Keles nodded. "But that story works even if you are not from here."

"But for how long, Keles?" She shook her head. "I know that the story is probably made up. At best it's a gross exaggeration of some minor historical incident. That being true, whenever I think about the valley, I can feel the cool grass under my feet and smell the flowers, and that makes it all real. Anyone can tell you the evils of greed. Objectively we all understand it, but I *feel* it because I can relate the story to a *real* place."

She stroked a hand over her belly. "What will my child *feel*? If he is connected to nothing, can anything have value for him? If he knows no hardship, can he have sympathy for those who are hard-pressed to survive? Can a man who has never known combat be a good general?

Could you be a good cartographer without experience of the world?"

"No, probably not; but experiencing something doesn't always make it beneficial." Keles arched his back and pops rippled up his spine. "Tyressa and I had a conversation once. She said she hoped your people could move on and find a home, not just keep fighting over this one. She said the struggle for Helosunde was what defined all of you."

"I'll grant she might be right, that being rooted here in Helosunde has warped some people." She looked over at him. "The Council's agents did not treat you the way we welcome guests and friends."

"I don't believe I was seen as a guest or friend." Keles coughed again. "Ieral Scoan saw me as a *xingnadin*. He wanted me broken. I don't think he's that different from anyone else in the Nine."

"You may have a point there."

"And your point is also well-taken, Princess." Keles shrugged. "The political climate in Helosunde shaped those who now chase us. The Council feared Prince Pyrust for a long time. Now they curry his favor by trying to capture you."

"This means that both Jasai and Tyressa are right." The Prince nodded firmly. "People need a place whence strong traditions can grow; and it would appear that Helosunde in its current state is not that place. Whether we find another, or reshape Helosunde, the task that awaits us will not be simple."

It seemed the Prince had more to offer on the subject, but the pounding of hoofbeats coming up the road from the south cut him off. Tyressa reined a well-lathered horse to a stop beside them. "There's a company of cavalry ahead of us. Scoan is leading them."

"How did he get south of us?"

Jasai waved away her brother's question. "How did he find so many horses?"

"They've been ridden hard, and no one has a spare mount that I saw. They must have paralleled us, then come east to cut us off when we didn't make for the coast." Tyressa leaped from the saddle and drew a sword. "Everyone into the woods. We'll hold them off while Keles gets Jasai out to the west."

Jasai shook her head. "No. These people are exhausted. I'll not have them die now so I can be caught ten miles from here."

"Jasai. Rekarafi can get you out of here." Keles looked around. "Where is he?"

"He was scouting to the west. He may have already run into them." Tyressa grabbed Jasai's reins. "Do not defy me, Jasai. Get out of here. Take Keles and your brother. Go."

Eiran slid from his saddle and grabbed Tyressa's wrist. "Let her stay."

"You can't do this, Eiran. You abandoned her once in Meleswin. You're not turning her over to him."

Eiran hesitated as Tyressa's words sank in. He ran a hand over his mouth, then looked up at his sister. "I was a coward then. I didn't know my own limits. I have a better idea of them now."

The Prince drew his sword and stepped further down the road. The thunder of approaching riders became unmistakable. The Desei warriors and Eiran's loyalists blocked the road, with Tyressa beside the Prince. A few people kindled torches and Eiran's wavering shadow weaved side to side over the roadway.

A mounted warrior burst from the dark forest tunnel. His sword hissed from the scabbard. The rider came on hard, his sword raised. It flashed down. Eiran's sword rose, caught the slash and turned it aside. The rider jerked his reins hard, spinning his horse around. Hooves gouged the earth but before he could make another pass, Tyressa darted forward and yanked him from the saddle.

The man yelped. Tyressa silenced him with a knee to the face.

Ieral Scoan drew rein. His men spread out. "Caught at last."

Eiran settled into a fighting stance, his sword raised by his right ear. "Not yet caught."

"Said as if you were the one who had unhorsed my man. I am not impressed."

"I don't care if I impress you or not, Ieral Scoan. My only concern is for true sons of Helosunde, not some creature given to obeying its Desei masters."

"I'm not the one consorting with the Desei, Duke Eiran."

"*Prince* Eiran, duly voted to that post by those you serve. Their failure to kill me did not remove that title." Eiran jerked his head back toward those behind him. "Desei these may be, but they are in service to my sister."

Ieral laughed. "And she is a Desei Princess, carrying Pyrust's child."

"But she's here, isn't she? A daughter of Helosunde, returning to her home to give birth." Eiran's head came up. He looked around at those who had ridden with Scoan. "How many of your mothers made the same journey so you could be born north of the mountains? How can you dishonor those brave women by stopping my sister?"

A few of the riders looked away, embarrassed. Ieral raised a hand to silence murmuring. "The world has changed, Eiran, and better you were dead than see it. We are Helosundian and are stronger for our unity with Deseirion. The Prince wants us to take custody of his wife and the Anturasi."

"So, it *is* Pyrust's bidding you do. The Council no longer even pretends to be Helosundian. What did he tell you? That you were riding after criminals? That you were stopping a Desei invasion? He dared not tell you the truth. No true son of Helosunde would join him in this foul task were the truth known."

Ieral slipped from his saddle and drew his sword. "I take offense at your words."

"I take offense at your actions."

"Very well, then we shall settle this here and now— provided you wish your sister to see you die. I am a swordsman of *Serrian* Tsuxai. I am of the eighth rank."

Eiran tightened his grip on his sword. "I claim no sword school."

"Then why do this?"

"Because I shall fight in his stead." Tyressa moved forward. "I am Keru."

"Keru? I am not afraid of you." Ieral waved her forward. "If you wish a spear, I will provide you one."

Eiran grabbed his aunt's shoulder. "You're not taking my place."

Jasai spurred her horse past both of them. "And neither of you acts as my champion." Her head held high, she reined up short of the ministers' man. "What price safe conduct for my companions? They mean nothing to you. I am the prize."

Ieral shrugged. "In exchange for you, the Desei can return home. The Anturasi, the Keru, they come with us. That is the only bargain that can be struck."

"And my brother?"

Ieral shook his head. "The Council has ordered his death."

"Why?"

The question caught Ieral off guard. "It is not my place to question their orders."

"But you know the answer, don't you?" Jasai shook her head. "Prince Pyrust pulls their strings, and they pull yours." She reined her horse around, showing him her back. "I withdraw my offer. I surrender to no puppet."

Eiran looked up at Ieral's men. "You allow him to pull *your* strings?"

"I don't pull strings, I cut them." Ieral Scoan flowed forward through the shadows. His sword rose and flashed liquid lightning. It swept down, passing in an arc beneath Eiran's parry. The blade came back up as Ieral spun. The leaping-dog crest on the back of his robe grew taut, then the blade fell again in a cut that trimmed a light brown lock of Eiran's hair.

The cut would have taken the Prince's head off, save that he'd stumbled forward with the momentum of his failed parry. His robe's sash, neatly cut across the knot, fluttered to the ground. The Prince pitched face forward onto the road. His sword bounced once, then spun, tracing curved lines in the dirt.

A booted foot stopped it.

Ieral shifted his stance and leveled his sword at the newcomer. "Who are you?"

The interloper hooked a toe beneath the hilt and kicked the sword into the air. Firelight gleamed from the lazily spinning blade. A hand plucked the sword from the air. He whipped it around, then snapped it forward with such force that the blade quivered.

He smiled. "This will do."

Keles' jaw dropped. *It can't be . . .*

"*Xidantzu?*" Ieral raised his head. "Begone, wanderer. You want no part of this."

"I am late of *Serrian* Foachin. I have apprenticed with Moraven Tolo." Ciras Dejote stepped from the shadow of the mechanical horse at the woods' edge and the Viruk standing beside it. "I have just seen a man claiming to be *serrcai* cut down a man who claimed no rank at all. This offends me."

"Your presence offends me." Ieral stepped back to allow Ciras onto the road. "Come, if you are so quick to embrace death."

"Draw a circle."

Even in the wan light of torches, there was no mistaking how the blood drained from Ieral's face. "You are *jaecaiserr?*"

"Is the circle done yet?"

"But this is not fair."

Ciras pointed the sword at Eiran. "You reap what you sow. The circle. Now."

Ieral lowered his sword. "I will not."

Keles dropped from his saddle and sank to one knee. He pressed his hand to the ground. The earth rippled. Pebbles danced. Stones erupted through the roadway and rolled into place. They formed a perfect circle, encompassing both swordsmen and the Prince.

Ieral pointed his sword at Keles. "There, swordsman, there is what you should kill. *Xingnadin. Jaecaixingna.*"

Ciras bowed his head. "Thank you, Keles."

The Helosundian swordsman's shoulders slumped for a moment, then he raised his blade again. "At least I shall die with honor."

Ciras shook his head. "The time for that is well past."

Chapter Twenty-one

2nd day, Month of the Eagle, Year of the Rat
Last Year of Imperial Prince Cyron's Court
163rd Year of the Komyr Dynasty
737th Year since the Cataclysm
Kelewan, Erumvirine

Prince Pyrust could not blame the people of the Illustrated City for lining the streets to jeer at him. The carnage surrounding the city, the ruin of the gates, and the hollow expressions on their faces marked them as defeated. While the Virine had never been particularly martial, they had not been useless either. Proud beyond reasoning, perhaps, but they claimed an Imperial legacy that every other of the Nine wished for itself.

Pyrust had never been favored in Erumvirine. Spies had reported that the Princes and populace feared him. He read that fear in their eyes now along with anger. *Had I come as a liberator, they would have welcomed me with flowers.*

He trudged along with others of his command. Count Vroan and his surviving Ixunites had entered the city triumphantly. Trampled flowers marked their passage. Vroan had pledged his fealty to the *kwajiin* quickly, and the Ixunites had even guarded the Desei fighters for Nelesquin's troops.

It would appear, Cyron, that someone else will have to rid you of that traitor.

The heavy chains linking Pyrust's wrists and ankles clanked with each step. It was not their weight that slowed him, but the short length of chain from wrist to ankles forcing him to shuffle stooped and subservient.

I am forced to walk as if conquered.

Pyrust felt anything but conquered. Exhausted, certainly, and bruised. Three horses had died beneath him in that battle. He'd gone down only after his sword had broken and the ax he'd appropriated got lodged so deeply in a *kwajiin* chest that he could not pull it free. He'd certainly been defeated, but conquered?

No.

"Not so proud now, are you?" A madwoman, with one eye wide and the other squeezed shut, broke through the edge of the crowd. She grabbed his chains and yanked. Spittle flecked her lips as she screamed. "We've an emperor here! You're a fool to defy him."

Pyrust shoved her away. "Then your duty is to the Empire, isn't it? Get out of my sight."

More of the crowd cheered her and jeered him. Virine warriors—old men, mostly—wearing blue sashes on their robes, forced the woman back. Someone in the crowd threw a rotten piece of fruit. Handfuls of mud, stones, and night soil followed, pelting Pyrust and the eighty warriors who were being paraded through the streets.

They have no idea what they are doing. Mud and feces missed the intended targets and instead splashed against the city's walls. The beautiful murals that had given the city its name added new stains to the blood that had dripped over them. They destroyed out of fear, and from that fear there was no recovering.

Pyrust raised his head. Cyron had warned him against destroying too much. Pyrust had not thought that possible. Kelewan showed him that it was. Out of fear the people cursed those who would have freed them. Men collaborated with their conquerors. Pyrust did not doubt that any armies marching north to lay siege to Moriande would have units drawn from the Virine and the Five Princes. Fear would unman the greatest of heroes, and surrendering to fear, in some ways, was the greatest of sins.

The old woman had understood that. To all others she had been a madwoman, but Pyrust had recognized her. Delasonsa, the Desei Mother of Shadows, had come in disguise. Others had seen her yank his chains, but she'd managed to slip a small garnet-and-silver ring onto his smallest finger. The talons clasping the edge of the garnet were sharp and poisoned. A casual scratch at his throat, and he'd die inside a minute.

Painlessly, too. She would not have me die an ignominious death.

She'd have rescued him, too, were that possible. Pyrust knew better than to think it was. Any effort to rescue him would doubtless kill loyal Desei agents. He would not reward their fidelity thus. With his comment to her, he'd turned Delasonsa over to Empress Cyrsa, to serve her as faithfully as the assassin had served him.

Prince Nelesquin might not have transported him to Kelewan to kill him, but it certainly wasn't to let him go again. Having Pyrust brought to heel would make for a great show, and would sow doubt among the opposition. Only by escaping could Pyrust salvage any victory from his defeat.

Nelesquin could not let that happen.

By dying when he wants me to be kept as a pet, I defy him.

Pyrust smiled grimly. His defeat hardly warranted a death sentence. In retrospect, Virisken Soshir's strategy would have been more effective—and might yet be. Even with reinforcements from the south, Nelesquin's army would be hard-pressed to lay siege to Moriande. Bleeding the army, hitting it where it was weak, these things could blunt the attack.

He'd fought on the plains because the Empress had ordered him to do so, but he could have easily overruled those orders. The fact was that he'd *wanted* to fight there. He had believed he could win. And he could have, save for a certain confluence of circumstances.

They did not defeat me, really, I defeated me.

Up to that battle, his southern campaign had been conducted flawlessly. He had used the superior intelligence and training of his troops to outwit the enemy. He'd crushed the Helosundians. He'd tricked Vroan. He'd overwhelmed Cyron.

But while his flooding of the plains had mirrored the tactic he used against the Helosundian Council of

Ministers, it had actually worked against him. It narrowed the battlefield, which gave the *kwajiin* an advantage by allowing them to concentrate their troops.

Marching through the city, he ignored the catcalls and curses. Instead, he once again envisioned the battle. He should have contested the enemy's entry into the plains. His cavalry could have made countless grazing attacks, raking the *kwajiin* with arrows. It would have made the invaders fear the cavalry, and that fear would have slowly killed them.

Weakened, the *kwajiin* would have had to choose battle or withdrawal. Pyrust could have retreated before them, then hit their supply lines. The invaders would have fallen apart.

So the question is not why *did I lie to Soshir, but why did I choose to* believe *the lie?*

Pyrust hesitated for a moment, then stumbled forward when pushed from behind. He had his answer and for that answer he thought he might, in fact, deserve to die.

Doing what he *should have done* was not the work of a *warrior.* Cyron could have run *that* kind of a campaign. It would not have been a military victory, it would have been a victory of logistics. He would have been doing to the *kwajiin* what Cyron had tried to do to him. Pyrust would have controlled the invaders by denying them supplies—a shopkeeper's war.

Victory was what they required of me, but I wanted a specific type *of victory—a* military *victory. More the fool, I. Never buy with blood what can be won with words, time, or rice.*

The parade of soldiers stopped at the Imperial Palace.

Kwajiin warriors pulled Pyrust from the midst of his companions and forced him up the stairs. At the top they allowed him to turn and look back. The crowd of Virine dwarfed the soldiers. As miserable as his men looked—Desei, Naleni, and Virine combined—they possessed more nobility than all the residents of Kelewan.

As the warriors marched Pyrust into the palace, he could not help but smile. He'd never seen the place before, but it lived up to even the most fanciful of descriptions. Nelesquin's new statue glared down at him, but did not inspire fear. In fact, Pyrust took heart in seeing it.

He filled that niche very quickly. The man clearly suffers from vanity.

The trek up the stairs and to the throne room confirmed Pyrust's assumption. Already murals had been repainted, rewriting Virine history. Nelesquin's face replaced those of legendary heroes—no matter that the events depicted occurred *after* the Cataclysm.

The guards stopped him at the throne room's entrance. They unlocked his chains. They stripped off the soiled robe and replaced it with a plain red one. They looped a gold sash around his waist and even tucked a short dagger in a wooden scabbard at his right hip.

Then the doors opened. A long strip of red carpet edged with purple connected the entrance to the foot of the throne dais. Nelesquin sat in the Bear Throne, backed by a huge stone disk with all the signs of the Zodiac carved into the edge. It transformed the Bear Throne into an Imperial throne and its presence did not surprise Pyrust.

What *did* surprise him was the fact that the disk was

taller than any door or window in the room. It had no seams. *How did he get it into this room?*

Tales of his *vanyesh* and their power tightened Pyrust's guts. *If his forces are backed by* xingna, *is there a strategy that will defeat them?*

Pyrust lifted his chin and began the trek along the carpet. Aside from Nelesquin and himself, only two others occupied the room. One, a slender man in an emerald-and-black cloak, stood to Nelesquin's left. The other man knelt at his right, on the floor, with a golden chain connecting his collar to the foot of the throne.

Nelesquin stood. "Of you, Prince Pyrust, I have heard much. My field general praised you and your effort. As you can see with your brother, Prince Jekusmirwyn, I am not without mercy. A man of your skills and standing could be of use in my Empire."

Nelesquin's rich, warm tones filled the room. Jekusmirwyn twitched at the sound. The man's eyes did not quite focus in the present. Pyrust had seen that look in the eyes of those Delasonsa had tortured. He understood the quality of Nelesquin's mercy.

Pyrust stopped shy of the throne and chose not to bow. "It has not been my custom to subordinate myself to a prince."

Nelesquin smiled slowly. "I am an emperor."

"A pretender. Empress Cyrsa sits on the Dragon Throne in Moriande. Her claim predates yours and is stronger."

The larger man's eyes narrowed. "I thought you were a warrior, but you speak like a bureaucrat. Tell the truth. You chafe beneath her orders."

Pyrust rubbed his raw wrists. "I would chafe beneath your orders as well."

"Brilliant." Nelesquin looked to his companion. "I told you, Kaerinus, there were men of this age that yet had steel in their spine. The worthy did not all die in Ixyll."

The cloaked man said nothing.

Nelesquin stepped from the dais and waved Pyrust over to a window. He slid a panel open. Down below, in the square before the palace, the eighty men who had marched in chains with Pyrust stood surrounded. Visible from that height, eighty wooden crosses were being erected on the city walls.

"I have need to show mercy to the people of Kelewan. I will pardon eighty men and women to celebrate our victory, and have your men crucified in their place. It's a most unpleasant way to die."

Pyrust nodded and fingered the ring. "I am not a stranger to crucifixion."

"Freeing the Virine will build loyalty, but I need them less than I need a man like you. If you join me, then Deseirion and Helosunde will come with you. This makes eliminating Nalenyr much easier. Cyrsa will be deposed and the rightful order can be reestablished." Nelesquin rested a hand on Pyrust's shoulder. "You will be much rewarded and your men will be spared."

"Your offer is most generous . . ." Pyrust's right hand came up and around in a backhanded slap that caught Nelesquin on the right cheek. The pretender staggered back. His hand rose to his cheek and probed the gash.

He began to laugh. His hand came away dry. The torn skin was not bleeding.

Nelesquin's blue-eyed stare bore into him. "Poison, I assume?"

"A noxious venom. Some sea creature, I suspect. It will be painless."

Nelesquin nodded. "I'm quite sure it would be. Have I anything to fear, Kaerinus?"

The cloaked man shook his head. "I can neutralize it, but what is the point?"

"True." Nelesquin smiled and ran a finger over the torn flesh. In its wake the flesh had sealed itself. "You see, Prince Pyrust, when I decided to become Emperor, I did not wish to leave anything to chance. Not even death. I took precautions. Were I as shortsighted as you are, I should now be dead and you would be a hero."

Nelesquin's fingers weaved through a sigil. Purple fire illuminated the character for a heartbeat, then Pyrust's silver ring heated up. It glowed, then melted through the Prince's little finger.

Pyrust clutched his hand to his chest, breath hissing between clenched teeth. Blood dripped, but the robe absorbed it. Then something hit him in the back of his knees, driving him to the stone floor. Nelesquin grabbed a handful of his hair and jerked his head back.

"I would have given you much, had you but worshipped me."

"What you would give, I would never want."

Nelesquin stooped and drew the dagger from Pyrust's sash. "Then I shall give you eternity to mull over your folly."

The Desei Prince caught his face flashed in reflection on the steel. He smiled. His eyes betrayed no fear and remained clear, even as Nelesquin drove the dagger into his throat and lodged it in his spine.

Pelut Vniel stared at the dagger lying on his tea table. He looked down at his reflection. A haggard man looked back. Dark circles haunted his eyes. His flesh had taken on a pallid hue.

His gaze flicked from the dagger to the note that had come with it. Prince Cyron had written it himself. Pelut recognized his brushwork. None of the others had come in the Prince's hand.

"The tragedy of battle now demands all take heart and unite to oppose the enemy. Those who do not do their utmost in opposing him, are complicit with him. Make this blade the sign of your commitment to the future."

Pelut shivered. Others who had gotten daggers from the Prince had proudly slid them into their sashes. The Prince had won them over. Praising them. Rewarding them. Making them feel important, but in doing so he had overturned the natural order of things. He had destroyed the safeguards that prevented the nation from lurching into anarchy or despotism. It did not matter that his efforts seemed necessary to oppose an enemy. They transformed the state into something that would always *need* an enemy.

Once Nelesquin was defeated—*if* he was defeated— where would Cyron turn next? Cyrsa would occupy the throne, but it would be Cyron's dream of empire that would be fulfilled. He would make his vision real, by hook or by crook, destroying the very structures that had kept humanity safe.

Every other minister's dagger had been sheathed, but not the one sent to Pelut. *Cyron acknowledges my threat.* The others had been invited to join Cyron, but Pelut was invited to kill himself. That was what the bared blade meant. If Pelut wanted to provide his own scabbard, if he wanted to acquiesce to Cyron's wishes and work with him, then he could be accepted.

My companions are all fools.

They failed to see the true import of the gift. They believed Cyron was raising them in status equal to warriors. He would allow them to wear a dagger in his presence—a privilege reserved for nobility and honored warriors. But this also bound them; Cyron could slay them if they failed. A few might have seen that, but they dismissed it. Nelesquin's threat made Cyron's plan seem acceptable.

It is not! I see the greater threat. Pelut reached for the hilt. In some ways it would be easier for him to pick it up and open a vein. He'd heard that cutting his wrists would be painless. Here, in a pristine room, wearing a white robe, his death could even be beautiful.

Far more beautiful than his current circumstance. He remained a minister of high rank, but in name only. Cyron had isolated him and hobbled him. Things were moving too swiftly to be controlled, and once the controls Pelut had labored his whole life to sustain were destroyed, they could never be slipped back into place.

So, there it is. The challenge. Join Cyron or kill myself.

Both options revolted him. Though he had been outmaneuvered, he had not been defeated. If he killed himself, the world he fought to preserve would die with him.

"You give me two choices, Prince Cyron. Join you or die." Pelut picked up the dagger and watched himself smile. "I see a third. Fight you. The world cannot surrender to you, nor can it survive you. So fight I will—from the shadows, from behind a smile, but fight I shall."

The man nodded to himself. "And when the time comes, this very blade will be your undoing."

Chapter Twenty-two

2nd day, Month of the Eagle, Year of the Rat
Last Year of Imperial Prince Cyron's Court
163rd Year of the Komyr Dynasty
737th Year since the Cataclysm
Wangaxan (The Ninth Hell)

Jorim backed away from Nessagafel, but his efforts put no distance between them. The other god had not moved, of course. The Viruk could have pounced on Jorim easily, but he refrained. He watched Jorim and fear trickled through Jorim's belly.

"There is no escaping this place, Wentoki, nor is there any escaping me." Nessagafel chuckled, raising goose-flesh on Jorim's arms. "I think you should want me to escape. I shall manage that trick with your help."

Jorim narrowed his eyes. "You want to destroy everything, kill everyone."

"You listen to Grija and the others? You believe them?" The Viruk god shook his head. "*They* have every right to fear, Grija most of all. He was my first, you know. My first child. I created him with a thought—a half thought, really. I was not paying much attention. I merely wanted a witness to my creation, and he was what I got."

Grija cowered in a grey heap, which shrank away to nothingness as Jorim watched. "Is he?"

"Dead? No. As long as he is remembered a god can never really die. His place can be usurped, he can become obscure or irrelevant, but die? No. I didn't allow for that."

"But Quun and Chado killed you. The constellation that represented you was ripped to pieces."

"As attacks go, it was masterfully done." Nessagafel clasped his hands together. "Had you helped them, I might have been so shredded that I could never have brought myself together again. You know you are the most powerful of them all. You are my most complete creation."

"Are you flattering me?"

"It is not flattery, Wentoki. They are limited. They take their aspects from ordinary animals, but you, you are a *dragon*. As a man, you have traveled the world enough to know there are no dragons, and yet you exist. Did you ever wonder why?"

"There are many creatures of myth."

"But none of them are gods, Wentoki." Nessagafel did not step closer, but the distance between them shrank. "When I chose to first visit my creation and walk in flesh, I made myself into a dragon. I did not visit often, but I found the Viruk and the Soth worshipping that image. I chose it for you, and I made you in that image. I made you in *my* image."

"But you are a Viruk."

Nessagafel shrugged. "When the Viruk became self-aware, they chose to believe that their god had made them in his image. I *had* made them, of course, and felt no need to disappoint them. Now this form suits me, but I can change."

In an instant the Viruk vanished and a young human boy took his place. "This should be more comforting to you."

"It won't make me forget."

"Forget what?"

"That you tricked me into divesting myself of my divine nature."

"That was unavoidable." The boy held up his right hand and flicked the little finger. A black ring circled the base of it, pinching the flesh. "I used your nature to unlock the chains binding me here. This ring is all that keeps me from my full power."

"It stops you from unmaking everything?"

Nessagafel nodded. "In fact, it does, but this should not be your concern. I would never unmake you."

Jorim arched an eyebrow. "No? Why not?"

"Because I need you. Do you know why I created you last?"

"No." Jorim watched Nessagafel and listened to his words. From the way the elder god was taking him into his confidence, the words were meant to beguile him. Flattery combined with sincerity and respect were intended to slip past Jorim's guard, and might well have, save for his Anturasi upbringing. Countless sea captains had used the same tricks to win charts from him, and Jorim had never surrendered so much as a sketch.

"Grija, incomplete as he was, was suspicious. He talked to the others and plotted with them. I knew they would come after me. They had to. The old and the new cannot exist together. So, I created you in my image, to be my ally and my revenge. By failing to join with them, you allowed me to return from the void. Together we can sweep them from the heavens. Had they killed me, you know they would have turned on you, too. But I made you strong enough to defeat them."

"If I could destroy them, I could destroy you."

The child-god smiled. "Yes, exactly. I meant you to be my rival. Think of it, Wentoki. You wanted to be so much like me because I made you so much like me. I became flesh; so did you. I created the Viruk; you created the Fennych to kill my Viruk. I know it was a symbolic attack on me, but I've forgiven you that excess because we are so alike. I gave the Viruk magic; you gave Men magic. You have made me very proud." His voice sank into a whisper. "And you have made them very *jealous*."

Nessagafel slipped his hand into Jorim's, and the dark void in which they stood melted as night before dawn. Green grasses grew up, and flowers thrust red and yellow blossoms skyward. To the right lay a swath of rain forest akin to that of Ummummorar. To the left the forests of Nalenyr. In the meadow, spotted antelope grazed. A clouded-leopard lounged in a thick tree branch. From the distance came the trumpeting of an elephant, and the coughed roar of a maned cat answering.

"When the others are swept away, Wentoki, we will reorder the world. You know that is what you have been doing. It's what your grandfather has been doing: making things over again. He's really doing my work—*our* work. We will make the world the way it is supposed to be. You and I, we can do that."

"What about those I love?"

The child's face brightened innocently. "We shall save them! We shall give them all they wish for. We will make them happy—happier than if they had died and gone to the appropriate heaven. We will do for them whatever you want. All you need do is unlock this last little restraint."

Jorim frowned. "How are you restrained?"

"It's a minor thing, really. I have my power back, I can travel to the heavens for a bit, but am still anchored here. I cannot reach the physical world, so my work must be accomplished through agents." Nessagafel held his hand up. "Just slip this ring from my finger and my will shall be done."

"There is one thing I don't understand." Jorim chewed his lower lip.

Impatience crept into Nessagafel's voice. "What is it, then?"

"If you created me in your image; if I am powerful enough to defeat the others, then I am powerful enough to challenge you. Perhaps even to defeat you. Aren't *I* the greatest threat you face?"

"You see? That's why it was perfect. You and I strive against each other. We push each other to be better."

"But don't you fear that I will someday depose you?"

Nessagafel shook his head. "No. I made you my equal in all things, and then I gave you something I have no use for."

"What?"

"Compassion."

The child's fist came around, changing from a pudgy hand to a Viruk claw. Nessagafel thrust his talons into Jorim's stomach and yanked. Blood splashed and entrails gushed.

Jorim dropped to his knees, scrambling to stuff his intestines back in. As he reached down, his hands filled with glass needles that punctured his bowels. He tried to scream, but thorned ivy shot up from the meadow and threaded its way through his body. A green tendril grew out through one nostril, then wrapped around his head, closing his jaw tight.

All around him the ground rippled. Anthills erupted like little volcanoes. Bright copper ants swarmed toward him, like spokes on a wheel. Each tore out a little piece of his flesh.

Dark birds circled overhead. Their fierce cries split his head with lightning. The ants traveled the ivy, crawling within. Their fire coursed through him. Their venom melted his liver and its dark nectar nourished and encouraged the vine.

Nessagafel, once again a Viruk, eclipsed his view of the birds. "Study the vultures while you can, Wentoki. They will come and eat your eyes soon enough. Then all you will be able to do is linger in darkness, feeling the ants pick you apart. The agony should be exquisite and without end."

The Viruk again raised a hand, and the ring around the smallest finger now appeared in white. "Unlock this and I shall unlock you. There is no escaping Wangaxan or me, Wentoki, save through granting me my freedom. The sooner you do this, the better for everything you have ever cherished."

Nessagafel vanished.

The pain did not.

Chapter Twenty-three

2nd day, Month of the Eagle, Year of the Rat
Last Year of Imperial Prince Cyron's Court
163rd Year of the Komyr Dynasty
737th Year since the Cataclysm
Kunjiqui, Anturasixan

Nirati woke with a start. Lingering traces of fire faded from her hand. She glanced down. An ant was walking across her knuckles. It tickled, and she laughed at the panic that had jolted her awake.

Takwee, a small furry primate that had been nestled against her stomach, picked the ant off her hand and ate it.

"I imagine there are plenty more of them to devour here."

Takwee rolled away and scratched at her golden fur. She stretched, then rolled onto her stomach. She crept along stealthfully, stalking more ants. She exaggerated her movements and glanced back, puzzlement slowly replacing the expectant delight on her face.

Nirati smiled and sat up, rubbing her hand. Normally the little creature's antics sparked laughter, but Nirati could not set aside the sensation of pain. Something had happened somewhere and echoes of it had reached her.

She looked around, half-expecting to see the ghost of her twin, Keles. She'd met him before, here in her paradise, while he was dreaming. That encounter had had a dreamy quality to it for her as well. Their being twins, and the blood link they shared as members of the Anturasi family, had enabled them to communicate—though she'd never managed it before coming to Kunjiqui.

Before dying to get here.

She shivered and Takwee ran over to hug her. "Nothing is wrong, little one." Nirati kept her voice even, but it could not hide the lie. Something was wrong. Someone was in pain. It wasn't Keles, but it was someone to whom she was close.

Holding Takwee tightly, Nirati stood and began to walk to the west. It really didn't matter which route she took. Here, in Kunjiqui, it was enough that she desired to go west. Her intent would take her there, and the length of the journey would only last as long as necessary.

She thought immediately of Nelesquin, but she knew he was in no pain. She loved him—or, at least, she believed she did. *Or had . . .* Since his departure for the Nine, she found it harder to remember him. It was as if he faded from importance as physical distance between them grew.

"But then, the dead are not known for their imagination." The details of her death had evaporated, but she knew that she had died. Nelesquin had returned to the land of the living, but she had been barred from accompanying him. This made her wonder if their love *never should have been.*

Her grandfather's condition was the next logical source of anxiety. Qiro had created Anturasixan and, within it, Kunjiqui, as a sanctuary for her. Nelesquin had used her grandfather's magical abilities to make Anturasixan into a womb for the forces he would use to conquer the Nine Principalities and reunite the Empire. He'd driven Qiro hard, wearing the man down until, in his free moments, he shaped armies of mud and set them loose on the sea.

But her grandfather was not in pain. That she would have known directly. As he cared for her, so she did for him. She cared for everything abandoned on Anturasixan—including the remnants of the nations and races Nelesquin had used to shape his army. If something was amiss, she would know, but the only thing out of place was the pain.

Nirati turned a corner and the landscape shifted. She stood on the edge of a mile-high cliff staring out at a huge, circular bay. An island sat in the middle; it looked completely out of place, as if a jagged stone thorn had pierced Anturasixan. Even the seabirds wanted nothing to do with it.

And below, dead fish washed up thickly on the beaches.

She caught sight of her grandfather down below and waved. The man waved back, then in three impossible strides was at her side. He smiled, lifting his head, letting his white mane dance in the breeze. Gone were any signs of fatigue. Instead his pale eyes pulsed with life.

"What is this, Grandfather?"

The old man glanced at the mountain as if he'd forgotten its presence. "You have heard of Mount Shanfa in Moryth?"

She nodded. "You said it was the tallest mountain there."

"Very good." He stroked her brown hair. "I was never satisfied with Jorim's measurement of its height. I brought it here so I could do the work myself."

"Jorim?" She rubbed at her hand again.

"Yes, he always relished the trips south. He pleased the Prince by bringing back animals to be caged—much as I was caged." Qiro peered past the mountain toward the Nine. "Cyron has yet to pay for the outrages he visited upon us. Yet I could have abided all of them, save for what he did to you, my pet."

"Grandfather . . ."

Qiro turned, caressing her cheek. "What is it, Nirati? I've disturbed you. Is it the mountain?"

Before she could reply, he gestured and the mountain slowly sank into a boiling sea.

"No, Grandfather. It's Jorim." She showed him her hand, but no physical evidence of the ant's passing remained. "I awoke feeling pain, Grandfather. Jorim is hurt. I have to help him."

Anger gathered on Qiro's face. "No, child. What you felt wasn't real. Don't I know your brothers better than you? Don't I share that special link with them; share their thoughts? Wouldn't I know better than you if Jorim was hurt?"

"Yes, but . . ."

"Do not question me." He opened his arms wide. "Have you forgotten what I have given you? Others abandoned you, but I did not. I built for you this paradise. Are you so ungrateful? Do my gifts mean so little to you?"

Nirati stepped away. "No, Grandfather. I love you—I love all you have done for me. So do my brothers."

Qiro laughed, but Nirati found no pleasure in the sound. "They have no idea what I have done or what I can do. They have no chance of understanding. Not your brothers, not Nelesquin, none of them. Even you refuse to understand who I am and what I am."

With a contemptuous flick of a finger, Qiro made the mountain rise again from the ocean depths. With another gesture he sliced the top from the mountain as cleanly as if he wielded an invisible sword. The stone rose in the air. It flattened into a thick disk, which hollowed itself into a wheel. Spokes connected the exterior with a hollow hub. In it hung a platform linked to the hub's rim by slender spokes and wheels. As the large wheel rolled through the air, the platform remained stable.

The ground shook when the black wheel touched down and rolled toward them. Takwee squealed and Nirati dropped to her knees. The wheel rumbled forward, stopping when Qiro raised his hand. Somehow the towering device remained upright and the platform slowly swung to a stop.

Qiro nodded at her. "They think of me as a cartographer. They cannot see more, even though I understand far more than they can even imagine. Jorim brought animals back for the Prince, and wrote reports. Did he think I could not understand them? And Keles, when he surveyed the Gold River, I understood. I understood how he wanted to transform the river, making it passable to commerce. Yet everyone thought I was just the one who made maps. Worse, they thought I was the one who presided over a workshop of others who made maps. They forgot that I had traveled, I had seen the world.

"They dared not imagine that I *understood* it." Qiro smiled. "And because I understood, I have been able to change it."

"Yes, Grandfather."

Qiro's eyelid twitched. "There are things going on, Nirati, that need not concern you. You should remain free of them, but I cannot. I am going to have to leave you here. I need to return to the Nine and set things to rights."

"You will stop Nelesquin?"

"Oh no, I have no desire to do that. He has value, your Nelesquin, and I shall use him."

Nirati looked up at him. "I don't understand, Grandfather. Nelesquin used you badly. You were . . ."

"Broken? Crushed?" The old man nodded. "I can remember that, but dimly. I was not myself then. But I do not expect you to understand."

"No, Grandfather."

"But I *do* expect you to obey me, however, so that the Anturasi family may take its rightful place in creation."

She nodded. "Yes, Grandfather, I shall obey. What would you have me do?"

"Nothing, child, nothing at all." Qiro bent down and kissed her on the forehead. "Knowing that you are here and safe will grant me the peace I need to deal with what I face. Will you do that for me, Nirati?"

"Yes, Grandfather."

"Very good. Thank you." He smiled. "Await my return, child, and all shall be well."

Qiro turned and rose in the air. White hair flowing, white robe flapping, he settled on the platform at the wheel's heart. The wheel lurched forward, then turned, leaning over. Nirati feared it would fall and her grandfather would be crushed, but then it righted itself and plunged down the cliff.

She scrambled to her feet and rushed to the cliff's edge. The wheel hit halfway down. The tremor dropped her back onto her knees again. The wheel bounced forward and splashed into the water. It continued to roll past the decapitated mountain, then sank beneath the waves.

Her hand rose to her mouth. Her grandfather would drown. *Or will he?* He clearly did not think he was in danger. Yet to travel from Anturasixan to the mainland rolling along the bottom of the ocean had to kill a man.

"But he is no longer a man."

Nirati shivered and Takwee hugged her tightly. She stroked the creature's fur, hoping its warmth would transfer to her, but to no avail.

Then something burned her foot. Another ant—this one bigger and copper-colored—walked across her foot. Its mandibles closed, tearing away flesh. Nirati smashed it with her hand.

She rose and backed away from the cliff's edge. Where the wheel had slammed into the ground, a rift had opened. Copper ants were pouring from it.

Already they were devouring the dead fish.

The pain began to fade and the blood to dry, but the impression of Jorim that seeped in intensified. The pain was his pain. She wanted to scream for him, but she couldn't. This frustrated her, but she knew it was for the best. If she gave voice to his agony, it would drive her mad.

But as Nirati stepped away from the cliff, a thorned vine caught at her ankle. The vine grew thicker, then tightened. Thorns pierced her flesh.

Takwee leaped from her back and uprooted the plant, tossing it away, but the vine stabbed its roots back into the earth and began to grow toward Nirati again. Takwee squealed in terror, extending bleeding paws to Nirati. The woman took the creature into her arms, stroking her fur, refusing to panic.

"This is my place. This is *my* paradise."

She drew a crescent-shaped line through the air with a finger. The section of the cliff described by her gesture broke away and slid into the ocean. It swept away the copper ants and the vine. It took everything save for the sense of her brother's pain.

Nirati looked off in the direction her grandfather had gone. "You didn't feel Jorim's pain because you cannot, Grandfather. I am closer to him now. I am dead. I belong in the Underworld, and this is where Jorim is trapped."

She turned from the ocean and began walking. It took her no more than a dozen steps before she turned to the right and arrived at her destination. Takwee leaped free, hooting delightedly. The creature crept up to the edge of the spring-fed pool and watched as little fish flashed gold and silver beneath her shadow.

Takwee circled the pond so she would not have the sun at her back, but Nirati remained, her shadow stabbing across the glassy surface. "From these depths Nelesquin emerged. I doubtless came to Kunjiqui through this portal as well."

She stared into the shimmering water and the pond began to drain. The water eroded a tunnel through the earth. Fish flopped. Springwater trickled down one wall. The tunnel opened out and spiraled down into darkness. A fetid breeze rose, smelling of things worse than dying fish.

Takwee backed slowly away from the tunnel's mouth.

Nirati smiled. "I want to go down there even less than you, but I have no choice. My brother suffers. I cannot allow this."

Takwee drew another step back.

Nirati laughed. "I understand what I am doing, Takwee. Though I may be dead, I am not stupid. We are off to lay siege to the Nine Hells, and we shall not go alone."

Chapter Twenty-four

4th day, Month of the Eagle, Year of the Rat
Last Year of Imperial Prince Cyron's Court
163rd Year of the Komyr Dynasty
737th Year since the Cataclysm
Kelewan, Erumvirine

It occurred to Nelesquin, as an afterthought, that leaving the crucified soldiers high on the city's walls might not give his visitors the correct impression of Kelewan. Yet, if any of the *vanyesh* noticed, they gave no sign. They had sailed across the Dark Sea and down the Green River, arriving at the quays with little ceremony. Dockworkers had known something was amiss when a ship came down the river faster than the current could have taken it, yet without oars, sails, or draft animals in sight. Most of them fled, making the sign of a circle to ward off magic, but one brave soul brought word of the ship's arrival to the palace.

Nelesquin made for the docks immediately, but without apparent haste. It would not do for him to seem anxious—though, in truth, he was. Kaerinus appeared unchanged despite the years. Nelesquin wondered how time had treated those who had waited with him in the Wastes.

The first of the *vanyesh* bounded from the ship, vaulting over the wales to land on the docks in a crouch. He appeared to be nothing more than a skeleton, his bones wrapped in silver. The metal had been etched with fine sigils and symbols. The creature—Nelesquin could hardly think of it as a man—rose to eight feet, and a second pair of whiplike arms uncoiled themselves from around his spine. A knot of fine silvery filaments rose from his skull like a warrior's topknot, and a pair of long swords crisscrossed at his back.

The only recognizable thing about him was his face. A metal mask replaced his flesh but moved with a fluid reality. The creature smiled and slowly stalked forward. When he reached a respectful dozen paces from Nelesquin, he dropped to a knee and bowed deeply, holding it for a very long time.

Nelesquin smiled. "Rise, Pravak Helos. Be welcome in Kelewan."

The metal man's head came up. "You are the dawn after a terrible night, Highness. We came as quickly as we could."

"And I am pleased to have you here." Nelesquin looked past him at the ship bobbing quayside. "How many of you are there?"

The giant lowered his head again. "Seventy-two. We had numbered more, but some did not survive the journey."

Nelesquin glanced at Kaerinus. "See what you can do for them."

"It has been a long time, brother." Pravak gave Kaerinus a smile. "Many will need bearers. If you take them to the circle outside the city, they will get better. In our form, we need the wild magic."

Kaerinus smiled, then headed back toward the gate to order bearers and other helpers.

Pravak stood and looked longingly at the small stone circle near the city gate. "If I could trouble you, Highness?"

Nelesquin smiled and led the way to the stone circle. Pravak stepped over the white stone rim and smiled with the satisfaction of a man entering a warm bath. "We stopped at a few small towns on the way downriver, but they have little enough magic trapped in their circles to help. We almost put in at Dreonath, for magic lingers there, but we could not countenance a delay."

"You anticipated my need."

"Circumstance forced our action. You won't remember Tolwreen, Highness, though you have been venerated there as a god for eons. We worked hard to maintain our number so we could rejoin you when the time came. We kept to ourselves but Turasynd Black Eagles found us. Since you had allied with them in the past, we forged our own alliance. Barely a month and a half ago we concluded an agreement. The Black Eagles and their allies already maneuver to attack Deseirion."

Nelesquin frowned. "At what cost?"

"They want Deseirion."

"Ha! I would never give them part of the Empire. Did you agree to this?"

"Yes, Highness." Pravak's metal flesh flowed into a smile. "We never had any intention of allowing them to keep it. Prince Pyrust, as near as we have learned, is the most capable military leader alive. We wished to distract him."

The Prince nodded. "Pyrust *was* the best. He's dead now."

Pravak shook his head. "The Black Eagles could not have reached Deseirion yet."

"He did not die in Deseirion. He died here. I killed him myself." Nelesquin rubbed a hand over his beard. "But, tell me, how did you learn of Pyrust and the state of affairs in the Nine?"

"There are wanderers in the Wastes who tell us much. We've used them in your service before." Anger etched deep lines onto Pravak's face. "One such was a man named Ciras Dejote. He bore the sword our brother Jogot Yirxan carried. We welcomed him and he told us much of the outside world. We thought him Jogot's reincarnation and believed his arrival was a sign that your return was imminent. Then he betrayed us and almost destroyed our alliance with the Black Eagles. Worse yet, we believe he and his companion were searching for Empress Cyrsa."

Nelesquin rested a foot on the circled edge, then leaned forward on his raised knee. "Cyrsa is in Moriande. Pyrust was her general. My troops defeated him and are on their way to lay siege to Moriande. I shall be leaving in a week and you shall join me. All who can travel will join me."

Pravak shook his head. "How did you . . . ?"

Nelesquin reached inside his robe and pulled out a

black leather sack. "The stones warned me. They warn me of many things."

The metal man laughed. "And I used to think you relied on them too much. They have served you well."

Pravak looked back at the barge and Nelesquin followed his gaze. Two of the *vanyesh*—one hopelessly slender and the other with a human torso grafted to a metal scorpion's body—carried a large wooden box off the ship. The scorpion bore it on his back while the other flitted to the left and right, steadying it. The nervous one calmed considerably once they reached solid ground and the box could not fall into the river.

Nelesquin's mouth went dry. "That is it, then?" Without waiting for an answer, he shook the stones in the pouch, then opened it and peered within. "Almost. Almost."

"As you wished, Highness."

The Prince nodded and forced a smile onto his face. "Kaerinus, see that the box gets to the palace, in the place we have prepared."

Kaerinus bowed deeply. "As you desire, my lord."

Pravak frowned and lowered his voice. "Kaerinus looks odd, Highness."

Nelesquin nodded. "He has spent much time away and has picked up some odd habits. He is yet as loyal as ever. Now how is it that you were taken in by the one who bore Yirxan's sword?"

"He and his companion slew some looters who were despoiling graves for corpse dust. They showed respect for the dead. We tested him and he *is* Jogot reincarnated. We had no means of knowing he would betray us."

"No, of course not." Nelesquin smiled slowly. "He returns and repeats the betrayals of before. We'd known there was a spy in our midst, Pravak, and now we know who it was."

"I would not have thought it was Jogot. I questioned him and never suspected."

"Kaerinus did as well, and so did I. He was good, but he failed to destroy me then, and has failed to destroy our cause this time." Nelesquin patted his comrade on the shoulder. "Think no more on it. You are here now. We have no more worries."

The two *vanyesh* smiled at each other and turned to watch their surviving comrades leave the ship. So many of them could barely move. Nelesquin was struck by the number who could be carried in a child's arms, hanging limply as rag dolls. These men had once been a proud company of sorcerers and warriors who feared little. Magic had become their way of life and now, for so many of them, it *was* life.

But when I employ them in battle, they will vanquish all they face. Cyrsa has nothing like them. They will crush her troops and my empire will be returned to its rightful owner.

Nelesquin nodded. "It will be good to fight together again, won't it?"

Pravak did not immediately reply. He stared past Nelesquin and slowly stood, drawing his swords.

Nelesquin turned and followed Pravak's gaze to the east. Something huge and black rolled along the river—a wheel of incredible size. Trees cracked and fell as it rolled closer. People and livestock ran from beneath it, then turned and stared as it rolled past.

The wheel slowed, then stopped at the foot of the furthest dock. The man in the center of it descended, drifting to the ground. Nelesquin caught the tingle of magic. Pravak clearly felt it, too, and straightened up as if newly energized.

Nelesquin recognized Qiro, but there was something different about him. He, too, seemed rested and years younger. *He comes as if joining his equals.*

Qiro bowed, but hardly deep enough, and certainly not long enough. As he came up, he nodded to Pravak. "It seems forever since we met, but it cannot have been more than fifty-four years. I am Qiro Anturasi."

Pravak's face grew animated. "I would not know you, save for your voice. This is Prince Nelesquin, my master. Highness, Qiro Anturasi played a big part in your return."

Nelesquin held a hand up. "I already know Master Anturasi, thank you. Qiro, I had not expected you to come here."

"Circumstances have changed, Prince Nelesquin. My presence is required." Qiro smiled and his voice remained even. "You move to conquer Nalenyr. Without me, your invasion will fail."

"Have you forgotten the troops we fashioned, my friend? The Durrani have already defeated a Naleni and Desei force."

Dockside commotion stopped Qiro from answering. The earth beneath the stone wheel began to sink and the wheel tipped. It hung in the balance for a heartbeat, then it went over. The wheel toppled, smashing the dock into kindling and exploding an old fishing boat. It splashed into the river, sending tall waves washing over the banks, which lifted the *vanyesh* boat and deposited it on the end of its dock.

Nelesquin frowned. "The wheel blocks half the river. Please move it."

Qiro nodded. "Of course, Highness."

The cartographer turned and slipped a foot out of his sandal. With his big toe he drew a straight line, then an oxbow curve, then another straight line. About six inches closer to the river he drew the same figure paralleling the first.

Magic crackled through the air. Blue fire played over Pravak's silver bones. Some of the somnolent *vanyesh* jerked and thrashed as if they'd been dashed with a bucket of cold water. The magic raked stinging nettles over Nelesquin's flesh. He dug fingernails in his own palms to fight the urge to scratch.

The Green River, four hundred yards wide and thirty deep, shifted in its bed. The water quickened, carving through the southern bank. The ferry dock tore away. Warehouses collapsed and debris began to flow downstream. People scrambled from houses mere seconds before the river consumed them. The water boiled black with mud. Fish floated to the top, flopping weakly before being sucked back down.

Inch by inch, foot by foot, the river changed course. What it inundated to the south, it left dry on the north. The *vanyesh* boat slipped off the dock and came to rest amid flopping fish and mud-covered pilings a good ten feet below the level of the dock. Children ran out, heedless of their parents' cries, to pull fish from the river and search for lost treasures. Here and there lay bones of men and horses or other beasts that had been washed away in spring floods, or tossed into the river to hide murders.

Finally, the water slid past the stone wheel and continued east to the ocean. The river calmed itself. Fish were able to swim again as the silt settled. On the far bank, one more warehouse collapsed, but the river nibbled away no more land.

Qiro turned back to the Prince and slipped his sandal back on. "You should have them make a garden here. The dirt will be rich and the garden will prosper."

Nelesquin shook his head slowly. "I merely wanted you to move the wheel."

"I know." Qiro smiled. "But I wished to move the river."

"Whatever for?"

"It is simple, Prince Nelesquin. Yours is the Empire, but mine is the world."

"That could be taken to mean, Master Anturasi, that you no longer serve me or my cause."

"Hardly, Prince Nelesquin." Qiro laughed easily. He walked over to a pair of puddles and gouged a channel with his heel that linked them. "There, I do you yet another service. You may not think so now, but you will see."

The cartographer's smile broadened. "Now, let us discuss this invasion of yours, and how I shall make it succeed."

Chapter Twenty-five

6th day, Month of the Eagle, Year of the Rat
Last Year of Imperial Prince Cyron's Court
163rd Year of the Komyr Dynasty
737th Year since the Cataclysm
Wentokikun, Moriande
Nalenyr

The last thing I wanted to do was to appear before the Empress at the head of a defeated army. The battle had not been mine to lose. My troops and I could not have salvaged it—I knew that, and so did they. Even so, I still bore responsibility.

Deshiel Tolo, Pasuram Derael, and Captain Lumel took charge of our force. They reorganized it, rounded up deserters, and deployed our meager cavalry as scouts. They ranged south to check on the enemy advance. For whatever reason, the *kwajiin* did not seem interested in pressing their advantage, but none of us were inclined to trust appearances.

Just over a hundred miles separated them from

Moriande. They could be there in a week. There weren't enough *kwajiin* to surround and isolate Moriande, so the siege would be nasty. Their very presence would cause a panic. It was easy to imagine streams of refugees heading north.

Messengers had been dispatched to Moriande with the dire news. Out of the forty-four thousand warriors we'd had at Tsengui, only a third survived. Desei line troops had taken the majority of casualties. The survivors—primarily cavalry—might well have been dead. Their prince had fallen. Though they never could have saved him, they all imagined they *might* have and that gutted their morale.

If there was going to be any hope for Moriande, we had to rebuild that morale. I focused them on vengeance. I told them that if Prince Cyron thought they'd been broken, he'd send them home. They'd never get their chance to avenge their beloved Pyrust. I also played on their contempt for soft southerners, using it to rekindle their pride. They would show us all how *true* warriors fought, and they would gain immortality because of it.

The Desei conscripts were little more than cattle. Most abandoned weapons and armor as they fled. They'd been reduced to exhausted, terrified wretches marching north through enemy territory. Their spirits had been completely broken. The surviving Hawks had nothing but contempt for them. And shunned by their own people, they had nothing to live for. They just wanted to go home.

Only I couldn't let them do that. Once we got to Moriande they'd be rearmed or used as forced labor. A handful might see Deseirion again, but war's voracious appetite made that doubtful.

The Virine and my *xidantzu* were in the best shape of all. They'd fought the *kwajiin* before and survived. They didn't share contempt for the other. I culled the troops from Tsatol Deraelkun for officers and imposed them on the Desei conscripts. This created sufficient structure that desertion dropped off and the conscripts' morale began to pick up.

I selected a valley about eight miles out from Moriande to house the army temporarily, then rode ahead to meet with the Empress. Resupplied, clad, and fed, they would look much better coming into the capital.

Tired though I was, just catching sight of the White City lifted my spirits. It gleamed, its tall towers unbroken. I reined my horse in and stared—wondering what Nelesquin or the *kwajiin* would make of the view.

Then three men stepped from the forest. Not even a year previous I'd stopped in the same spot.

Back before all this had begun.

Back before I knew who I was.

The largest stepped to the fore. "There's a toll on this road, friend."

"Blood or gold?"

"I'm sure you'd rather be paying gold instead of blood."

I shrugged and shifted in the saddle. "I've killed your like on this road—in this spot—since before the Time of Black Ice."

Two of them laughed, but the third slowly clasped his hands at the small of his back.

I glanced back over my left shoulder. "In half a week

an army will be coming up this road, to lay waste to Moriande. Now you can go to Moriande and be useful, or you can die here."

The leader laughed again and looked at his two comrades. One laughed with him, but the other kept his hands behind his back. The leader frowned at his companion. "What's with you?"

"My mother lives in Moriande." The goldfish crest on his robe shimmered as he shifted from foot to foot. "If what he says is true . . ."

"He's lying to save his skin."

"But we saw the army head south."

"That was Pyrust, and good riddance to him. Let him rule in Kelewan. He's never coming back this way."

I straightened up and looked at Goldfish. "Come to Moriande. Find me through *Serrian* Jatan. I'll give you honest work."

The other underling, who wore a crest of a seated dog—probably stolen from a Helosundian deserter—looked up. "Me, too?"

"Hurry." I smiled at the leader. "Coming to Moriande, or do we make the road a little less thirsty?"

His companions stepped away, isolating him. His hand went to the hilt of his sword. "I'm not afraid of you."

"The quiver in your voice suggests otherwise."

"I'm not afraid of you. I'm afraid for my mother." He brought his head up. "S-she lives in Moriande, too. I think."

"Good. Wait here for my army. Ask for Ranai Ameryne. She will bring you into Moriande. Dunos will take you to *Serrian* Jatan. I'll find you there."

The three of them straightened into a line and bowed. I returned the bow and rode on. I would see two of them again. This gladdened me, but only for as long as it took them to disappear into the woods. A month from now, none of them would be alive.

I doubted, a month from now, that Moriande would be alive.

Prince Cyron greeted me in Wentokikun's throne room. He looked different than when last I'd seen him, and it was not just the half-empty sleeve. He'd lost weight and had that haggard look of a man with too little sleep. Yet his blue eyes still possessed an inquisitive quickness that marked the sharpness of his mind.

He waved me forward and came halfway down the red carpet to welcome me. "I know it's not me you wanted to see, but I needed to see you. Are you prepared to direct the city's defenses?"

"Absolutely not."

"What?"

"I have no skill at defending against a siege, Highness. I will be on the walls fighting the *kwajiin,* but if I had any skill at resisting sieges—or any inclination toward that art—I'd have died in Kelewan."

Cyron stared at me. "But you were the leader of the Emperor's Bodyguard."

"You've forgotten. He died. Not much of a recommendation." I smiled. "I sent you the best man for the job. Count Jarys Derael."

"Yes, but he's . . ."

"Crippled?" I frowned. "His body's hurt, but not his mind. You *must* have an appreciation for that situation."

Cyron's face flushed crimson. "Point well made. I *have* been sending him information. Humoring him, really, since you sent him. I thought ... but, never mind. I will consult with him."

"And act on his plans?"

The Prince laughed. "Yes. No need to twist the only arm I have."

"He'll know how to defeat them."

"What of Pyrust?"

"Dead, probably. I don't know. I sent a messenger offering to ransom him."

"And Vroan?"

"He survived. I did not like him, so did not extend the same courtesy."

"Pity. We could have spared a bucket of warm horse piss." Cyron sighed. "I had planned to monopolize you to go over facts and figures, but I shall leave that for Count Derael."

"I am interested, but ..."

The Prince nodded. "She waits for you in my sanctuary. She hopes you won't be angry with her."

"Why would I ... ?"

"There are some things, Master Soshir, that only the Empress knows." Cyron smiled. "Best not to keep her waiting."

The palace's sanctuary made it easy to forget the horrors to the south. Lush plant life filled several acres, drawn from throughout the Nine. Flowers clung to trees, and sweet fruits I'd not seen in eons hung from branches. The thick vegetation deadened sound from beyond the walls. The yowls of exotic animals echoed through the jungle, and if not for the white stone pathways, I might have thought myself in the depths of Ummummorar.

The scent of one flower, *paryssa,* conjured memories that carried me further away. I smiled and drifted deeper into the sanctuary. Lost in memories, I saw little of it. Wrapped in enchantment, I really didn't care.

I first saw Cyrsa in Kelewan, at an elegant brothel called the House of the Jade Maiden. The big, rectangular building possessed an interior courtyard garden very like the Prince's sanctuary. I'd spent the night with a woman Nelesquin had recommended—his taste in women had always been exquisite. I had awakened and stepped into the garden very early, before the sun had evaporated the dew. From deeper within I heard girlish giggles and the clacking of sticks.

The garden path opened onto a crushed marble circle. Two young women played at sword-fighting. Paryssa had red hair back then, and her silver eyes flashed brightly. She circled the other girl, stalking her, then struck quickly.

Her foe shrieked, then ran past me, sucking on her fingers. I could only smile, amazed, as Paryssa saw me, bowed, then struck a pose meant to be fourth Tiger. How odd it seemed, her being trained for pleasure when she could fight skillfully.

I had been taken with her immediately. In free moments I would school Paryssa in the way of the sword, indulging her, praising her. She incorporated what I taught into a dance, which delighted warriors. They, like me, came to enjoy her company in all ways.

And then, at Nelesquin's urging, I bought her and gave her to our father, the Emperor, as a gift.

I entered a marble-strewn clearing and my guts tightened. She stood still, her back to me, bearing a willow switch. I allowed the stones to crunch beneath my feet, but she did not turn. Her head sank just a little, then she looked back shyly—again the young girl even though we had known each other for eons.

"Do you think, Master Soshir, you can come to love me again?"

I bowed to her deeply, as befitted the Empress, and remained low as befitted the one who had long since captured my heart. I slowly straightened.

"Your question presumes I stopped loving you."

She turned to face me. She wore a white robe trimmed in green. Black thread had been used to embroider crowns on the breast, back, and sleeves. The same thread tiger-striped the hem, and worked hunting tigers onto the ends of her sash. Her open gaze searched my face. The slight narrowing of her eyes betrayed concern.

I waited, not reacting, leaving myself open to examination. I had no idea what she was looking for, but she seemed not to find it. She smiled and idly twirled the switch in her hand, then turned away from me and began to walk deeper into the sanctuary.

A twitch of the willow branch invited me to follow.

"How shall I address you, Highness? Do you answer to the name my father gave you, or . . ."

"Or have I taken to changing my name as you warriors often do?" She spun and lashed me playfully with the switch. "Here you may address me as you wish, but formality shall be observed at court. And how shall I call you?"

"I think a return to Virisken Soshir will most discomfit our enemy."

"Then it *is* Nelesquin?"

"I saw him at Tsatol Deraelkun."

"Has the grave taught him anything?"

I caught the switch on its next pass and tickled her nose with the tip. "He is as ever he was: arrogant and confident. He also appears to be somewhat wiser. Years in the grave have made him more dangerous."

Again she studied me for a heartbeat, but the smile did not leave her face. "We prevailed against him once."

"And we shall again."

I offered her my hand. She dropped the switch and took it. I drew her to me and luxuriated in her warmth. "Prince Cyron said you feared I would hate you. Is that because you knew who I was but never told me?"

She laid her head against my breast. "I knew who you *had been*. Who are you now? Virisken Soshir?"

"It's a name." I frowned. "It's one of the people I've been. Who am I? I don't know. By the time this is over, I certainly hope I will have found out."

She kissed my throat and said something softly, but the raucous cry of a creature flying overhead stole her words. A large, cold shadow passed over us.

I thrust her behind me and filled my left hand with steel.

One of Nelesquin's flying beasts, stinking of carrion, landed heavily in the stone circle. A *kwajiin* rode at the base of its neck. Behind him sat a mad artist's conception of a human-Viruk hybrid, rendered as a silver skeleton. Two tentacles unwrapped a canvas-shrouded package and unceremoniously tossed it clear of the beast's furling wings.

"There is your general, dead by Prince Nelesquin's hand."

I recognized the voice. "Pravak Helos. You've looked better."

"Virisken Soshir." The metal man threw his head back and laughed—a haunting sound that elicited angry growls from the sanctuary's other animals. "I'm glad you're alive. Had I leave from my master, I'd harvest your head."

"Step down. We have a nice little circle here."

"You dishonor yourself, tendering an offer you know I must refuse."

"Another time, then, after the puppet master has cut your strings."

The monster's silver face closed. "Is that the little whore who led us to ruin hiding behind you?"

The Empress stepped from my shadow. "You followed Nelesquin into ruin. It's an error you compound."

"We will undo what you did." The *vanyesh* tapped the *kwajiin* beastmaster on the shoulder. "We shall meet again, Master Soshir, and I will kill you."

"And I, Master Helos, will melt your bones and give the silver to beggars." I bowed respectfully.

He did not.

The beast spread its wings and beat skyward. The blast of air staggered us. I slipped an arm around Cyrsa as the creature faded into a dark spot against the sky.

She snorted. "Some of the *vanyesh* have survived."

"Nelesquin wants us to fear their return."

"I do."

"Wise woman." I hugged her close. "There is no good to come of it."

Chapter Twenty-six

6th day, Month of the Eagle, Year of the Rat
Last Year of Imperial Prince Cyron's Court
163rd Year of the Komyr Dynasty
737th Year since the Cataclysm
Helosunde

Ciras Dejote laughed happily. "When Rekarafi found us, he told us you were alive. I scarcely believed he was able to find you, but I never should have doubted."

"He tracked me from Ixyll to Felarati." Keles coughed. "Such as it is, I *am* alive. Barely. My travels have not been kind."

The swordsman nodded, keeping his true feeling hidden. When they first met, Keles Anturasi had been a quiet man. He had endured the hardships of traveling in the Wastes without complaint. He'd even accepted a bit of sword training from Ciras, despite the slender likelihood of ever needing it. The expedition had toughened Keles up some, but he had still been soft.

No more. Where there had once been hints of fat, bones were easily visible. His hands were not healing quickly. His body bore bruises. Wrinkles radiated from the corners of his bloodshot eyes. The cough, though dry, never really stopped. Where his flesh was not purple, brown, or yellow, it was grey. Strands of white shot through his brown hair.

Even Prince Eiran looks better than he does.

Scoan had wounded the Prince, but not mortally. The blade had to slice through the Prince's knotted silk sash, his silk robe, and the garment beneath. Only the tip had caught flesh. The wound had been a handbreadth long, but had not run deep. No internal organs had been damaged. The wound had been stitched and, against his protests, Prince Eiran had been forced to travel on a stretcher borne by two of Borosan's *gyanrigot* soldiers.

The pink of Eiran's cheeks compared favorably with the pallor of Keles' flesh, but both men needed rest. Getting through the mountains was not going to be easy, especially if the Council of Ministers had more hunters in the passes.

Ciras squeezed Keles' shoulder. "Rest, my friend. We will see you safely to Moriande."

Keles smiled weakly. "And you, Master Dejote."

Ciras slipped away, threading through the camp. Tyressa nodded in passing. Keles had always been her charge, but her manner toward him had changed. Ciras would never have thought gentleness was a Keru trait, but Tyressa softened when she dealt with Keles.

I wonder if he knows how lucky he is? Ciras shook his head. *How lucky we've all been?*

The soldiers who had been under Scoan's command

quickly professed undying fealty to Prince Eiran, his sister, and the nation of Helosunde. They immediately offered up all they knew about plans for the fugitive's capture and suggested routes for escape.

The various factions—Eiran's rebels, the Voraxani, Jasai's Desei, and the newly loyal Helosundians—made camp nearby and planned to travel to the Valley of Rubies in the morning. Borosan spent his time compiling all the geographical data he'd collected for Keles in Ixyll. Warriors set watches and an odd sort of normality settled over the camp.

Ciras sought out the Viruk and bowed. "Master Rekarafi, I would ask of you a question."

The Viruk, who crouched with his back against the trunk of a huge oak, nodded. "You wish to know if I was aware of Voraxan's location."

"Yes."

"I was. I helped them find it." Rekarafi picked up an acorn and crushed it between thumb and forefinger. "I was with the Empress and her expedition."

Ciras' jaw dropped. "You fought with which side?"

"Neither side. This struggle between barbarians and civilized men has defined Men. You endure hardships because to surrender would somehow diminish the nobility of those who fought to protect you. This is nonsense. There was no nobility. Imperial forces and the *vanyesh* did as much to hurt one another as the Turasynd did; and even they had their squabbles between bands."

"But the *vanyesh* were evil."

"Perhaps, yes, but what does it matter to me? I am Viruk. I have lived since before Virukadeen destroyed itself. I remember a time when the Viruk could bear chil-

dren. I remember a time when Men were our slaves—
cherished, yes, but no more to me than a horse or a barn
cat might be to you. Your ideas of good and evil are
meaningless."

Ciras' eyes narrowed. "I don't believe you."

Rekarafi waved his comment away. "I would not waste
a lie on you."

"You lie to yourself." Ciras pointed back toward the
encampment. "You would not have gone to watch the
battle if you had no feeling for those fighting. You were
acquainted with Prince Nelesquin. You knew Virisken
Soshir."

The Viruk nodded. "The one you knew as Moraven
Tolo, your master."

The confirmation of what Vlay Laedhze had said surprised Ciras. "You knew, and you said nothing?"

"If he chose no longer to be known by that name, who
was I to chain him to it again?" Rekarafi half lidded his
eyes. "Perhaps I *have* lied to myself. I *did* care for the outcome. I grieved for the dead. I helped those who survived."

"Did you know that the Empress had left Voraxan and
returned to the Nine?"

"It does not matter, Ciras Dejote. Your path was
meant to touch Voraxan. It has."

"I don't understand. Can you see the future?"

"I am not a Gloon. I have just lived many of your life-
times. Just as dogs circle before they lie down in grasses,
so the affairs of Men circle. There are currents in time,
and roles that must be played."

Ciras shook his head. "No, I refuse to believe that. In

the past, I struck Virisken Soshir down, but I would never dishonor my master that way."

"But, in the past, Virisken Soshir was not your master."

"Who was?"

"It does not matter." Starlight sparkled in the Viruk's dark eyes. "All that matters is who your master is now."

You're upset at being called a Gloon, but then you give me a Gloon's riddle!

Rekarafi's parting comment puzzled Ciras. He could come up with a half dozen ways to apply that question and get three times as many answers—none of which made the future any more clear. To complicate matters, travel south was hopelessly uneventful, which left him plenty of time to ponder the permutations.

That changed at dusk on the second day. Ciras had been with the vanguard scouting the road, and had sent back reports of what they had found. Now he took some delight in seeing the Viruk's green flesh turn as grey as Keles' as he beheld the phenomenon.

"Here's a riddle better than yours, Rekarafi."

The cartographer slipped from the rear of the wagon. "This isn't supposed to be here."

"I didn't think so."

Keles crouched and looked south. The land had been torn in half. Bits of turf and trees on the far side still fell from jagged edges. No river had softened the banks or carved the rift. A god must have pulled the land apart, splitting it suddenly. There could be no other explanation.

The cartographer looked up. "At least a mile across, and half of that down. No trails. Did you look into it?"

Ciras nodded slowly. "I did not like it."

"Me, neither. There are spots where the bottom doesn't exist." Keles threw off the blanket and rocked forward onto his knees. He stripped off his bandages, then rubbed his palms together. He shifted his shoulders, then placed both his hands flat on the ground.

His eyes closed for a second, then he recoiled, jerking his hands up as if burned.

"What's the matter?"

Keles looked at his hands. "When I touched the earth, it felt wounded. Slashed open like Prince Eiran's belly."

Rekarafi crouched. He extended a single talon and scraped a circle around Keles. "Try it now."

The cartographer gingerly put one hand down. His fingers lightly stroked the ground. Keles pressed that hand flat, then carefully put the other hand down. Then his eyes closed and his body jerked. It jerked again, but he hunched his shoulders and blood slowly drained from his face.

He knelt there for a minute or more, then his eyes fluttered open. "There is something very wrong here."

Ciras crouched. "You have a gift for the obvious."

Keles laughed. "Your voice, my grandfather's words."

"What is it?"

Keles scratched the back of his neck, smearing dirt. "I don't know. When I touch the ground, I can usually get a sense of the surrounding area. Everything is where it is meant to be. Does that make any sense?"

Ciras nodded.

"This is the opposite. If an earthquake had opened this rift, it would feel natural. Or if a river had carved it. Whatever did this wasn't natural."

Keles flipped a small stone into the rift. "The really bad thing—the thing that *hurts*—is the thing at the bottom. I've never felt anything like it before. It is *wrong*, blasphemous. And I can't tell you what it is because it really isn't anything. It's the absence of anything. It's as if, down there, nothing has ever been."

Ciras stood again. "I guess we camp here, then look for a way around tomorrow."

Keles shook his head. "There is no way around. It travels in both directions."

"From the Dark Sea to the ocean?" The swordsman stared in disbelief. "The continent has been split? Will water fill it?"

"Eventually, if it does not drain out through the bottom." Keles chuckled. "At least we have trees to build some ships to sail across."

"That won't do." Ciras raked fingers through his hair. "We have to get south. The *vanyesh* have doubtless already reached Nelesquin. We have to reach the Empress. We've got to get to Moriande."

Keles began wrapping his hands again. "There is nothing I can do, Ciras."

Rekarafi toed the edge of the rift, then looked at the cartographer. "Yes, there is. Make this elsewhere."

"What?" Keles frowned.

"You did it in Ixyll."

"This isn't Ixyll. We were moved, I moved us back. And this isn't like Tsatol Pelyn. I just remade a fortress that had fallen to ruin." He held up his hands. "I'm still healing from that."

"In one, you reconnected things that had been severed. In the other, you rebuilt something that was broken." The Viruk pointed at the rift. "This is severed *and* broken. Fix it."

"You don't understand, Rekarafi . . ."

The Viruk crouched. "I understand you are stopping yourself from succeeding."

"This rift is a mile across and . . . and at least six hundred miles long. Do you have any idea of how many tons of stone and earth that is?"

"Don't tell yourself why you cannot do this, Keles. All you need to do is see how it *can* be done. Make it connect again."

Keles massaged his brow, smearing dirt over his forehead. "There is *no way* . . ." He leaned forward, again placing his hands on the roadway. His chest heaved and his breathing slowed. His head came up and he looked across the rift, to the Viruk, then nodded.

"All right, maybe. There's a chance. Get rid of this circle."

Ciras scuffed half of it away. "What else do you need?"

Keles screwed his eyes shut. "We need everyone ready to travel quickly. This isn't going to be an easy path. If Borosan can outfit some of his *gyanrigot* with ropes or some of the soldiers with axes, that will help. The wagons might not make it."

Ciras nodded. "I will get things started."

"Good. This is going to take a while." Keles smiled bravely. "Oh, one more thing. Remove everyone from the edge."

The Viruk nodded. "Did you figure out how to heal the land?"

"Not exactly. Not the way you're thinking. But my mother's talent is for plants. See those flutterleaf trees? They propagate when suckers grow up off the roots. Roots were snapped when the land came apart, and it is time to connect things again."

Keles pressed his hands to the ground and Ciras' skin tingled as the magic flowed.

Flutterleaf trees grew with incredible rapidity. Roots spread, suckers rose and flourished. Older trees fell, ripping great root balls from the earth. Some of the trees slid into the rift. Others toppled in after them, rolling to a stop parallel to the rift. They trapped falling dirt. New suckers grew up on the narrow terraces. Other trees fell and crossed them.

The sun set and the *gyanrigot* moved in, shaping the trail into the rift. With ax blades for hands, they chopped trees and pruned branches. They carved earth from the canyon walls and packed it down with flat metal feet. They dragged tall trees to bridge the gap above the slowly closing rift. Bobbing blue lights on their chests marked their passage. By the time the black moon had completed half its journey through the sky, they were hard at work on the path up the other side.

By midmorning, trees grew at the rift's far side. Before noon, the first of the refugees began the trek across. The void had closed, but the trees that had grown above it had been stunted and twisted. A few bore fruit which, while perfect in shape, stank of rotted meat. Dying crows twitched below, their sharp beaks melted away.

Save for a single narrow column, the rift's edge had

eroded. Keles sat hunched on it and the Viruk crouched over him, steadying him. Ciras couldn't tell if Keles were alive or dead, and Rekarafi might as well have been a statue.

Then, finally, the rear guard started the journey across and Ciras with them. The track they traveled twisted back and forth, torturously and treacherously steep at points. The different shades of the earthen layers and the different scents surprised him. Likewise did the itching of his flesh as he descended.

Before he ascended the other side, Rekarafi caught up with him, bearing a limp Keles. Tyressa covered a look of horror quickly and raced on to prepare a litter for Keles.

The swordsman's eyes narrowed. "He's not dead, is he?"

The Viruk shook his head. "Exhausted. Imagine growing a forest. The work of a lifetime in one night."

Ciras shivered. "It would be like fighting a war forever."

"This is a conclusion you can test, Master Dejote. When Nelesquin lays siege to Moriande, it will seem as if you've been fighting him for all time."

Chapter Twenty-seven

12th day, Month of the Eagle, Year of the Rat
Last Year of Imperial Prince Cyron's Court
163rd Year of the Komyr Dynasty
737th Year since the Cataclysm
Anturasikun, Moriande
Nalenyr

Keles Anturasi awoke with a start and was determined to stay awake. For too long consciousness had come in lightning strikes of brilliant clarity etched in pain, such that he surrendered to the sweet comfort of oblivion. Despite Tyressa's ministrations, exhaustion had refused to surrender its hold on him.

His work at the rift had stripped him of any human identity. He wondered why he'd been stripped of bark. He had no leaves to shade and feed him, no roots to seek moisture. His limbs had been pruned back to a paltry four. He had no words, because trees cared not for words, only wind-songs. And things seemed to be moving very quickly, too quickly. Even *he* was moving, and somehow that was not possible.

But, slowly, enough people said the word "Keles" that he came to associate it with himself. That realization unlocked dreams and they, in turn, led him back to himself.

That said, awakening in Anturasikun shocked him. The place felt right, and that made it feel alien. The person he was now had never been there before. He recognized everything and its presence pleased him, but he could not shake off a feeling of lurking menace.

He threw off the blanket and cool night air puckered his naked flesh. He glanced down at his feet, half-expecting to see rootlets, but they only ended in toes. His bandaged hands and fingers had no leaves attached. He smiled as if it were all a fading dream.

"Keles, don't try to get out of that bed."

The voice came from the chair by the door. His mother smiled and came around to the side. She poured him a cup of water, then supported his head as she helped him drink. "Slowly, slowly. How do you feel?"

Keles just nodded, then pushed the cup away with one hand. Water rolled off his lower lips and sank through several days' growth of beard. He swiped at it with his hand, then looked at her. "Are you real?"

Siatsi Anturasi smiled, and her violet eyes sparkled. "I am real. You are back in Moriande. Geselkir has seen you. Your bones will heal, he says."

"There's more?"

She nodded. "There is news, Keles, and it is not good."

Keles slid back on the mattress and leaned against the headboard. "Tell me."

"Your grandfather is missing. We don't know where."

Keles nodded slowly. He'd seen Qiro not a month ago. *Was that a dream, too?* Keles looked at his mother and finally noticed she was wearing a white mourning robe. "That's not why you are wearing white."

"No. Majiata is dead. Murdered. She died shortly after you left Moriande."

A jolt shook Keles. He and Majiata had been engaged. He had loved her. She'd loved the access to Anturasi maps and charts that their marriage would give her family. Their breakup had been less than amicable, and Keles had been happy to leave Moriande shortly thereafter. That seemed so long ago. *So many things have changed.*

"Keles, you have to listen to me. The murderer also killed your sister. Nirati is dead."

"No, she's not, Mother."

"Geselkir was right. It was too soon to tell you."

"No, Mother, I have seen Nirati."

Siatsi's eyes narrowed warily. "Keles, I washed her body. I stitched it back together. I wrapped her in silk and lit the pyre myself. Nirati is gone."

Keles reached up and brushed the tear from his mother's cheek. "She is alive, Mother. She is well. She is my twin; I would know if she was dead. I've seen Grandfather, too."

"But . . ."

Keles shook his head slowly. "I have a link with him. He is out there." He hesitated for a moment, then concentrated. The same linkage of roots he had used to make the trees grow came back to him, and he felt his grandfather's presence. "He has come closer than before. There is something wrong with him. Worse than before."

"Keles, this can't be."

"Mother, it *has to be*. If it is not, then I am insane." His hazel eyes widened. "Have they told you what I've done?"

She looked away. "I didn't want to believe them."

"It is *jaedun,* Mother, not *xingna*. It's not evil."

"I know." Siatsi pulled the sheet up and wrapped it around him. "Come to the window."

Keles got out of bed unsteadily and leaned heavily on her arm. "Uncle Ulan is quicker than I am."

"Only for a little while." She smiled and guided him to the window. She reached for the latch. "I had heard, but I did not want to believe. Then I had no choice."

She unlatched the window and pushed the panel out and up. Or she tried to. Thick green vines tugged at the edges of the frame. The sweet scent of flowers came through the narrow opening. Keles even caught sight of a thick, green vegetable dangling from a vine.

He looked at her. "That's *tzaden*. It doesn't grow this high. And it can't be flowering if it's already borne fruit."

"But it has, in the two days since you've been here. It only grew this high on this side of the tower. It bore fruit. It's good for restoring health and building stamina." She shook her head. "It is as if the plant itself wants to get to you."

"But you are a *bhotridina*. You understand plants. You must have helped."

"No, Keles. In fact, I cut some of it back." She tugged to close the window. "I cannot explain this. Nor can I explain how you made the trees grow, or rebuilt the fortress or changed the people."

Keles leaned against the wall and clutched the sheet

around himself. "But there have to be stories of *jaecaibhot* who have made plants grow faster."

"There *are,* but not at the rate you have." She caressed his cheek. "And think what you are saying: that you have become a Mystic with plants, a Mystic at building, a Mystic at, what, *healing*? No one has ever mastered so many things."

"No one outside the *vanyesh*." He'd said it aloud. He'd admitted to himself what the Helosundians had feared. He'd become one of the monsters capable of destroying the world. The realization surprised him, but his reaction to it surprised him more.

Half of him expected a wave of evil to wash over him, as if acknowledgment of his power would instantly corrupt him. The other part of him wanted to protest his innocence, so his mother could look at him without suspicion or fear. For eons the *vanyesh* had been defined as evil incarnate; and his mother—like every other right-thinking person—was afraid of their return.

He levered himself off the wall and stood as straight as he could. "Mother, I am not *vanyesh*. I do touch magic; there is no denying that. But I begin to understand what I am doing. When you use your knowledge of plants to prepare a tincture or elixir, your goal is to help someone by restoring them to a normal state, yes?"

She nodded. "It takes many years to achieve mastery."

"But when you started, how did you know what your talent would be?"

Siatsi frowned. "My mother was skilled with plants. I used to help her."

"But didn't you always tell us that there was a day

when you were making a sleeping draft and added something extra because it felt right?"

"Keles, I may have said . . ."

"No, listen, aren't there times when you look at a formula and add something more or take something away?"

"Depending upon the season when a herb is harvested, or how long it has been since it was harvested, its strength varies."

"Yes, and your sense of things tells you what is correct."

His mother nodded. "I will grant that."

"What if I tell you that, when you do that, you are touching magic, setting your formulation to what it is meant to be? What's right for it."

She shook her head. "I don't . . ."

Keles licked his lips. "The people were not turned into the warriors I needed. They became the warriors they would have been, or had been, or would become. The magic simply let them reach their proper potential. And, I think, because an attack was coming, it became easier to fit them into that role because that role was right for that place and time."

Her eyes tightened. "Go on."

"Out in the tea market, you can buy dozens of varieties, different preparations. They will always taste the same, but sometimes they taste *better.* On a cold, cold day, a smoky black tea will warm your bones. On a hot, muggy day, jasmine tea will refresh. When your stomach is upset, *pu-ehr* is perfect. They become right because of time, place, and circumstance."

"But, Keles, who decides what the circumstance is? A dark alley might terrify someone approaching it, but a thief who knows he is the only threat therein will not feel fear. Who is right? Whose perception takes precedence?"

Keles scratched his head. "I don't know. I guess it would be whoever has the strongest conception of what is real. I mean, the strong-willed often impose their will on those who are weaker. Grandfather was a prime . . ."

Oh, by the gods . . .

He slumped back against the wall for a moment, then grabbed his mother's shoulders. "You have to take me to Grandfather's workshop."

She took his elbows in her hands and guided him back toward bed. "You need to relax. You need more sleep."

"No, now. I have to go now."

She looked at him, then nodded. "Sit. I will get you a robe and some slippers."

He started to protest, then looked down at the sheet tangled around his legs. "Very well."

Siatsi returned quickly, and Tyressa with her. The look of concern on the Keru's face brought a lump to Keles' throat. She'd clearly not slept much, and was knotting her robe's sash as she entered.

Keles smiled. "It's good to see you, Tyressa."

"And you, Master Anturasi."

Siatsi shot her a glance. "You are not fooling me, Tyressa."

The Keru looked surprised. "Mistress . . ."

"Be quiet. Lift him up and help him on with this robe."

Keles smiled. "Someone who gives orders better than you or your niece."

"She is Mistress of the tower."

Keles shot his arms through the robe's sleeves. "Where is Jasai?"

Siatsi looped the sash around his waist and knotted it. "She is sleeping. The journey was hard on her and the baby. She had benefited from *tzaden*-flower tea, as shall you. In fact, let me go make you some . . ."

"No, Mother, I must go to the workshop."

Tyressa steadied him as he slid his feet into slippers. "Why the urgency, Keles?"

"I'll tell you as we go." He staggered toward the door. "Mother, perhaps you can bring that tea to the workshop?"

"I'll get him there, Mistress."

"And I will meet you quickly."

"Well, at the rate I'm moving . . ." Keles laughed and shuffled through the doorway. His mother slid past, hurrying off to her own workshop. Tyressa fell into step with him, moving at his pace, ready to catch him.

The stiffness eased with each step, but he'd grossly overestimated his condition. He kept one hand on the wall and slowed as he came to the first short set of steps.

"The rift in Helosunde wasn't natural. I felt it."

"You mumbled about that in your sleep."

"My mother just asked whose perception would take precedence in a conflict. See, if you take two Mystic swordsmen, and they fight, they get the measure of each other. They learn who is better and who is worse."

"You don't have to be a Mystic to learn that."

"No. It's true in almost everything, but here's what's important. When two opponents agree that one is better and the other is worse, who will win?"

Tyressa reached the bottom of the stairs first and

eased him down the last few steps. "Presumably the better swordsman."

"Exactly. And he's better because both of them agree on the circumstance—or the reality—that says he's better." Keles looked at her. "But skill is only one dimension. What if the lesser swordsman is *luckier*? And what if the better swordsman has seen omens that make him think it is not a good day for him? Could their shared perception of luck and omens change the circumstance and make the lesser swordsman the victor?"

"But reality isn't subjective, Keles."

"Isn't it?" He paused for a moment and caught his breath. "When I was young, I worked for my grandfather and drew maps. Thousands of them. Sometimes I wanted to do other things, or I was having a bad day. I would draw a map and I would think it was horrible. I hated it. I was certain my grandfather would reject it and beat me. And then he'd take that map and praise it. He would use it as an example for all my cousins to show them what they should be able to do. And I would look at that map and it wouldn't be as bad as I thought. In fact, it would be pretty good."

She looked hard at him as they started up the spiral ramp to the workshop floor. "You seem to be saying that your grandfather's perception of the map changed it from being flawed to good."

"I am."

"But that's impossible."

"Why?" Keles held his hands out. "I saw the ruins the way they should have been and rebuilt Tsatol Pelyn. Why couldn't his looking at my map refine it to be the map he said it was?"

Tyressa frowned. "But that would mean that there is no bedrock reality."

"No, I think there is. The same way there is a mattress, though sheets and blankets may hide it. Perhaps, after time, the weight of perception shifts reality, but it takes a long time and requires a lot of magic."

They topped the ramp and came into a vast, circular chamber with high, vaulted ceilings. A dozen pillars supported the chamber's dome, and a ring of windows below it allowed sunlight. Desks and drafting tables, cabinets, and shelves predominated, with young Anturasi men and women working so hard, that none of them noticed Keles' arrival. Aside from a hissed curse here and there, or the crackle of a map being scrolled open, the chamber remained quiet.

To the north, a pair of curtains had been used to slice a wedge out of the circle. With Tyressa's help Keles pulled aside the first set of curtains and passed through.

"Beyond this is where my grandfather worked on his map of the world. He used to say that a place did not exist until he put it on the map. Right here, he told my brother, 'I *am* the world!'" Keles shivered, remembering Qiro's rage. "His is the strongest perception of the world, Tyressa, and I don't like the implications of that."

Keles drew aside the last curtain, and his heart sank. "Look, there, where the rift was."

"It's a channel linking ocean to sea. The coastal lowlands in eastern Helosunde are flooding." She pointed. "You can see the blue expanding."

"And no one but us knows about the rift, so no one could have put it on the map. This is Qiro's world." Keles shook his head. "And that, there, the continent where none ever existed before, that's a piece Qiro added."

"Looks like it was drawn in blood."

"I have no doubt. His blood." Keles' shoulders slumped. "With a whim, he created a continent. And with malice aforethought, I believe he means to destroy another."

Chapter Twenty-eight

14th day, Month of the Eagle, Year of the Rat
Last Year of Imperial Prince Cyron's Court
163rd Year of the Komyr Dynasty
737th Year since the Cataclysm
Kunji Wentoki, Moriande
Nalenyr

The only thing Pelut Vniel liked about the suffocating weight of the ceremonial white mourning robes was that others hated wearing them even more than he did. Sleeves, leggings, and hems had been so exaggerated that everyone looked like children wearing adult clothing. He'd not been required to march through the street with the wagon bearing Prince Pyrust's body to the Temple of Wentoki. This was good, because his refusal to join the procession would have caused a stir.

Or should have.

His objection to the whole funeral had excellent grounds based on tradition. Pyrust's body should have been tossed onto the plains south of Moriande for carrion

birds to pick apart. He failed to defend the Empress'
holdings, so he was hardly worthy of a state funeral.
Moreover, the people of Nalenyr had lived in fear of him
for years. Their sons and daughters—or at least their
gold—had gone to opposing him. To grant him the long
procession that wound through the streets had been
absurd.

It had also been quite the spectacle. The buildings
along the route had been whitewashed overnight. People
wore white—or as close as they could get to it. Many
people caked their faces with white cosmetics, or
painted white tears on their cheeks. White ribbons hung
from branches and fluttering strips of white paper
drifted to the streets. Pelut had seen the reports. He
knew the expense of it all. It was pure silliness.

Cyron had organized it. Pelut was certain that the
Prince did so because he would never have gotten such a
funeral had the assassin succeeded in killing him. His
body would have been dragged through the streets and
torn apart by dogs. It would have been a fittingly ignominious ending for someone who had all but destroyed
the bureaucracy.

Pyrust served as his surrogate.

Cyron had gotten all the funeral's details wrong as
well. Pelut cast a sidelong glance at the procession and
barely contained his anger. It was one thing to have
Pyrust lie in state in Shirikun, but *six* days? Cyron's own
father had only been on display for three. True, six days
was the correct amount for an Imperial Prince, but
Pyrust wasn't born of Imperial loins. Like the Komyr
Dynasty, the Jaeshi had begun with bloody-handed bandits usurping a throne. Cyron decided to show Pyrust

that honor to further the fiction of the Empress having returned—especially when everyone knew it was Nelesquin who was coming to reestablish the Empire.

And Cyron's graciousness utterly belied the fact that Pyrust had come to Moriande to kill him and claim the Dragon Throne as his own.

Then Cyron—not content with offending tradition and sensibility—decided to compound his errors by affronting *Heaven*. By rights, Pyrust's pyre should have been built in the square in front of Kunji Shiri. Granted, the Temple of the Hawk was decidedly run-down and small, but to use that as an excuse to honor him in front of the Temple of the Dragon? It beggared credulity. Wentoki would want nothing to do with Pyrust. Better they held the funeral at the Temple of Death, for Pyrust was clearly one of Grija's favorites. Even the Temple of Kojai would have been more appropriate—Pyrust did rule Helosunde, and the Dog god was the god of War, after all.

All the begging Cyron might do, or the sacrifices he might offer, would not make the Dragon open the gates of Kianmang to accept Pyrust. The man might have been a warrior, but he was a nasty one who had never hesitated to inflict as much damage as he could. Vicious in war and fierce in retribution, the man deserved perdition.

And damned he shall be.

Cyron might well have thought he had completely neutralized Pelut, but the Prince never really understood the complexities of running a bureaucracy. Part of it was finding things for people to do, and not always meaningful things. By keeping them working, but not allowing them to see the overall picture, you maintained power. And that power could be unleashed as needed.

Wood had been assembled in the square before the broad and tall Temple of the Dragon, creating a pyre. Logs had been stacked in a cube that rose eighteen feet high. White silk banners had been tied to the cross-pieces. Simple prayers for Pyrust had been drawn on each one. And there, visible beneath the platform, were thousands of other written prayers that had been folded up and tossed amid all the kindling. The prayers would burn along with Pyrust, and Wentoki would read them before beseeching Grija to admit Pyrust to Heaven.

Cyron had been content to allow Pelut to handle the production of those prayers. The silken ones asked the gods to be fair and just in their judgment of Pyrust. His clerks had used some of the more archaic symbols to express this message because it was appropriate to the gravity of the ceremony. He doubted Cyron could read but half of them, yet had the Prince had them translated, he would have seen nothing duplicitous in the messages.

The folded prayers—which had been produced by a cadre of young ministers—were slightly different. They implored Wentoki to forget Desei atrocities, while describing them in great detail. After reading countless messages about the evil Pyrust had done, the gods would have no choice but to interpret "justice" in his case as sending him into the most hideous of the Nine Hells.

The procession spread into the square, and Pelut clenched fists hidden in voluminous sleeves. First came the cart bearing the body. It wore an empty saddle that had been draped with white. The body, which had been wrapped in white silk, lay buried beneath a blanket of flowers and paper strips from the street. As it drew up, four strong priests of the Dragon moved in to convey the body to the platform atop the pyre.

Behind that wagon came a simple carriage carrying two women. The Empress wore white, including a porcelain mask.

Pyrust's widow rode beside her, likewise in white. She did not hide behind a mask, but her face had been made up in white and her hair bleached. Save for the dancing of a wisp of hair and the red-rimmed icy blue eyes, she might have been a marble statue. Her robes hid the signs of her pregnancy, but there was not a person present who did not know her womb nurtured the dead man's child.

Jasai's presence galled Pelut. Was there anyone in the city who did not know that Jasai had loathed her husband and was escaping his realm when she arrived in Moriande? Pelut gladly spread rumors that the child she carried was not Pyrust's, but that of Keles Anturasi. While Jasai's attendance at the funeral—and her apparent distress at her husband's death—thrilled the romantics in the city, it would be her undoing.

Pelut would see to it.

After that came another carriage, with Prince Cyron and Virine Count Derael. The latter looked little better than the corpse, and Cyron was not much healthier. Their hats tapered to abrupt points and, had there been a following breeze, were wide enough to propel the wagon.

The men's presence was meant to inspire the people. In Pelut it inspired hatred. How could the people take heart in these men? Two cripples were Moriande's defense? Already, people were grumbling that Nelesquin had killed one cripple, so throwing two more at him would mean nothing.

Pelut encouraged that effort, and was pleased at how little he had to spend manufacturing fear.

Once the four priests had placed Pyrust high on the pyre, they carried Count Derael to the broad landing halfway up the steps to the temple. Cyron slowly mounted the steps as the troops who had marched behind the procession filled the square. The Desei troops had painted their shields white and had added the clipped feathers back to the hawk on their crests. Virine and Naleni troops had white silk strips dangling from their helmets. The company of misfit *xidantzu* had relaced half their armor with white cords.

Standing a step below the Empress, Prince Cyron raised his arms—emphasizing his deformity. Pelut did not doubt the Prince had planned the gesture to make some other sort of point, but it was moot. The lot of them looked like the ghosts they would be soon.

"People of Moriande, Nalenyr, Deseirion, Helosunde, and Erumvirine—people of the True Empire—today we release the spirit and soul of Prince Pyrust of Deseirion. Prince Pyrust's greatest wish was the re-creation of the Empire sundered so long ago. The Jaeshi Dynasty came closer than any other to accomplishing this task. Just over a month ago he arrived here, ready and able to add Nalenyr to his realm. I would have been slain by his hand. His vision of the future would have prevailed."

Cyron half turned toward the Empress. "The Empress revealed her presence to the both of us—I had no more knowledge of her identity than he did—and drafted us both into her service. We both gladly agreed. Pyrust's dream had come true, and he accepted the charge to be her warlord. His goal was to preserve the Empire and this he fought to do against an evil so ancient and potent, even Death could not contain it."

Cyron faced the pyre again and lowered his arms. "There is no one within the sound of my voice who did not, in some way, fear Prince Pyrust. I did. When he came to kill me, I saw the fire in his eyes, the steel in his spine, the strength of his dream. He came to unite Deseirion, Helosunde, and Nalenyr, not only to reestablish the Empire, but to face a greater threat. He never intended to be defeated by it, or to surrender to it, but to destroy it. That his effort did not bring success is not a failing on his part but a mark of the cunning of our enemy. Prince Pyrust killed many of them. He bought us time that will guarantee our victory."

Pelut dug his fingernails into his palms to keep from falling asleep. Of course Cyron had to deify Pyrust. That would appease the cowardly Desei troops who let their prince die. It might even convince them to die for Nalenyr—Cyron all but ceded it to Pyrust in his eulogy. And the rest of the people learned that while Pyrust had been bad, Nelesquin was worse. The message was clear: all the energy you'd have put into resisting Pyrust must be redoubled to resist Nelesquin.

But the people had done nothing to resist Pyrust. The Lords of the West had allied themselves with him against their own ruler. Cyron should have ceded the westrons to Nelesquin outright, since they'd cause nothing but trouble. And, ultimately, Cyron was telling everyone that things would be fine since he was in charge of things—he and a whore, plus the man who lost Tsatol Deraelkun. He might be speaking from Wentoki's Temple, but those words wouldn't inspire courage.

Cyron finished speaking and accepted a torch from the hand of Wentoki's high priest. He descended the steps slowly—thwarting Pelut's desire that he trip—and respectfully approached the pyre. He, at least, spared the crowd the maudlin display of looking upward and uttering unheard words that thousands of wags would be happy to invent.

In fact . . .

Pelut turned to a notoriously gossipy minister standing next to him. "What do you think it was that Prince Cyron just said to Prince Pyrust?"

The light of crackling flames illuminated the surprise on the man's face. "I do not believe, Grand Minister, I heard him say anything."

"No, of course you didn't. He spoke too softly." Pelut glanced at the pyre and the thick, white smoke rising from all the burning prayers. "But just before he lit the pyre, he looked up and said something. I couldn't hear, but his expression, it wasn't . . ."

"Wasn't what?"

"Appropriate." Pelut shook his head. "You must have seen that flash of jealousy. Maybe it was fear. What did you think it was?"

The man shuddered. "I don't think I could say."

"No, of course not, best for the morale of the people we forget it." Pelut nodded conspiratorially. "It would not do for the people to know Cyron thinks all is lost."

"No, Grand Minister, it would not."

"Good. Be certain to squelch that rumor whenever you hear it."

"Of course, Grand Minister."

Pelut turned away, fighting to appear impassive. Whatever gains Cyron had made in the temple square would be eroded in the public houses. The mere act of correcting an impression would give it life. By the end of the day, that minister and any he talked to would remember seeing Cyron lift his face and say something to his vanquished foe. That would undercut the nobility of his sentiments and wither his support.

Never once did it occur to Pelut Vniel that weakening Cyron might hasten the fall of Moriande. The Grand Minister had already assumed Moriande would fall. The white city would be bathed in blood. But as long as it was Cyron's blood and not his, both he and the ministries would survive.

And, he was certain, that was something of which both the gods and Emperor Nelesquin would approve.

Chapter Twenty-nine

RUNDE 14th day, Month of the Eagle, Year of the Rat
Last Year of Imperial Prince Cyron's Court
163rd Year of the Komyr Dynasty
737th Year since the Cataclysm
Wangaxan (The Ninth Hell)

Nessagafel understood very little about his children. He forced Jorim to maintain full clarity of mind during torture. Every ant bite, every twist of the thorned ivy, each rake of a talon, remained stark in Jorim's mind. He could catalog them and sort them, rank them and order them.

Nessagafel intended the torture to be unendurable. Clarity of mind provided a means for putting the tortures in context. The context was simple: the agony would endure until Jorim released Nessagafel.

Every twinge underscored this point. As they built and thrummed through him like bass notes, they reached and passed the point at which Jorim would have acquiesced to Nessagafel's demands.

Jorim's clarity of mind made one thing apparent: he had absolutely no clue how to release Nessagafel. Moreover, if the first god had been restrained with something that took Jorim's divine nature to unlock, it stood to reason that whatever this last restraint was had nothing to do with Wentoki or Jorim. Another of the gods must have secretly restrained Nessagafel, trusting neither Grija nor Wentoki to keep him in check.

It had to be Tsiwen. Only the goddess of Wisdom would have such foresight. She was probably also wise enough to suspect something very strange was happening with Nessagafel. She would stay well away from him. Nessagafel would remain trapped and the world safe.

Clarity of mind allowed Jorim one other realization. No matter his physical pain, what truly tortured him was Grija's simpering moans. When the blood cleared from Jorim's eyes, the god of Death became visible. He lay on the ground like some discarded scrap of cloth. Even the ants marched around him, though they greedily devoured the dead vulture that had tried to nibble on Grija.

Eternal pain is one thing, but being trapped here with him is too much. Jorim would have told him to leave but the vine wrapped around his head and the thorns piercing his tongue severely limited his conversational abilities. He did manage a grunt, however.

The grey scrap rolled over, looking much like a doll that had been crushed beneath cart wheels. "It is your fault, Wentoki. If you would release him, he would free us. Can you not see how I am tortured?"

Jorim, who at that moment was having difficulty

discouraging a vulture from plucking out an eyeball, wanted to laugh. Yet all he managed was a snort. He had never, in all his life, known anyone so pitiful—save, perhaps, his brother's ex-fiancée.

Majiata actually had a lot in common with Grija. They both were self-centered schemers who accepted no blame and took no responsibility for their actions or the consequences thereof. Had he a choice, he'd have preferred to be trapped forever in Wangaxan with Grija only because her presence would mean she was a goddess— though he couldn't imagine what her aspect would be.

He snorted another half laugh, then thought for a moment. Wangaxan was the Ninth Hell. It was the one meant for gods. But he was no longer a god. He was no longer Wentoki. He was just Jorim Anturasi—a cartographer, maybe a warrior, maybe a magician. Though a god couldn't escape Wangaxan, a mortal couldn't possibly be trapped there.

The paradox vibrated, engulfing him. Pressure built. His ears popped. He felt himself being squeezed, then the sphere imploded, crushing him. Stars exploded before his eyes. He was falling, then he hit the ground, bounced, and landed on his left arm.

He opened his eyes. He lay on a cracked and dry plain the color of amethyst. The moment he described his surroundings that way, a thousand amethyst crystals poked up through the earth. He moved carefully off them and they receded.

The sky was the color of sulfur. The pungent scent followed quickly so he changed his mind, likening the color to that of a *zaomin* flower. Oval petals began to drift down like snowflakes. The temperature began to drop as well, and wind whipped petals into drifts.

Hunching his shoulders against the cold, Jorim walked. The sky changed color—this time to a blood-red hue, which began to fall. It washed away the yellow snow and turned the purple earth into stinking mud, but only for a circle nine feet in diameter, centered on Jorim.

He wiped away the blood. "I am in Tolwreen, the Eighth Hell, the one designed for magicians."

The place shifted constantly. New colors and sounds, new scents and tastes, gravity becoming heavier or lighter. It was designed to challenge magicians to imagine. Whatever they imagined became real and presented more challenges. The more clever you were, the more frustrating your torment. Imagine escape and you create a prison. Magicians would become trapped in a maze of their own invention.

You had a hand in this, Tsiwen, but you must have left a way out. Tsiwen's wisdom would dictate that no torture should be eternal. If one could demonstrate a lesson had been learned, a reward would follow. Whatever misdeed had doomed a magician, regret, atonement, and change would certainly be sufficient for release.

Of course, one might have countless lessons to learn.

The blood rain abruptly ended, but from the last drops that hit, thirty-six ministry clerks sprang up, each with sheaves of rice paper. They peppered him with innumerable questions, never waiting for an answer. They pressed in on him, their voices rising, the questions becoming more and more absurd.

Jorim laughed. As daunting as they were, they were

nothing compared to his grandfather. *No, wait, don't think...*

Too late!

The clerks all flowed together into a colossal version of Qiro Anturasi. The giant stamped his foot, but Jorim dodged. The earth cracked and Jorim fell. He rolled, just avoiding another stomp. More earth cracked and Jorim latched on to the sound. He linked it with breaking ice.

Qiro stomped again and his foot went through. The giant plunged into an icy sea. The resulting wave pitched Jorim ninety feet. As he flew through the air he tried to think about growing feathers so he could flap his way to a soft landing.

When he did hit, it was on a bed of feathers, but they were all made of obsidian. They crackled and sliced, opening his flesh. He rolled off the bed and tried to blank his mind. He tried to think of nothing but pleasant thoughts. Still, the stinging cuts reminded him of the copper ants.

"No, anything but!"

His mind would have summoned the ants, but a gangling figure clawed its way over the edge of a nearby rise. The Viruk started to run, but he'd developed a limp. A cast-iron mask covered his face, blinding him. His ears rose through the metal and he swung his head side to side, listening for pursuit.

A half dozen Fenn came boiling after him. They snapped and hissed, totally feral. They'd shifted into a shape perfect for killing Viruk. Long claws would slice flesh. Their teeth—longer than he'd ever seen on Shimik—would punch through bony armor. Their shape even changed with the terrain, their limbs growing longer to speed them.

Being chased by Fennych was torture for a Viruk, *but it would be paradise for the Fenn.* Something was not right. The punishment was totally out of keeping with Tolwreen's nature.

What's happening here?

Facts cascaded together. Jorim cupped his hands around his mouth.

"Talrisaal, this way!"

The Viruk and his pursuers turned toward him. Jorim looked up and smiled. He imagined the sky looked the color of rice beer. *Let's make Tolwreen work for us.*

Thunder cracked and sheets of the liquid sloshed up around his ankles. The Viruk slipped and slid past in the beer pond. The Fenn all happily dove into it, plunging their muzzles in deep. They greedily sucked up the frothy liquid then flopped onto their backs. Their little distended bellies pointed skyward. They opened their mouths, drank themselves insensible.

Jorim splashed over to the Viruk. "Let's get the mask off."

The Viruk held still while Jorim checked the mask. *No seams.* He applied magic, looking for the mask's *truth.*

Very clever! He smiled. The mask didn't really exist. It consisted entirely of resistance to Viruk magic. Talrisaal could never have removed it. Jorim rebalanced the *mai* and the mask vanished.

The Viruk stared at him, then rolled over and buried his face in the mud. "I thought hearing your voice was another illusion of this place. You have saved me again, Wentoki."

"I'm not Wentoki, Talrisaal." Jorim frowned. "I have *been* Wentoki, but now I am just a man, trapped just like you. Do you know how long..."

The Viruk looked up. Rice beer washed mud from his hair and face. "A long time. Nessagafel consigned me to this place. I betrayed him to you. He made your creatures my torment."

Jorim glanced over his shoulder. "They're not real Fenn, just demons. Nessagafel doesn't understand real Fenn."

Thunder cracked again and viscous sheets of rain poured down. The Fenn melted into skeletal demons with hooked horns and gnashing incisors designed to strip flesh from the bone in seconds. Another blast of rain completely drowned them in a quagmire.

The Viruk slowly stood and the rain tapered off. "If you are not Wentoki, how did you come to be in this place?"

"You and I have a common enemy. Nessagafel."

The Viruk bobbed his head. "A nasty enemy."

"None worse." Jorim looked up. "No more rain. I think that's because we're not thinking about ourselves anymore."

Talrisaal's honey-colored eyes tightened. "This may be true. Self-centeredness is punished here."

"If acting selflessly is all it takes to get out of here..."

Even as Jorim spoke, the landscape changed. Cool green grass grew beneath their feet and a small, spring-fed pool formed. A small stream began to trickle out of it and back toward the rise over which Talrisaal had run. It eroded the ground and created a massive mud slide. The purple wave cut a swath through the valley nearly a mile wide. Bodies bobbed and sank. People screamed and, for a heartbeat, the unaffected escaped their torments. Demons evaporated. Flames vanished. Chains fell away and the sticks impaling so many evaporated.

Drowning people begged to be saved. Many just watched. Then one heaved a heavy stone at a drowning person. The stone rebounded from the target. It accelerated and snapped the thrower in half. His torso landed in a tangle of crystalline cactus while his lower half crawled aimlessly across the ground.

Talrisaal held a hand out. "If they would just help one another, they could escape."

"It won't happen."

"Why not?"

"Look at them. They have so long used the power of magic that they think themselves gods. You see, that's the ultimate jest here. They all thought to rival the gods. When Tsiwen created Tolwreen she made it a place where you had to fight yourself. The only way you win that battle is to admit you can't win. You accept your limitations, work to change them, and move on. They will never escape."

The Viruk slowly nodded. "But we are not trapped here?"

"No. A god put you in here to punish you. You're not part of this."

"And you?"

"I got here by accident." Jorim pointed toward the ground. "I've got to return to Heaven and get Nessagafel back under control. But first, I have to go through seven more Hells."

"Might I accompany you, Lord Wentoki?"

"I'd be glad to have the company." Jorim smiled. "When we get to the Fifth Hell, we can hunt down the demons who were chasing you."

The Viruk grinned and, for the first time ever, Jorim could appreciate the display of sharp teeth. "This would please me."

"Good. By the way, my name is Jorim." He pointed to the pool. "I think we dive in, swim all the way to the bottom, and we'll come out the other end in the Seventh Hell."

The Viruk scratched at his chin. "That is the one we call Icsdayr. For us, it is the land of predators."

"Mungdok is what we call it." Jorim shook his head. "Blasphemers, murderers, politicians, and dishonest merchants are what we have there. Predators sums it up pretty well."

"We shall not be prey." The Viruk leaned forward and dove into the water. A few bubbles rose.

"No indeed, not prey." Jorim smiled, dove, and escaped the Eighth Hell.

Chapter Thirty

16th day, Month of the Eagle, Year of the Rat
Last Year of Imperial Prince Cyron's Court
163rd Year of the Komyr Dynasty
737th Year since the Cataclysm
Imperial Road North, Moriande
Nalenyr

Nelesquin caught himself on both hands. Weakness would *not* prostrate him. Sweat coated him and stung his eyes. He tried to raise his left knee from the carpet. He failed and sank back, taking most of his weight on his shins and thighs. His arms still threatened to buckle, then another jolt of pain ripped up his spine.

A cough wracked him. Lightning shot through his vision. His eyes threatened to burst. He gasped, gulping air. The pain drained and muscles quivered, but he still refused to collapse.

I will not have them find me thus. He licked his lips, tasting salt.

He forced himself to breathe normally. The drumming

of his heart gradually faded. He resisted the urge to thrust himself to his feet. He'd faint. He'd done it twice so far on the trip and would not repeat the mistake.

The outer tent flap snapped open, splashing dawn light over the thin inner curtain. He forced himself up and caught the edge of his cot, but couldn't summon the strength to pull himself onto it.

Kaerinus slipped quietly into his sleeping chamber. "Another spell, my lord?"

Nelesquin nodded, then shifted to sitting on the edge of the cot. "I know *why* they are happening, but I do not understand why they become more debilitating as we move closer to Moriande. I did not suffer at all on Anturasixan."

"Proximity means nothing, my lord. You have been parted from your soul for a very long time. You seek reunion with it. Your body, your spirit, they reach out constantly, and this drains you. The sooner we reach Moriande and take it, the sooner we can locate the vessel and reunite you with your soul."

"Yes, that must be done." Nelesquin reached over and pulled a blanket around himself. "I pray the search will not take much time."

"I imagine we shall find it directly. I shall perfect a spell to find it, though my lord's precautions have not made that simple."

Nelesquin snorted. "But they were necessary. You successfully severed my soul from my body."

Kaerinus nodded. "I bound it into a ruby."

"And you passed it to another who bound it into something else, and he passed it to yet another."

The slender *vanyesh* tugged on the ends of his emerald

sash. "And so on, through a half dozen, all of them slain afterward. Their deaths kept your soul safe."

"But we know it is in Moriande. This much I can feel." Nelesquin stood and rubbed a hand over his beard. "The taking of Moriande will accomplish two things. My Empire will be reunified, and I shall be reunified. Then even the gods will tremble."

Kaerinus bowed his head. "I have no doubt they tremble even now, my lord."

"Flattery does not become you, Kaerinus. You were not a flatterer when I knew you before."

"I have spent much time alone, Highness, and have practiced flattering myself." The *xingnaridin* smiled. "I do not know why your spells did not affect you on Anturasixan, but I suspect it is because, in that place, the rules governing death were blunted. It allowed you to escape from the Underworld."

"You're doubtlessly correct. The sooner we take Moriande the better."

The blanket slipped from Nelesquin's naked body. He shuffled across to the wooden stand from which hung his golden skeleton. It, naturally, stood almost as tall as he did. He turned and pressed his back to it. The cool metal chilled his flesh, then he invoked a spell.

The metal warmed and the skeleton flowed onto his flesh. The heavy bones split, armoring shin and thigh, forearm and upper arm, with their halves up and back. Thin gold bands linked them at three points, holding them in place. Golden ribs plated his chest, and vertebrae thinned into overlapping strips covering his spine. Where collarbones joined they pooled into a gorget and below the pelvis covered his genitalia. Gold gauntlets

warded his hands and the entire skeleton took on a supple vitality that supported him even when he felt weak.

"It would not do for them to know I suffer."

Kaerinus shook his head. "It might dishearten them."

Nelesquin laughed shortly. "Not my Durrani. Nothing
could take the fight out of them. No, I meant my enemies. Imagine how Soshir would laugh at my infirmity."

"He would laugh at his peril." Kaerinus brought a
hand up and a black-and-green butterfly picked its way
over his knuckles. He watched it for a moment, then
smiled. "There is news, my lord. The Anturasi arrived
last night."

Nelesquin drew a robe on and belted it quickly. "Why
was I not informed?"

"None of us noticed." Kaerinus pulled the curtain
aside, then sped ahead of Nelesquin to open the tent
flap. "When I awakened, I found *this*."

South of the army camp on a hilltop—a hill that had
not existed when they had made camp—a pavilion had
been erected. It dwarfed Nelesquin's tent, and appeared
to be made of granite. This feat was rendered even more
remarkable by the fact that the walls fluttered in the
light breeze.

"This could be a problem." Nelesquin's expression
darkened. "I had not expected Qiro to follow me, and I
certainly had not expected his power to come with him.
In fact, when I left him on Anturasixan, he was a broken
old man."

"No more so."

"Agreed." Nelesquin looked around. "Wasn't there a
Durrani regiment camped on that spot?"

"I believe there was. The Sun Bears. They have been

moved to the other side of Count Vroan's Free Naleni Battalion. Better you had spared Pyrust, I think."

"Pyrust's eventual rebellion would have been dangerous. Vroan will die in the first wave we throw at Moriande."

Kaerinus smiled. "I have little doubt Pyrust intended him to die at Tsengui, my lord."

"But Pyrust also thought Vroan had more than mere political value. I do not labor under such an illusion." Nelesquin straightened his scarlet robe. "Shall we see what the Anturasi desires?"

Kaerinus' butterfly preceded them, riding nearly imperceptible breezes like a tiny ship on a storm-tossed sea. The pair threaded their way through the endless rows of tents. They'd been gathered beneath their unit standards, with slit trenches dug to the east and water drawn from streams to the west. Smoke from cookfires created a low haze hiding some of the more-distant tents, and Nelesquin enjoyed the fact that his army was so vast he could not easily see from one end to the other.

Qiro's hill did provide him more perspective, and that pleased him. In addition to his Durrani troops, he had levies from the Five Princes and mercenary companies joining him. New groups came on in the army's wake and, to the south, an encampment swelled with those who habitually follow armies.

The question of how to announce himself was rendered moot when the stone flaps slid apart like theater curtains. Guttering torches illuminated a spare interior that appeared, at first, devoid of luxury. The grass underfoot, however, grew thickly and was of no native variety. Flowers blossomed, though hidden in the shadows of stone folds. Two dwarf trees had grown and bore fruit—though on one tree the fruit came in the shape of roasted capons.

Qiro, wearing a white robe featuring a simple gold circle as a crest, bowed his head in greeting. "Your visit pleases me to no end, Highness."

Nelesquin smiled, hoping Qiro's good mood would last. "You have no idea how much your joining us pleases me, Master Anturasi. You should have informed us of your arrival."

"I did not wish to disturb your rest, Highness."

"You must have news. Have you prepared another womb-land to breed more of my creatures?"

Qiro nodded, but his white brows contracted in a frown. "It was not easy. I cannot bring them to maturity rapidly."

"How can that be?"

Qiro shrugged dismissively. "You know the nature of magic, Highness. Anturasixan was a place of my creation, so I was the supreme master there. What I wished to happen, *did* happen. Here, there is a complication. You see, in Moriande, in my tower, I created a map of the world. It was exacting in every detail. I created it with *jaedun,* before I realized what I was doing. It has become an artifact of great magical power. It is a focus of power, even, and it limits me."

"It did not limit you splitting Helosunde and Nalenyr. I saw you do that digging your heel through mud."

"True, Highness, but it is because no one else understood my map and its significance." Qiro plucked an orange fruit from the other tree and sank long fingernails into it. "It seems that someone who does understand has studied it. Before, it was completely mutable. Now, with another in possession of it, my control is not absolute."

"You are powerless because of a map in Moriande?"

"Powerless?" Qiro bounced a piece of the rind off Nelesquin's chest. "Was this hill here yesterday? No? Will it be tomorrow? Only if I will it to be. I have power beyond your wildest dreams. And the meddler will know my power, my wrath."

Nelesquin plucked a bit of white rind from his breast, sniffed it, then cast it aside. Their gazes met: Qiro's, angry and resolute; Nelesquin's so very cold. It would have been the work of a heartbeat to cross the room and snap Qiro's neck, but Nelesquin needed him still.

"Master Anturasi, when I ask you a question, it is not done to embarrass you, but rather as a solicitation of information. If another's possession of this map causes difficulties, then I shall take all steps necessary to remove the obstacle. Now, you have said this map is in your tower in Moriande. We must not destroy the building then, correct?"

"Yes, true." Qiro frowned. "It must be taken intact. No Anturasi blood may be spilled. That must be clear. You shed none of my blood."

"I shall pass the word to my commander. The focus of our assault is to the west of your tower. If you would be so kind as to draw us a map . . ."

"Absolutely not."

Nelesquin's nostril's flared. "You try my patience."

"Have you not listened? I told you the map I created is hampering my ability to effect change in the world. If I were to draw you a map of Moriande with the walls in place, the walls would be *in place*. Your creatures could vent their fury on them for eternity and they would not fall."

"Then draw me a Moriande with no walls."

Qiro's fist convulsed, spraying juice, then he flung the pulped fruit away. "You do not listen! My map already shows Moriande with walls. They exist. I cannot stop them from existing by drawing a new map. I can add details. I can make the unknown known. I cannot make the known unknown. I cannot render the unreal real with the stroke of a brush. Not now, not before I possess the map."

Nelesquin scowled. He wanted to remind Qiro that he'd mastered magic eons before Qiro had ever set brush to paper. For Nelesquin, magic was simple. He looked at reality, then imagined a different reality. Through an act of will he created what he desired. The process was not always a simple one, but as strong-willed as he was, it had always been effective.

He understood Qiro's plight with the map, even though it was no true problem. Having a focus for working magic was common enough. Kaerinus and his butter-flies were a minor example. Nelesquin had come to magic through swordsmanship. He saw a sword as his focus—at least at the beginning of his career. He had since moved beyond it.

Qiro might, too.

A chill slid down Nelesquin's spine. Qiro was wielding power that was all but unimaginable. In fact, it was un-stoppable. This critical map might be the only means of controlling Qiro and that would be valuable beyond belief.

In that moment, Nelesquin realized that either he or

Qiro would be master of the world. Qiro was incapable of sharing power, as was Nelesquin. He would have to destroy Qiro.

And he was equally certain Qiro had come to the same realization about him.

Nelesquin smiled. "Master Anturasi, if it is your old home that you seek, with your kith and kin hale and hearty, so it shall be. We shall secure it and keep your chattels safe against all onslaughts. Doing that shall be the first installment on repaying the debt we owe you."

Qiro nodded as if he were already the Emperor. "It is the key to the world. If you wish to rule, you must possess it."

"Possess it? Not I." Nelesquin bowed his head. "Inside a week, you shall be in your home again. The wrongs of the past shall be made right again, and a brilliant future shall be ours to enjoy."

Chapter Thirty-one

25th day, Month of the Eagle, Year of the Rat
Last Year of Imperial Prince Cyron's Court
163rd Year of the Komyr Dynasty
737th Year since the Cataclysm
Moriande, Nalenyr

This year, Moriande would host no Harvest Festival. Crops that could be taken early had been. Though premature, the harvest had been generous. Storehouses bulged with grain. Cattle, sheep, and swine had been slaughtered.

And to the south, in the stubble- and chaff-ridden fields, Nelesquin and his vermin had taken up residence. They had taken their time setting up. Nelesquin always had liked a parade and spectacle. He put on quite a show for us, though few in Moriande truly understood their peril.

His army did look impressive from atop South Gate. The *kwajiin* made up the bulk, but he also employed human regiments from the south and even Nalenyr's western provinces. The Free Naleni Regiment fought beneath Count Linel Vroan's banner, which surprised no one. Prince Cyron had exclaimed that the man was hardier than a cockroach. There wasn't a warrior on the walls who hadn't boasted he'd be the one to crush him.

Nelesquin's slow advance allowed us to complete most of our siege preparations. Pilings had been driven deep into the river and vast chains stretched between them to bar all passage. We'd also sown the known channels with stout spikes that would stave in hulls. Where channels were too wide for that, we'd scuttled a ship or two.

Under Count Derael's direction, the river's edge had become fortified. Barricades covered both approaches to the nine bridges. The ferries had been cut off. Streets leading up from the river had also been blocked. He stationed soldiers at key points in case the *vhangxi* were infiltrated through the river.

Children had all been issued nets and sticks, and been trained how to smash the winged toads. Derael suggested the best way to combat fear was to give people something to do. Only the helpless truly feel afraid. I marveled at little gangs of feral children marching in good order, patrolling their neighborhoods. I wished their parents would take soldiering as seriously.

Our defensive plan had three components. The first and most important was the defense of the walls. Keeping Nelesquin's troops outside the city would be best for all. We were prepared to defend them, but chances were the walls would be breached. We had to assume they *would be*.

From the walls we would fall back to the towers.

Three of the city's nine provincial towers lay south of the Gold River. From west to east, they were Kojaikun, Quunkun, and Wentokikun. Initially it was assumed that we would surrender the Dragon Tower only after every defender had been slain, but Prince Cyron demurred. He'd already evacuated the animals from his sanctuary to the north end, housing them in the gardens adjacent to Shirikun. While we were expected to defend his palace, the plan was simply to bleed the enemy and buy time so people could escape north across the bridges.

After the towers, we'd hold the bridges' southern ends, then get driven back to the north ends. We already had catapults, ballistae, and trebuchets ranged and sighted for sweeping the long archways. If Nelesquin's troops got that far, the slaughter would be horrible.

"Master, I should like to say . . ."

I turned and smiled. Ciras Dejote stood before me in a full suit of armor. A flame had been painted on the breastplate in yellow and orange. The armor's lacings likewise alternated those two colors. He wore a pair of swords, one long, one short, and a fierce armored mask hung by its lacings from his shoulder.

I clapped him on the shoulders. "Ciras, I am no longer your master. You traveled to Voraxan and came back with the Empress' loyal retainers. It was an act that shall be sung of for a long time."

"Only if we win, Master. If not, we shall be sung of as the *vanyesh* are now."

I nodded. "Then we cannot let that happen."

"Master Tolo—I do not know if I call you that or Master Soshir . . ." Ciras frowned and slid the long sword, scabbard and all, from his sash. "This blade belonged to

Jogot Yirxan. There is some indication that I may be him, reborn. Using the sword, out there in Ixyll, I had visions. And one of them was . . ."

I held up a hand, then extended it. He laid the blade's hilt in my palm and it was as if ice encased me. My vision blurred and night came on fast. I knew I was me—Virisken Soshir—but my body felt alien. It was as if I were wearing a costume, pretending to be someone I was not.

Nelesquin's camp in far Ixyll had been laid waste. My brother's body stretched out in front of me. I tangled fingers in his hair and lifted his severed head. I held it high, laughing. He had thought to oppose me. He had thought himself my better.

I spat in his face, then kicked his head into the darkness.

I don't know how I knew he was there. A sense? *Jaedun,* perhaps. I think it may have even been deliberate on his part, a tiny sound, just a hint of warning. Not that it availed me much, because his sword—the sword connecting me with Ciras—connected the two of us. It bit through me, carving into my left side from spine to breastbone.

My hand fell from the sword. I found myself on my knees. The scar ached as it had not in a long time.

"Master, are you . . . ?"

"I'm fine, Ciras." I got to my feet, steadying myself against the wall. "You had a vision of almost cutting me in half."

Ciras could not meet my gaze. "It dishonors me."

"It should not, no more than the scar does me. Jogot and I had been as brothers—truer brothers than

Nelesquin and I had ever been, or so I thought. When he joined the *vanyesh* I felt betrayed. I did not realize *why* he had gone."

I looked past him, north, to Shirikun, where the Empress had taken up residence. "When first I saw her again she looked for something. She wanted to believe she could trust me, but I had broken her trust before."

Ciras shook his head. "You never would have done that."

"I am afraid I would have." I pointed to the sword. "I saw Nelesquin as *my* rival for Imperial power, not hers. I'd struck him down, just as I would strike down anyone who stood between me and the throne. She knew that. She sent you to kill me. You did."

The blood had drained from Ciras' face. "But in a most cowardly way, Master. I struck you from behind."

I shook my head. "Not cowardly. Prudent. Your vision ended after you struck me down?"

"Yes."

I reached out and tipped his chin up, exposing his throat. "I was a very dangerous man then, Ciras. You paid dearly for your fidelity to the Empress." I hesitated. "There was just enough life in me to take your head."

Ciras swallowed hard. "This explains many things. If you demand satisfaction of me, Master . . ."

I let his chin fall again. "Do not be silly. I know better than to want to tangle with you."

He blinked.

"If you wish me to say it, I will. I fear you, Ciras Dejote." I laughed and he joined me, albeit slowly.

"Fear me? I would think you hate me."

"Hate you? No. You acted bravely for the Empire. And

that's good to remember, now that we're here, fighting a war we thought we had fought eons ago."

Ciras leaned on the wall and peered south. "You could challenge Nelesquin to combat in the circle and be done with it."

I shook my head. "He'd not accept."

"He fears you would kill him."

"Nelesquin fears nothing, which has always been a problem." I shrugged. "I have had many more years of practice at this point, but he has his magic. It would probably be an even fight."

"Then why refuse the challenge?"

"His war is with the Empress. Killing me is for later." I chuckled and patted Ciras on the shoulder. "I'm glad to see you ready to fight. They will come tonight, just after the sun has gone down."

"We will show them no mercy."

"Exactly. You're already a hero, Ciras Dejote. Today you'll become a legend."

The assault came even later than I expected. I'd forgotten Nelesquin favored a short nap after his evening meal. I sat with my back against the wall, sharing a bowl of rice and some warm soup with Dunos, wondering what Nelesquin supped on. He'd always enjoyed the finer things. It surprised me that he'd limited his extravagances to the gold gauntlets I'd caught glimpses of.

When their drums began pounding, and some of their odd creatures started hooting, I sent Dunos off with our bowls. He protested being sent away, but I also gave him a message for Count Derael. That errand mollified him somewhat. He promised he'd return soon with an answer.

Trumpets answered on our side. Torches flared along the walls. Warriors—veterans and conscripts alike—donned circle talismans or drew ashen circles around their eyes to ward off magic. I couldn't feel the tingle of *jaedun,* but the *vanyesh* were out there, somewhere. I couldn't fault anyone taking precautions.

Melodies shifted. Our catapults launched oil-filled flaming urns. They streaked through the sky and exploded against the ground. None found a living target, but the burning pools cast enough light for us to see the enemy.

The *xonarchii* loomed forward and hurled boulders in high arcs. Several eclipsed the stars. Two or three landed well shy of the city. Others struck sparks from the stone and bounced off, gouging the walls.

One sailed completely over and collapsed a hovel into a pile of shattered kindling.

It had been hurled by the largest of the *xonarchii.* A massive beast, it had been painted with black stripes over its blue flesh, like a tiger—Nelesquin's way of mocking me. It did make for a terrifying display. The driver turned the beast and it disappeared into the shadows to retrieve another rock.

I glanced at Penxir Aerant. "Three hundred yards."

"Three and a half." The giant twirled an arrow. "Next throw if it comes to the same spot. The one after if it does not."

"Perfect."

A loud clacking filled the street below. I smiled. The Derael spikes were working as intended.

No one who had been at Tsatol Deraelkun could forget the giant moles. Count Derael named them *danborii* after one of the Rat god's more odious aspects. He'd made ready to give them the welcome they surely merited.

Every nine feet along the entire length of the wall we'd dug postholes another nine feet deep. Each hole had a bamboo shaft in it and an old man or woman holding it. Above the hole we positioned the same sort of pilings we'd used to stop the river, with three yards of hooked-iron spike on the downward end. They'd been hoisted into position with a pulley and angle-frame. When the sentinel felt the bamboo shift, he or she clapped two shorter lengths of bamboo together and a wall warden cut the Derael spike loose.

The piling shot down into the posthole. The iron spike pierced the *danbor*'s skull, pinning it in the tunnel. As the beasts thrashed out their deaths, the muffled thumps made us smile. Soldiers sighted back along what they imagined was the tunnel's line. Archers nocked arrows, ready to feather anyone trying to dig his way free.

The *xonarchii* returned to hurl more stones. Penxir drew his great recurve bow and held it. Firelight danced over the razored edge of the broadhead. He waited, his muscles never quivering, the arrow rock still.

The tiger-striped *xonarch* turned.

Penxir released.

The arrow spun out into the night. It was ridiculous to think that so small a missile could hurt such a massive creature. Yes, warriors had suggested that driving an arrow through an eye might get into the creature's brain, but the head was as wide as most wagons were long. A cloth-yard shaft would completely disappear into the thing's skull before it had a chance of hitting the brain.

But then, as we'd discovered before, finding the monster's brain wasn't the only way to stop it. Penxir's arrow passed through the rider's armpit. There was no mistaking the dark spray of arterial blood. The arrow poked out the other side, completely transfixing the *kwajiin*. He fell back and to the side, to hang by one foot from a stirrup.

The beast yelped and swiped a hand at the control sticks. It missed. The *xonarch* rolled onto its back, then over, staining itself with the driver's pulped remains. On its feet again, it tore off across the ground, going low and fast, barking out furious challenges.

I smiled. "Nice shot."

He shook his head. "Next time I will not kill a driver. I will kill one of the creatures. It will be the perfect shot."

"You'll get the chance tonight."

"I know." He nodded toward a spot further down the wall. "It will be from there."

"Go."

As he departed, Dunos reappeared. "The count thanks you. If you feel plans are in error, he bids you send me to him with new information."

"There's no mistake."

Dunos drew my old sword. "Then I am ready."

The determination in his voice made me smile. I guided him to a crenel. "Watch what arrogance will make a man do."

The enemy's drumming shifted tempo, announcing a new attack. Troops marched forward through the darkness. They had to see the walls and the fires. They doubtless breathed prayers to Wentoki or Kojai or even Grija, hoping the gods would see them through the fight. Officers shouted orders and encouragement, but many wanted to run.

I knew because I could remember that far back.

As the enemy reached the edge of the firelight, their ordered formations melted into screaming masses. Men bearing long ladders, swords, and bows raced forward, yelling fiercely to scare those they faced. Men in their midst bore standards identifying troops from Moryth and the other of the Five Princes or Erumvirine or even western Nalenyr.

Nelesquin, having lost any advantage of surprise, sent our own people against us. "He'll let us destroy our brothers, Dunos, to learn what we have in store for his *kwajiin*."

"Teach him a lesson, then, Master."

I snapped a fan open and raised it. Trumpets blasted. I brought my hand down sharply and nines of small siege engines launched their missiles. The ballistae lofted clouds of arrows. They cut swaths through the charging soldiers. Some men died pierced by three or four, which then held them upright—bloody, twitching scarecrows guarding fields of carrion.

Catapults hurled earthenware globes. These had not been filled with fire. I would have gladly immolated *kwajiin*, but men, no. Instead we used other things. These vessels shattered, scattering caltrops. They always landed with a spike pointing upward, and that spike punched through sandals with ease. Soldiers screamed and limped back, or sat and pulled the spikes from their feet.

Elsewhere along the line, tightly wrapped bales of smoldering *vaear*-root arced through the air. So effective at settling the stomach when brewed as a weak tea, *vaear*-root burst into flame as it flew. The riverine breeze sent the thick smoke south and east, choking the battlefield. When inhaled it induced vomiting and dizziness in some, blindness in others. The truly unfortunate saw horrible visions. Coughing men staggered and fell, some clawing at their eyes.

Most retched and wept.

Our archers stepped up to display their skills. They shot anyone who came into range—putting arrows through their limbs. That was by Count Derael's order. A dead man is simply dead. A wounded man has friends who hear his screams. He must be rescued and a wounded man eats as much as a hearty one but doesn't fight.

Nelesquin's drums beat a retreat. Men abandoned their ladders. They formed chains, dragging themselves and their compatriots south. Soon enough, all that remained on the battlefield slithered, crawled, or begged to die.

"Have we won?"

I shook my head. "Not yet."

The drums changed their beat. "Now he comes in earnest."

Chapter Thirty-two

25th day, Month of the Eagle, Year of the Rat
Last Year of Imperial Prince Cyron's Court
163rd Year of the Komyr Dynasty
737th Year since the Cataclysm
Moriande, Nalenyr

Ciras relished the tight press of the battle mask against his face. The mask's long white fangs jutted down and blood stained the corners of his mouth. He knew well the effect of such a fearsome visage, yet Ciras wished he could go into battle without it.

The mask hid him from the enemy. He *wanted* them to know whom they faced. He wanted to be feared not for what he wore, but for his skills in combat. He was worthy of their fear.

He sat astride his mount with the other Voraxani. He'd not yet hit the switch that would extend the armor and spikes. While there was no pretending that he was on a real horse, he didn't want to be part of a war machine. The other champions of the Empress seemed to have no trouble with it, but it still didn't feel right to him.

At the further end of the plaza, crews operated their ballistae. They drew the arms back and locked the pusher plates in place. Some they loaded with stone or cast-iron balls. Others took sheaves of arrows with broadheads fully a handspan long. At a signal from the wall, lanyards were yanked, missiles flew into the darkness, and the whole process began again.

The ballistae crews fought earnestly and hard but he could not think of them as being his equal. They dealt death, but did so anonymously. They did not see their enemies die.

That made them no more honorable than the *gyanrigot* soldiers lined up in the plaza. The machines could not care. They could not grieve. They could not consider mercy, nor could they beg for it. They knew no fear. They just killed until destroyed themselves—inexorable, implacable harvesters of souls.

Courage and discipline were vital. The automatons were slaves to their commands. Some took that for perfect discipline, and some mistook their lack of fear for courage, but it was the antithesis of courage. Courage was to face down the very fears the *gyanrigot* could not even recognize. Courage was to fight on in spite of looming disaster.

Trumpets blared, calling the Voraxani to alert. Guards stationed at the western sally port hauled away on thick ropes. Crossbars swung up. Sweaty, loincloth-clad men turned capstans. The gate swung outward.

With Vlay Laedhze in the lead, the Voraxani poured onto the battlefield.

Things *had* developed much as Moraven Tolo had predicted. The city's main southern gate was its weakest point, so the assault had been concentrated there. The first wave of humans had broken. The battlefield lay littered with casualties—be they still or crawling back toward their own lines. They had been a distraction while the boring beasts had tried to tunnel beneath the walls. Neither of those ploys had worked, so Nelesquin had shifted tactics.

Conventional siege machines rolled along the Imperial Highway. A massive ram mounted within a long wagon led the parade. A roof over the top and shields covering the front and sides protected the men as they pushed the creaking machine forward. Two siege towers came next, each as tall as the city's walls. A long line of *kwajiin* soldiers propelled the towers along the road. Once they had them in position, they'd mount the towers and hurry across bridges to top the wall. Soaking-wet hides covered both the towers and the rams' roofs to repel fire.

The *kwajiin* were the antithesis of the *gyanrigot* warriors. Their standards, terrible and yet glorious, had been affixed to the machines, proclaiming pride in past deeds. The warriors chanted rhythmically and the engines moved in time with that music. Even the rams' steel-shod points swayed with the tempo, seeming eager to pound the city's gates to pieces.

Formations of men flanked the engines, though marching through the corpse-strewn fields slowed their advance. Nelesquin's monsters and conscript attendants hemmed them in, preventing defections. The hammer-headed *xonarchii* pulled wagons, like children's carts, bulging with smaller stones. They'd dig a hand in, raise it, and throw, scattering rocks against the walls and battlements. Men toppled, screaming, and the *kwajiin* cheered.

The men of Moriande answered with well-aimed arrows and flights of their own stones.

The mounts' hoofbeats pounded up into Ciras. The Voraxani drove at the monsters. The conscripts shouted warnings and bared swords. The warnings turned to screams as the Voraxani appeared on their metal mounts, festooned with spikes and blades.

Ciras deployed the armor and spikes barely a dozen yards before the conscript line. He squeezed his knees and rode over the first man. His sword flicked right. A bloody geyser spurted into the night, then he was through.

A *xonarch* towered over him. Ciras had known they were big, but hadn't appreciated just *how* big. The creature could have easily grasped the top of the city's wall and hauled itself over.

Ciras drove in hard, then rose in his stirrups and slashed mightily at the thing's left ankle. Fur flew and blood flowed. He'd hoped to cut the tendon and hobble it, but he would have had an easier time hewing through oak.

The creature roared furiously and flung a handful of stones. They crushed a dozen of its allies, smearing broken bodies across the ground. By then Ciras had ridden far enough forward for the driver to see him. The driver jerked a lever and the beast swiped a hand at him.

Ducking the blow, Ciras slashed the creature's palm. The *xonarch* roared again and sucked on the wound. The driver worked the control rods. The *xonarchii* stopped midlick, then smashed both fists against the ground. It gathered itself to leap.

Too close. I'm dead.

The tingle of *jaedun* accompanied an arrow's flight from the walls. The shaft passed through the beast's right nostril and burst through the thin bone wall separating sinus from brain. The razored broadhead sliced through nerves and arteries, plunging deep into the brain stem.

The *xonarch*'s left arm and leg collapsed. It mewed, stricken, crashing on its left side. The impact bounced the swordsman and his mount into the air. The right arm clawed weakly at Ciras but missed. Then the only visible eye fluttered and rolled up in the broad, bony head.

He landed astride his mount in the gap between its arms and thighs. The war mask's visage concealed his surprise. He brought his mount past, thinking to cut around the body and deal with the driver, but he never got the chance.

The ground opened beneath him.

Ciras rode a dirt-and-grass avalanche into a breached tunnel. Four yards down, the mount found its feet. It kicked at dirt-covered men. In response to Ciras' commands, it started scrambling back to the surface. Ciras clung to it, but a flying stone struck him full in the chest. It glanced off his breastplate with enough force to somersault him backward, casting him again into the darkness.

He landed on one knee, somehow retaining the *vanyesh* blade. He rose and placed his back against a tunnel wall. Surprise pulsed through him, chased by fear.

Many men emerged from both sides of the darkened tunnel. They all brandished swords, their lethal silhouettes intent on his death.

Ciras invoked *jaedun*. What he saw and heard took on secondary importance. He concentrated on what he *felt*. He parried. His blade came around and up, then thrust through a throat. He pulled back, and slashed left. The *vanyesh* blade clanged off a battle mask, then chopped down. Blood splashed black and hot. Shift left, parry with a hip and twist, letting another thrust pass wide of his ribs. Slash up through an armpit. A limb drops, a scream echoes.

The battle shifted. Close quarters had favored his foes initially. Quickly, however, fear constricted the battlefield, dictating their movements. Their desire to elude death just made them easier to kill.

One man lunged from the darkness. Ciras sensed him only as a point of fury in that sea of fear. Ciras parried the thrust, then riposted. His blade arced up and around, slashing at the man's head.

His opponent ducked, whipped his other hand around. His blade's wooden scabbard cracked against Ciras' knee.

Pain exploded and the swordsman danced back, eluding another slash. Ciras gingerly planted his right foot. More pain, but his knee held. Then something grabbed his ankle. A dying man, blind and desperate, curled himself around Ciras' leg.

I am rooted in place like an oak! A vision flashed before his eyes. His feet extended roots into the earth. His limbs stiffened like branches. His skin became bark.

Then came the killing stroke. It passed beneath Ciras'

left elbow, aimed at his waist. Sliding below the breast-plate, the blade sliced cleanly through armor lacings and his robe.

It will open me cleanly. My guts will pour out in one steaming mass.

He prepared himself for the sting, for the gush and flow, but it never happened.

The cut *splintered* flesh and caught firmly in the wood beneath.

Ciras' blade fell, driven by the weight of an oaken limb. It drove the man to his knees, crushing his shoulder. He looked up, disbelief in his eyes. Ciras hit him again, scattering his brains, then slashed down and rid himself of the man hugging his leg.

Three thumps heralded the arrival of *gyanrigot* reinforcements. One killing machine began working its way south, while the other two charged into the tunnel's north end. Men screamed, and the machines clanked. Both sets of sounds grew distant quickly.

Alone save for the dead, Ciras probed the wound at his left hip. His glove came away darkly stained, but he smelled no blood.

And those pale flecks . . . they are *splinters.* Oak *splinters.*

He wiped the glove against his thigh, then scrambled out of the tunnel. His mount awaited him, standing stock-still behind the breastwork of the *xonarch's* body. Ciras pulled himself into the saddle and guided the mount around the hole.

He hadn't been underground for that long, but already the invaders were in full retreat. The ram burned fifty yards shy of the gate, and one of the towers had fallen over—also the victim of a collapsed tunnel. The other tower still stood tall, abandoned on the road.

The Voraxani had regrouped and were heading back. Vlay Laedhze hailed him heartily. The man's right arm hung limp, transfixed by a pair of arrows. Most of the Voraxani had made it back, with a few worse for the fight, but most just spattered with the blood of others.

Once through the sally port and safe again, Ciras studied his stained glove. *What happened?* He understood the magic of the sword, he could invoke it as needed but this was something else, something strange.

He did not like it.

If magic can make me invulnerable, how then am I different from war machines that cannot be destroyed?

Chapter Thirty-three

26th day, Month of the Eagle, Year of the Rat
Last Year of Imperial Prince Cyron's Court
163rd Year of the Komyr Dynasty
737th Year since the Cataclysm
Anturasikun, Moriande
Nalenyr

Keles practically lived on *tzaden*-flower tea. His hands had recovered significantly, and he practiced each day at drawing maps. His lines became strong, even bold. While nothing he drew created a physical change in the world, the clarity of his charts heartened Moriande's defenders. Word had gone out that Prince Cyron was using Anturasi maps.

Keles spent much of his time in Qiro's observatory atop Anturasikun. To the south, beyond the battlefield, lay the hills where Nelesquin's troops waited. Those hills had not actually been quite so close—at least he did not remember their being so close—but their location matched the available charts.

Remembering how Qiro's perception of a map might have transformed it, Keles had sketched out a new map that pushed the hills back to where he remembered them. He made a show of taking as many measurements as he could—scaling the map precisely—then had his cousins copy the map again and again. He wanted them to believe it was accurate, too.

But in drawing the hills, Keles had met resistance. His hand didn't want to move forward. Something inside him screamed that what he was doing was wrong. The voice sounded like Qiro, which steeled his resolve to continue.

It also left him uneasy.

His grandfather was out there. He sensed Qiro strongly, but Keles could not connect with him. Something else was blocking him. Keles felt another presence—someone who was bending Qiro's will to his own. If Nelesquin could do that, it would be impossible for Moriande to stand against him.

More disturbing was the void behind the hills. His sense of it had grown since the battle. Keles tried to push his sense into it, but did not get far. A staggering array of images assaulted him, but he could make little sense of any of them.

Keles spent the vast majority of his time in the tower. His uncle, Ulan, and his cousins accepted his commands without question. Qiro had so cowed them that they were unable to function without forceful leadership.

Yet as much as he found them cloying and annoying in equal measures, he preferred his kin to the people of Moriande. The stories of what he had done had spread like wildfire. Some people took hope from the tales, but most were simply terrified. They said he was *vanyesh* and would betray them. The wilder tales suggested that he and Kaerinus were actually the same person. After all, their names began with the same initial and no one had ever seen them both at once. Kaerinus had vanished at the same time Keles had. Some wags went so far as to suggest that the creation of "Keles Anturasi" had been a plot by the princes to allow Kaerinus his freedom, and that Nirati Anturasi had been slain because she knew the truth.

He could have dealt with the speculation easily, except people's behavior revealed their true nature. Drinking *tzaden*-flower tea became wildly popular—though crediting it with Princess Jasai's recovery helped immensely. People did wear circles on their clothing and a dead zone formed around Anturasikun, but at its edges little shrines blossomed. Elsewhere they venerated Prince Cyron, but near Anturasikun they offered bribes so Keles would leave them alone.

Had he the luxury of time, he might have hated the foolishness. In fact, as he walked in his grandfather's footsteps, he understood his grandfather's contempt for people. From the chamber below, he could study the whole world. For most of the people on the streets, however, Moriande's north half was exotic territory. Helosunde was a fabled and distant land. Keles, Jorim, and Qiro before them, had traveled further and seen more than hundreds of thousands of their fellow citizens. Anturasi knowledge of the world allowed Nalenyr to prosper and brought fantastic trade goods to Moriande.

And, in return for all this, they were feared. *And my grandfather was trapped in this tower. He resented those who* had *freedom and did not exercise it, while those who deserved freedom were trapped.*

Keles leaned on the railing, alone save for a family of bats roosting beneath the roof's eaves. "We are alike, aren't we? You are wise, yet often feared for your appearance. Tales abound about you and the evil you can do but I bet all you want to do is fly freely, eat bugs, and enjoy your life."

The bats, perhaps confirming his assessment of their wisdom, continued to ignore him.

Keles laughed and wandered around to the south again. Bodies littered the battlefield, though burial-detail teams from Moriande tossed them into collapsed tunnels and buried them. Other bodies were tossed onto pyres made from the siege towers. The dead *xonarchii* had decayed overnight. Their ivory skeletons swam in a sea of black putrescence, frustrating the efforts of an intrepid crew trying to drag bones clear.

The cartographer smiled. They were out there at the behest of Prince Cyron. The Prince would want the bones to study. Jorim had brought Cyron countless animals—mostly alive, but some preserved carcasses, too. Cyron's intellectual curiosity had driven Naleni exploration and prosperity—both of which the invasion had ended.

I wonder what happened to Jorim and the Stormwolf? Keles had tried to connect with his brother, but their link had become more ephemeral. He was certain Jorim was still alive, but his location and condition were uncertain. As it was, given the sense of distance, Keles assumed his brother was on the other side of the world. He hoped, for Jorim's sake, he would never return.

A small bell rang, summoning him back to the workshop. Keles descended and emerged from the Master Cartographer's sanctuary. Ulan, seeming smaller and more frail than Keles remembered, smiled timidly.

"Nephew, there is a man to see you. Ciras Dejote awaits you in the audience chamber."

Keles frowned. "Qiro might have received people there, but Ciras is my friend. Send someone to bring him to the room at the ramp's base."

Ulan's eyes widened. "You'll not bring him up here, will you?"

"Be calm, uncle. I shall not violate the Prince's rules."

"Yes, nephew, of course." Ulan started down the ramp. "I shall fetch your guest myself."

"Thank you."

Ulan paused as if Keles had spoken in Viruka or Soth, then nodded and scurried off.

Keles looked around and smiled. A few of his cousins looked up. The youngest ones even smiled back. The others, trained by Qiro, distrusted the smiles and returned to work nervously. They measured more carefully and took a bit more time with their drafting. Had he not been Qiro's grandson, he would have been doing the same, so Keles spared his cousins any disdain or pity.

But the next generation will not be afraid.

Keles slowly descended the ramp. Qiro had not been allowed to walk down the ramp and pass through the golden gate. He had remained a prisoner within his own tower for fear that what he knew would be shared outside Nalenyr. Keles had not been placed under any similar prohibition, but outsiders were still not allowed into the workshop. Though he would have welcomed Ciras and thought the man would have enjoyed a visit, rules were rules.

He stopped halfway down, then returned. "Dricol, fetch me our most recent map of Tirat, please."

The dark-haired boy brought one quickly. He presented it to Keles with a flourish. "I drew it myself. Would you like it sealed and with a ribbon?"

"This will do nicely for now, but I do wish to have another drawn up. Add color and pinpoint the location of the Dejote family land."

"Yes, Keles."

Something clicked in the back of Keles' mind. He raised his voice. "I have a project to be undertaken immediately."

He waited for his cousins to set their brushes down. "I wish to have copies of all of our charts made to the size of nine by eighteen. They will be bound into a folio, so leave room for the binding. I wish a two-inch margin all the way around and in that margin you are to draw the flora and fauna or landmarks found there. Include family crests and any other details you can think of. You will consult with *bhotcai* and other experts. You will make certain the images are perfect. I want color everywhere, lots of it. Start with Moriande, then Helosunde, Deseirion, and the islands. Do the Five Princes after that. Finish with Erumvirine."

They nodded in understanding.

"Two more things. You will work in teams, a minimum of two per team. Make a record of anything too difficult to finish. You will know what I mean. You may leave those areas of maps blank, but you will bring them to my attention immediately."

They agreed silently, then set about to work.

Keles took the map and wound his way down the ramp. He passed through the golden gate, and nodded to his uncle, who locked the gate behind him. *Old habits die hard.*

Ciras waited over by one of the tall windows. Sunlight illuminated a serious expression.

"So thoughtful."

Ciras blinked, then bowed. "I beg your pardon."

"No need. I've been lost in thought before, too." Keles presented him the map. "It's of Tirat, obviously. I'm having a better one prepared for you."

"You are most kind." Ciras studied it briefly and smiled. "Beautiful."

"I shall let my cousin know." Keles joined him at the window. "It's good to see you, and a surprise. A welcome one, in fact. I had heard you were wounded in last night's action."

"This is why I came." Ciras slowly rolled the map into a cylinder. "I had a most disturbing experience, and I would ask you about it. I don't know if you can help me."

Keles nodded. "I will do what I can."

"While fighting last night, I invoked *jaedun.* A dying man grabbed my leg and I thought, to my horror, that I was rooted like an oak. Before I could do anything, another man tried to cut me in half."

The swordsman loosened his robe and exposed his left hip. Sunlight shone on the wound. Ciras had definitely been cut, but there wasn't any blood. Moreover, the wound's edges weren't clean. It looked as if an ax had been taken to wood.

Keles dropped to one knee. "May I touch it?"

Ciras nodded, but did not watch.

Keles probed the wound. The flesh was warm and somewhat supple, though it had the texture of a callus. The splintering definitely resembled wood, but the edges felt more like fingernails. Even so, within the wound, the flesh felt perfectly normal.

Keles stood. "You thought you were rooted like an oak?"

Ciras closed his robe. "It was more than that. I pictured the transformation. My body was the trunk, my skin was bark, my arms were limbs.

"He should have killed me, Keles, but it was as if I *were* oak."

"But you weren't really rooted in place. You couldn't be here if you had been."

Ciras nodded. "Out in the Wastes, at Opaslynoti, we saw many odd things. In Ixyll, too. Magic had changed things. Amid the *vanyesh,* I saw even many stranger sights. The *vanyesh* had long ago surrendered their humanity."

Keles nodded. "And you figured that, because of what I did with the trees, I might know what happened to you?"

"Do you?"

The cartographer folded his arms. "Magic can change people. It's not easy, but it can be controlled. Magic emphasizes the true nature of things."

Ciras frowned. "But I'm not an oak tree."

"No? Oak trees are strong and hard. They're dependable. Durable, noble even. You have those same qualities. You were using magic, and defined yourself as an oak.

The magic flowed through you. In that place and moment, you *became* an oak."

"Is that possible?"

"Your flesh splintered. You're alive. It's possible." Keles smiled. "You may have been an oak for a heartbeat, but you've already begun to reject that notion. And see what has happened? Your body is no longer wooden. Your flesh has taken on the nearest normal equivalents, even though a callus on the hip is something I've never seen."

"I don't understand your point."

"You have the mental strength magically to transform yourself both into an oak and back again. You use magic in a way that has nothing to do with your training."

Ciras frowned. "I didn't think that possible."

"Everything we were raised to believe says it isn't." A tingle ran down Keles' spine. "But magic is more complicated than we imagined, and far more powerful. The *vanyesh* already know that. If we don't find a way to master the magic we *do* command, we will be helpless before them."

Chapter Thirty-four

27th day, Month of the Eagle, Year of the Rat
Last Year of Imperial Prince Cyron's Court
163rd Year of the Komyr Dynasty
737th Year since the Cataclysm
Dientan Hills, south of Moriande
Nalenyr

"I have no tolerance for bad news today." Nelesquin tugged a robe closed over his golden exoskeleton. "Vex me, and there will be repercussions."

Kaerinus opened his arms, displaying an ephemeral jet-and-emerald webbing between his robe's sleeves and body. "I believe all parties understand this, Highness, but each believes the *other* will suffer beneath your ire. Despite the conflict, progress has been made."

"Very well." Nelesquin sighed. "My father had the patience for this sort of nonsense. I do not. We are at war!"

He led Kaerinus from the tent and stalked toward Qiro's hill. The tent remained atop it, and the pennants flapped in a breeze that was felt noplace else. The gaiety with which they danced did not lighten Nelesquin's mood.

The Prince could not shed his ire. Nelesquin had not expected his first assaults on Moriande's walls to succeed. He'd simply been probing, seeing what the defenders would do. He'd learned a great deal—in fact, he had learned all he needed to guarantee the city's conquest.

But the vulnerability of his moles and the *xonarchii* had surprised him. He'd not expected the moles to bring the walls down, but the simple efficacy of the countermeasures had gone unanticipated.

The vulnerability of *xonarchii* riders had been obvious, but he could always train more riders. He'd not expected a single arrow to kill one of the beasts, and this led him to rethink his weaponry.

The bright spot in the whole operation had come when one of Moriande's mechanical warriors emerged from a tunnel and attacked the camp. It had been relatively simple for Durrani with polearms to disable the device. The *vanyesh* had recognized it, so Nelesquin set them to the task of finding a way to replicate it.

Kaerinus paused at the base of the hill. "It would be best, Highness, if you were to calm yourself before proceeding."

"Yes, of course." Nelesquin drew in a deep breath, held it, then slowly exhaled. He did his best to purge himself of anger. Qiro's realm concentrated and accelerated time. He could exhaust himself fairly easily.

I tire too quickly these days.

He nodded, then stepped forward, piercing an invisible shell and entering the heart of the hill.

Steel chains encircled his chest. His eyes bulged.

Unseen forces crushed in on him, sheathing him in steel, then the heat began. His flesh started to burn and itch. If he lifted a hand to scratch, he'd peel his skin off. Millions of glass needles burrowed into him, impaling flesh and bone.

He staggered through and dropped immediately to his hands and knees. Cool green grass brushed his cheeks, caressing away the pain. He gasped, finally able to breathe. A wave of fatigue passed over him. His arms buckled, but he held himself up on his forearms. *I will not pass out*.

"Welcome, Prince Nelesquin."

Nelesquin looked up, at first seeing only Qiro's sandal-clad foot and the hem of his white robe. The fabric shifted from homespun wool to embroidered silk and back, as if the breeze were changing it. The tingle of *jaedun* undulated with the robe's transformations.

A shadow covered Nelesquin, then strong arms slipped beneath his and raised him up. "Thank you for coming, Highness."

Nelesquin patted the silver bones that held him. "Thank you, Pravak."

The giant *vanyesh* steadied the Prince, then withdrew. Nelesquin forced a smile onto his face. "I have not come because of reports of discord. I wish to see progress."

Pravak laughed. "We have done much in the months here."

Qiro smiled, but Nelesquin ignored him. "I see the building there, belching smoke. Show me what you have done."

"I am honored, Highness."

They began walking to the distant black building, but reached their goal only after a handful of steps. Nelesquin could feel Qiro's smile grow, but his ability to manipulate time and space no longer amazed Nelesquin. Qiro had created a whole world inside a hill so modest as to go unnoted on any map. Given that starting point, how could anything else be truly surprising?

Pravak opened the factory door. Metallic clanking and clanging filled the whole building. The red-gold glow of molten iron gushing from furnaces lit the interior. *Vanyesh* labored, channeling heat from the liquid metal back into the furnaces. Mechanical creatures hammered and shaped the metal; others hauled the various pieces away to assemble weapons.

Pravak's silver smile twisted his thin lips. "In Tolwreen, these mechanicals shaped many things, but we had not made them autonomous. Borosan Gryst appears to have made that possible. We were able, in the first month, to decipher what he had done. Then we surpassed it."

Nelesquin frowned. He'd not been informed that they had gone beyond creating automatons. Annoyance surged through him. He could still guide the project. Even if this meant it took years in the pocket world, the citizens of Moriande would only have won a week or two of respite.

"Show me, please."

Pravak led the way through the factory. "It was your brilliance, Highness, that allowed us to make this break-through. You see, Borosan Gryst inscribed instructions for the automatons on *thaumston*-alloy slates. *Thaumston* provided the magical energy and channeled it into specific tasks. The automatons, however, were limited in their actions because they had a limited number of strategies to choose from."

"I understand, but I had nothing to do with that."

"No, Highness, your brilliance was in how you created the Durrani. They cannot use magic as we do, but it is as if they are living *thaumston*." Pravak pushed another door open. "And with all they know, they are able to do much more than any automaton."

The door opened onto an enormous arena. Below, on the sandy arena floor, two dark steel bears circled, fully three times Pravak's height when they reared up. Metal flesh moved fluidly over muscles, and paws blurred as they flicked out toward an enemy.

Nelesquin forced himself to breathe calmly. *Never have such weapons walked the earth.* "Explain what these are."

"Your Durrani have called them *dari*. The Durrani drive them from within, fully protected and very powerful."

"*Dari*, of course. It means *fierce* in their tongue." Nelesquin's eyes narrowed. "What determines the shape?"

"It is what we have chosen, Highness." Pravak smiled. "We chose to honor Quun and Erumvirine."

"Splendid." Nelesquin glanced at Kaerinus. "What do you think?"

"Impressive, though they lack in one regard." The *vanyesh* opened a fist and a butterfly rose from it. It beat its wings twice, then disintegrated into jeweled dust. "They're not terrifying."

"You're right." Nelesquin pointed at the bears. "They

need to be nastier. Make them man-shaped, with animal's heads and paws."

Pravak nodded. "You are wise, Highness."

"Craft for them suitable weapons. Clubs and axes." Nelesquin frowned. "How vulnerable are they?"

"They are not invulnerable, but neither are they easy to kill. Sink one in a river, the pilot will drown. A ballista can drive a bolt through him or a big stone will crush him. Fire will roast the man inside."

"Yes, yes, all risks to be avoided." Nelesquin smiled. "Can others use them?"

Pravak's face darkened. "It is possible. Within them we have placed many cards and tablets, each of which allows a warrior to invoke a spell. A few of the *vanyesh* have found it possible to operate one of them, but . . ."

"What?"

"Several of them have vanished within the machines. We open the *dari* and there is no trace of them."

Nelesquin frowned. "You will test more. Use conscripts. And you will train more. Create nine armies of these *dari*. We will burst Moriande wide . . . What is the problem?"

Pravak sank to one knee and bowed his head. "Master, I have sought to create *one* army, but Master Anturasi tells me this is impossible. He says we cannot create more than a handful."

"What?" Nelesquin spun on Qiro. "Why do you thwart me?"

The old man's eyes blazed. "I have done everything you ask. I create this place. I make time move faster. I facilitate the creation of these *gyanrigot*. I have done everything, and I get nothing in return. I have asked only to be given my workshop again, but do I have it? No!"

Nelesquin pointed to the bears wrestling below. "Do you not see that these are the means to attain what you desire?"

"Do you not see that you don't need an army of them to end this siege?" Qiro waved off Nelesquin's concern. "You can have a company of them. It is enough."

"How dare you tell me what I can and cannot have?" Nelesquin lunged for Qiro, but the older man backed away. Kaerinus grabbed Nelesquin's belt and held him back. The Prince spun, slapping the *vanyesh*'s hands away, but it was enough to vent his anger. He snarled, then turned slowly and regarded Qiro carefully.

"This is not, Master Anturasi, about what I need. It is about what you can provide, isn't it? You have created this world, but you did not anticipate the need for iron."

Qiro's chin came up. "I was led to believe you wanted to breed more of your creatures."

"Fair enough. Neither of us anticipated this windfall, but it should not be a problem." Nelesquin brought his hands back together. "Create us another world, one with enough iron."

Qiro's nostrils flared. "I cannot."

"Cannot or will not?"

"Do not use that tone with me. I told you that I needed my tower, my workshop. I told you another controlled it and that limited me. When I created this place, I was able to make it a microcosm of Nalenyr. I drew upon the riches of this nation to shape this place. Had I wanted to, I could have dragged all the iron in the world to this place as if I were a magnet."

Nelesquin spoke through clenched teeth. "And now you are prevented from doing that?"

"Yes. Whoever controls my tower has anticipated me. He has found a way to define the lands, locking them. Because I created this place before he worked his mischief, it remains largely unaffected."

"But once I return you to your tower, you can undo this meddling?"

"And I *shall* undo it."

Nelesquin ran a hand over his face. The coolness of the gold felt good. It provided him a moment's respite. The brush of metal over his face also gave him an idea.

He peeked out from between golden fingers. "Iron is not the only metal you have here. We have gold and silver, tin and copper. Lead, too, I suppose, but that will never do."

Qiro nodded. "I have all those things."

"Good. Pravak, you will create these machines of whatever metal you can find. We will use salvage. I want two regiments. Use wood if you must, and bones. Grow me many *xonarchii* and harvest them for their bones. I will equip two regiments of my best Durrani with these things and let them open the city. I will get you your tower, Master Anturasi."

"This is all I have asked, and all I require."

Nelesquin shook his head. "No, you require one more thing."

Qiro raised an eyebrow. "Yes?"

"The death of the one who opposes you."

Surprise lit Qiro's face for a split second, then vanished as his expression sharpened. "Yes, yes, I do." He eyes rolled back in his head and he swayed. His eyes snapped back down and he smiled. "It is Keles."

"I will have him destroyed. But you need to provide Pravak with the tools for our success."

"Of course, Highness." Qiro stepped back and waved a hand toward the arena. The earth shook, toppling the combatants, and almost upsetting Nelesquin. The sand at the arena's heart boiled, then a dagger of iron thrust up through the earth. Around it, bursting through the stands, came another of gold and one of silver. A tin spike shattered rock and was, in turn, blunted by it. And copper leaked up through all the rents and pooled in a rising lake.

The bears, looking more like animals than warriors, scrambled up the iron plinth and leaped to the golden spike. They traveled along it to safety, their claws leaving curls of gold in their wake.

Nelesquin wanted to curse, but even thinking about it sapped his strength. *So much power used so cavalierly. Does he not realize how powerful he is, or does he merely bide his time?*

The smile slithering over the lower half of Qiro's face suggested he served only because it amused him. He would continue to be a problem—more so than he had been already.

Perhaps killing Keles is not the wisest choice. Nelesquin let weariness swallow his smile and the appearance of weakness hide his thoughts. Yes, Keles might be a problem, but he was a problem for Qiro. Nelesquin was certain

Keles had no more love for his grandfather than he himself harbored. *Perhaps we shall have to see if the dictum that the enemy of my enemy is my friend holds true. If so, Keles Anturasi will be very valuable, and his grandfather will cease to have any value at all.*

Chapter Thirty-five

27th day, Month of the Eagle, Year of the Rat
Last Year of Imperial Prince Cyron's Court
163rd Year of the Komyr Dynasty
737th Year since the Cataclysm
Mungdok, The Seventh Hell

Talrisaal and Jorim emerged from the depths of the pool and dried off almost instantly. The landscape shifted, swallowing the pool. A dark, apparently well-trodden, road appeared beneath their feet.

Mungdok itself felt very small, as if it existed no further than they could see in the darkness. With each step along the road, Jorim imagined the shadows gobbling up reality behind them.

The Viruk squatted and sniffed the air. "Something is cooking around the bend."

"Maybe that's the nature of this Hell—we'll be hungry and the meal will always be around the corner."

"Given the nature of the people sent here, I do not think it is a suitable punishment."

"Good point." Jorim led the way down the road and shortly rounded a bend. The landscape opened into a widening valley dotted with thousands of lights. Each light marked a building, and each building was a public house. The structures varied, from dugout hovels roofed with scrap to incredibly ornate places easily mistaken for a prince's palace.

The Viruk pointed at the first few places. "They have a path, but no door."

Jorim rubbed a hand over his chin. "Perhaps we're not welcome there. Maybe we won't be welcome anywhere."

Talrisaal laughed. "The only people who have never felt predatory hunger would be unwelcome here. I wish I could say I did not belong, but I have taken advantage of others."

"By that measure, I definitely belong." Jorim sighed. He'd used his status as Qiro's grandson to get cousins to do his work. And, more than once, he'd let his family's status bedazzle a woman into his bed. On a scale where the most heinous acts were murder and torture, his offenses might barely register, but he certainly was not innocent.

He shivered. "Was anything you did sufficient to *keep* you here?"

"I hope not."

"Good." Jorim smiled. "The faster we get through, the more I'll like it."

"Haste will make it more difficult for Nessagafel to find you."

Jorim looked around quickly. It did strike him as odd

that Nessagafel hadn't come after him. The irregular flow of time might have meant he wasn't missed yet. He couldn't count on being that lucky.

"Perhaps he'll come hunting and get trapped along the way. Wouldn't that be nice?"

The Viruk bobbed his head in agreement. They hurried on through the town. A couple of the taverns had doors, but while they looked inviting, the travelers continued past. As they progressed toward a luminous silver sea, the establishments became bigger and more spectacular. They found themselves irresistibly drawn to the largest, since it alone allowed access to the sea.

Jorim paused, reading the sign over the open door. " 'The Broken Crown.' It conjures images. I'm not sure I like them."

"In Viruka it is 'Nesdorei.' " The magician's dark eyes glittered. "It means the place where the mighty have fallen, and not in a good way. It is the spot where the arrogant have been brought low."

"I'm going to have to study Viruka. Lots of nuance there."

"Viruka's time is long past. The world no longer welcomes nuance."

"A pity, but you're right." Jorim stepped back. "After you."

The palatial Broken Crown was immense in every respect. Whole trees had been stripped of bark and transformed into pillars whose branches supported vaulted ceilings. The golden wood floor appeared seamless, as if a single log had been peeled into a continuous surface. Along the walls, and down the center, massive stone hearths blazed. Rough wooden tables—some set with

benches and others with heavy chairs—packed the floor.
The vast hall defied any attempt to count tables.

Meat roasted on spits. Servants bearing trays groaning
beneath the weight of cups of ale and wine or steaming
platters of meat wandered through the endless hall.
Occasionally a servant would pause, pass his burden to a
patron, then slip into that patron's place at a table.

"It would appear, Wentoki, that those condemned for
using others are made to serve them."

"That's part of it, certainly." Jorim drifted forward,
trying to recognize some of the patrons. A couple of the
crests seemed familiar. They marked minor tyrants or
ministers who had thrived on corruption. Often as not,
the patrons wore no crest at all, marking them as anony-
mous abusers, murderers, and pedophiles whose crimes
had gone unnoticed by anyone save the gods and their
victims.

"Trying to find an acquaintance probably isn't the
most intelligent strategy."

"I agree." Talrisaal's eyes narrowed. "I would also suggest we do not sit down, do not take a tray, nor partake of
food or drink. We can pass through, but if we become involved, we could be trapped."

"Agreed."

Jorim's wanderings brought him close enough to a
hearth. The warmth proved inviting, and the scent made
his stomach rumble. He began to smile, then he got a
look at what the servants were roasting.

A patron stripped off his clothes and bent over. Another thrust an iron skewer through him. The spike completely transfixed him, emerging with a gush of blood at
an angle from the man's neck. Other spikes secured him

tightly to the skewer. Two servants carried him to a set of
hooks, then bound him up like a suckling pig. Two more
people, grimy and glowing with sweat, hefted the man
into the hearth. His flesh began to sizzle as he slowly rotated on the spit.

Jorim didn't know *that* man, but the one next to him,
the man whose flesh was blackened save where cooks
had sliced off long strips, looked familiar. "Count
Aerynnor?"

The roasted man thrust his hands toward the sound,
cracking flesh at elbow and shoulder. "Who's there?"

"Why are you here?"

"I'm innocent. I didn't murder any of them. Not my
family, not Majiata, not Nirati, none of the others! Help
me."

"Nirati?" Jorim's stomach knotted. "Nirati Anturasi?"

"Not her, not her. I'm innocent!"

Jorim's eyes narrowed. He'd accepted that his sister
was dead but hearing that news as Wentoki had stripped
it of all emotion. It was just a fact—one tempered by her
still being "not-dead." He'd never even wondered about
the circumstances of her death. An accident or illness he
could have understood. He'd even assumed that much.

But murder?

Aerynnor's denial trivialized her death. He'd done it,
else he'd not have been roasting. The utter lack of remorse in Aerynnor's voice chilled Jorim's blood. He was
well and truly deserving of his punishment.

The person beside Aerynnor had been carved to the
bone. Servants dumped the bones into a pile. The skeleton began to move and collect itself. Several more servants rushed food and drink to it. The skeleton quaffed

ale and gobbled down great hunks of meat. Instead of splashing to the floor, the masticated victuals flowed over the bones, sheathing them in muscle and flesh. The transformation revealed the skeleton as female.

Again whole, with lustrous long, dark hair, she picked up the robe the most recent patron had discarded. At her touch it became a brilliant green silk, bearing a gold tiger crest. She cinched it around her waist with a golden sash, then moved through the crowd and joined a table.

"It would appear, Talrisaal, they serve and serve again."

The Viruk pointed after the woman. "No one seems particularly distressed at either serving or roasting. It is not much of a punishment."

"True." Jorim cut through the tables and made his way to the table where the woman had taken a seat. Based on her crest and the style of embroidery, she was some minor Moryth princess. There were stories about a branch of the royal family who indulged in unnatural vices with peasants and later murdered them. The princess sat with others of royal blood, one of whom was well known in Nalenyr.

Prince Araylis?

Prince Cyron's older brother had a breadth of chest and robustness of features not found in Nalenyr's current ruler. He bore no sign of the sword cut that had split his skull, though he did sound a bit nasal. He wore a robe with the Naleni crest and an Imperial crown hovered above the dragon.

"If only I had been more patient. I think that is it, really. The Desei were weak and would have grown weaker had I waited. Pyrust could not have held his throne much longer. I could have done it. I could have forced him out of Helosunde and brought that realm fully under my control."

Jorim frowned. He'd been a child when Araylis died. He'd worked on some of the maps the Prince had carried on his campaign. Curiously, the campaign had only ever been praised as one in which the Prince would free the Helosundians from the shackles of Desei domination. There was no hint of taking Helosunde for Nalenyr.

"No, no, patience would have availed you nothing." The man who spoke wore a brown robe with a white hawk in flight. "The battle goes to the swift. I made my mistake in waiting. I wanted your dynasty to fall apart in civil strife. I wanted you weakened, but it did not happen. If only I had struck when your grandfather first took the throne. Quick, decisive action would have won me your nation."

Another woman focused on a reality only she saw. "If only I had not forced peasants to grow blue lilies. Then that child would not have been stung by the bee and died. And his parents would not have started the rebellion. My family would yet rule . . ."

"No, that's not right." Prince Araylis wiped spittle on his sleeve. "If only I had been patient. That would have been the thing. The Desei would have weakened . . ."

Jorim slowly backed away. Doing so, he picked up other snippets of conversation. Everyone had a complaint. Each one of them had a regret—some trivial, some monumental—which they cited as their undoing.

But Prince Araylis was wrong. Impatience hadn't killed him. Arrogance had. The same arrogance that told him that he could take Helosunde was what told him he could defeat Prince Pyrust. No matter how long he waited he'd probably never have been able to defeat his Desei rival.

Jorim turned to Talrisaal. "The punishment here is not serving or even being roasted alive. It's reliving your failures over and over, for all time."

"Does it fit the crime?"

"I suppose. These people went through life without second-guessing themselves. They believed in their infallibility. They acted based on it." Jorim shook his head. "Forced to relive mistakes without finding a solution. I can't imagine."

One of the servants, bowed by the weight of a sloshing tray of cups, cackled. "If you can't imagine, you'll be back here soon enough. As you serve, you see what fools they all are. What a fool you were. And there is no escape."

Talrisaal pulled Jorim back. "Do not engage him. He would trade places with you, much as they all seek to foist blame on others."

"What a terrible place."

The Viruk nodded. "Being roasted and carved must be the most acute punishment, but I would suffer beneath the rest as well."

"I hope all their victims know pleasures equal to the pains down here."

"We must move on, Wentoki."

"True. The door is over there. I'll meet you."

The Viruk regarded him curiously. "What are you going to do?"

"Magic will work here, yes?"

"Yes."

"Good, this will only take a minute."

True to his word, Jorim rejoined the Viruk and they marched to the sea. They waded into it and dove down, heading for the Sixth Hell. It was only as the waters closed over his head that the screams of Junel Aerynnor left Jorim's ears. The man had asked for help, and Jorim had been glad to oblige. The healing spell had taken immediate effect, returning his flesh to pink and sealing the wounds left by the carving knife.

And it would continue working, forever, so Nirati's murderer would spend eternity on a spit, screaming out his innocence for any who cared to listen.

Chapter Thirty-six

27th day, Month of the Eagle, Year of the Rat
Last Year of Imperial Prince Cyron's Court
163rd Year of the Komyr Dynasty
737th Year since the Cataclysm
Kunjiqui, Anturasixan

Nirati knew not how many days had passed in the real world since she had made her decision to save Jorim. In her realm, days passed at a whim. Time could even be reversed—at least, she believed it could. She seemed to recall reliving a number of days. She grew so frustrated at the end of each that she wished they had never taken place.

In Kunjiqui, her wishes were law.

But there were some things she could not wish into existence. She'd told Takwee that they would not travel into the Underworld alone. She needed an army and set out to raise one. The task should have been easy, since

Nelesquin had created his army on Anturasixan and sent it off to invade the Nine.

More important, he had left her some of his creatures. As he worked with Qiro to create lands that were conducive to breeding fierce warriors and terrifying weapons, some creations were not quite what he wanted. Nelesquin and her grandfather had simply wiped those lands away and started over, but Nirati had collected the orphaned strays, like Takwee, and made a home for them. Because it gave her so much pleasure, Nelesquin had taken to giving her larger and larger populations of creatures to house in what he called the Land of Lost Toys.

Hopeful, she had gone there, seeking to replicate the Durrani. She concentrated on the things she knew. Proto-Durrani—small, brutish men with blue skin and heavy muscles—took well to riding deer with golden horns. They used their mounts to herd other creatures, including the giant and quite docile hammer-headed rock-throwers.

A whole race of emerald-furred apes with bats' wings flew down from the mountains. They called themselves the Nighfor. They imitated the formations Nirati put her troops through. Within four or five generations, they understood commands and had become very loyal. They couldn't use bows, but spears suited them, and they were very good at dropping rocks on things.

Other creatures, like her long, reptilian wolves, also developed a rudimentary intelligence. They seemed to flock by instinct and sprinted quickly. They had a nasty bite and were happy to hunt as long as the day was sunny and warm.

In fact, all of her troops were happy to do whatever

she required of them. She'd found shrines built in her honor, with flowers and sacrificial offerings. She became as devoted to them as they were to her. As their eldest died and were laid to rest, she would come to ease their passing and promised loved ones they would be reunited in the Underworld.

All the creatures would indeed lay siege to the Underworld at her command. The problem was, she didn't know *how* to command. While she could breed creatures as well as Nelesquin, she had no clue as to what generals did. Like every other young girl of Nalenyr, she'd watched plenty of military parades and learned all about the Keru when she was younger. Parades and drills were useful for establishing discipline, but did nothing to teach creatures how to attack and use strategy or tactics. As for killing... Nirati really didn't like the idea of killing much.

Her army was made up of innocent creatures who would do whatever she might ask—*but there are just some things that should not be asked.*

Nirati found herself firmly stuck between two unacceptable alternatives. She could let Jorim remain trapped in the Underworld, or she could lead inexperienced and insufficiently trained creatures into a war that she had no skill to execute. Either would be a disaster, but doing nothing would not work either.

"I need a general." Nirati frowned as she stared out at the silver ocean into which the land's azure river poured. A wave crashed and flowed up the beach to wash her feet. As it retreated, the sand buried her to the ankles. She twiddled her toes, laughing at the sensation, then remembered something.

Her grandfather, exhausted and quite insane, had shaped a small army of mud. He'd placed his little warriors in boats and sent them off. They were meant to free Keles from the Desei capital. He'd even shaped a leader for them, taking a single hair from Nirati's head to complete the creation.

Nirati smiled and dropped to her knees, piling up handfuls of wet sand. Takwee and her two Nighfor bodyguards fell in and helped. They heaped wet sand into an oblong six feet in length and three high.

Nirati plucked Takwee from atop it and patted it all smooth. She began by generally outlining the shape of a tall, well-muscled man. She'd studied a little bit of sculpting in her long quest to discover her talent, but took heart in the fact that her grandfather's mud soldiers had been quite crude. She worked on the details, right on down to individual finger- and toenails.

She saved his face for last. She sought in vain for any image of the Emperor Taichun—the man who had created the Empire. The few surviving pictures had been idealized and melded easily in her mind with images of Jorim. She knew of other generals from stories, but had no clear images of them. She could conjure up an image of Prince Araylis, but she remembered that he'd died with his head split in two and didn't think he'd be very useful that way.

Nirati knelt and closed her eyes. She laid her hands on the empty face. Instead of trying to imagine a specific person, she concentrated on the traits a great general ought to possess. A strong jawline, certainly. High cheekbones, strong brow, and high forehead. A nose with a bump, perhaps having once been broken. And eyes, set not too deeply.

As she cut the eyebrows in with a fingernail, her entire body tingled. She focused on her need, her desire, for a warrior who would lead her army and save her brother. It had to work.

Then a huge wave hit. It caught her in the back, breaking on her. The water knocked her sprawling on top of her sand general, then the undertow plucked her away. Nirati tumbled down the beach. She clawed at the sand. It melted from between her fingers. A second wave drove her into the sand. Grit ground beneath her teeth. She sputtered, then inhaled water. She started coughing and the retreating wave sucked her into the silver waters.

She struck toward the surface, but the boiling water rolled her over and over. Hair wrapped her face and throat. Her lungs burned. She coughed. Precious air bubbled out. She thrust a hand toward the surface. She felt air, but also felt herself slowly sinking.

Then a hand closed on her wrist. Her savior dragged her from the depths and held her dangling childlike. Nirati coughed some more, sucked in air, then vomited all over herself. She gasped and struggled as he lowered her into the water, washing her off before hauling her free again.

Finally, she swept hair from her face. She recognized the man holding her aloft. His face—it had the strengths she'd sculpted, and much more. The eyes, a green of a deeper hue than Nighfor fur, glowed intensely. His gaze flicked from her face to the two charging apes.

The beasts stopped abruptly, snarled, and retreated up the beach.

He set her down, then looked at his left hand. He flexed it, studied it, and flicked his thumb against the ring on the fourth finger. He smiled, quite pleased. "I've lost my beard, but regained two fingers. It's a bargain I'll take."

Nirati covered herself with a gown of seaweed. "Welcome to Anturasixan, Prince Pyrust."

Chapter Thirty-seven

30th day, Month of the Eagle, Year of the Rat
Last Year of Imperial Prince Cyron's Court
163rd Year of the Komyr Dynasty
737th Year since the Cataclysm
Moriande, Nalenyr

I dropped to a knee before one of the shrines to Cyron and tossed a beggar a silver coin. From within his dirty robes, he produced a small wedge of incense and lit it. The self-appointed priest of Cyron began mumbling a prayer, making up in fervency what it lacked in coherence.

The shell-shaped shrine was like nine thousand others scattered throughout Moriande. It had the requisite picture that looked a lot like the Prince and a couple of toy soldiers standing vigil. My priest had a small finger bone purported to be from Cyron's lost arm. This hardly made the shrine unique—if only a ninth of the enshrined bones had actually come from Cyron, the man's left hand would have once sprouted at least eighty-one fingers.

I'd seen no harm in offering a prayer for Cyron's well-being. The Prince's directives gave people a purpose. That purpose gave them hope. My hope was that the prayers would help us to keep Nelesquin out of the city.

Kneeling there, I felt their approach before I heard it. Vibrations rose through the ground. The finger bone danced, which the beggar-priest took as a sign of divine favor. We stood at the same time—he to pray more loudly and me to race up the wall.

Metal hooves and the thunder they made had me wishing my priest would pray just that much harder.

Giant metal beast-men, reminiscent of the *gyanrigot* but much bigger and more ornate, charged from Nelesquin's camp. The lead rank of nine ram-headed men bore double-bitted broadaxes. Ranks of elephantine warriors flanked them, trunks trumpeting, and steel spikes capping ivory tusks. Tigers and wolves, bears, bulls, and lions raced north. Some were gold, others bronze, and some looked like wood and bone.

I'd never seen anything like them. I'd never even imagined war machines so large. My mouth went dry. Pirates, Viruk, Turasynd, and even the *vanyesh*. I'd killed them all. *But here, these things . . .*

"What will we do, Master?"

Dunos' question brought me back to reality. "We fight, boy. Get down there. Clear the courtyard."

"But the fighting will be up here."

"Not for long. Go."

I ignored his grumbles and plucked the fan from my sash. I snapped it open and gave the signal.

Our trumpets blared louder than the elephants. Hammers struck. Catapults and trebuchets lofted missiles that grazed the low-hanging clouds. Smaller stones just rattled off the metal creatures, but a large stone hit a bull in full charge, crushing its skull, dropping the metal beast. A following bull leaped over his comrade's shell and kept coming.

A ram sprinted for the city's gates. I expected it to lower its head and slam into them, but it stopped short. Shrugging off a hail of arrows, the ram hammered the gate with its ax. The heavy blow spun me around and dropped me to a knee. Wooden splinters shot through the courtyard. Men reeled away, stuck through with lethal fragments, and a big hunk of wood knocked Dunos down.

A tower crew levered a small ballista around and wedged it up. They had no real chance to aim, but the machines were thick at the gate, so they simply shot. Their iron-tipped spear pierced a ram, entering at the left shoulder, lancing down. The ram froze, tottered, then collapsed in a tangle of arms and legs.

More chopped at the gates. Others pounded the walls. Mortar cracked, stones shifted, and men fell. Below, in the courtyard, men loaded their ballistae and trained them on the gates. More splinters flew, then a hinge screamed.

I sped down the stairs. Stone cracked and iron bolts snapped. A piece of metal shot past my head and ricocheted off another man's battle mask. He went down hard.

A heartbeat later, half the gate went down harder.

Time slowed. The crossbeam securing that half of the gate splintered, ripping the brackets from the other half.

The door landed heavily, pulping an archer. His red-fletched arrows clicked and bounced over the cobblestones. The other door, tortured by incessant pounding, surrendered to the rams.

Nelesquin's monsters framed themselves in the gateway. Ballistae loosed their bolts. Coiled cords groaned and torsion bars clacked. The missiles reached their targets in an eyeblink. One spear skewered the lead ram's thigh and another took it through the gut. That ram went down, its forehooves covering its stomach before it sagged to the side. The third bolt stuck another ram through the hip.

It limped back, but two more entered.

And there I stood, alone, swords drawn, the faint scent of incense filling my head.

Ciras Dejote stood on the walls aghast as the war machines charged. The elephants drove directly at his position. He immediately recognized them. *Gyanrigot!*

All my skill, all my discipline, is nothing against one of these.

Beyond them, coming hard in their wake, *kwajiin* and human warriors screamed out challenges.

Penxir Aerant drew an arrow and let fly. It glanced off the lead elephant's broad head, leaving a bright scar in the dull iron.

Ciras grabbed the archer's sleeve. "You can't do anything against them."

The taller man pulled his arm free. "Not at that range, but they will get closer."

He drew again and shot, this time driving a shaft through the same elephant's breastbone. The mechanical beast stumbled and went down. The tusks carved deep furrows through the earth. Another elephant stumbled over the first. It hit hard, gouging up dirt, and rose slowly, giving the archer an easy third shot.

But Penxir never took it. Two *kwajiin* arrows crossed in his throat. Hot blood splashed over Ciras' battle mask, blinding him. He reeled back, swiping at his eyes. Another arrow pierced his left hand and clanked off his battle mask. Pain shot up his arm, then something hit the wall hard.

Ciras went flying.

He hit one of the mole-catchers' frames, partially breaking his fall. Twisting in the air, he landed on his back and smacked his head. His helmet bounced away. His battle mask hung askew. He tore it off.

High in the sky, one of the winged monsters sailed over the wall. Of more immediate concern, however, was the sally port gate. The first blow from an elephant's club had dented both halves and cracked the bar holding them shut. A second blasted both from their hinges. The metal doors whirled into the courtyard. One cut a man in half. The other exploded water barrels intended for fire-fighting.

Ciras tried to get up, but slipped in the new-made mud. Someone further back screamed, "Stay down!" Durrani warriors swelled through the sally port, their war cries fearsome, only to be answered by the staccato clacking of spring engines.

The oldest of siege machines and the least sophisticated, the spring engines consisted of a stout post sunk into the earth. A man's height remained aboveground, and the top had a V-notch a handspan across. A plank had been bound to the post at the bottom with thick cable, then bent back and secured. A sheaf of arrows had been stuffed in the notch. When the trigger cord was cut, the plank sprang up and struck the arrows hard on the end.

A cloud of arrows passed above Ciras. The first *kwajiin* fell back as the arrows passed through them. Those behind had arrows sticking in armor or flesh. Some paused to snap the arrows off. Others kept coming.

The spring engine's design did little for range or accuracy, but it sped reloading. Ciras rolled clear as the wood clacked again and again. *Kwajiin* warriors groaned and cursed, but too few died.

Ciras gained his feet and drew his *vanyesh* blade in the same motion. Remaining low, he scythed through a blue-skinned warrior's legs. Another *kwajiin,* this one with an arrow through the meaty part of his shoulder, slashed wildly. The swordsman parried the attack wide, then snapped his left elbow into the warrior's face. Bones cracked. The enemy staggered back, blood pouring through his fingers. Ciras' lunge took him through the throat.

Ciras leaped back to invoke *jaedun* but couldn't. The pain in his hand, the ache in his back, the pounding in his head, and the shock at seeing an elephant squeezing into the sally port made concentration impossible. He knocked another lunge aside, then kicked out, catching the warrior in the knee. It went sideways, breaking loudly, then an overhand cut clove the *kwajiin*'s skull in two.

From further down the street, one ballista shot, then another. The first slammed a ten-pound iron ball into the elephant's chest, cracking the armor. The other launched nine iron-tipped spears, several of which took *kwajiin* right off their feet. Two of the spears struck the elephant, and—doubtless guided by Kojai's hand—one punched through where the ball had hit.

The spear went deep and quivered. The elephant jerked. Its head snapped up, a tusk impaling a writhing *kwajiin*. The elephant froze in the sally port with the dying warrior wriggling helplessly.

Moriande's warriors sent up a shout. More spring engines shot, and archers picked specific targets. The trapped *kwajiin* sought and killed warriors, but without reinforcements, they died quickly.

Other elephants pounded on the walls. *Won't be long before this whole section comes down.*

Ciras broke the arrow and drew it from his hand. He filched a strip of fabric with a prayer on it from a Cyron shrine and bound the wound. He barely acknowledged the thanks of others as they scurried off to other posts. They invited him to join, but he declined.

Despite the pain and the victory, he'd not forgotten the winged beast flying over the city, skimming the clouds. He looked up and saw it circling to the west. Ciras knew in an instant where it was headed—Anturasikun—and he could make a good guess what its mission was.

For some reason Nelesquin wanted Keles Anturasi, and Ciras was not going to let them take his friend.

"We must get closer." Nelesquin took another glance at the handful of augury stones, then tapped the *kasphana* driver on the shoulder with a riding crop. "I can see what is happening, but I need to hear, too."

Kaerinus shook his head. "Get too close, and you can smell it."

Nelesquin smiled, returning the stones to their pouch. "I had forgotten you never developed a taste for war."

"I have just healed so many wounds that it no longer holds a thrill for me, Highness."

"And you do that very well, Kaerinus."

Stones flew over Moriande's walls, crushing some of the *dari*, but already the main gate had been shattered. Smaller gates east and west had gone down as well, and the elephants were close to bringing down a major piece of the wall. To the east, the effort to use the wooden *dari* as siege ladders seemed to be working. They linked themselves together and clung to the wall like ivy, allowing warriors to swarm up.

Nelesquin spoke into the bag of stones. "It's going better than you predicted."

"Did you say something, Highness?"

"A private joke." Nelesquin smiled broadly. "You see, my friends, warfare is what makes Men unique. Are the Viruk mighty warriors? Of course, there is no denying it. But they had stopped fighting wars well before True Men reached these shores. We were able to drive them back from their empire and establish our own. Yes, some have suggested the Viruk were tired of war and felt their age was passing, but this is the whining of those who do not understand how important warfare is. It kills the weak and rewards the strong. It makes us better."

"Winning me my tower will make us *much* better,

Prince Nelesquin." Qiro studied the distant battle with sharp, pale eyes. "Your effort in the west falters."

"Patience, Master Anturasi." Nelesquin grasped the crop in both hands at the small of his back. "This war is a work of art. Savor it. It will bring you what you desire."

The Prince nodded to himself as a *jarandaki* began its descent. "And once we have what we desire, there will be no stopping us."

Chapter Thirty-eight

30th day, Month of the Eagle, Year of the Rat
Last Year of Imperial Prince Cyron's Court
163rd Year of the Komyr Dynasty
737th Year since the Cataclysm
Moriande, Nalenyr

I threw myself from beneath the ram's ax. Its blow pulverized cobblestones and crushed the shrine where I'd prayed. Stone shards ricocheted off my armor. Sparks exploded as a second blow just missed me, skittering low and taking off another warrior's legs.

"Master, this way!"

I scrambled up and sprinted after Dunos. Another ram missed me, but blasted through the corner of a building. Roofing tiles cascaded, shattering, but I didn't look back. The ground shook with every hoof fall. Fear was lending wings to my feet, but that still wasn't going to win me this race.

Dunos darted left and I came hot on his heels. We cut

left down a narrow street. One of the ram's horns caught the edge of a roof, scattering more tiles. We ran beneath clotheslines hung with sheets. Rope snapped as the ram came on. I leaped over an abandoned bundle of clothes and ran past a crossing alley.

Only then, with the thunder of the ram's pursuit faltering, did I dare glance back.

Red and blue rags hung from its horns and the ram pawed them from his eyes. He paused at the crossroads, ignoring the east and west alleys. They were too narrow to permit his passage and Dunos and I were still out in front of him.

Though this was a creature of metal, the trap we'd planned for the *xonarchii* worked perfectly against it. Ballistae hidden in each alley shot from close range. One spear skewered both thighs. The other entered at a hip and came out at the opposite shoulder. The ram jerked, then sagged against a building. The wall crumbled and the war machine disappeared within the rubble.

Dunos tugged at my sleeve. We ran east and the ballista crews reloaded. We fought our way through crowds of panicking people streaming north. People shouted questions, but I had no answers they wanted to hear. I pointed to the bridges and told them to move quickly.

They did, praying to Cyron or anyone else who might listen.

I wonder who Cyron is praying to right now? Cyron might have planned on the walls coming down, but certainly not that quickly. No one could have. Nelesquin had managed in seconds what should have taken months.

My *xidantzu* company had assembled quickly.

Ranai pointed southeast. "We should fall back to Wentokikun and hold it."

I shook my head. "We have to protect the innocent. Deshiel, get your archers to the rooftops. Kill what you can, but I want you to track the enemy. Bait them. Lead them into our traps. Ranai, get your people moving refugees to the bridges. Get them out of here."

She frowned. "But, Master . . ."

"I know, it doesn't sound like a warrior's job, but it must be done. Do you honestly think there won't be enough bloodletting later? Clear the refugees, and you can fight to your heart's content."

She nodded and they both moved to relay orders to their people.

I looked down. "Dunos, go with Ranai."

He shook his head adamantly. "You'd be dead if I hadn't been at the gate. I stay with you."

I had no time to argue, especially when he was right. "If we get separated, you head north, understand?"

Dunos' bright smile managed to summon a twin to my face. "Head north; got it."

I promised to see my people on the other side—and most of them assumed I was talking about the river. Smoke had already begun to rise near a small gate usually reserved for the Prince, so Dunos and I headed that way. Almost immediately, we ran into people streaming from that direction, many of them cut and bleeding. They'd been fending off sword blows with their bare arms, which spoke to their courage and the incompetence of the invaders.

Dunos and I entered a small circular courtyard centered on a fountain. Two men wearing the crest of the

Free Ixunite Company had pinned a woman against the fountain. Her husband lay in a knot of his own entrails. Two wide-eyed toddlers cried silently, hidden in the shadow of an overturned wagon.

Jaedun sizzled through me. I crossed to the fountain, hamstringing the first man, then harvesting his head. His accomplice turned, eyes wide. His gaze shifted from me to the stumps of his handless arms. That was the last thing he saw before he fainted in a pool of hot arterial blood.

A dozen Ixunites occupied the courtyard's southern half. They gave up looting and came at us, swords bared. I spun into them, both blades flashing. Muscles tore and ligaments popped as razored steel slid through. Gasps and groans, curses running into gurgles. and screams warred with the clatter of metal, as swords dropped from nerveless fingers or in the grasp of severed hands.

Two of the men went for Dunos. There was no mistaking him for a man. He was a child, and a crippled one at that. They decided he would be easier to kill than I, proving they were, in fact, more stupid than they looked.

Dunos, though small and early in his formal training, had seen much combat. He dodged left, blocking one man with his companion. Dunos caught the first man's overhand slash on his sword, then darted in. He stabbed his dagger into the first man's groin. Blood gushed bright red. The man stumbled back. Dunos ducked low, sweeping a leg out. He caught the man's heels, sending him over backward.

The other coward, watching his friend's life spurt out, hesitated.

Dunos lunged, striking like a cobra. His sword slipped

beneath the man's breastplate and into his guts. The boy wrenched his sword hard, then yanked it out. The man coughed his last words into a bloody cloud, then flopped lifeless to the cobblestones.

Dunos' second foe hit the ground about the same time as the last pieces of mine. The woman had crawled to where her children cowered. The tinkling of the fountain's water covered most other immediate sounds, save for the ordered stamp of soldiers blocking all avenues of escape.

Count Linel Vroan entered the square, accompanied by two of the *gyanrigot*. They'd been constructed of wood and shaped like mantises. Though not as heavy as their metal counterparts, their footsteps still shook the ground. They flanked the leader of the Ixunite troops.

The tall man bowed. "Virisken Soshir, I remember you. Will you allow me to please my master, or will you force me to regretfully offer him your corpse?"

Prince Cyron snarled. He looked south from the heights of Shirikun. "How can they have breached the walls so quickly?"

Count Jarys Derael sat immobile in his wheeled chair. "Nelesquin has something new. We must hope to find vulnerabilities, or all is lost."

Cyron raked fingers back through his hair. "My city. We can do nothing."

"We have prepared well, Highness."

"They are through the wall. There is a fire in the southeast. It could consume everything."

"It is unlikely Nelesquin will let it rage. He wins nothing if it does."

"But how can he..." Cyron shook his head. "The *vanyesh*, yes. Perhaps they used their magic to bring the gates down."

"If they are that bold and that foolish, then all is lost no matter what we do." The count flicked a finger. "Please, we have a decision to make."

Cyron turned the wheeled chair toward the massive map spread over the center of the tower's floor. Cyron's grandfather had credited his penchant for playing with toy soldiers as the source of his military acumen. Toys had been painted to represent the various units stationed throughout the city and placed appropriately on the map.

"Highness, we must assume that the units at the gates are gone or soon will be gone. Likely our second line of defense as well. We can already see people coming over the bridges."

Cyron glanced back south. The nine bridges were choked with refugees. Here and there a cart was pitched over the side. Occasionally a body fell from the spans.

"Perhaps we should have evacuated everyone."

The count's voice came in a firm whisper. "We could not have anticipated Nelesquin's weapons. He did not have them at Tsatol Deraelkun. He did not have them five days ago."

Cyron shook his head. "But we knew he was coming."

"It does not matter. It would have been wrong to evacuate everyone."

"How can you say that?"

"Prince Cyron, I lived my entire life in a fortress. My

sole reason for living has been to kill the enemy. Those who lived with me knew no quarter would be asked or given. Had Tsatol Deraelkun fallen, survivors would have been slaughtered. To assume it would be any less here is folly."

The Prince frowned. "Because everyone is at risk, we shouldn't make them safe?"

"No. We are at war. To allow any segment of the population to pretend it is *safe* is dangerous. It makes defending the nation a task for warriors alone. People come to regard them as they might gardeners or other servants. They allow themselves to become insulated from the reality facing them. Either a people is united behind a leader to guarantee the destruction of its enemies, or its effort is futile. If anyone is allowed to think he is exempted from involvement, the war is lost."

Cyron regarded the sharp-eyed man trapped in a dying body. "There are a lot of children out there."

"And we shall mourn every single dead child. Our job is to determine how we can best prevent the enemy from killing them."

Cyron nodded and turned back to the window. He gazed out at the city. He saw it less as a collection of stones piled one on the other than as a web. To the south, strands were fraying and snapping. The city took on a glow—at least the parts of it his forces still controlled— and the disease that was Nelesquin's invasion darkened the edges.

The bridges over the Gold River, the high arches with their blue *gyanrigot* lights, they glowed the strongest.

"People produce that glow."

"Did you say something, Highness?"

"Thinking out loud." He returned to the map. "We have no choice. We recall our third and fourth lines across the river, then we cut all the bridges save one: the Dragon Bridge."

Count Derael closed his eyes. "We will get as many people across as we can first, but you are right, this must be done."

"And so it shall be." Cyron sighed and waved a clerk forward. "We'll cut the bridges and anyone caught on the far side, may Grija be kind when he welcomes them into the Underworld."

Through the book, Keles measured the enemy advance. He clutched the oversized folio against his chest and waved his cousins from the tower. They ran with arms full of charts and maps and diagrams. As long as Keles had his Secret Atlas, he could re-create anything that was lost.

And make sure nothing that has been created will *be lost.*

His cousins had worked tirelessly. In three days they had largely completed the world atlas. The pages came to him swiftly, and it seemed that each cartographer had pushed to make his chart better than any other. They worked together, adding illustrations and bold legends. Some of the youngest clerks wrote out notes from Jorim's adventures, and even Qiro's, which were bound into the atlas in the right places.

Keles had mentioned the project in passing to his mother, and she noted that it was a pity that they'd not done the work on paper made from plant fibers native to the appropriate places. She had some of the plants in the tower garden—the portion of it not yet overrun with *tzaden*—so they pressed petals between sheets and used some oils to provide scents.

He had to make the world of the book as real as possible. He needed everything—sight, scent, texture, folktales, all the things that gave a place its unique identity. As the pages came in, he studied them and bound them himself. Only he knew all that the book contained, but his cousins were certain they could reproduce their pages. It was this task they were set upon completing when the enemy hit the walls, and the horns and drums from the north sounded a general retreat.

Keles hurried the last of his cousins out of the tower, then shut and locked the golden gate. Tyressa found him there, her armor on and spear in hand. "We have to get going, Keles."

"Have you seen my mother? She was going to get *xunling* root for one of the maps. She thought she had it in her workshop or might have to dig it up from the garden."

"I haven't seen her." Tyressa pointed to the stairs. "Go. Check the garden. I'll check her workshop."

"I'll wait for you."

"No, keep going. I'll catch up. Kojai Bridge. If you get over it, go to Shirikun. You'll see your mother there again, I promise."

"I'll hold you to it." He reached a hand toward her face.

She stiffened, then smiled. She took his hand in hers and squeezed it. "Get going. Hurry."

Keles took the stairs two at a time, then leaped to the landing. He raced out into the garden, bursting through a green tangle of *tzaden* vines. He fought through, but a few still clung to him.

He stopped. "Mother?"

At the base of the garden steps, a silver skeletal monster held his mother's broken body. One tentacle wrapped her throat, the other encircled her thighs. Her neck was bent unnaturally.

Behind him a large leathery-winged creature nibbled fruit from a *naranji* tree.

The monster let his mother's body spin to the ground. "She wouldn't tell me where you were. Now it doesn't matter." The creature stalked forward and slid a scabbarded sword free of the harness on its back.

"Prince Nelesquin sends his regards, Keles Anturasi. He begs you to come visit him." The monster grinned. "He has a conflict with your grandfather, and believes you to be the solution to that particular problem."

Chapter Thirty-nine

30th day, Month of the Eagle, Year of the Rat
Last Year of Imperial Prince Cyron's Court
163rd Year of the Komyr Dynasty
737th Year since the Cataclysm
Moriande, Nalenyr

I glanced left. "Dunos, escort that woman and her children north."

"No, Master, I am staying with you."

"Dunos, do as I ask."

Count Vroan waved dismissively. "Go, child, you will be safe. I shall send a runner with you."

Dunos thrust out his chin defiantly. "I'm not a coward."

"So says the blood dripping from your weapons." The count bowed briefly in his direction. "But you must obey your master. Go."

I nodded. "Yes, Dunos, go. We must all obey our mas-

ters. The count obeys his, and will pay a fearful price
for it."

"Then may I hope, Moraven Tolo, that you will obey
your master."

The voice came softly, yet surprisingly strong, from a
small, ancient man huddled beneath an old blanket and a
conical straw hat. He moved slowly, supporting himself
on an oaken staff taller than he was. He could have been
any old man out wandering, save that gauntlets encased
his hands.

I started toward him. "Master!"

Vroan laughed. "*This* is your master? If you learned to
fight from this thing, Prince Nelesquin has no reason to
fear you."

Phoyn Jatan laughed with that dry rattle so common
among the ancient. "Has my lord never understood that
looks can be deceiving?"

"How am I deceived? You are three. I have many. You
might think me deceived, but I have no fear of your
killing me."

My master, small and shrunken, shook his head. "You
are not deceived, for I did not come to kill you." He
pointed his staff at the wooden *gyanrigot*. "I came to kill
them."

I reached his side. "Master, you don't need to do this."

He looked up and his hat slipped back. He smiled, his
eyes youthful despite his craggy face. "Will you tell me to
obey *my* master?"

"You have none, Phoyn Jatan."

"But I acknowledge one. You denied me a chance to
fight for our empress long ago. Will you do so now?"

A lump caught in my throat. I shook my head.

He unlaced his hat and handed it to me, then shrugged off his blanket. Beneath he wore brilliant golden robes with a coiled dragon in black. Below it rested the Imperial crown. Aside from the gauntlets, however, he wore no armor, and he bore no swords.

"You cannot go into combat without arms and armor."

He raised his voice, directing his comment at the enemy. "Were I fighting Men, I would be dressed as a warrior. These are wooden soldiers, thus I shall be a woodcutter."

Count Vroan raised a hand, forestalling the *gyanrigot* advance. "You realize your valor will not save your student?"

"I have no fear for the welfare of my students." Phoyn smiled at me. "Do you think this courtyard enough of a circle?"

"Yes, Master." I backed away. A few of Vroan's men likewise moved back. Word spread through the army, and they withdrew to the courtyard's edge. They all wanted to watch a Mystic battle the war machines, but none wanted to be caught in the magic.

I handed the hat and blanket to Dunos. "Keep the women and children close. You'll guide them to the bridge when the time comes."

"I won't leave you."

"I'll be right behind you, I promise."

Phoyn Jatan kept the fountain at his back. One of the wooden mantises came forward to oppose him. My master did him the honor of assuming the fourth mantis position, raising the staff to shoulder height and grasping it in both hands.

The wooden machine dwarfed him, mandibles clacking. Its arms ended in the insect's crushing claws. Limbs had been sharpened and festooned with spikes that could easily impale a man.

Phoyn Jatan remained undaunted. He bowed to his foe, took a mandible-clack as a suitable reply, and began slowly spinning the staff. The motion began clumsily, as one would expect of an old man with stiff joints and atrophied muscles, but as the staff moved more quickly, the motion became fluid. The golden-hued staff blurred into a circle. The air hummed. A golden nimbus surrounded my master. *Jaedun* surged.

The mantis drew back a half step, almost crushing a hapless Ixunite, then stabbed a claw forward. Phoyn shifted the spin, angling the staff up, as if to parry. The idea that he could succeed defied logic—the staff was a twig deflecting a battering ram. Staff struck claw with a terrible crack. Splinters flew. Two huge chunks of claw bounced past me. My master stood unaffected as the small sawdust cloud settled in a open circle around him.

The mantis pulled back and examined its arm. The ragged stump gave the warrior pause for a heartbeat, then it struck again. It raised the stump as a club and swung hard, intending to pound my master into paste.

Cobblestones shattered under the assault. Count Vroan fell. I went to a knee. Master Jatan did not falter. He leaped forward. The staff whirled left, then shot out to its full length. The knob hit the mantis' elbow.

Gold fire surged. The limb exploded like a lightning-struck tree. Ixunite warriors reeled away, bristling with splinters. The forearm bounced free, crushing two others.

Master Jatan stepped forward, moving almost too

swiftly. Golden flame wreathed him. The staff lashed out to the right, then left. The mantis' legs disintegrated. More lethal splinters flew.

The mantis, unbalanced and broken, flopped onto its belly. The impact knocked me flying. Its left arm flicked out, crushing the fountain's basin. Water gushed like blood.

Master Jatan whirled and raised his staff for an overhand blow. He smashed the stick down, catching the mantis at the base of its spine.

The crack came as crisp as that of a well-seasoned log caught beneath a woodsman's ax. The wood parted just as easily, splitting from pelvis to crown. What had previously been a seamless wooden construct collapsed into a collection of boards and pegs.

And somewhere within its midst, the warrior who had piloted it was crushed by the weight.

The second mantis darted forward, snatching Phoyn Jatan up in its right claw, plucking the staff away with the left. Contemptuously, it snapped the staff, then raised my master toward the sky. The claw contracted, all but cutting Phoyn Jatan in two.

Even his death did not matter. The fire of *jaedun* gushed down along the wooden arm. It splashed over the body. Droplets spattered thighs and feet. The wooden war machine smoldered for a moment, then exploded in fire. It burned brilliantly for a heartbeat, then imploded into a cloud of fine black ash that choked the courtyard.

And, swords bared, I strode into that cloud.

*   *   *

Keles backed away from the monster. "You expect me to serve a man who condones my mother's murder?"

"You're a grown man. You're well rid of your mother." The monster smiled. "You will be compensated."

Keles' eyes blazed. "You *murdered* my mother! How could anything compensate for her death?"

"Get away from him, Keles!" Tyressa burst through the *tzaden* vines and drove at the monster. Her spear whirled in a great arc. The monster tried to parry, but she slipped the head beneath his sheathed sword and brought it up in a slice. The blade quivered and carved metal from its pelvis. Had the monster been anything but a living skeleton, that single blow would have left him kneeling in his own intestines.

The monster's tentacles lashed out. She ducked one, but the other caught her right ankle. The monster yanked, pulling her down before the spearhead swept through the tentacle. It parted with a ping. Metal rings flew. Tyressa leaped back, kicking the tentacle from her ankle.

The monster bared both of his swords and bore in on her. Tyressa dodged right and left, letting the swords strike sparks from statuary and paving stones. She lunged, snapping a rib, then ducked beneath a tentacle. She favored her right ankle, but moved quickly enough that the monster couldn't touch her.

"Keles, go. Flee."

"No, Tyressa, get away from him." Keles' flesh had already begun to tingle from the magic pouring from them. He focused on that, working past the shock of his mother's death. "Go! I will save you."

The monster's tentacle snaked out and snapped

against Tyressa's left thigh. It dented the armor plates and knocked her back. She planted her right foot to steady herself, but her ankle broke. The Keru went down awkwardly, her right ankle twisted beneath her. Her spear came up to bat away one sword.

But the other blade passed beneath her desperate parry. Nelesquin's monster stabbed straight down, piercing the breastplate and punching out past her spine. The blow drove her back hard against the ground and the blade sank to a third of its length in the earth.

"Tyressa!" Keles crashed to his knees. He couldn't breathe. Tyressa writhed around the sword and pain twisted through his guts. *She can't die. She can't.*

The monster turned, his face a snarl. "No more games, Keles Anturasi, you're coming with me."

The black cloud parted. I stood above Count Linel Vroan. The family crest had bubbled and peeled off his armor. The same thing had happened with much of his face. The fire had blinded him, but he didn't need eyes to know who I was.

He held a hand up. "Let me stand so I can die like a man."

"To die like a man, you once had to be one." I took his head in one stroke. It rolled away. I kicked his body for good measure, then I stalked forward, looking for more men to kill.

A few of them came, imagining themselves to be braver than their master. This does not say much for them. Those were the stupid ones, and they died easily.

The smartest had run when my master had engaged the war machines.

I quickly exhausted my foes, but there were screams and the sounds of combat to the northeast. I sprinted over, straight into the ass end of a Ixunite formation. Though the Ixunites were grown men and trained as soldiers, a small group of students drove them back. With their master slain, the students of *Serrian* Jatan had no reason to grant mercy.

Nor did I. A thrust here, a slash there, and men went down screaming. Suddenly aware of an assault from the rear, the last of Vroan's soldiers panicked and fled.

"*Serrdin* of *Serrian* Jatan, join me." I pointed a bloody sword north. "We must cross the river."

Their leader, Eron Jatan, saluted me and sent his charges toward where Dunos waited. Beyond them lay Ixunite corpses and a few wounded, each feathered by Deshiel Tolo's archers. I noticed an arrow stuck in a building further along. "Follow those arrows north."

I ran with the others through streets strewn with the debris of war. Wounded people limped along, sometimes helped by friends and strangers. Others, mostly the elderly, sat beside buildings, heads tucked between their knees, their hands wrapped over their heads, sobbing. Dogs ran free, forming the packs that would feast on the dead. One mongrel even raced past me with Vroan's head held by an ear.

Things became worse the closer we got to the span of the Tiger Bridge. The Wolf span, parts of which were visible around a shallow curve in the river, wavered and twisted. I couldn't tell why, but the reason was soon apparent. The whole bridge collapsed much as the first wooden mantis had.

The crowd wailed at the bridge's failure. People shouted. Fistfights broke out. Men knocked aside children, old women, and pregnant girls. A gang lifted one cart and threw it over the River Road South wall. People surged into the opening, but the crowd barely moved any further.

"Dunos, Eron, with me. We're going to the bridge."

I invoked *jaedun,* reading the crowd as I would an enemy formation. I watched them jostle each other. Where two people bumped together and rebounded, I passed through their point of contact. I slid sideways between ranks, then darted forward. A nudge here, a push there, and I gained the bridge in short order.

I found the problem.

A gang of armed men controlled the bridge's approach. Bared steel and nocked arrows gave them all the authority they needed. They let a trickle of people through, making sure panic wasn't going to get anyone crushed.

I would have applauded their efforts, save that they were charging for passage.

I squeezed through and made for their leader. One of his underlings planted a hand in my chest. Dunos emasculated the bandit before I had a chance to take that hand off at the elbow.

I stepped past the screaming man, my eyes hard. "I haven't the time to draw a circle, so you have a choice. Die where you stand, or follow my orders. Choose. Now."

The man, whose eyes had widened at the mention of a circle, bowed his head. "How may I serve you, Master?"

"How high can you count?"

He looked at his hands. "Through the Nine Gods and one for me."

"Good. Pick nine people. They go." I nodded to Dunos and Eron. "Pick nine and send them. Stagger it."

Word of what I'd said passed back through the crowd. People took heart and grouped themselves in sets of nine. They started moving quickly over the bridge, which was just as well. Looking back into the city, seeing the smoke rise and the growing crowd heading toward the bridge, getting them all across was going to take a long time.

And we were going to run out of time long before we ran out of people.

Chapter Forty

30th day, Month of the Eagle, Year of the Rat
Last Year of Imperial Prince Cyron's Court
163rd Year of the Komyr Dynasty
737th Year since the Cataclysm
Moriande, Nalenyr

Ciras Dejote leaped over Tyressa's body and smashed both feet into Pravak's face. The *vanyesh* giant stumbled back, unable to free the sword in Tyressa's belly. The swordsman landed and dashed forward. His slash rang loudly, notching Pravak's thigh.

The tentacle swept out, but Ciras sidestepped it. He twisted away from a cuff by Pravak's open hand, then blocked a slash aimed at his back. He forced the blade up and over his head, then slashed again and scarred a shinbone.

"Ciras, get away from him."

"No, Keles, I know this one. Get free."

Pravak, bootprints still denting his profile, withdrew

and settled himself in fourth Scorpion. "You show me no respect, attacking without warning."

"You deserve none, conspiring with Turasynd and fighting against the Empress."

"And I thought you truly were Jogot reborn."

Ciras raised his sword in a salute. "I am, in more ways than you could ever imagine." He invoked *jaedun* and set himself. "And I am your better."

"Don't do this, Ciras!" Keles screamed at him.

"I have no choice, Keles."

Pravak launched himself. He came hard, raining blows down on the swordsman. Ciras retreated, step by step, dodging some blows, parrying others. The few he blocked sent shivers down his arm. Ciras' ripostes would have sliced muscle from arms and legs, crippling a normal foe. Against Pravak the worst of the cuts only curled silver off bone.

Ciras ducked. A wild cut lopped a branch off a tree. Ciras exploded through the shower of leaves and kept low. Pravak's sword whistled above his head. Ciras cut around, then slashed at the giant's knee, carving through the silver bands that bound the joint together.

The woven silver band snapped, then *jaedun* pulsed, and the tiny metal threads wove themselves back together.

Pravak spun and laughed. "I remembered how you defeated me before. I have taken precautions."

"Ciras, leave him alone!"

The swordsman ignored Keles' plea. He drove forward, his blade a blur. A cut swept through a knee and even before it had begun to heal, he slashed at the ankle. His sword came up and around, denting the smaller arm bone, then poked a vertebra to the side and chopped through a low rib. He disengaged from every parry, eluded every thrust, and constantly attacked, forcing Pravak to devote time to straightening limbs and repairing joints.

It became a battle of attrition. Pravak became battered; Ciras just became tired. Yet even as his muscles ached and his lungs burned, the magic filled him. He moved more swiftly than ever, reading intention in the slightest movement and countering strategies before they had even begun. Pravak could not defend and repair himself in the same moment. It would be a matter of time before the *vanyesh* lay scattered over the garden.

Pravak clearly realized this. The swordsman's blade slashed through the giant's left knee. The shin fell away and Pravak's femur jabbed into the ground. Ciras pivoted, bringing his sword back up for a strike at the monster's head but, as he turned, Pravak's right fist slammed into his face.

Ciras went down, landing hard on his tailbone, legs tingling hotly.

Pravak's sword came down. Lacquered leather bracers snapped and ring mail pinged as the sword chopped through it. Blood gushed and bones cracked. Ciras' sword flew as his hand spasmed, then Pravak bore down, using his weight to take Ciras' right forearm off.

"Being a *vanyesh* reborn is still not being a *vanyesh*, Ciras."

In shock, Ciras stared at his severed forearm lying two feet away. The hand still moved and clutched, but at nothing and weakly. Blood spurted from his stump, the severed artery pumping his life out with each thundering heartbeat.

I am dead.

Then a vine wrapped itself around his arm at the elbow. It just grew there, up through the ground, and tightened. The bleeding stopped.

Pravak grabbed his lower leg and fixed it back into place. *Jaedun* flared and the silver bands became whole again. The *vanyesh* patted the leg lovingly, then stood. "You tried, Ciras, and failed. No loss of honor in that."

Then the *vanyesh* turned toward Tyressa, presumably to recover his sword, but he couldn't lift his right leg. Vines similar to those that had formed the tourniquet had grown up through his feet and wrapped around his ankles. He tried to pull his foot up, but he couldn't escape the plants' tenacious grasp.

"What is going on here?"

"You *murdered* my mother." Keles Anturasi stood deeper in the garden, his fists clenched, his face closed. "You've hurt my friends. You didn't expect me to let you get away with that?"

Pravak turned, ripping one foot free. "You have no idea whom you are defying."

"And you have no idea whom you have angered." The cartographer raised a hand, then brought it down swiftly.

The carpet of *tzaden* vines fell in a wave from the tower. The green avalanche smashed Pravak to the ground. The sword flew, but vines rose and plucked it from the air. Then the whole plant flowed back up the tower, carrying Pravak's head high, but leaving his feet on the ground, and spreading the rest of his parts in between.

Keles gathered up a book and stood. He clutched it tightly to his chest with both arms. He closed his eyes.

In garden beds behind him the earth boiled. Plants clawed their way out of the ground. The rootlets formed arms and legs. As tall as a man, they stalked from the beds.

Two of them marched to where Siatsi Anturasi lay and lifted her up. They bore her to the garden and laid her in the hole from which they had emerged. They covered her with dirt. In an instant, fiery red and gold flowers carpeted her grave.

Two more of the plants reached Ciras and helped him up. One recovered his sword, but left his arm on the ground. The other plant ground the nub end of its hand against a paving stone, scraping away purple flesh. Liquid oozed up, and the plant painted both Ciras' stump and his punctured left hand with sticky darkness. Pain eased.

Ciras found concentrating difficult. "What is this?"

Keles opened his eyes. "*Xunling* root. My brother brought it from Ceriskoron. My mother cultivated it— the only *bhotridina* to succeed this far north. She'd come for some when . . ."

The last two roots reached Tyressa's side. They cut themselves on the sword in her belly, letting their sap run down the blade to her wound. They also dripped fluid over her lips.

Keles nodded and plants grew thickly beneath Tyressa. She rose and Pravak's sword came with her. Turning her on her side, the roots treated the exit wound as best they could.

The two that had buried Siatsi joined the ones tending Tyressa. Rootlets sprang from the ends of their arms and wove together into a thick mat, creating a litter. A few roots grew over to secure her to it, then the four bore her to Keles and Ciras.

"Come, Ciras, we must quit this place." Keles looked back at the tower and Pravak glittering amid the vines.

Ciras pointed at the winged beast. "What about that?"

"Oh, right." Keles gestured at the *naranji* tree. A branch stabbed out, impaling the beast. It flapped its wings, then collapsed. In the tree's shade, fungus began to consume the creature's body.

"Thank you for reminding me." Keles headed down the stone steps toward a garden gate and didn't look back. "Never again will Anturasikun be my home."

A captain in the Prince's Dragons found me on the south side of the bridge. "We have to bring this bridge down now."

Stonemasons had already been lowered to pound away at keystones on the central arch. Once they were knocked out, the center of the bridge would collapse.

"Look at the people, Captain, they still need to cross."

"It doesn't matter; the order has been given." The captain pulled a folded message from within his breastplate. "Prince Cyron's seal."

Muttering prayers and making all haste, people kept crossing. Most of the hale and hearty had already made it, and we were down to the sick, wounded, and lame. Carts lay abandoned, cargoes picked over. Somewhere, a child was crying.

"I've got my warriors out there, Captain. You can't expect me to abandon them."

"No, but they're not going to cross the Tiger Bridge. I have my orders."

I signaled Dunos to back away and the boy resheathed his knife. "What do I tell them?"

"The Dragon Bridge will remain open. We'll hold it. Same goes for your men. I have no choice."

"I have to get more across."

"You have until I'm back on the other side."

"Walk slowly."

He nodded and departed.

We sent as many more as we could across, but it wasn't nearly enough. While double the size of any other, the Dragon Bridge couldn't handle all the traffic. Moreover, Nelesquin would have made taking it a priority. How anyone thought they would hold it against the war machines, I had no idea.

"Eron, I need you and your students to start herding people west. They have to go to the Dragon Bridge."

He looked at the crowd, then back at me. "They will never make it. Look at the River Road. Twenty yards wide, a four-foot wall on the river side. It's a slaughter yard. And if anyone decides to go over the wall, it's a twenty-foot drop to the river."

"I know—and that's why you have to get them to the Dragon Bridge. I'll see how close the invaders are."

"Don't lie. You're going to buy them time." Eron rested a hand on my shoulder. "Let us come. We can fight, too."

"I know. I just need you here." I shook my head. "I'm counting on you."

"It shall be done. May the gods smile upon you."

"I'd rather they frown on the enemy. Dunos, with me."

We fought our way through the thinning crowd and raced into a tannery and onto the rooftop. In a city like Moriande, with so many buildings set so closely, one could travel swiftly from one point to another across the roofs.

Dunos stood beside me and slipped his right hand into my left. "This is bad. Very bad."

A woman, naked and bleeding, had leaped from a tower window and hung herself. Soldiers — Men and *kwajiin* alike — pitched riches to people waiting below. Warriors fought, screaming and dying, and fires had accidentally sprung up in several places.

And here and there, glimpsed between buildings and along streets, the *gyanrigot* giants stalked victims. A small congress of the machines had gathered where Phoyn Jatan had destroyed two of their number. I dearly wished we had a trebuchet capable of hurling a stone into their midst.

I gave the boy's hand a squeeze. "Let's go, Dunos. We have to find the enemy, then convince them to stay away from the bridge."

If not for the *xunling* warriors — for this was how Ciras had come to think of them — he would not have made it to the Dog Bridge. Their juice, which smelled bitter, had seeped into the wounds. Aside from dulling the pain, it induced a mild euphoria, against which part of his mind fought. He'd lost his sword arm, but somehow that seemed of questionable importance.

The unlikely group moved quickly through the city streets, most of which had been left to the dead. Many of the dead had been looters. The valuables that lay beside them were scattered or smashed, and clearly not worth dying for. One dying thief had crawled to a Cyron shrine, offering loot for mercy.

That prayer had gone unanswered as dogs fought over his corpse.

They came around a corner and saw a lovely young woman sitting in a doorway, playing the *necyl*. She drew a bow across the five strings, creating a mournful sound that made dogs howl and even seemed to wilt the leaves on the *xunling* warriors' heads.

Keles invited her to join them, but she never even acknowledged their presence. They moved on, yet as long as the melancholy notes echoed, they knew the girl still lived.

They reached the expanse of the River Road and stopped. Carts and boxes lay abandoned at the bridge's approach. People, no more than eighteen of them, huddled against the wall, arms wrapped around their knees, crying. At first Ciras could not figure out why, then he looked beyond them.

The only thing left of the Dog Bridge was four sets of pillars rising from artificial islands in the river. The Bat and Eagle Bridges had been similarly destroyed.

Ciras straightened and flexed his left hand. It felt good. "My sword."

Keles glanced at him. "There is no need."

"The *kwajiin* will find us before we ever reach the Dragon Bridge. We might as well die fighting."

"No. My mother has died today. I'll not have you or

Tyressa die." He pointed to one of the *xunling* roots. "Go."

The root left Ciras' side and ran toward the empty bridge footing. At river's edge, it leaped into the air, stretching its arms out. Even in his addled state, Ciras could see the creature would never make it, then rootlets shot out—slender filaments that reached the pilings ahead and back to the footing. The root thinned and reshaped itself, becoming a web that grew thicker with each heartbeat.

Keles addressed those who had given up hope. "If you wish to live, come now."

Half of them roused themselves and followed him out onto the root web. At the next pillar another of the *xunling* leaped and bridged that gap. The first one contracted back into its original form, then created the next section of bridge.

They crossed the fourth section and reached the north bank unmolested. The refugees fell prostrate and thanked Keles. They begged to be of service, but he sent them on their way. Ciras watched them go, then followed Keles and lost himself in what was left of Moriande.

Chapter Forty-one

30th day, Month of the Eagle, Year of the Rat
Last Year of Imperial Prince Cyron's Court
163rd Year of the Komyr Dynasty
737th Year since the Cataclysm
Moriande, Nalenyr

Finding the enemy was not difficult, but convincing them to stay away from the bridge was impossible. Though looting was prevalent, it seemed largely limited to the province of Men, not the *kwajiin*. The latter seemed more interested in combat than trophies.

The *kwajiin* leader, rather ironically, fought from within one of the *gyanrigot* tigers, looking the very incarnation of Chado. I wondered how long it would take for Nelesquin to resent that. The *kwajiin* deployed his lightly armored skirmishers to fan out through the city ahead of his war machines. They flushed some of our ambushers and exchanged arrows with Deshiel's men.

When their advance slowed, the war machines came

up to break through resistance. More heavily armored foot soldiers followed them up. Their advance north was steady and inexorable. The tigers were definitely the point of the spear, and it was driving straight at the Dragon Bridge.

We did what we could to slow them, but it was like cursing lightning, for all the good it did. Deshiel and his archers could stop the skirmishers, then Ranai or a unit of Mountain Dragons would push forward and try to flank the *kwajiin* tigers. The war machines would smash their way through a building or two, accidentally starting fires, which conscripts came up and fought with bucket lines. We could have attacked and easily slain them, but they'd been enslaved, and none of us wanted to see the city burn.

Our foot soldiers had to be careful, however, lest the other forces moving through the city flank them. We would hit, then fade back, hit again and fade, always retreating toward the bridge.

Dunos proved most helpful in that regard. He scrambled over rooftops and climbed the highest pinnacles to report on the crowds and how swiftly traffic flowed over the bridge. Many people were making it across, but more showed up. It became clear that many people would be trapped in the south side. There was nothing we could do to prevent it.

So I pulled my people back as well.

I read the dismay and disappointment in Dunos' eyes. For him and so many others, war is a simple thing: kill or be killed. You have orders and you carry them out, trusting the decisions of your leaders. If an order required you to make the supreme sacrifice, you did so, contented, knowing you would be revered for your bravery.

Dunos had an excuse for believing that—he was but a child of ten years. Adults who believed it had never fought, or had never had to make a life-or-death choice— at least never one that affected them directly. A minister might quarantine a village so some fever would burn it- self out, but he did so at a distance, never having to hear the moans of the dying or see the haunted faces of sur- vivors. If you have not seen blood, you do not know war. If you do not know war, you cannot make the right deci- sions in war.

But then, having seen war was no guarantee you'd make the right decisions either.

We threaded our way through the city. The crowds thickened and we had to force our way to the bridge. I felt trapped by bodies pressing in around me. Any sec- ond an arrow would find me. A war machine would pluck me up and crush me like Master Jatan.

And, though I fought it, panic won. I shoved my way through the crowd. I was strong and they were weak. Heedless of protests, I reached the bridge and sent my people across. I ran after them and once safely behind the first line of ballistae, I turned, drawn by the screams rising from the south shore.

The *kwajiin* skirmishers appeared on the rooftops. They nocked arrows and shot, not even bothering to aim. People wailed and surged toward the Dragon Bridge, but Naleni guards had overturned wagons and set them on fire. Still people tried to climb around, and one man even tossed a young boy through the flames.

The child landed, miraculously unburned, but broke a leg. Dunos darted out and dragged the child to safety.

Along the River Road, people scrambled over the wall and leaped into the river. At least one man made the mistake of standing when he topped the wall. Two *kwajiin* arrows lodged in his chest. Some people hit the water badly and never came up again. Bodies bobbed and floated eastward. Other people struck for the northern bank, swimming furiously. Many exhausted themselves, slowly sliding below the grey water.

Kwajiin archers reached the River Road to the east. They set up in a simple line. If swimmers had made it to the middle of the river, they were safe, but those just setting out had a choice of drowning or dying with arrows in their backs.

Then the *gyanrigot* arrived. A mantis kicked aside the burning wagons. Two ballistae shot. They were not small machines. They'd been loaded with timbers as thick around as my thigh and capped with triangular steel points half a yard long. The first blew through the mantis' chest, knocking the *gyanrigot* back several steps before it exploded like a crushed barrel.

The second shaft glanced off the mantis, then whirled into a human soldier. The blade decapitated one cleanly and the shaft broke nine more. A cheer rose from behind us. I helped reload the ballistae. We could kill another couple here, then the ballistae line behind us could kill a few more. The ballistae on the north shore could sweep that half, killing even more.

Even so, we couldn't stop them all. If they came, they'd win through.

But they did not come. The *gyanrigot* melted back into

the city and *kwajiin* warriors took up positions commanding the foot of the bridge.

The war for Moriande was half-over, and we had been soundly defeated.

The green light in Qiro's tower suggested decay to Nelesquin. The conditions within the tower certainly agreed. *Tzaden* vines had broken through windows and proliferated wildly. The workshop was a shambles. The weight of vine and fruit had collapsed desks and drafting tables. Charts had been crumpled by grasping vines and curtained partitions had been ripped down.

Yet as Qiro preceded him into the jungle, it seemed he noticed none of the destruction. He drifted through it, irritated only by the occasional vine that tugged at his ankle. The plants shrank from his curses.

Nelesquin stopped at the chamber's heart. "I will, of course, assign people to clean this up."

Qiro spun. "No, under no circumstance shall anyone enter."

Kaerinus, who had trailed in their wake, left off sniffing a *tzaden* flower. "Does this mean I should leave, my lord?"

Qiro nodded, but Nelesquin forestalled that command with a flick of his hand. "No, not yet. When you do go, you can tell Pravak we have found his left hand." Nelesquin kicked the thing free of a tangle of vines, but more grew to trap it.

Kaerinus bent and retrieved the bones. "Most aggressive, these vines. They render your tower quite uninhabitable."

Qiro laughed aloud. "That doesn't matter. The tower is mine again."

Nelesquin surveyed the wreckage. "It is not much of a prize, Master Anturasi."

"If you believe that, you are a fool." He walked to the far wall and sank a hand deep into the vines. "Behold the world."

With seemingly no effort at all, Qiro pulled and a whole tapestry of vines fell away. They revealed a white wall with a map of the world drawn on it.

Nelesquin's mouth went dry. As the son of the last Emperor, he had been privy to what was known of the world. While they had traded with the lands beyond Ixyll, little was known of their culture and nothing of their political structure. Fleets had sailed south and west, trading at islands or a few seaports, but those distant ports defined the edges of the known world.

"It's beautiful." Nelesquin walked toward it, his blue eyes shining. "That's Aefret? It's much larger than I could have imagined. And Tas al Aud, I didn't think it was that far west."

Qiro turned slowly, his fingers intertwined and pressed against his breastbone. "Yes, Prince Nelesquin. This is the world. *My* world. It is the place I have created. You see there, Anturasixan, my continent, wrought by my hand and my will."

The cartographer pointed toward the top of the map and the blue line running above the Helos Mountains. "There is the Imperial canal connecting the Dark Sea with the ocean. No, not a canal, a river. Yes, a river. The River Nelesquin. There, my lord, I name it for you. I made it. I name it for you now."

A chill ran up the Prince's spine. "You are most kind, Master Anturasi."

Qiro spread wide his arms and turned to the map again. "You have returned to me my tower. I am not ungrateful."

"I am pleased that you are pleased. And you have given me a great gift."

"What is that, Highness?"

"The world, of course." Nelesquin smiled broadly as he studied the map. "We shall restore the Empire once the pretender is destroyed. And then, well, look at how much we have to conquer. Your name shall be exalted in all the lands, Master Anturasi. My legions will bring all this under control."

Qiro turned, a thin smile on his lips. "But it is already under control. This is my world, Prince Nelesquin."

"I understand that, Master Anturasi, but it shall be my *Empire*. Look there, where your knowledge of Aefret ends. I will push into those lands, and you will add them to your map. I will bring you more of the world."

"You will bring me more of what is already mine?"

"Yes, Master Anturasi." Nelesquin smiled indulgently. "And I have given an order that the gates of gold are to be ripped away. You are prisoner here no longer."

"You are most kind, Prince Nelesquin." Qiro gave him an odd smile, then returned to studying his map.

Nelesquin led Kaerinus out of the tower. He paused, catching his companion by the sleeve, fighting the fatigue washing over him. "He is too dangerous. He will have to be destroyed."

Kaerinus nodded. "And you shall destroy him, my lord."

"But not until I am whole. Hurry, Kaerinus, find what I need." Nelesquin raised his head. "If I am to be Master of the World, I must be whole. The sooner I am, the sooner our new campaign begins."

Keles hugged his arms around himself. "You have tried everything, Master Geselkir?"

The rotund man wiped sweat from his brow with a square of stained silk. "There is nothing more . . ."

"Perhaps the Viruk ambassador. She healed me."

The Prince's physician shook his head. "I consulted her and even begged her to use magic, but she said that too much damage had been done. The sword split her spine and ruptured her bowels, poisoning her blood."

"But the *xunling* root, it helped."

"But a body can only take so much of it, Keles. It numbs because it is poison." Geselkir patted Keles' shoulder. "We have tried everything."

Keles grabbed the man's sleeve. "There must be something more." Tears leaked from his eyes.

"You should say good-bye."

Keles nodded, his throat thick. He swiped at tears, then entered the darkened chamber. Tyressa, her flesh as pale as her hair, lay on a bed. The only light came from a candle on the table next to her. The *xunling* roots stood sentinel against the walls. Rekarafi huddled in the far corner, his face hidden in shadows.

Keles approached the bed quietly and drew up a chair. Tyressa looked so innocent, so beautiful. Gone was the wariness and ferocity that had always been a part of her.

She'd been dressed in a black silk robe, embroidered

in gold with the rampant hound crest in which all Keru were laid to rest. A white sheet covered her to just beneath her breasts. Her breathing came regularly, but shallow and rasping.

He took her hand in both of his and shuddered. Her flesh was so cold. He looked at his hands, now healed in part because of her ministrations, and held on more tightly. He closed his eyes, searching for a way to summon the magic to make her whole.

Her hand tightened on his, briefly. He looked at her. Her blue eyes fluttered open, but only halfway.

"No, Keles. Your magic won't work."

"Tyressa . . ."

"You make things *whole*. I already am." Her eyes closed for a second. "I have outlived Pyrust. I served my Prince and kept you safe."

Keles nodded, determined not to cry.

"And I have been loved."

Keles' tears fell on their hands.

"Do not cry, Keles." Again she squeezed his hand weakly. "I became Keru because hatred filled me. There was no room for love in my heart. You made me whole."

"You can't die."

"I must. Kianmang awaits. There are Hells for warriors who only know hate." Tyressa struggled for breath. "I will know paradise because of you."

"Tyressa, I love you." He held on tight. "Don't leave me."

"You will be cared for, Keles. Better than I could have managed."

Her grip slackened as the Viruk's hands clasped Keles' shoulders. "Come."

"But . . ."

"Her niece is here."

Keles nodded and stood. He wiped away his tears, then bent and kissed her lightly on the lips. "Good-bye, Tyressa. To Kianmang swiftly."

Keles let himself be led from the room. He tried to look back, but Rekarafi's broad body eclipsed his view. He nodded to a red-eyed Jasai as they passed in the doorway, then attempted to shrug off the Viruk's hands. But Rekarafi directed him through a doorway and onto a balcony that overlooked Moriande to the south.

Keles refused to look at him. "Why wouldn't you let me stay?"

"She did not want to have you see her die."

"She shouldn't die alone."

"Jasai will be with her. Prince Eiran, too, if he comes quickly enough." The Viruk came up beside him and looked out over the city. "She was a warrior. She would not have you think of her otherwise. We will mourn her, you and I, then I will avenge her."

"I already tore him apart."

"But you didn't kill him, Keles. You do not kill. But I know the one who did this to her. He also maimed Ciras Dejote. That I did not kill him when I had the chance long ago is an error I shall soon remedy."

Chapter Forty-two

31st day, Month of the Eagle, Year of the Rat
Last Year of Imperial Prince Cyron's Court
163rd Year of the Komyr Dynasty
737th Year since the Cataclysm
Shirikun, North Moriande
Free Nalenyr

Cyron Komyr stared at the wall-mounted map of his divided capital. Despite a few scattered fires, it had not been significantly damaged by flames. Eight bridges had come down with a minimum of casualties, though too many of his people had been trapped on the far side.

A semicircle of tables surrounded him. Reports of all types lay on them, some scrolled, some bound into folios, some just notes scribbled onto scraps of paper. He'd perused them all, had Eiran sort them into piles, and sent his clerks out for more.

He scratched at his stump as he studied the map. It was hardly a remarkable specimen—certainly not an

Anturasi chart—which he had marked up with numbers and symbols and ideograms of his own invention.

He turned from the map and frowned at the Empress and Virisken Soshir. "The news is not as dire as could be expected. The *kwajiin* came straight north. Other troops secured the wings. A few Dragons, some militia, and *xi-dantzu* put up a spirited defense of Wentokikun. They repulsed two assaults by Virine Bears. *Kwajiin* were diverted to kill them, but failed to get them all. Nelesquin has made his headquarters in the Bear Tower. There are scattered pockets of resistance in the south. Black Myrian and his family of bandits are contesting control of the docks. A small boat went across last night. I hope to have word back tonight."

The Empress nodded and would have spoken, save for a quick knock on the door. A clerk stood there and bowed deeply, extending a folded and sealed note through the door. Eiran crossed and took it, then delivered it to Cyron. He pressed the paper against his thigh, then broke the seal with his thumb.

Shaking it open, he studied it for a moment, then handed it to Eiran. "The developing-situations pile, please. Majesty, you were going to say something?"

"Count Derael provided a realistic view of our ability to hold Nelesquin's forces back. Within the city we are well defended. If Nelesquin were to send his war machines west, cross the river, and come back on the north side, we would face a repeat of yesterday's assault."

"I have taken steps to deal with it." Cyron rubbed at his eyes. "The *gyanrigot are* a significant problem. They can overwhelm our defenses, but they cannot hold territory.

They must have support troops, and we can kill those. The *gyanrigot* are not invulnerable, either."

Virisken nodded. "So you don't believe he has the troops necessary to conquer the north?"

"Not right now." Cyron jerked a thumb at the map. "Prince Pyrust stripped his nation and put weapons in the hands of everyone who could carry them. Similarly, I am arming as many of my people as we can. The *kwajiin* may be formidable, but they're not immortal. With every citizen armed, taking the whole of Moriande will be difficult."

"He had Virine soldiers and troops from the Five Princes fighting for him." The Empress' eyes narrowed. "Can he bring more up?"

"It will take the better part of a month." Eiran fished through a pile of papers and glanced at a sheet. "He has to feed his army in the interim. There's not enough food in the south to do that."

Virisken's eyes narrowed. "How do you know that?"

The Naleni Prince patted a stack of folios nearly a yard tall. "It's all in here. Erumvirine shipped us a million *quor* of rice, and we shipped nearly that much north to Deseirion. We left minimal stores in the south. He has a week, two at the outside."

Even as he spoke, Cyron began to revise his assessments. It was as if just touching the ledgers and inventories refreshed his memory. He could see the stores shrinking as they were consumed. Every theft, every grain nibbled by a rat, every bit of waste; it all came to him easily. Heavy rains or abnormally hot days would alter things in different ways. Even the way the *kwajiin* ate and what they needed was different, or could be. *I have to find out about that.*

He looked up at the Empress and the swordsman, and found them regarding him curiously. "What?"

The Empress smiled. "I believe your assessments. You will send a messenger to me if you have cause to revise them."

"Of course, Highness."

Another sharp rap on the door panel presaged its opening. The same clerk appeared at the door and bowed deeply. He shuffled into the room and handed the folded paper to Cyron before withdrawing.

Cyron glanced at it, then extended it to the Empress.

She stared at the wax seal. "Nelesquin's crest." She slipped a thumbnail beneath the seal and broke it. She carefully unfolded the message, then read it aloud.

"Greetings, Cyrsa, harlot who would be Empress. I possess the Imperial capital and everything south of the Gold River. I will soon possess it all, but war against my own wearies me. Three days hence, I would meet with you on a barge in the middle of the river to discuss terms. Please send your reply to conclude negotiations.
Yours truly,
Nelesquin
Emperor"

Virisken smiled. "If he had the troops to take the north, we'd not have gotten a message. Refuse to meet him."

"No, I will meet him." The Empress looked at Cyron. "How much preparation will three days buy you?"

Cyron's head immediately filled with figures and images, orders to be written and reports that would come back. "A great deal, Highness."

"Enough to keep the north safe?"

"Quite possibly."

She nodded. "Then figure out how much more time you need. We shall find a way to charm it out of Nelesquin. I want the middle of that river to be as far north as he ever gets."

Chapter Forty-three

32nd day, Month of the Eagle, Year of the Rat
Last Year of Imperial Prince Cyron's Court
163rd Year of the Komyr Dynasty
737th Year since the Cataclysm
Wandao (The Sixth Hell)

Jorim's quest to win through the Nine Hells almost ended in Wandao, the Sixth Hell. It had been given over entirely to the torment of bullies—from the abusive father and spouse, to the aging shrew who emotionally tortured and manipulated everyone she knew. They had all been regressed to the age of nine—the point at which they should have grown out of such behavior—though their voices and vocabularies betrayed the age at which they died.

In this Hell of children, the copper ants and thorned vines with which Nessagafel had tortured Jorim abounded. Again and again, the children kicked over the anthills. When the ants erupted in copper geysers, the children would run screaming through nettles, brambles, and the vines. Thorns would tear at them and burrs would thicken their hair. Eventually they would stumble and fall. Screaming and thrashing, they would sink beneath a wave of ants.

Clean piles of bones dotted a landscape which—aside from these grim monuments and the abundance of anthills—appeared quite pleasant. Plants would arise from amid the skeletons, flower, then produce a strange fruit that resembled a cocoon. It would fall to the ground and a child would emerge to begin the cycle anew.

Seeing the ants and vines stopped Jorim. He dropped to his knees and hugged arms around himself. "There has to be another way around."

The Viruk hunched beside him. "What is it?"

"Nessagafel." He looked up. "He used the ants and vines on me."

"I understand." Talrisaal nodded. "Even his kindnesses were tinged with cruelty. Our priests said it was to toughen the Viruk. Our philosophers thought it a reflection of the world we grew up in."

"What do you mean?"

Talrisaal laughed and Jorim took pleasure in the sound. "How do I say this to a god? You, your brothers and sisters, were long acknowledged as Nessagafel's creations. Even when he manifested himself and became the God-Emperor in Virukadeen, he reinforced this thought. It was a core precept of our religion, but there were heretics among us. In fact, until the day you saved me, I was one."

The Viruk got his hands under Jorim's shoulders and hauled him to his feet. "Wentoki, I have been watching.

If we do not anger the ants, I believe we will pass unharmed. Look, over there."

Two children played together amid the grasses. They laughed and plucked blades of grass. They held them between their thumbs and blew, making funny sounds. This increased the laughter. The children slowly regressed, shedding years, and when they reached the point where they could no longer stand, they vanished altogether.

Jorim arched an eyebrow. "You think they are off to be reborn?"

"Thus is the cycle of life completed." Talrisaal urged him forward. "We will get out of here soon enough."

"You're right." Jorim walked on, placing his feet carefully. "I want to go back to something you said. What did your heretics believe?"

"I don't know that it was belief, really, as much as a point of discussion. People wondered why cruelty existed in the world. If Nessagafel was a perfect and generous god—as he claimed—and creation was a reflection of him, then cruelty had to be part of him or something he introduced consciously. Why would he do that? No one could answer, and he remained silent on the point. So some began to wonder if he was a flawed god. When that was taken a step further, we wondered if he was a god at all."

"How could they question his being a god? He was there in Virukadeen."

"Actually, that was the source of the question. There was no way to tell if he had discovered magic and it had made him as powerful as a god or—and here is the heretical bit—if the very discovery of magic made us believe there had to *be* gods. That belief, perforce, led us to create a god—either of whole cloth, or by channeling our belief into a Viruk who claimed he *was* a god."

Jorim stopped. "But if he wasn't the god who created everything, then how is it here? How am I here?"

"Two separate issues and, believe me, your existence caused me no end of sleepless nights. The existence of reality could imply a god, but does not require one. Our *creation* of a god could have imbued him with the power to create you and his other children, as well as other bits of creation you all claim. Some have suggested, in fact, that we created a god to be a mechanism for working magic before we understood how it worked. We invest power and belief in a god, we ask for boons, and when they are granted, we rejoice. What this means, ultimately, is not that Nessagafel created us in *his* image, but we crafted him in *ours.*"

Jorim followed the Viruk around a silken pouch that was just beginning to open. "But why would your god, your vessel, then create us?"

Talrisaal nodded grimly. "Here is where it gets very odd. If we created Nessagafel in our image, and if his very life depended upon our worship of him, then our growing understanding of magic and how to control it became a direct threat to his existence. If you can work miracles yourself, how or why do you need to worship something that no longer seems so powerful? Nessagafel was, in effect, a parasite. By creating you for Men to worship, Nessagafel was guaranteeing his continued existence. He creates nine of you, he waits to see which is the most powerful or well liked, then allies himself with you or supplants you."

"Then why the plan to destroy all creation and start over?"

Talrisaal shook his head as they neared a shimmering lake. "There was not much time to discuss this as the end came, but the idea was advanced that one of you, his children, might bestow magic upon Men. Tsiwen had gifted foresight to the Soth, and you allowed the Fennych to shift shapes. Magic for Men was but a matter of time."

"Which would put him in the same situation all over again: losing power because Men would become miracle workers." Jorim frowned. "But the *vanyesh* and the Cataclysm ended that problem. Magic is feared, and the power is limited."

"But limited only by the minds of those who wield it."

"If he had influence over the *vanyesh*..." Jorim shook his head. "All of this is predicated on his ability to influence affairs in the mortal realm, but he was destroyed with Virukadeen."

"He may have been destroyed, but his worship was not." The Viruk sighed. "No matter how horrible something may be, there will be those who refuse to see its reality. Change terrifies them, so they refuse to acknowledge it. They cling to the old ways, repeat the old rituals, and through that imbue new life into an old evil."

Jorim rubbed both hands over his face. "What you've said makes a dreadful sort of sense. Among the Amentzutl, the pantheon has undergone contractions and the channels for worship have been merged. For instance, Tsiwen and Kojai have been merged into Tlachoa, a monkey god which, in more recent representations, has sprouted bat's wings."

"They shape the gods to their needs." Talrisaal shrugged slowly. "If the gods do for us that which we cannot do ourselves, it makes sense that we reshape them and their aspects to address our current needs—for good or ill."

Jorim looked down at himself. "Then am I being reshaped?"

The Viruk flashed bright teeth. "You are courage, and it is forever needed and lauded."

"The ants tested that courage. Thank you for helping me."

"I have returned a favor you did me." Talrisaal waded out into the lake. "And now to Quoraxan, to repay the demons who had been tormenting *me* for their kindness."

The Viruk dove beneath the water and Jorim went after him. They both swam down, going deeper and deeper until a current began to draw them along. It picked up speed and suddenly sucked them into a tube.

Then a heartbeat later, Jorim shot out of a tunnel, free of the water. He flew into Quoraxan, a world of red lands that had been scoured and scarred by savage winds and volcanic flows. Lava erupted and burning lakes lit the landscape. Even the water burst into flames halfway down its nine-hundred-foot descent.

Jorim began falling and falling fast. His companion had suggested that worshippers shape gods to their needs, and Jorim sorely needed wings. He reached out, finding magic and shifted its balance. His robe ripped as wings thrust out and beat hard. He took heart in the fact that they were bat's wings, and he came to hover just above the tallest of the pool's licking flames.

Talrisaal, on eagle's wings, hovered beside him, riding the hot air.

Jorim laughed. "My bat's wings are for Tsiwen and wisdom. But you? Eagle's wings for Sisvoc and love?"

"I *love* not being burned."

"Good point."

The two of them looked down. The pool had collected in a bowl-shaped depression, the edges of which eclipsed their view of the surrounding area. Demons, tens of thousands of them, in a variety of colors—some dotted with warts, others striped with ulcerating wounds oozing pus and maggots—packed the shores. Some bore tridents, others studded clubs, but the nastiest just gnashed serrated teeth and flexed claws.

"And I think, Wentoki, I love flying above them."

Which is when the demons all sprouted wings and launched themselves into the air.

Chapter Forty-four

32nd day, Month of the Eagle, Year of the Rat
Last Year of Imperial Prince Cyron's Court
163rd Year of the Komyr Dynasty
737th Year since the Cataclysm
Shirikun, North Moriande
Free Nalenyr

"Keles."

The cartographer turned slowly. He already knew she'd entered the garden. The plants had reported it to him—and not just the *xunling* roots. And it was not that the plants were able to sense Jasai specifically, but when she eclipsed light, the sensation passed through the plants like a slip of cloud passing before the sun. Her tread, though gentle, created pressure. Unconsciously, he factored in height and weight, leaving him with only one possible option.

Besides, he'd known she would come.

"Good afternoon, Highness. Please, sit." He waved a hand toward a bench. The trees shading it drew limbs away, allowing sunlight through. "Are you warm enough?"

"Yes, thank you." She nodded, pulling a cloak about her, and accepted his invitation. "I hope the rains do not start again."

"I've heard it said the weather turned because of disturbances in the Heavens and Hells." He sat beside her. "I fear the weather has broken, as has my heart."

"My aunt's death was a blow to us all, Keles. For my entire life, she was an example for me. My greatest disappointment was when I realized the Keru would never accept me because I was too small."

Keles shook his head. "You are fierce enough to be Keru."

"Ferocity counts little when you are tiny." She stared into his hazel eyes. "When I realized I could not be Keru, I sought to prove I should be. Do you know what I did?"

"I can't imagine."

"You're not even trying." She took his hands in hers and squeezed firmly. "I ran away. I ran off into the mountains. I was going to prove myself worthy. I was going to survive out there, perhaps kill a bear or a tiger or something to prove how tough I was. Now, mind you, my prior experience of the wild was herding cattle and sheep in meadows. But, off I went.

"Tyressa followed me. For a week she watched—she never admitted it, but I was able to piece things together later—then, when I was hungry and tired and cold, she came wandering down the trail in front of me with a deer she'd killed. She showed me how to skin it and butcher it, then how to make a shelter. She taught me which plants were edible and which were poison. We stayed out for a week, talking, getting to know each other."

Keles smiled. "I spent time like that with Tyressa on the way to Ixyll. She knew a great deal, and was wise in so many ways."

"I know, Keles. She was very wise. In that week she taught me a lot about herself. She told me she envied my mother for having married well and having had such wonderful children. She promised me never to tell anyone, but that there were times she longed for love. I asked her why she didn't love, and she just said, 'The Keru love and serve Helosunde, and that has to be enough.' And yet, we both knew it wasn't enough.

"She chose a hard life, Keles, one I never could have chosen, because I wanted more. She and the other Keru put nation and service before self. You have to respect that."

"I respect it, Highness. I understand it. I just don't want to. I feel hollow. My heart beats, but is gone."

Jasai tipped his face up with a finger under his chin. "She died to keep you alive. She died happily, having fulfilled her mission."

"I know that." He looked at her but, seeing too much of Tyressa in her face, closed his eyes. "Why couldn't she tell me she loved me? She did love me, didn't she?"

A finger brushed away his tears. "Keles, oh Keles, of course she did. She loved you terribly. It elated her and scared her. Eiran says she insisted that he save you from Vallitsi—getting me out of there was almost an afterthought."

Keles shook his head. "You know that's not true."

"An overstatement, perhaps, but not much of one. She

loved you. You had to have seen that in how she cared for you and acted around you."

"But then why, on her deathbed, could she not bring herself to tell me she loved me?"

"If she admitted to it, perhaps she thought she would be abandoning her identity as Keru. Keru put people and nation before self. In dying, she thought she had failed, and did not want one last failure."

"But she didn't fail."

Jasai clutched his hands tightly. "And I think, perhaps, by not telling you that she loved you, she hoped to spare you some of the pain of her death."

Keles wiped away his own tears and stared at her. "How could she think it would spare me anything?"

"The Keru are not perfect, Keles. Strong in war, weak in love. Had she thought about it, she would have done the right thing. She never had the chance to. You can't hold that against her."

"No, you're right, I can't." Keles reached out and brushed a tear from her cheek. "I've been selfish, mourning my loss and wallowing in pity."

He laughed for a second. "I was thinking . . . Well, I was thinking all sorts of stupid things."

"Like what?"

"That the four women in my life who loved me—or pretended to at least—all have died in the last year. Majiata, Nirati, my mother, and Tyressa. And not just died, but died horribly. Who would be stupid enough to come near me, now? I've lost everyone who loved me. I'll forever be alone."

"Keles, I . . ."

He pressed a finger to her lips. She looked down, but

he raised her face again. "No, Princess, no need for the charade. You've seen me as a means to an end, and I understand that. I accept it—applaud it, even. I know Tyressa thought you loved me and thought I should fall in love with you instead of her. It's enough that I see how pitiful I am for myself. I don't need your pity, too."

She refused to meet his stare. "It's not pity, Keles. You have no idea how much I admire you and what you have done."

"I've done nothing worthy of admiration, Princess."

"How can you say that? I was at Tsatol Pelyn. I was there when you enabled us to cross the rift. I've benefited from the *tzaden* plants that grew to help you."

"None of that means anything, Highness." Keles stood and looked south. Low clouds and smoke darkened the landscape. Lights burned in the windows of Quunkun. *Gyanrigot* lights in Qiro's workshop created a blue halo around the top of Anturasikun. Through the smoke, the huge, hulking metal warriors strode along the River Road. Above them, bare smudges in the distance, resisters' bodies hung from crosses.

"Nothing I did stopped Nelesquin, or made the world safer. Your husband died trying to stop Nelesquin. Because of him, your aunt is dead. My mother is dead. Half the city is gone. You should save your pity for someone worthy of it."

Jasai caught his right hand and brought it to her lips. "Those I pity, Keles Anturasi, are the people who never do anything. They never act, they just *wish to have acted*. You will always be one who acts. My respect and admiration for you will never end."

"Respect and admiration. Thank you. Do not tell me you love me."

"You still believe you are unworthy of love?"

"It is best if I am, Highness. I kill those who love me." Keles frowned. "You know they say I am *jaecaixingna*. Everyone fears me. Everywhere I look I see circular amulets."

"They do that because they fear the *vanyesh*."

"They fear me more." He slowly shook his head. "Or they will."

Her eyes narrowed. "What do you mean?"

"You said I act. I only do that because your aunt showed me how. Before her, I was an observer. But now, you're right. I have to stop this nonsense. If I don't, love won't matter. There won't be anyone left alive to love."

Ciras Dejote huddled under a cloak, less to ward himself from the cold than to conceal the stump. He wouldn't even put it through a sleeve. He just hid it inside his robe.

It struck him as curious that what he noticed more than not having a right hand or forearm was the lack of weight at his left hip. He no longer wore a sword. *What is the purpose?*

It really didn't matter that his left hand was still healing from the arrow. He certainly had been trained to use a sword in his off hand. One couldn't reach a level of mastery without that, and though he did not fight with two swords, he could certainly defend himself. But the ability to use a sword did not bring with it the *will* to use one, and it was that will which had abandoned him.

No, not abandoned. I left it behind.

He peered south across the Gold River's sluggish breadth, where crucified soldiers moaned on their crosses. They'd continued fighting even though they'd been hideously wounded. Such was Nelesquin's idea of justice that one soldier who had lost a leg had it nailed knee and ankle to the crossbeams along with his body.

Smoke and clouds swirled. Archers lurked on both sides of the river, occasionally taking shots. They couldn't hit anything. Even with a tailing wind, the arrows fell short of either shore. But as futile as the task was, the archers had to try occasionally, relieving tension and venting fear.

Ciras would never have done that. Engaging in a futile act revealed weakness. If a warrior perceived himself as weak, he would die.

A tugging at his cloak brought Ciras around. "Yes, boy, what do you want?"

The young boy wore a white robe with a red bear crest. The long sword tucked into his red sash almost scraped on the ground after him. His left arm, wrapped though it was in leather and ring mail, clearly was withered.

"I wish to know why my master sent me to watch you."

"Your master?"

"Moraven Tolo, though some call him Virisken Soshir."

"I don't know why he sent you."

The boy shrugged. "I was watching him. He asked why and I said I was studying to be a hero. He told me

I should study a real hero. That's when he sent me to find you."

Ciras sagged against the river wall. "I am afraid your master has made a big mistake."

"He doesn't make mistakes." The boy shook his head adamantly. "If he says you're a hero, then you're a hero."

"No." Ciras threw the cloak back, revealing his half arm nestled against his chest. "I'm a broken man."

The boy shrugged again. "Well, I only have one good arm, too. But I'm going to be a hero."

"Are you?"

"I'm already on my way. I've killed some *vhangxi*. Couple of men, too." The boy jumped up to peer over the wall. "Haven't killed any *kwajiin* yet, but I'm going to. Maybe one of the *vanyesh*, too. You think I should?"

Ciras squatted down. "If you think killing is all that makes one a hero, you have not studied your master enough."

"Oh, I know. He says that, too." The boy smiled. "But he's awfully good at killing."

"Sometimes it is more important to know when not to kill."

The boy nodded. "Is that why you're not wearing your swords? It's not time to destroy anything?"

"No, boy, it is because I have been destroyed."

"Oh." The boy frowned. "Does that mean you're going to leave the city with the old people and the kids and the sick ones?"

"I hadn't thought to."

The boy nodded solemnly. "All right. Well, if you need help, like if the *kwajiin* are chasing you or something, you let me know. My name is Dunos. That's my only

name, but when I'm a hero I'll ask the Empress to give
me another one. It'll be good."

"I'm sure it will." Ciras patted the boy on the shoulder. "Please give your master my best regards."

"All right. Take care of yourself." Dunos nodded once,
then smiled and ran off. "Bye."

Ciras watched him go, distantly remembering a dream
in Voraxan where a nephew had similarly run off. He almost reversed his decision and sought a horse—a *real*
horse, not some mechanical mount. He could ride to the
coast and get a ship to Tirat. He could join his family and
spend time with them.

*And then die in front of them when Nelesquin comes for
Tirat.*

"Master Dejote, I'm glad I found you."

Ciras stood, pulling the cloak around himself. "Master
Gryst, good to see you again."

"And you, Ciras." Borosan frowned. "I was wondering
if I could ask your help in something."

One of the *gyanrigot* foot soldiers had accompanied
the inventor, and the silence with which it moved had
not betrayed its approach. It had taken on even more of
the shape of a man, with decorated armor plates covering
gears and hiding command-slates. The thing even wore a
battle mask—far too slender ever to hide a real face, but
impressive and haunting despite that.

Ciras smiled. "I see you have made great progress with
your machines. I fear I will be of little use to you, however."

"No, you're the perfect person." Borosan nodded
toward the other side of the river. "I have collected reports about the big *gyanrigot*. They have warriors inside

them, guiding them like you do with the mounts, only more direct. They use thoughts the way you use the pressure of your knees."

"It makes for formidable armor." Ciras shrugged. "I doubt they are putting their halt and lame in the suits."

"Probably not. What I want, what I need, is some measurements."

"Of?"

"Your arm."

Ciras' eyes narrowed. "My arm?"

"Yes, I think I have a way to fashion a substitute arm for you. It would work just like your real arm."

"My arm?" Ciras staggered back against the wall. "You would replace my arm with a *gyanrigot* device?"

"Yes, exactly. You would be able to fight again."

Ciras turned away and hugged his half arm to his chest tightly. "No, Master Gryst. Ninety-nine times no. I have respected you. I have tried to understand you. I even have achieved an appreciation for your machines, but I will *not* become one of them."

"No, Ciras, it is not like that . . ."

"Yes, it is!" Ciras turned back and threw the cloak off. He slipped his robe down, thrusting it aside with his cloth-swaddled stump. "You mock me, sir, in a most horrible way."

"No, Ciras . . ."

"You know not the depth of the insult you have paid me." Ciras shook his head adamantly. "Leave me, Master Gryst. It is out of respect for all you have done that I do not challenge you to a duel. Trouble me no further with your artificial warriors. I may be half a man, but I am still a *man*! And I won't let you take that away from me."

Chapter Forty-five

34th day, Month of the Eagle, Year of the Rat
Last Year of Imperial Prince Cyron's Court
163rd Year of the Komyr Dynasty
737th Year since the Cataclysm
Gold River, Moriande
Nalenyr

Deciding how he would get to the barge turned out to be the most difficult choice about the meeting for Nelesquin. The Naleni ministers had agreed immediately on the size of the barge and how it should be anchored in the middle. They proved most agreeable on details about the boats that would carry the delegations. They even allowed that no one would bring weapons, but that his golden armor would not be ruled a weapon.

Their concession on so many minor points meant that the north accepted their cause as lost. Cyrsa and Virisken could not have forgotten that, as a *xingnadin*, he was capable of killing them. That such exertion was momentarily beyond him was something they did not need to know. He'd gone so far as to make a great show of sparring with some *kwajiin* while keeping the northern ministers waiting. He'd done so to impress them with his strength, but he ended up enjoying the fights and continued the training even after the negotiations had been concluded.

It was remotely possible that Virisken would try to secrete a sword on the barge and kill him. That would surprise everyone—especially when Nelesquin didn't die. To preclude that happening, Nelesquin had insisted that everyone be attired in formal robes which, with their oversized sleeves and long hems, hampered anything but the most slothful movements.

And this, then, was the source of his problem. He could easily use magic to float himself down, but if he had one of his spells, he'd land in the river. Soul or no, he'd die of embarrassment. Stairs were out of the question, even if they were carpeted. One misstep would have the same result. Ramps were only slightly better, but were too common and hardly suited to someone of his stature. His manner of conveyance demanded elegance yet needed to display his power.

So plans were made, and even though the day started cold, with grey clouds hovering just above the Dragon Bridge's arches, no one present could possibly question his supremacy. Four of the *dari* bears bore an open palanquin upon which the Prince sat. He wore robes of red with the Erumvirine bear in white, rampant, crowned in gold. The same design had been worked on the chair, though white had surrendered to silver and gems sparkled from the points of the crown. The Durrani carrying the palanquin had drilled endlessly to keep it level at all times, which they did throughout his transit to the river.

South Moriande was not completely under Nelesquin's power. Durrani warriors thronged to his route, and more lurked behind closed windows. The three routes to the river had been swept and occupied—the Prince used his scrying stones to choose the final route at the last minute.

The cast of the stones had not been particularly auspicious, but did not hint at anything as dire as assassination. The most generous reading suggested the negotiations would be difficult, but that was to be expected. The Empress would offer little and demand much. It would avail her nothing, for Nelesquin was not of a mind to concede her anything.

Nelesquin actually expected nothing from the negotiation. In offering to meet, he merely wanted to show the citizens of North Moriande that he had *tried* to save them. With the full might of his *dari* armor arrayed in ranks on the River Road, his victory would be obvious and inevitable. Given the chance, the forces in the north would revolt and turn that half of the city over to him. In fact, negotiations with dissident elements had already begun.

As his palanquin passed by, troops melted into the city to quell any unrest that might arise while he was on the river. The last thing he wanted was to see a group of misguided peasants attack his soldiers. He required complete peace in South Moriande and the Durrani would see to it.

The procession arrived at the River Road. Nelesquin did nothing to suppress a smile. His troops had arrayed themselves in good order, in twelve companies of one hundred. Nelesquin had decided to modify the standard organization of nines. One each of the legions still honored the gods, but the tenth, the bears, honored him.

The bears bore his platform to the edge of the river. Two more bears stood at river's edge, holding long poles fitted with block and tackle. Ropes suspended a platform over the river. Two more bears were poised to turn the capstan to play the rope out.

Nelesquin stepped onto a platform inside the river wall, then onto the suspended platform. Kaerinus, wearing formal robes of black and green decorated with his butterflies, stood back and to the Prince's left. Qiro Anturasi, wearing gold with purple bears on it, took up a position at the other aft corner. Slowly, and without a hint of sway, the platform descended.

Nelesquin suppressed a smile as he stepped onto the flatboat. Cyrsa waited for him on the barge. She wore purple, trimmed in red. Four circles of varying size trapped within a larger one formed her crest. It represented the sun, the world, and all three moons, proclaiming her Empress of everything. It was a bold choice, and he did admire the tiny woman for making it.

Virisken wore a black robe, trimmed in orange, with a gold crown embroidered beneath the hunting tiger. Though he had seen his half brother at Tsatol Deraelkun, it had been from a distance. He appeared to have weathered the years well but had lost the edge to his glare. The years had sapped something from him.

Prince Cyron occupied the third position on the barge. He wore purple robes trimmed in gold and wore the Naleni crest as his own. An Imperial crown had been added to it. Save for the emptiness of his left sleeve, Cyron would have been a handsome figure, and Nelesquin might have been inclined to keep him much as he had Prince Jekusmirwyn. He might yet consider it if Cyron gave good counsel.

What Nelesquin had not quite expected was the density of the crowd on the river's northern side. People of every stripe had crowded together and even pushed their way onto the Dragon Bridge. They huddled in windows and lined rooftops. The northern breeze tugged at a few banners—either old Naleni flags or family crests. While he did get some sense of their anxiety, he caught no hint of surrender.

No matter. They will learn.

The flatboat bumped against the barge. Durrani boatmen steadied it. The Prince disembarked and crossed to his position at the barge's heart. Little more than a wooden stage linking two flatboats, it had been covered in rice mats and red carpeting ringed with purple. To Nelesquin's amusement, Qiro stepped onto it with no hesitation, while Kaerinus employed magic to float a handspan above it.

Nelesquin bowed to Cyrsa for a respectful amount of time, though the bow could have been deeper. Cyrsa returned the gesture, but the duration again seemed a bit short. Doubtless some minister of Protocol could tell him that she held it long enough to honor a prince or a master potter, but not the Emperor. A transgression, yes, but one he was inclined to let slip, since she had many more for which she would pay fully.

The two of them settled to their knees and smoothed their robes. Their courtiers remained standing.

"We are pleased, Prince Nelesquin, that you have come today."

"You have forgotten, Cyrsa, that I invited you. You have come to me."

She smiled. "We six know this, but to the people watching, *you* came to *me*."

Nelesquin chuckled. "Still full of games. And deceit. You deceived my father."

"No, I *murdered* your father. I did so to save the Empire."

"Had you succeeded, we would not be here now."

"And had *you* succeeded, Nelesquin, there would be nothing here now."

"More games." Nelesquin shook his head. "I am not here to play games, whore. There are many things that should be evident. I look past your shoulder and I see people. If you look past mine, you see the machines that will kill those people. You cannot stop the conquest of Moriande. The only hope these people have is for you to surrender."

"Toward what end?" She glanced up at the bridge arching above them. "Will you crucify me at its highest point?"

"I might have to, to make a point. My preference is to strangle you with my own hands."

Cyrsa's voice shrank to a whisper. "If death at your hands is my destiny, what do I care if others suffer?"

"I can ensure *you* will *not* suffer."

She laughed. The sound raked claws over his flesh.

"You have forgotten my talent, Nelesquin. I will never suffer." Her expression hardened. "If you brought us here to trade insults, you have wasted your time."

"That was not why I brought you here." Nelesquin stood in one flowing motion and opened his arms. "People of Moriande, I am the Emperor Nelesquin. I have reunited the Empire. I have restored the order lost when this woman murdered my father and usurped his throne. I now offer you that which she denies you: a chance at life. You see my army. You see my war machines. You know the havoc they have wrought. They shall only come north if you support her. She offers death. I offer life and, beyond that, riches and glory. It is yours if you will but hail me as your rightful ruler."

Hoots and hollers, jeers and other rude noises began sporadically, then built. People laughed at him. Stones and half-gnawed food splashed in the river. People began to chant all manner of discordant things, but it quickly resolved itself into pulsed shouts of "Never the bear, never the bear."

Cyrsa looked up at him. "Had you expected a different outcome?"

"No. This was exactly what I expected." He raised a finger and brought it down again.

The *dari* rams marched forward, turned left, then sprinted toward the end of the bridge. They reached the footing and tore apart the barricades. Ballistae shot, but most of the bolts rattled harmlessly off their metal hides. Men shouted orders and reloaded, waiting.

The rams remained on the south bank, having pulled back after clearing the path. They could have easily reached the next line of defense, and the one after that. They could have burst free and killed thousands.

And the crowd knew it. People screamed and fled. A

few pitched over the bridge's side and plunged into the river. People vanished from windows, pulling shutters closed. At least one man tumbled from a rooftop. The milling mob hampered the arrival of a company of Naleni Dragons.

Nelesquin's eyes narrowed. "There, Cyrsa, now your people know what awaits them. You do, too. You could take that bridge down, but I would just ford the river and lay siege from the north. If you want me to be generous, now is the time to speak, because when I leave this barge, we will speak no more."

Before she could reply, a man on the bridge shouted down at them. "No! You shall not win. I shall not allow it."

Nelesquin looked up. The man stood on the bridge's railing. Two soldiers tugged at his legs to pull him back, but they might as well have been trying to shift stone.

Qiro and Cyron both shouted at the same time. "Keles, get down!" The Prince begged, the grandfather commanded, but each had the same luck as the soldiers.

"You've destroyed too much. No more."

Keles bared a silver blade with a flick of his wrist. The scabbard spun through the air like a falling autumn leaf. He stroked the knife over his left wrist. His hand tightened. Blood spurted.

Red rain spattered the river.

Magic pulsed with each heartbeat, each wave of it stronger than the one before. A million scorpions scuttled over Nelesquin's flesh. Vast amounts of magic surged through him, shocking him.

A red mist rose from the river, stinking of copper. It washed over the barge, infusing blood into the white parts of the Prince's robe. Nelesquin staggered, crashing to his knees. Kaerinus and Qiro fell with him.

The mist swept past them and thickened. It swirled up into the clouds, then pulled them down as well. The clouds took on the red-brown of dried blood. Nelesquin expected lightning as the clouds descended on the River Road, but none flashed.

And the only thunder was that of the poles crashing through and sinking Nelesquin's elevating platform.

The clouds lifted again, then parted, allowing a shaft of sunlight to sweep the southern shore.

The *dari* armor had vanished.

Virisken started forward. Kaerinus interposed himself between the swordsman and Nelesquin. "There is yet a truce here."

Virisken nodded and righted the Empress. Behind them Cyron gained his feet.

She remained kneeling, but began speaking before Nelesquin had time to gather himself. "Your advantage is gone. Do you wish these fraudulent negotiations to continue, or shall we speak of something substantive?"

Her offer tempted him, and he might have agreed to an arrangement, save for two things. He *did* know her art, and knew she could be quite persuasive. No doubt she would take any advantage she could.

The other thing, however, was the note of unease in her voice. She had not known what Keles was going to do. None of them had. It surprised them, and the sheer power of it frightened them. She might pretend to be in a strong position, but he had taken Tsatol Deraelkun without *dari*. So the rest of Moriande would fall.

He levered himself into a kneeling position. "This

changes nothing. A week. I give you a week to consider surrendering the rest of Moriande. It is half a city against an empire. If I am forced to take it, Moriande will be destroyed and, like you, will be forgotten well before my Imperial reign ends."

Chapter Forty-six

34th day, Month of the Eagle, Year of the Rat
Last Year of Imperial Prince Cyron's Court
163rd Year of the Komyr Dynasty
737th Year since the Cataclysm
Anturasikun, South Moriande
Imperial Nalenyr

"Stop saying he's a clever boy!" Nelesquin upended a desk in Qiro's tower, scattering papers and brushes. "He bleeds in the river and my army vanishes. Twelve hundred warriors in *gyanrigot* armor, Keerana among them! The best of the best were in those suits, and they are *gone*! And all you can say is that he is a *clever boy*?"

Qiro's arms remained hugged around himself, and he chuckled. "Far more clever than I had imagined. More clever than his father, by far. No, Ryn never could have figured this out. It was very good."

"No, Master Anturasi, it was very *bad*!" Nelesquin balled a fist and took a step toward the cartographer, but his left leg didn't want to move. Weakness seized him.

He leaned heavily against a table and discovered his fist would not unclench.

Qiro did not notice. "Keles really doesn't understand the power. He has little experience, but he always was sensitive. He always tried to shield his brother from me. But now he's hit on something and he's feeling his way through it. It's remarkable, actually, that he was able to do what he did. And, if we asked him, I doubt he would know how he did it himself!"

Nelesquin snarled and smacked his fist against his thigh to loosen it. "He's probably dead."

"No, I would know." Qiro tapped his temple. "I would feel it if he died. He's very weak now, but his mind still functions. They're dosing him with *xunling* root and *tzaden*-flower tea. He will recover."

"So he can do this again." Nelesquin pointed north. "He'll fill that bridge with mist and my soldiers will never make it across."

"Fear not on that account, Highness. I won't let that happen."

"Won't let it happen? Why didn't you stop it in the first place?"

"Because I didn't know what he had done." Qiro sighed with a schoolmasterish air that made Nelesquin want to choke him. "Keles was in Felarati, then he came south. He passed by the new channel I cut. But I acted in haste when I did that. Instead of piling the earth up on either side, I made it go away."

"Away?"

"Out of this reality. I am uncertain if it ended up in one of the Hells or in some other place entirely. But Keles must have been close enough to get a sense of the void into which the earth vanished." Qiro stroked his chin and glanced at the map of the world. "Keles, in his urgency to get rid of the *dari* armor, must have picked up on the idea that it was not really part of this world. It had been formed in a pocket world—another creation entirely, much as his sister's paradise, Kunjiqui, was."

"I remember." Nelesquin slowly flexed his fingers. "So the *dari* are there, then. Bring them back."

"I can't."

"Why not?"

"You don't understand, Highness." The cartographer paused for a moment, then smiled patronizingly. "The world, as I have drawn it, is a chessboard. Keles and I each understand the board on one level or another. My mastery is much greater than his, of course, but he has learned much. In our game we have the ability to shift aspects of the board—but only aspects that have not been identified. While each of us is capable, the board remains the same."

"Then how did he make the *dari* disappear?"

Qiro smiled, proudly. "He sensed the alien nature of the *dari* armor and sent it to a place where it would be at home. This is why I cannot bring it back. I do not know where that place is."

Nelesquin took a deep breath and let it out slowly. "You cannot bring it back. I accept this. Make me more *dari*, then."

Qiro opened his hands. "I cannot do that either, Highness, and you know that. Our resources have been exhausted."

"Your answer does not please me, Qiro Anturasi."

"And your tone does not please me, Prince Nelesquin.

Have you forgotten that we are united in this campaign to destroy Nalenyr?" Qiro snorted. "There are things I *can* do for you, and I am doing them."

"If you could rip a channel from the Dark Sea to the ocean, you can build me more bridges."

"I could, but that would be rather inelegant. I shall do something else for you instead."

"Yes?"

"The world in which the *dari* armor was created still exists. Have your Durrani round up all the fertile women in South Moriande. Bring them there and get children upon them. You've given Cyrsa nine days. In that time, you shall have thousands of troops ready to die for you."

"I want them to kill for me."

"I have no doubt they will."

"All the troops in the world will avail me nothing if they cannot cross the river. I can take them outside the city and lay siege to it, but that will take too long."

"Fear not, Highness, for I am no more patient a man than you are." Qiro bent and rooted about in the maps Nelesquin had scattered. He pulled one from the pile, eyed it carefully, then nodded. "I think this will do nicely."

Nelesquin frowned. "It is an old map of Moriande."

"It is a beginning." Qiro smiled, then nipped the pad of his index finger. A bright red droplet welled up. "And now, if you will forgive me, I must go to work."

Pelut Vniel huddled beneath a heavy canvas shroud, which reeked of vomit and dead fish. The small boat's rocking did nothing to quell his queasiness. The butter-flies in his stomach grew bolder with every creaking pull on the oars.

Such nervousness surprised Vniel, for he'd not felt it in many years—perhaps not even since he took his first ministry exams. Once he had entered the bureaucracy, he had been supremely confident. He appeased those who could destroy him, destroyed those who would appease him, and carefully worked connections that allowed him to rise to Grand Minister of Nalenyr.

But Prince Cyron had changed all that. He'd isolated Vniel and pared away his power. Granted, he'd made the bureaucracy more efficient, and those reforms did have their uses. But Cyron had made one mistake: he fought to preserve his nation. He had forgotten that the bureaucracy was bigger than Nalenyr, that it assured the continued stability of the world.

Pelut acted for interests beyond Nalenyr's. He'd researched Prince Nelesquin. He'd known all of the folktales, of course, but he looked beyond them. Certain histories from before the Time of Black Ice had praised the Prince for his battles against pirates and his campaigns to preserve the Empire's integrity. Had Cyron been one-ninth the man Nelesquin had been, Nalenyr would have long since re-created the Empire.

The new Empire was precisely what the bureaucracy needed, so Pelut had actually given thought as to whether or not he should betray Nalenyr. He set aside his personal dislike for Prince Cyron. He viewed things rationally and dispassionately. Moriande had to fall eventually—and probably sooner rather than later. Its conquest would effectively unite the Empire. Helosunde and Deseirion had made their stand in Nalenyr. Once the forces here were crushed, their annexation would be but a formality.

Cyron will not look to the future, so I must.

Keles Anturasi's disappearing Nelesquin's *gyanrigot* warriors had given Pelut pause. That raw display of power inspired hope, but the aftermath killed it. Keles had collapsed. And though Cyron's physician, Geselkir, cared for him, the young cartographer was reported to be very sick: feverish and delirious. What he had done once he likely could not do again.

All of his considerations left but one path open for Pelut Vniel. Cyron had waged war against the bureaucracy, and Pelut would have to fight back. He saw no other choice, yet betraying his nation did not come free of anxiety. It had to be done, of that he had no doubt, but . . . *if I fail* . . .

He peeked from beneath the canvas. "Why so long, boatman?"

"I'll get you there, *Grandfather.*" The man said the word without a hint of respect. "Must have been rain in the uplands. The river's running a bit faster than usual this time of year."

The man grunted and pulled harder at the oars. The south shore lights bobbed. Pelut ducked beneath the canvas again, returning to the close and fetid sanctuary in the bottom of the boat. Bilgewater sloshed. He fought to keep his gorge down.

The thing that most frightened him was not the chance of being discovered. He'd already laid the groundwork to suggest he was undertaking an independent mission of peace to save lives and reunite families. He'd made inquiries, ordered reports, all of which would back up this contention. If Nelesquin killed him, or if he was discovered and killed by Cyron's troops, the fiction would redeem him in the eyes of his people. His effort would be thought good-hearted, if misguided.

The prospect of meeting Nelesquin scared him. Pelut would have one chance to read him, find his weakness, and exploit it. There was no doubt that the man was vain—the manner in which he'd come to the negotiation that morning made that quite clear. Were Nelesquin stupid, vanity would be the way into his mind; but intelligent men always suspect treachery from flatterers. While they believe they deserve the flattery, they also know it is a means to an end. If they spy out the end and do not like it, their retribution is often swift and harsh.

The boat bumped against the quay. Cool air rushed over him as the canvas was peeled back. Pelut quickly mounted the ladder to the dock. He looked in vain for the agent who was to meet him. Then he felt the gentle flutter of a butterfly's wings against his cheek. He turned and bowed.

Kaerinus shook his head. "No time for formalities. Follow me."

Though the route they took through the riverside district seemed fairly direct, Pelut quickly found himself confused. This especially discomfited him, as he'd lived his entire life in Moriande and knew it very well—including the nether regions given over to Black Myrian's control. He'd even met with a Desei agent in an opium den, arranging the failed assassination attempt against Prince Cyron.

The *vanyesh* brought him to a darkened doorway between a teahouse and a tavern. They ascended the stairs and entered a small room lit with a single lantern. As the door closed behind him, the light brightened, revealing Nelesquin eying him suspiciously.

Pelut bowed low and held it for even longer than protocol required. Instead of rising, he sank to his knees and pressed his face to the floor.

Nelesquin grunted. "So courtesy has not died in Moriande."

Pelut shook his head. "Imperial Highness, I shall not waste your valuable time. I am your man, ready to serve you."

"Sit up."

Pelut did as he was bid.

Nelesquin, arms crossed, towered above him. "One pledged to me would do anything I asked of him. Is this true of you as well?"

"Ask, Imperial Highness."

The Emperor's expression tightened. "You are direct. It is a rare quality among bureaucrats. It pleases me. I would have you please me further."

Pelut said nothing.

"And you know when to keep your mouth shut—another rare quality. I will have a use for you, Pelut Vniel; but you must prove your loyalty."

"Of course, Imperial Highness."

"So, I shall be direct with you." The Prince's expression hardened. "I want Prince Cyron dead. Make that happen, and you shall find a high place in my Empire."

* * *

Dunos giggled. He'd never seen a butterfly quite like the one walking up and down his left arm. It was black and green. The geometric designs on its wings shifted shape with each beat. That wasn't what made him laugh, though. Its journey up and down his arm—over the top of his robe and ring mail—*tickled*.

"Dunos?"

The boy smiled and held his hand up. "Hi, Ranai. It tickles."

"What tickles?"

"The butterfly, see?"

"I don't see it, Dunos."

He glanced at his arm. The butterfly had gone, though he could still feel the tingle of its steps. "Well, it was here."

"I'm sure." The swordswoman smiled and joined him at the river wall. "What are you doing here?"

Dunos shrugged. Her voice had that mother tone to it, so he knew he had to answer. "Well, Master Tolo told me to find Master Dejote. I saw him here a couple of days ago. He's not here. I decided to wait. And then there was the butterfly."

"I didn't see the butterfly, but I think it's a good thing you're exercising your arm. Does it feel better?"

The boy shrugged again. "I guess." He brought his hand across his belly to the dagger at his right hip. "Easier to draw. My grip is tighter. We don't have to tie the dagger into my hand anymore."

"Well, we might still do that, just in case." Ranai squatted down. "I remember you from the road, you know."

"When you were going to rob me and my father and my grandfather?"

"Yes. You were the only one willing to step up to fight my companions and me."

"And Master Tolo."

"And Master Tolo." Her eyes grew distant, as if the memory was years old, not months. "You remember he sent me south, to study at *Serrian* Istor?"

"Yes. And he sent me to *Serrian* Jatan with the robes of the man you'd killed."

"True. The reason I ask is this. At *Serrian* Istor, I helped train boys just like you."

Dunos' face lit up. "You want to train with me? You've never wanted to before. We can do it right here. I'm good at Tiger and Dragon, you know."

She held her hands up. "Slow down. Yes, I will train with you, but not just now."

Dunos frowned. If she didn't want to train with him right then and there, why mention it?

"Dunos, do you remember before the invaders came?"

He nodded. "Like when I found the glowing rock and it hurt my arm?"

"Yes, but not exactly." Ranai went to a knee and rested her hands on his shoulders. That meant she was serious, so he had to listen. "Do you remember playing with friends and, you know, just having fun?"

She jerked her head in the direction of the Dragon Bridge. A half dozen ragged children capered and shrieked as Naleni Dragons made faces and roared at them. A couple of the boys started wrestling, and two of the girls whispered to each other.

"I remember."

"Don't you sometimes just want to go and have fun?"

Dunos' eyes widened. "I have fun all the time. I really like killing *vhangxi*. It's like cleaning fish, sort of, but they're stinkier."

"Dunos, killing is not supposed to be fun."

Oh, this is going to be one of those talks. "I know that, Mistress Ameryne. It's not fun. It is satisfying."

That didn't wipe the concern from her face. This puzzled Dunos, because the word "satisfying" usually worked with adults. She wanted some other answer, but she wasn't very good at telling him what it was. Most adults were. If he said the right things, they would go away happy.

"Dunos, when I was your age, I didn't worry about fighting and killing. I had fun. Just like those kids over there." Ranai studied his face. "You've been through a lot. Don't you ever just want to have fun?"

He rested his hands on her shoulders so she had to listen. "Yes, I want to have fun. I remember the days before. Before the invaders, before I hurt my arm. I had fun. I ran around like them." He smiled at the playing children. "I had lots of fun."

"Good. That's good."

"But, Mistress, I also had work to do. I hauled water. I swept up. I cared for horses and mules and oxes."

"Oxen, Dunos."

"Oxen. I collected eggs from our chickens. I fed the hogs. I helped butcher one once. That wasn't fun. I did lots of things to help my family. Some of those were fun. But I still had work, just like I do now."

"But this is butchery, Dunos."

"It's work, Mistress, and it must be done. If we don't do our work, no one can have any fun."

A sharp cracking cut off any reply. Dunos spun. Even in the twilight there was no missing the puff of dust as mortar split on the Dragon Bridge. Soldiers hurried to where a piece of stone railing had shifted. More mortar crumbled and a piece fell into the river.

Ranai stood and peered over the river wall. She gasped.

Dunos leaped up and caught the edge with his good arm. His feet scrambled against the stone and he got his belly on top of the wall. He balanced there, staring down at the river.

Something was not right. His left arm itched, and that didn't feel anything like tickling. "There are little waves everywhere."

"There are. And there's a tingle. *Xingna*, a trickle of it."

He looked up at her. "What does it mean?"

"Faster water." Her eyes slitted. "The river is narrowing."

He slid back to the ground. "I'll go find Master Tolo. There will be a lot of work for everyone now."

Chapter Forty-seven

35th day, Month of the Eagle, Year of the Rat
Last Year of Imperial Prince Cyron's Court
163rd Year of the Komyr Dynasty
737th Year since the Cataclysm
Shirikun, North Moriande
Free Nalenyr

Cyron knew the answer the second the piece of paper touched his hand. "The rate of closure is constant, then. Eight feet an hour."

Prince Eiran, who had slipped seamlessly into his role as Cyron's deputy, nodded. "Prince Nelesquin gave the Empress a week. In nine days the river walls will touch. We'll be fighting everywhere."

Cyron closed his eyes. In three days, the largest ballistae and trebuchets would be able to shoot across the gap. In six days, archers could exchange arrows. In a week, warriors would be sword to sword. He could see it all, including the fires, the wounded, the dead.

He set the paper down and raked a hand through his

hair, scratching where his scalp tingled. "This changes everything. Tonight, in darkness, have a work crew slip out and undercut the river's north bank just west of the city. I want the river flooding the western approach. The increased flow means they won't find a ford downstream. Send another team east. I want every bridge cut and every ferry on the north side of the river."

A clerk blew on a sheet of rice paper, bowed, and hurried from the room.

"They'll be building siege towers." The image appeared in Cyron's head. The towers would be solidly constructed, but out of material salvaged from the south. Beams from buildings, pieces of furniture, planking from floors or bits of wagons would be hammered together. At best, they'd have ramps that extended twenty-four feet, so the *kwajiin* could cross three hours before the river walls touched.

"I want the range from the river wall to each siege engine paced off exactly. Get Borosan Gryst to measure the distances with his *gyanrigot*. I want ranging shots taken so we know where those stones will land."

Eiran frowned. "Wouldn't barrels of oil be more effective? It would burn up the towers."

"I don't want to burn the rest of my city. We're not using fire. We will, however, need sand to put out fires. We will need work crews—they can use the sand piles to block streets. We want to channel the *kwajiin* into killing areas. Count Derael has worked out how best we can trap them. Get his charts and coordinate placement of ballistae, spring engines, and barricades."

Two clerks, one working logistics and the other on fire precautions, bowed and withdrew. As they passed through the doorway, a replacement for the first clerk appeared and dropped into place at a desk. As she did, heat poured through Cyron.

His vision faded, yet he continued to see. Each of the clerks became a bright spot, a *star* in the night sky of his vision. Little white lines connected them with others, creating three-dimensional constellations, with himself in the middle. Energy pulsed from him to them, and from them out to the others. Stars shifted. People re-arranged themselves, resources were re-ordered, and what had begun as a tangled skein of lines and points re-solved itself into a flexible and resilient matrix binding North Moriande together.

Cyron heard no sounds, but he knew he was speaking because energy pulsed out of him. Clerks rose and de-parted, sharing that energy with others. New clerks ap-peared and locked into place in the matrix. More orders were communicated and more people moved.

Because the pattern appeared so clearly, Cyron changed his orders. He reemphasized some things, or set up redundant systems. He found bottlenecks and allevi-ated them. He ordered water to be brought in smaller casks to combat stations. He demanded carts be requisi-tioned so meals could be brought to soldiers at their posts.

He reached out and the city seemed to fit him like a formal robe. There was so much there, but it all had to be perfect. He smoothed a wrinkle here, tightened a lace there, folded, and tucked. In the rush of things it took him a moment to realize he had his left arm back and was using it with the skill of a musician teasing notes from a *necyl*.

I am whole again.

He laughed and his joy poured through the matrix. A prince born of princes, it was assumed his talent had been for governance. He had done well in his post, but the thing he did best was organizing. His father had begun the program of exploration, but Cyron had formalized it, set goals, and encouraged it even before he'd reached the throne.

I was a minister without a ministry, working at my talent without ever realizing it.

He began to work faster. Clerks came, but before they had spoken or handed him a report, he knew their questions, had found solutions and communicated them. Some clerks looked at papers and found marginal notes they'd not seen before, then acted on them. Others suddenly remembered a fact he'd mentioned. Upon checking, they found a solution.

The matrix pulsed with life—his life—and energized him in return. The sheer joy of seeing things work, of watching them unfold and simplify, provided him with the same deep satisfaction as hearing a bird sing, or watching a sunset.

"Highness."

Eiran's voice reached him. Cyron blinked, and the world returned. The room had emptied of clerks and the day had passed into twilight. "Where is everyone?"

"They are off on the missions you gave them." The Helosundian prince shook his head. "I was here for it all, but I never noticed time passing. I heard every word . . ."

"You heard it? I was speaking?"

Eiran hesitated. "I *remember* hearing, but that is the only way I can understand what has happened. You did not stop and there was no problem for which you could not find a solution. Some so elegant that we would never have thought of them ourselves. Organizing militia by neighborhoods and using those neighborhoods as rallying points was brilliant."

Cyron nodded. "That's where they will run to when the line breaks. It was right."

"The whole thing was right, Highness." Eiran jerked his head to the south. "With your plan in place, and you in command, Nelesquin's invasion is finished before it begins."

Pravak Helos hated premonitions. He'd never been inclined to trust them back before the Turasynd expedition. Whenever he felt good about something, it always went wrong. And when he felt bad about it, it just went worse.

The only things worthy of trust were his skill with swords and his strength. He'd come to the study of *xingna* through his mastery of the sword, though he'd never devoted himself to it fully like some of the others. He'd learned minor magics—things to keep his blades sharp or to heal small cuts. But he'd refused to be seduced by magic, as others had, keeping himself grounded with his continued study of the sword.

The problem with premonitions was that they were irresistible. He'd come to awareness in midevening when something jolted him. It actually made him feel energized, which he took as a good sign. Then he decided it was a premonition. From there he had to follow his sense of things.

Well, his sense, and the stones.

There had been a dozen of them so far. Black pebbles—unremarkable save for their uniform smoothness. They reminded him of Nelesquin's scrying stones, which Pravak had grown to hate more and more. They *generated* premonitions, and Nelesquin relied on them too heavily.

Pravak slid his swords into the harness on his back and set out. He found the first stone in the corridor outside his chamber in Quunkun, and the next in the road. He followed them as he would a trail, knowing that someone leaving so obvious a set of clues intended him to follow. That raised the spectre of an ambush, but this did not concern the *vanyesh*. Aside from Nelesquin, Qiro, and perhaps Qiro's grandson, he feared nothing in Moriande.

He sighed—or, rather, his shoulders slumped as if he were sighing. His lack of lungs had done nothing to strip away the habit. He had imagined Ciras Dejote would give him more of a fight, but the young man had not. If he truly was the reincarnation of Jogot Yirxan, the rebirth had been flawed. Now the swordsman was flawed—another useless enemy.

Pravak was aware that Virisken Soshir lurked beyond the river, but wasn't concerned about him. The man was, after all, mortal. Though they had never seriously come to blows in the past, Pravak had seen him fight. While Soshir was good, he was hardly invincible.

The stones led Pravak across South Moriande and to Kojaikun. Here the *vanyesh*'s dread deepened, because he recognized what had awakened him. Many of the *vanyesh* harvested the magic from the city. The *thaumston* fibers he wore as a long queue dragged magic from the circles. Pravak's new vitality meant he was drawing more power because no one else was harvesting it.

The others are dead.

That shook him. The *vanyesh* had hardly been immortal. Down through the eons, survivors had changed—abandoning their physical forms for constructs they'd created in Tolwreen. Many of his comrades had ridiculed him for having his skeleton wrapped in a silver/*thaumston* alloy upon which magic formulae could be inscribed, but he'd outlived those who doubted him.

Even as he bent and picked up the final stone, he realized he was the last of those who had preserved Nelesquin's legacy.

The Grand Hall in Kojaikun had been transformed into barracks for the *vanyesh*. Not only was it spacious enough, and pleasingly decorated, but the Keru had used it as a place to train. Magic lingered there, making it a welcome sanctuary.

Now a mausoleum.

A Viruk waited in the center of the hall, armed with a Keru spear. Around him, the rest of the *vanyesh* lay scattered as if a child had destroyed them in a tantrum. The *vanyesh* sparkled in the wan lamplight, each one beyond repair.

The Viruk grinned with a mouthful of ivory needles. "I would have killed you at Quunkun, but I thought you should see this."

"Is it your work?"

The Viruk toed a hawk's feather. "The Desei shadows. You killed their prince. The Mother of Shadows has avenged him."

"I am not afraid of you, Rekarafi. I have killed Viruk before."

"I know. I have heard the tales." The Viruk slowly began to spin the spear. "Two at once, it's been said."

"Both bigger than you." Pravak dropped the stones, drew his swords, and let his tentacles snake out. "You are a fool to avenge them after so many years."

"It's not them I seek to avenge." Rekarafi opened a hand. "You slew a Keru of my acquaintance. I avenge her."

"Then you shall die just as quickly as she did." Pravak darted forward, his tentacles whipping low back and forth. The moment the Viruk leaped above them, Pravak would cross his swords right through his midsection. The tactic had worked before and the Viruk didn't give off a sense of *jaedun,* so he knew the fight was over before it began.

Only Rekarafi never leaped. He lifted one foot, then the other, bringing each firmly down on a tentacle. He thrust the spear forward, catching the swords before they reached him, then snapped the spear's butt end up. The iron cap just missed his pelvis, but caught his spine solidly and drove him back.

The Viruk retreated, crouching. "The stones, do you know what they are?"

Pravak slid into a tiger stance. "Scrying stones?"

"No. *Ghoal Nuan.* Soulstones. They will weigh you down in the grave. You'll remain in the Underworld forever."

Pravak laughed. His tentacles withdrew and wrapped around to armor his spine. Metal talons scraped on the stone. He inched forward, both swords raised. "*If* you put me in the grave."

He attacked, his blades a blur. The spear spun, battering the blades away, but Pravak moved with them. From the first form to the fourth, then the fifth and the ninth, following no pattern, but flowing from one moment to the next. The Viruk ducked and deflected, blocked and riposted, but always gave ground.

Like a tiger's claws, Pravak's blades tore into whatever they touched. They clove through tables and shattered benches. Down from shredded bedding filled the air. Teapot shards crunched underfoot. Sparks flew as swords gouged the floor and further scattered bits and pieces of dead *vanyesh*.

Faster and faster the swords flew. Pravak shifted from Tiger to Mantis, then Scorpion and back. Rekarafi remained on the defensive, retreating around the room. Occasionally the spear's blade might score a rib, and the butt end slammed fully into his sternum once, but it did not stop the *vanyesh*'s offensive. But for everything he threw at the Viruk there was a counter, and the Viruk looked no closer to tiring than he was.

Pravak lunged with both blades. Rekarafi brought the spear down and around in a parry that trapped the blades on the floor. The combatants snarled, faces close enough that Pravak could feel the Viruk's moist breath.

The Viruk laughed. "They may have been bigger than me, but they were not me."

Pravak whipped one tentacle around the Viruk's arms, binding his elbows together. The other wrapped around an ankle and yanked. The Viruk started to go down, but Pravak caught him by the throat and lifted him from the ground.

"But they were both as stupid and died just as easily."

He began to tighten his grip, intent on snapping the Viruk's neck. Muscles bunched, thwarting him, so he redoubled his effort.

What's happening? It shouldn't have taken this much effort. He'd broken iron posts in his grip. Something was *very* wrong.

The Viruk spread his arms and the lifeless tentacle slid off easily. The other one slithered from his ankle. Pravak's knees buckled. He dropped into a kneeling position, but only remained upright because the Viruk had grabbed his wrist and steadied him.

I don't understand. Pravak wanted to say the words, but the mechanism that allowed him to speak had failed.

"You forgot something, Pravak Helos. You made yourself into a creature of magic." Rekarafi tore the *vanyesh*'s hand off and flung it against the far wall. "The Viruk existed *before* magic. We discovered it, learned how to use it. How to contain it. We also learned to absorb it. I have absorbed it from you."

The metallic tinkling of his skeleton's collapse sounded distant. Pravak tried to keep shock from his metal face. He would not wear a surprised expression to the grave.

The Viruk plucked his skull from his spine and everything crashed to the floor around him. Rekarafi held it high and peered up at him. "Your head, I'll take. I'll place it at the highest point in the city, and you will live long enough to watch your dream die."

Ciras winced as a cadre of *gyanrigot* soldiers marched through the factory. The sight of *gyanrigot* smiths making soldiers still made his flesh crawl. No mercy in them, just efficiency. The same blows that shaped metal would break bone and spill blood. It might be necessary this time, and even the next, but what would happen when it wasn't and someone used them anyway?

He worked his way across the floor to a small bench. Borosan Gryst sat hunched over a drawing. He waited, hoping Borosan would notice him. When the inventor did not, Ciras remained quiet. He'd seen Borosan concentrate like that before. He had learned to respect it as much as Borosan had respected his training regimen.

The crash of metal from deeper within the factory brought Borosan's head up. He blinked, then rubbed his eyes. "Ciras? Master Dejote?"

Ciras nodded. "I wanted to speak with you. I have wronged you. I accused you of wanting to make me into a monster. Though I am half a man, I thought you wanted to take that away from me."

"No, Ciras, that was never what I wanted."

The swordsman raised his left hand. The arrow wound was still healing. "I know."

Borosan shook his head. "I didn't think, Ciras. I have become consumed with my machines. I see the elegance and intricacy. When I make something move, it excites me. And your wound grieved me. I wanted to help so I . . . Well, I disregarded everything you ever said about *gyanrigot*. I know you hate them. They have no judgment, they can only follow orders."

Ciras nodded. "And all the command-slates in the world will never equal what a man knows in his heart and head."

"Well, actually, I am working on some small *gyanrigot*

that can write in very tiny script on command-slates, so there are more orders . . . but, well, that isn't really practical right now."

"And you are correct, Borosan. I hate *gyanrigot* because they have no judgment. They have not learned the things I have learned. They do not know to make the decisions I know to make. That's not your fault. It is not a failing of your work; it is just the conditions of the machines."

Borosan nodded. "Perhaps someday."

"Perhaps indeed." Ciras shook his head. "Someday, however, will not come soon enough to stop Nelesquin."

"You're right."

"I know. This is why I've come to you." Ciras threw his cloak back with his half arm. "Make your measurement. I have the judgment your machines lack. Right now, I am half a man. Make me a whole swordsman again, and we'll live to see your someday."

Chapter Forty-eight

35th day, Month of the Eagle, Year of the Rat
Last Year of Imperial Prince Cyron's Court
163rd Year of the Komyr Dynasty
737th Year since the Cataclysm
Quoraxan (The Fifth Hell)

The demons of the Fifth Hell launched themselves at Jorim and Talrisaal. They filled the bowl and choked the air above the burning lake. All scaly skin and irregular ebon teeth, with blazing black eyes and talons that put a Viruk's claws to shame, the demons came for the two magicians, undaunted by the sudden appearance of their wings.

Jorim immediately folded his wings and dropped toward the lake like a stone. Claws tore at his clothes but missed the flesh beneath. Part of him wanted to conjure magic armor, but all the armor in the world wouldn't kill demons, and killing them was the key to getting free.

If, of course, they actually can *be killed.*

He put the consequences of that idea out of his mind and snapped his wings open barely twenty feet above the burning lake. He swooped back toward the falls, diving through a sheet of flame, then summoned magic and *pushed* hard. His head came up and he shot skyward.

The demons winging hard after him couldn't follow that sharp a turn. They plunged straight into the falls. One or two burning bodies rebounded from the cliff and trailed oily black smoke down to the lake. There was no telling if they were dead or not.

Talrisaal opted for armor and found a way to destroy demons. He surrounded himself with a blue sphere upon which the demons descended immediately. Once they'd covered it in a living carpet, blue spikes shot up and out, impaling them. The sphere then tripled in size, becoming a hexagonal lattice spiking at each point. A similar, marginally smaller lattice caged the Viruk.

Demons flung the bodies of their incapacitated comrades away and squeezed through the first lattice and started on the second. Talrisaal gave a wave of his hand and the second lattice started spinning. It pulled the demons apart, slicing off limbs, which pattered down like rain on the fiery lake.

That gave Jorim an idea. He flew up to the mouth of the river and the demons came after him. Just as they reached his altitude, he ripped a hole into Wandao. The river gushed, bringing with it a storm of the copper ants. Wet and angry, they poured over the demons, biting flesh and gnawing through wings. Thousands of demons fell to the fiery lake.

Jorim smiled. "We might get out of here."

The Viruk shook his head. "This isn't a lake. It's a womb."

Demons crawled from the lake like insects emerging from cocoons. Some now had copper mandibles. Other sported extra pairs of limbs. Some were even wreathed in flame. Whatever had killed them just made them stronger, and they were still intent on ripping the two companions apart.

A new flight of demons launched itself, then something odd happened. A volley of arrows arched up over the basin lip. Some demons, stuck through, spiraled down into the flames. Others fell to the ground and melted away.

More took to the air, but odd, winged creatures—apes of an emerald hue—soared up to engage them. The fleet among them flew high and hurled rocks, while the heavier ones soared up to meet the demons retreating from the stones. Demons and apes both fell, but far more of the demons.

Then below, ten-foot-long lizards poured into the basin. Sharp teeth filled their mouths. One lunged high enough to pluck a demon from the air. The lizards munched and demons screamed.

"If they don't make it back into the lake, they're not reborn!"

Jorim nodded to his companion. "That could be, but I'm not eating them."

"Jorim!"

Jorim's jaw dropped open, and it wasn't just the giant hammer-headed ape cresting the basin, or the fact it had a demon clutched in a paw like a snack. The beast had been fitted with a bridle and he knew the driver saddled between its shoulder blades.

He swooped down immediately. "Nirati!" He avoided the ape's slothful swipe at him, and landed on its spine. "How?"

"I knew you were in trouble. I came to help. Kunjiqui has a gate to the Underworld." She beamed. "Here we are."

In the wake of the lizards' sweep rode a company of the oddest mounted archers Jorim had ever hoped to see. Blue-skinned men rode golden-antlered hinds. Leading them came a man riding in a chariot pulled by four of the hinds. He barked orders in some guttural tongue and the cavalry complied. Arrows flew, demons fell, and Talrisaal swooped down.

Jorim looked at the man. "Prince Pyrust?"

The charioteer nodded. "We can't stay here. They *will* overwhelm us eventually."

Nirati pointed off to an odd blue spot. "We came in through there. It will take us back to Kunjiqui."

Jorim shook his head. "We can't escape. We have to push on through the last Hells. Nessagafel, the first god, wishes to undo all of creation and remake everything. He'll succeed unless we stop him."

Pyrust ran a hand over his jaw. "Fight our way through the Hells so we can assault the Heavens and throw down a god?"

Talrisaal nodded. "As daunting as that sounds . . ."

Pyrust laughed. "Not daunting, challenging. A worthy fight for a worthy reason. What have we got to lose? We're already dead, and if we fail, we'll be unmade with the rest of creation? Lead on."

Chapter Forty-nine

36th day, Month of the Eagle, Year of the Rat
Last Year of Imperial Prince Cyron's Court
163rd Year of the Komyr Dynasty
737th Year since the Cataclysm
Quunkun, South Moriande
Imperial Nalenyr

Kaerinus' expression made clear the fact that he was not bringing good news. If possible, it was even worse than word that the *vanyesh* had been destroyed. That had hit Nelesquin particularly hard because the *vanyesh* were crucial to generating more troops.

The Prince knotted his robe's sash. "What is it now?" He held up a hand. "No, wait, I know it has to do with Qiro."

"It does, sire, and your troops."

Nelesquin shook his head. He took the small leather pouch from inside his sleeve, poured the scrying stones into his palm, then let them dribble through his fingers. They bounced across a tabletop. He read the pattern, the play of black and white stones, the angles at which they rested, and let go a large sigh.

"Not a complete disaster. Tell me."

"I wish telling would suffice. You need to see it."

"I have no desire to ride south at the moment."

"No need. He brought a company here." The magician led the way through the corridors of Quunkun. Pairs of Durrani warriors had been stationed every twenty feet to deal with intruders. They snapped to attention, hammering right fists to left shoulders as Nelesquin passed.

"Remind me, Kaerinus, to choose a new Dost. I should have done that already."

"That, Highness, is perhaps the only bright spot in this whole affair. Holgaara of the Ox clan has worked tirelessly to drill these new soldiers. Working in the pocket world has not only aged him, but apparently made him wiser. The new soldiers follow him almost fanatically."

If they follow him that closely, I will eventually have to destroy him.

They descended broad circular stairs to a vast storeroom just below street level. It had been cleaned out of anything useful. There had been some rice available and, when it turned out that it was not poisoned, it was distributed to the troops. *Still, I would have thought there would have been some of it left.*

Qiro awaited them, Holgaara beside him. The new troops waited behind them, arrayed in neat ranks ten wide and deep. They contrasted poorly with Holgaara. *They contrast poorly with* Qiro.

Nelesquin glanced at Kaerinus. "I thought you said they brought me troops. These are shallow-skulled, stoop-shouldered wildmen. We've not seen their like in these parts for eons, and these are more brutish than ones that haunted the jungles of Ummummorar."

Qiro smiled. "You will find, Highness, that you are mistaken." The cartographer joined him at the base of the stairs, then nodded to the Durrani.

The blue-skinned warrior turned and shouted orders in some pidgin tongue. The soldiers split evenly and with precision in their movements. Half of them bore spears, the other half cudgels. The weapons had been crudely manufactured, but had a brutal quality to them that intrigued Nelesquin. The spearmen attacked when ordered to, and the clubbers parried, then attacked in response. Most of the spearmen blocked the blows, but several of those who failed went down hard.

The drill continued. The sharp clack of wood on wood echoed within the storage chamber. More soldiers went down and a few would never rise again. The injured, when they could, crawled away and the survivors paired up again.

Nelesquin clapped his hands once and Holgaara shouted an order that ended the fighting. The warriors sprang into their ranks again, with little concern for their fallen comrades.

"You have done well, Holgaara. Take your troops back and continue training."

The Durrani bowed, then shouted another order. The injured and dead were hauled away, leaving the three men alone in the bowels of the Bear Tower. Nelesquin descended the last step to the room's floor, spread his arms wide, and turned back to face Qiro.

"How is it, Master Anturasi, that I ask of you a simple

thing, and you fail to deliver it even after you tell me you can?"

"You asked for an army, and I found it for you."

"I wanted you to *build* me an army. You said you could breed Durrani and women here. What happened?"

Qiro's expression hardened. "What happened, sire, is that no one took into account what we did when we created the Durrani. On Anturasixan we had ample food. We did not have enough here to grow another army."

"Not enough food?" Nelesquin frowned. "Our stores, Kaerinus?"

"Running low, but we have more food coming up from Erumvirine."

"Good." He rubbed the center of his forehead. "How, Qiro, did you find these brutes?"

"Be careful calling them brutes, Highness, for they have more claim to this land than you do." Qiro smiled slowly in the manner of men pleased with their own genius. "The pocket world encompasses all that was Nalenyr, if you will recall. We have stripped it of metal for your *dari* armor, and I wondered if we might be able to strip it of food. Harvests are cyclical, of course ..."

"I am aware of the vagaries of agriculture, Master Anturasi."

"I'm sure you are, Highness. So I wished to explore reaping more grain. My limits here, of course, pertain to things that are known, so I wanted harvests that were unknown. Records have been kept throughout the Imperial period—rather exact ones, if one knows which minister to bribe. I had to delve past that, so I did, into the time before."

"The time *before*?"

"Yes." Qiro's smile grew. "You yourself noted that men such as these had not been seen in this area for eons. This is because I have opened a path to history and have brought them forward into my pocket world. They breed prodigiously. Half of them I have slaving to gather food, the other half train as soldiers."

"How many do you have?"

"Twenty thousand."

Nelesquin's jaw dropped. "Twenty thousand? When did you start?"

"Just after I began the river's narrowing." Qiro nodded. "Ten thousand more become available each day, fully trained and armed. You will have ninety thousand when the walls collide."

Nelesquin covered his mouth with a hand. As crude as they were, the brutes might work, making up in numbers what they lacked in quality and endurance. Waves of them pouring over the river wall and invading North Moriande could sweep away all resistance. There was no way the Empress could kill all of them.

"Kaerinus, work with Holgaara. He is the new Dost. Have him reorganize the forces. I want Durrani in charge of each brute unit. Have the brutes work with our remaining creatures so they get used to each other. I cannot have panic break my army."

"As you wish, Highness."

Nelesquin nodded, then graced Qiro with a bow. "You have done well, Master Cartographer. My victory shall owe much to you."

"*Our* victory, Highness." Qiro returned the bow. "And this is not *all* I shall do for you. The enemy might prepare themselves for what you will bring, but they never can be prepared for what I bring."

Urardsa, the Soth Gloon, lurked like Grija's shadow in my room. Pale, with an oversized head and seven eyes, black and gold, he watched me pull on a clean robe and tie my hair back. I caught his reflection in the mirror, as I dabbed at a bloody droplet on my neck—a remnant of shaving.

"Say whatever you have to say, ghoul, and no riddles."

"Virisken Soshir dies soon."

I laughed. "You can't even pretend to be direct."

"This mission to assassinate Nelesquin will be the end of you."

I turned. "The end of *me,* or the end of Virisken Soshir?"

The Gloon opened his hands but remained mute.

"When I recovered the memory of who I had been, you told me I could die, but I think I was already dead. I think Virisken Soshir died when Nelesquin did, and was only resurrected because Nelesquin was. What started so long ago has to be finished. If that means I die *again* if he does, too, my life will have served well."

The Gloon rose from his crouch and paced to the window. The owl moon's bright light limned him. "Frustration is not my goal, Master Soshir. Once I, too, was blind to the future."

"I remember. You were Enangia. You came on the Turasynd expedition. You fought, and well."

"In the city are many life-threads. Too many. And too many end quickly."

"Mine included, I assume."

The Gloon grunted. "There is more to life-threads than beginnings and ends. Colors and textures. Patterns. The pattern could continue, or it can change. Something old, something new, or nothing."

He stared at me. Though shadow hid his face, his eyes glowed. "Nelesquin would repeat the pattern of the past. Cyron, the Empress, they would make a different pattern. The past we understand. It has problems for which we know solutions."

I frowned. "The problems of the past are never the same as those in the future."

"If you know this, then why do you believe you are the solution now?"

I started to answer, but words stuck in my throat. Nelesquin and I had been friends who grew to be rivals. I had chafed beneath his superior attitude—which had been born out of nothing but his birthright. This had led me to resent him, resent my father, and desire power for my own. I knew the stories of my past, and I had been every bit the petty tyrant Nelesquin was.

But this time it was different. I was no longer Virisken Soshir. My sense of who I was had been shaped by my training and the years I'd spent as *xidantzu*. Soshir had spent his life in service to the Empire and himself. I had served many, shielding them from evil and misfortune.

It struck me that I really did feel Virisken Soshir was another person. I could not escape responsibility for who he had been and what he had done, but I didn't need to be imprisoned by it, either. Nelesquin might well have been an old problem, but applying an old solution would only kill me along with him.

I regarded the Gloon carefully. "I am the solution because Nelesquin will never make himself vulnerable to another. No one else could even get close. He wants to defeat the Empress, but he wishes to crush me personally. It's the only way he corrects the mistake that killed him in Ixyll."

"This explains access, but not reason."

"The reason I am the solution is that I will stop him to save others, not for myself."

"You may well succeed." He cocked his head to the side.

"What? What do you see? Tell me."

"I see the futures, Master Soshir. I do not decide them." He shrugged. "But if you wish to succeed, remember, this mission can only be accomplished by those who should be dead."

Chapter Fifty

36th day, Month of the Eagle, Year of the Rat
Last Year of Imperial Prince Cyron's Court
163rd Year of the Komyr Dynasty
737th Year since the Cataclysm
Shirikun, North Moriande
Free Nalenyr

Keles did not come fully awake until someone dragged him upright in the bed. The *xunling* roots had done nothing to keep the shadowed stranger away from him, which was odd. They never let anyone near him until ordered back, not even Geselkir or Jasai.

Who?

The man wrapped a sheet around him and lifted Keles into his arms. Being carried like that felt at once alien and yet normal. He worked a hand free and rubbed his eyes. Keles stared at the man, then knew he must be in a fever dream. The square jaw, the beard, the half smile—all very familiar.

"You look like my father."

"I am your father." As untrue as the words had to be, the voice triggered all sorts of memories. "Easy, Keles, don't struggle. I don't want to drop you."

"You can't be. My father's dead."

"Not dead. Just lost, for a time. In time."

The man carried Keles to his suite's antechamber. A wooden platform with a gold railing and eight gold disks filled the room. Pieces of furniture had collapsed beneath it. A huge globe, six feet in diameter, on a gimbaled stand dominated the platform.

"What is this?"

"Your grandfather has his map. You have your book. I have this." He lowered Keles to the platform, then sprang over the railing and got a chair. He placed Keles in it, then ran back to the bedroom and dragged the heavy blanket to drape over him. "It can get cold."

Keles weakly shoved the blanket off. "I can't . . . I have to wake up."

"Keles, you have to trust me."

"Trust you? I don't know you. I don't know this thing. I am delirious. This is a dream."

"No, it's not, son." The man started the globe spinning. A sphere of brilliant light surrounded the platform. It became opaque, hiding the world. Keles' stomach lurched. They were moving, and the tingle of magic pricked his flesh with needles.

The word "son" resonated through him, distracting him. He'd heard it said in that tone, in that voice, over eighteen years before. Ryn Anturasi had bent down, smiled reassuringly, and used that very sentence to quell Keles' fears about his father's last voyage.

"You never came back."

"I couldn't."

"Mother is dead."

"I know."

Keles looked over at him. "How?"

"I did something I was not supposed to do. I saw things I was not supposed to see." Ryn Anturasi slowly shook his head. "One of them was your mother's death."

"But . . ."

"It happened in the future, yes." Ryn rested his hands on Keles' shoulders. "My father sent me to the Dark Sea not to kill me, as many have supposed. He sent me to look for something very specific. He knew it was out there, on one of the islands, buried deep in the ruins of a Viruk fortress. I went, I dug, and I found it. It was an opaque sphere as big around as my head. I was told to find it, put it in two sacks, lock it in a chest, and bring it to him. You know how Qiro gives orders."

Keles nodded. "You disobeyed."

"I did."

"Jorim takes after you."

"And you after your mother." The man's voice caught. He squeezed Keles' shoulders. "I studied the stone. I caught visions. I saw many things from the past, all fascinating, and then I dared look into the future."

"What did you see?"

"Nothing."

"How can you see nothing? Doesn't it work?"

"It works too well." Ryn came around and sat back on the railing. "I was looking too far, so I refined my vision. I saw the future we are in now. I saw your mother die. So I looked for other futures, but she always died. So I began to look into the past.

"There was a god, Nessagafel, the first god among the Viruk. The creator. His children cast him from the Heavens and trapped him. On the earth, Virukadeen was destroyed. Nessagafel was no more, or so everyone believed. But it wasn't true. Down through the years he has attempted to engineer plot after plot to free himself so he could start over. There are dozens of people—human, Viruk, Soth—whom he has used as his agents. Prince Nelesquin was one and your grandfather is another."

"Have you seen us here, now, together?"

"No, which is why we can be here, now, together." Ryn smiled. "I took the stone and used it as the heart of my timeship. I can use it to slip into places where there are no observers because once something has been seen, it exists. Your grandfather makes things exist by putting them on maps or imagining them in his head. I look for open places where I can venture. Since I last saw you, I have slipped in and out of time, working to balance Nessagafel's influence."

"Couldn't you have just gone back and prevented your father from becoming an agent? It happened when he traveled to the Wastes, yes?"

"Yes, but that was before I was born. As tempting as it might have been to kill him then, I wouldn't have existed." Ryn frowned. "I was able to spend time with him on that trip. One night, in a teahouse in Sylumak. We were just travelers talking. He was so enthusiastic about his journey. He was a different man."

"Now he has become very dangerous."

"Nessagafel has regained a degree of freedom. He augments your grandfather's power."

"Nessagafel created the stone?"

"He or one of his minions. Had my father gotten his hands on it, disasters would have unfolded much faster."

Keles nodded, then glanced right. "The globe, it's slowing. The lights, too."

Ryn pulled the blanket up around him. "It will be cold. We will be quite high." His father tucked it in around Keles' shoulders, then moved to the globe's controls.

The sphere faded completely and Keles grasped the arms of the chair. The platform hung many feet in the air. They faced the east, with the sun coming up. Its light had just touched the eastern shore, but already mountains north and south blazed with light reflected from snowcaps. Long rivers ran through lush valleys and emptied through sparkling deltas.

"Do you recognize this place?"

Keles leaned forward. "Nalenyr? But I don't see Moriande. And there are forests everywhere."

"This is Nalenyr before there *was* a Nalenyr."

"I never could have imagined . . ."

"But that's what's important, Keles. You have to study this. Your grandfather *does* imagine, and everything he imagines shifts what you see below."

Keles shook his head slowly. "This is incredible."

"Just wait." Ryn worked two levers. "Look at this."

The timeship came around, putting Keles' back to the sun. Before him, where the Dark Sea should have been, a massive mountain thrust its peak into the clouds. Snow girdled the base but, above, the mountain became alive with green plants and flowers and flocks of colorful birds. Islands with beautiful palaces orbited and small airships passed from one to another.

Keles stood and staggered to the railing. "Rekarafi

said Virukadeen was a paradise. He didn't lie. I've never seen anything more beautiful."

"And Nessagafel would have eliminated all of it. The Viruk fought him and ended up destroying it. That won't be for eons yet. Here, they have just mastered magic. This is what the Viruk lost, and why they feel they deserve no more future."

Keles looked back over his shoulder. "They don't deserve a future?"

"They destroyed paradise, Keles. They have no more children, and build no more empires, because they can never again have what they lost."

"And that is what will happen to Men? That's why you could not see a future?"

"That's why I've brought you here. To *guarantee* we have one."

Keles nodded. "Bring me lower. Let me study the world. Let me know how the land once was—how it is meant to be. I want to know everything. I can't let Qiro change anything."

Ciras spun, ducking beneath the whistling blade of a *gyanrigot* warrior. He twisted his wrist and it clicked into place. He slashed up, severing a control wire. The *gyanrigot*'s sword arm went limp, but the weight of the arm spun the machine around in a circle.

Two more cuts, parting similar wires where a man's hamstrings would have been, and the soldier went down.

Ciras leaped past him, blocked another sword blow, and stroked his sword over a *gyanrigot*'s stomach. It folded around the cut. Its sword clattered to the ground.

A metallic scrape against the floor betrayed another attacker. Ciras whirled, bringing his sword up in a back-handed slash. The *gyanrigot*—an unconverted smith—caught the blade with tongs, then smashed a hammer on the swordsman's blade. The sword spun from his grip.

Both Ciras and the *gyanrigot* stared at his empty hand for a moment, then Ciras lunged. He stabbed his stiff-fingered hand into the warrior's chest and came away with a handful of wires and tubes. Hot oil sprayed. The *gyanrigot* crashed to the floor in a horrible din.

Ciras shook his hand, then let the oil drip from it. The black fluid drained away, revealing silver skin covered with lines of tiny script. He flexed his fingers. They did what he ordered them to do, and he could almost feel with them. Borosan had yet to work out heat and cold, but pressure functioned very well.

And, at least, I do not feel pain. Ciras smiled. *Neither in my flesh nor in my heart.*

Borosan lifted Ciras' sword and wiped the oil from it. "I can make the grip tighter, if you want?"

"I don't think that will be necessary." Ciras rested the metal hand on Borosan's shoulder. "It works very well."

"There are some other improvements I'd like to make. I can put a compartment in the forearm that will open and shoot darts, just like the mousers."

"No, my friend, I am a *swordsman.* I am *jaecaiserr.* All I need is a blade. You've done enough already to make sure I'll never be without one. I am happy." He took the *vanyesh* blade from the inventor. "A strong arm and a good blade to wield. That is all I have ever really needed in life. I have them now, and my enemies, once again, have ample cause for fear."

Chapter Fifty-one

1st day, Month of the Bat, Year of the Rat
Last Year of Imperial Prince Cyron's Court
163rd Year of the Komyr Dynasty
737th Year since the Cataclysm
Shirikun, North Moriande
Free Nalenyr

She stood at her bedchamber's southern window, so serene despite the turmoil in the city below. I wondered at her composure and drew strength from it. All Moriande did and I hoped she had enough to see us through.

With the setting of the sun the biggest of the siege engines had come within range of the far shore with modest projectiles. Dozens of men hauled on lines, raising the counterweight, lowering the arm. Someone locked the arm into place, then others rolled an iron ball forward. They'd wrap it in a sling, then the engine's captain would order the trebuchet levered to the left or right, as if an inch here or there could drop the missile on a specific target.

He'd shout an order and the men would scatter. The captain would yank a lanyard. The weight would fall, the arm rise, and the sling would hurl two hundred pounds through the air. The ball arced over the river. Sometimes it would pound the river wall and sometimes it would fly over. The iron balls struck sparks and bounced through buildings.

I had been down there, watching; but from her vantage point Cyrsa could see none of the hurried action. She'd just hear the shouts, might catch a flash of the weight falling, hear the distant echoes of stone striking stone.

Though I had tried to be quiet, she knew I was there. Her long, dark hair covered the five-circle crest on the back of her robe. She shook her head and highlights shimmered through her hair.

"This is what I hoped to prevent back then. I didn't want a civil war."

"I know."

She turned, a tear on her cheek. "That's why I ordered you killed."

"It was a wise choice."

The Empress smiled. "It was an unfair choice. I didn't give you a chance to change your mind."

"I wouldn't have."

She hesitated, then lowered her eyes. "Perhaps we speak about different things."

"Perhaps." I reached out and she placed a hand in mine. "I have not recovered all of my memories, but I know enough of them. I would have supplanted you. My desire was that great. I paid for that greed with my life."

The Empress brushed her other hand over my chest, smoothing a wrinkle. "Then you don't remember. I knew what you desired. I knew what it would mean. I knew the decision it would force upon me. But I gave you a choice. I loved you that much."

"What choice?"

"I asked you to marry me, to become prince-consort."

That sent a thrill through me. "You asked me to marry you even though you knew I wanted to overthrow you?"

"It was the only way." She rested her cheek against my breast. "You would have been Emperor in all but name when we returned. You loved me. I knew that. You loved the idea of being Emperor. I had to know which you loved more."

"What did I answer?"

"You said you would tell me your answer when you returned with Nelesquin's head." She traced a finger down my cheek. "That meant no."

I closed my eyes and tried to remember. I couldn't, but I could imagine it easily enough. The throne had to be mine, all mine. I could not accept it from her hand.

I enfolded her in my arms. "Is it too late for me to give you my answer now?"

Her fingers slipped into my hair and pulled my mouth to hers. We had kissed before, many times, but this was like the first kiss all over again. Soft and hesitant, questing and curious, and warm, so very warm. Our lips brushed past each other's once, then returned more firmly. Her breath warm on my cheek, my arms tightening around her, pressing her to me.

Our kisses became more urgent, tasting each other's lips. I kissed her throat, then the hollow at the base of it. She wrapped her arms around my neck as I lifted her up, burying my face against her neck. Her tears splashed against my cheek. She hung on tightly and I carried her to the bed.

We freed each other of our clothes, teasing and playful in the revelation, but ardent in exploration. We touched and tasted. My fingers tingled as they ran over her silken skin. Fingertips danced over her softly, then my nails traced the same path more sharply.

Her touch was like fire, her breath ice. Her kisses inflamed me, her whispers seduced me and carried me down with her into a world where words ceased to have meaning. We became who we were before we existed, and what we would become after we were gone. Laughter became gasps, sighs became moans, heat and motion and emotion fused us together in more than flesh, more than soul and spirit.

And then we lay together after, her nestled on my chest, a finger lazily tracing the scar. I brushed hair from her forehead and kissed it. I smiled against her flesh.

"What?"

"Paryssa. I smell it."

"It is who I am for you." She smiled. I felt it against my throat. "Who will you be for me?"

"Not Soshir. No longer Moraven Tolo." I closed my eyes. "Someone else, someone new. Someone who would be your consort, your champion, your lover and friend. Someone you can always trust."

Her head came up. She studied my face. A smile slowly grew, then she kissed me. "That would please me very much. When shall we choose your new name?"

I stroked her hair and cradled her head against my chest. "After I bring you Nelesquin's head."

Chapter Fifty-two

4th day, Month of the Bat, Year of the Rat
Last Year of Imperial Prince Cyron's Court
163rd Year of the Komyr Dynasty
737th Year since the Cataclysm
Inn of Nine Fishes, North Moriande
Free Nalenyr

"You didn't think we would let you go alone, did you?"

I should not have been surprised at their presence. They'd each been through a great deal with me. Captain Lumel, Deshiel Tolo, Ranai Ameryne, and Dunos. Each wore an oilskin suit bound up tight, with robes in a watertight container, and similar sheathings for their swords. They stood between me and the stairs to the cellar.

I smiled and bowed in genuine respect. "I did not expect you to meet me here."

Deshiel bowed. "We understand that, Master. Perhaps it was because you gave us another time and point of rendezvous by mistake."

The others smiled, and I bowed my head again. "It was because you have no intention of letting me go alone, and I have no intention of going accompanied. Deshiel, Captain Lumel, your archers are out there now trading arrows with the *kwajiin*. Neither they nor Moriande can afford to be without your services."

The Virine warrior shook his head. "They've fought well enough without me. This is important."

"As is the battle that will come." I nodded to the woman. "And you, Ranai. They may have once been my *xidantzu*, but they answer to you now. As well they should. You are needed here."

"Master, you told me that I should be *xidantzu* for nine years. You said I should wander and entertain bandits. Is there a greater bandit than Nelesquin?"

"No, but his entertainment is mine to provide." I dropped to a knee and met Dunos' unwavering stare. I caressed his cheek with a hand. "If I could take anyone, I would take you."

"I will get across the river. I can hold my breath real good. I've been practicing." He sucked in a big breath and held it.

"No, Dunos, don't. I know you could get across. I know all of you could get across. I know all of you would fight like tigers on the other side, but that isn't where the fight will be waged. We've traded shots for days and that will continue as the cities grow closer. If I fail, if Nelesquin lives, his invasion must be beaten back. You are the ones who can do that."

"But, Master, I will help you kill *kwajiin*."

"Yes, Dunos, you will. Knowing that is what gives me the courage to do what I have to." I stood and studied all their faces. "Virisken Soshir would have found you here and thought you doubted his abilities. He would have thought one of you a traitor. He would have thought nine million things, but the one he wouldn't think is what I think now. You are all friends who would fight and die with me. I would do the same for you, but here we must part company. It's not going to be safe on the other side. This whole mission may have been betrayed."

Deshiel frowned. "What?"

"How did you know when and where I'd be crossing?"

"There were rumors, Master. We had you watched and when you headed this way, well, arrows travel faster than even the swiftest of runners."

"Arrows can cross the river, too. Nelesquin may be expecting me. If we have traitors giving him information, we may have already lost the battle for Moriande."

The line parted and they bowed. I returned their bows, then began my descent of the stairs. I heard a step behind me and turned. "No, Dunos, you can't come."

"Master, if you go without me, you will die."

A shiver ran through me. "Dunos, I won't die."

"Master, please. I feel it. I know it."

I went to a knee on the stairs. "I won't die, I promise you."

The boy shook his head and a tear splashed on my face. "You can't make that promise."

"I can and have. You will have to help me keep it." I glanced past him to Ranai. She rested her hands on his shoulders and gave me a nod.

"Farewell, my friends." I smiled bravely and started down.

Dunos shouted. "No!" He didn't come after me, but ran out of the Inn.

"I'll find him, Master."

"Thank you, Ranai."

I descended into the Inn's basement. A rusted grating stood open above a round brick hole. I climbed down, finding corroded steps with my boots. Twenty feet later, I splashed through sewage and entered a taller pipe slanting downward.

My fingers located a thick rope tied off just below the surface of the dirty brown water. I took several deep breaths in rapid succession, exhaling quickly, then drew in a normal one. Ducking my head beneath the water, I pulled myself along the rope as quickly as I could.

Figuring out how to get into South Moriande hadn't been easy. I finally settled on the idea of passing from one sewer pipe to another. It was only two hundred yards, and with practice I'd been able to make the journey. Getting the rope in place was going to be a bit more difficult, but Borosan Gryst's *thanatons* had no problem. One was sent across with the cable and anchored itself on the south side.

Once free of the pipe, I had to fight the river. The current wasn't that strong, but the occasional arrow that had fallen short sank past me. I pulled myself along as quickly as possible. My lungs were on fire by the time I entered the far pipe.

I broke the surface and breathed as quietly as I could. The first impulse was to gasp and gulp air, but I couldn't afford to make that much noise. If traitors *had* revealed my place of crossing, I'd be dead well before I got a chance to dry off.

Breathing more normally, I squeezed past the *thanaton*. I climbed up the sewer pipe to the storage cellar of another inn on the river's south side. I looked about before I emerged, but darkness reigned. I came up and lowered the grate back in place, but just before it lay flat, one rusty hinge squealed like a murdered cat.

"Don't worry, Master, there is no one about to hear."

Crouched, with one sword already drawn, I faced the shadows from which the voice had originated. "Ciras? How?"

"Master Gryst told me about the *thanaton*'s task." He unshuttered a small lantern, revealing himself in dark robes with the flame pattern as his crest. He picked the lantern up with his right hand, and enough light reflected from it to reveal its true nature. "And I came over early to guarantee there would be no surprises waiting."

"And because you knew I'd not let you come *with* me?"

The young man smiled. "It is better to ask forgiveness than permission."

I laughed lightly and began to shuck my oilskins. "Then I beg your forgiveness for having kept you waiting. Let me get dressed, then we shall do something Prince Nelesquin will never forgive."

Four Hells prevented Jorim and his companions from reaching the plane of Zhangjian—literally, the place between the Heavens and Hells. The Fourth Hell, Landao, almost proved their undoing.

It was the Hell given over to the punishment of the slothful and greedy. Their dreams would hang in front of them like fruit on low branches, but no step taken in that direction would bring them any closer. Then, when frustration boiled over and they really exerted themselves, they would shoot past their goal in the blink of an eye. They'd turn around and try again, repeating the whole process.

Talrisaal figured out how to beat Landao. He made his goal the desire to get as far away from something as he could. That brought it into reach, and he plucked it. His action frustrated many of those trapped there. However, the more they wanted to come close and bash his brains out, the further from him they were sent.

Pyrust immediately made it his goal to lead everyone as far away from the gateway to the next Hell as possible. The army passed through into the icy plains of Shanchu. The whole of the Hell seemed to be made of floating ice islands on slushy seas. Wayward souls bobbed shrieking in the water and got ground between colliding islands.

The army moved pretty quickly along a chain of islands and into Ji-bing. Disease ravaged the people trapped there. They seemed mostly to be people involved in heretical and fundamentalist cults. They seemed to spend a lot of time gathering together groups to worship. A disease would spring up, covering them in boils. The entire congregation would catch it and literally fall apart. In fact, leprosy would have been kind in comparison to what they suffered.

When they finally expired, pus puddles would boil. The rising steam created ghosts, which solidified into people. They'd wander about until they heard someone preaching a message and join that group. Then the boils would rise, mucus would run, and things would get ugly from there.

Maintaining discipline in the second and third Hells had not been difficult. This was just as well because the last Hell, Chong-to, was the realm of warfare. From the moment they began to assemble, pulling themselves from a shallow river in the center of a verdant valley, warrior bands began attacking them.

The ferocity of some combatants surprised Jorim. Chong-to was not meant for warriors, but for the warlike. Those politicians and bureaucrats who had been content to create wars without ever shedding their own blood ended up in Chong-to. Cowards also landed there, as well as men who had greatly exaggerated their exploits or warriors who'd only carried hate in their hearts. It was a place where men who thought of war as a game were trapped for eternity, seeing that it was not.

Jorim pointed. "Some of the bands are joining together over there."

Pyrust nodded. "I've heard it said that if you die with honor in battles here, you win your way to Kianmang."

The Viruk shook his head. "But since they are fighting to serve themselves, they cannot die in honor."

"Which is why they will be here forever." Pyrust snarled as one of the winged apes fell from the sky, shot through with an arrow. The moment the beast hit the ground, he vanished. "Our troops, on the other hand, will be flooding Kianmang."

Pyrust formed his army up with the lizards on the wings, and the hart-cavalry in the center. The winged apes hung back, waiting to flank the bands and harass them. The formation moved ahead in good order and blew through the small gathering of bands. Potbellied men wheezing into battle ran as the lizards swarmed.

Skeletal spearmen fled before cavalry charges and the apes kept opportunist bands from hit-and-run raids.

When Chong-to's denizens died, the earth swallowed them, leaving old, rotten armor and helmets on the ground. The lizards sniffed at the relics and shied from them. Pyrust had the apes gather the weaponry into piles and the army marched on.

As they came out of the valley, the landscape changed into one lit with purple balefire. The blue river that had brought them flowed into a dark swamp tangled with broken trees and marsh grasses deep in black mud. Big bubbles appeared across the swamp's surface like giant frogs' eggs.

The eggs popped and warriors emerged. They dug through the mud, salvaging old armor with slimy, half-rotted leather harnesses and weapons that were composed more of rust than metal. They waded from the swamps and ran off along hidden pathways.

Jorim watched them go. "They're not stupid. They've seen us fight. They'll pick a place they can do the most damage."

"There are only narrow paths through the swamp. They'll ambush us there."

The Viruk turned to the Prince. "Can your lizards swim?"

"They can, but I wouldn't want to swim in that mess."

Jorim smiled. "Using the lizards to flush the ambushers is a good idea. I have another one. Just get everyone back over the ridge."

Nirati glanced at her brother. "Whenever you get that look on your face, you do something dangerous. Please, don't."

"You worry too much." He stood on the crest of the ridge above the swamp and set himself. "You, too, Talrisaal, get behind the ridge."

"If you're going to do what I think you are going to do . . ."

"It will be fine." Jorim frowned. "I'm a god, remember? I probably helped design this place."

Nirati was too far away for him to hear her clearly, but he thought she said something like, "I don't find that particularly reassuring."

He grinned and closed his eyes, beginning to manipulate the magic. When the Amentzutl first taught him magic, he had learned to find the *truth* of things. As he reached out, he sought the truth of the swamp gas that gathered and burned. Using the *mai,* he gathered it together, squeezing it into a sphere, then used magic to shift its elements. He unbalanced them and injected a lot of heat.

A brilliant sun dawned over the swamp.

Then the fireball exploded. The shock wave blasted him off the ridge. He tumbled back through the air, his robe smoking. He hit hard and bounced, but a winged ape caught him.

Nirati hurried over, but already the light in the sky had begun to dim. "Jorim, are you all right?"

"Yes, I'm fine." He slapped at a smoldering bit of cloth on his thigh. His ears were ringing, but he scrambled up the hill. A couple of the winged apes charged after him, but they hung back well shy of the crest.

Talrisaal helped him to his feet. "It was a good idea, in theory."

"Yeah." Jorim turned around. "Get ready. They're coming!"

The blast and fire had destroyed the swamp, baking the ground black and cracking it as if it had been dry for nine hundred years. Reborn warriors dug their way out of shallow graves and ran off in the other direction, joining a horde of easily nine thousand or more.

Pyrust joined him on the ridge. "Remember those wings you had when we first found you?"

"Yes."

"Sprout them again. Go that way." Pyrust stepped down and began shouting orders. "Let the enemy see you. You're bait."

Bat's wings sprang from his back. Jorim rose and moved off to the left, with Talrisaal rising beside him. The enemy, which came on in a ragged mass, shifted to follow them. Below, Pyrust led his army back down and around, poised to hit the horde in the flank.

The Viruk pointed toward a shimmering curtain between two tall mountains. "The pass into Zhangjian?"

"I hope so. So very close."

Pyrust's army came around the hill and blasted into the lost souls. The hammer-headed apes tossed huge boulders that rolled to a stop along a trail of pulped bodies. The hart-archers lofted volley after volley into the attackers, cutting down huge swaths, but it didn't seem to make much difference. The dead were springing back up and coming on stronger.

"They aren't reacting like a normal army."

The Viruk pointed. "They're swarming like a flock of birds."

It was true. When the archers cut down whole ranks,

the others flowed around them. There wasn't even an attempt to keep a disciplined line, just a wave of flesh that kept coming. Some of Pyrust's troops died in each skirmish, never to be replaced. They couldn't win the war of attrition.

"Come on!" Jorim swooped low and began manipulating the *mai*. Death and dying were painful, but the enemy knew they would be reborn in no time. Interrupting *that* cycle was impossible. Rebirth was part of Chong-to. To change that, he'd need all the power of a god, and he had but a fraction of it at his command.

But there is an answer.

One of the enemy took an arrow through the chest. He fell, clutching at it. When the arrowhead emerged from his back, it cut a nerve. The man's left arm hung limp.

Jorim manipulated the *mai*. He used just enough of it to stop the man from dying. He didn't heal the damage, just insulated the man from death. He did the same for the blinded man next to him, and a man who had lost a leg. The magic staunched the wound and sealed the stub.

Talrisaal, seeing what Jorim had done, swooped in after him and did the same. Jorim came around and shouted to Pyrust, "Maim them; don't kill them!"

The wounded clogged the battle line, but the mass continued to flow. More and more warriors appeared to join the group. The edges made it past Pyrust's lines and threatened to surround him. He pulled his lines together, maneuvering to a small hill, but the horde pressed tighter around them, nibbled away at Pyrust's troops.

Then horns blared and drums pounded. A cavalry force slammed into the horde's flank. War chariots with

Naleni archers ranged around behind the enemy. And heavily muscled warriors wearing masks of jade and gold, wielding war clubs edged with obsidian, slashed their way into the horde. The war clubs harvested limbs, and then Amentzutl *maicana* cast spells to heal the maimed.

The horde shifted, turning to face the new threat. Pyrust ordered his troops forward, catching the enemy in midmaneuver. The wounded were driven back into their own troops and the horde began fighting with itself. It disintegrated into mobs of half-dead warriors limping as far away from others as possible.

Jorim flew down beside Pyrust. "I bet you never thought Naleni cavalry would be saving you."

"No. Who are the others?"

"The Amentzutl. They live on a continent far to the east, across the sea. The *Stormwolf* expedition found them."

"How did they get here?"

"I have no idea." Jorim's wings grew back into his body as the Amentzutl line parted. A black-and-gold bundle of muscle and fur bounded up the rise and tackled Jorim.

"Jrima, Jrima, Shimik comma. Shimik here!" The Fennych hugged him tightly, then leaped up, did a backflip, and landed on his chest again. "Shimik happy happy happy."

Then Fennych caught sight of Talrisaal. His ears flattened back against his head and a growl rose from his throat.

Jorim caught the Fenn by the scruff of his neck. "No, Shimik. Talrisaal is a friend."

Shimik sat back down, then did another back-flip, landing at Jorim's side.

And beyond Jorim's feet, previously eclipsed by the Fennych, stood Nauana. She had her hands clasped at her waist, fear and joy warring on her face. A single tear glistened.

Jorim sprang to his feet and gathered her into a huge hug. He hung on tightly, burying his face against her neck. The scent of her, the silken brush of her hair against his face, her arms enfolding him, her little gasp and sob made him wish this moment would never end.

He kissed her neck, tasting his own tears. "I'm so sorry, Nauana, for all the pain."

She took his head in both hands and kissed him. "How can it cause pain to have a god sacrifice himself so you may live?"

"But . . ."

"You are a god, Tetcomchoa. You cannot die." Nauana kissed him again, then opened an arm to indicate the troops behind her. "We knew you needed help, so we came."

"You knew we needed help?"

"Of course. It is *centenco*."

Jorim shook his head, then slipped from Nauana's arms. He bowed to the woman approaching them. "Captain Gryst, how did you get here?"

"You disappoint me, Cartographer, god or not." The *Stormwolf*'s captain smiled. "Have you forgotten we found the Mountains of Ice on our expedition? There have always been stories told of an opening to the Underworld there. We found it. A big fireball pointed us to the battle."

"Jrima, fire, whoosh." Shimik clapped his hands.

"I believe he's expressed our thoughts rather aptly."

Anaeda pointed back along their line of attack. "We can leave whenever you desire."

"We're not leaving. Not yet. There's a rogue god who wants to unmake all of creation. He needs to be stopped. Care to come along?"

Anaeda Gryst frowned. "It's not exactly within the purview of *Stormwolf*'s directives from Prince Cyron."

Pyrust smiled. "I doubt marching into Hell was either."

"Good point." Anaeda nodded. "You're the cartographer, Jorim Anturasi. Lead, and we shall follow."

Chapter Fifty-three

4th day, Month of the Bat, Year of the Rat
Last Year of Imperial Prince Cyron's Court
163rd Year of the Komyr Dynasty
737th Year since the Cataclysm
River Dragon Inn, South Moriande
Imperial Nalenyr

Ciras nodded and shuttered the lamp, plunging the Inn's cellar into darkness. He kept his voice to a whisper. "When I first arrived, I checked the ground floor. I saw nothing. A stone had blasted through a corner, but the street looked empty, too."

"That's all good, but we may have been betrayed. Ranai and some of the others tried to come with me. They knew where I'd be."

"How is that possible?"

"An educated guess. A clerk somewhere made a note, and once into the bureaucracy . . ." Moraven snorted. "Are you ready?"

"Yes, Master." Ciras hesitated. "Master, you don't think I've betrayed you, do you?"

"Because of Jogot Yirxan?" A hand found his upper arm and squeezed. "No. In fact, I hoped you would be here—at least at my side in the battle against Nelesquin."

"Is that why you sent the boy to watch me?"

"Sometimes there are things we learn best when others watch and we teach—even if we don't know we're teaching. Dunos is a brave boy, and he would learn much from you. And you would learn from him, as I learned, teaching you."

"You learned from me?"

"I did. You maintain the idealism of youth. Older heads would say that such idealism is impractical and must give way to pragmatism and compromise. But compromise that strips virtue and rewards vice is evil. I learned that from you."

Ciras nodded, unseen. "You sent the boy to remind me who I was."

"Who you *are*, Ciras."

"Thank you, Master."

Moraven squeezed his arm again. "I think it is time we show Nelesquin who we are."

They crept up the stairs to the Inn's ground floor. Tables and stools had been scattered haphazardly. They picked their way through the disarray and waited at the eastern door. The street outside remained dark and quiet, save for the occasional rattle of an arrow against cobblestones.

Ciras searched the opposite skyline for signs of the enemy. He saw nothing. Moraven shook his head, so they slipped through the doorway and padded quietly along the wooden sidewalk. At the corner, they darted across the street, heading southwest toward Quunkun.

The trap closed about them on the second block. Men slipped from the shadows bearing long tiger-spears. With twin barbed heads on either end of a curved shaft and wooden haft, they more closely resembled pitchforks than weapons. They'd been chosen more to mock Moraven than for their efficacy. *Kwajiin* warriors commanded each squad, and Virine archers appeared on rooftops. They nocked thickheaded, blunted arrows that would batter and stun.

Ciras and Moraven immediately drew their swords and stood back to back—two men and three swords facing a horde of misshapen creatures that would have sent the demons of the Fifth Hell running. Their *kwajiin* leaders rested hands on sword hilts, obviously eager to test themselves.

"You bear two swords, Master, so I expect you will kill twice as many as I do."

"But I am older than you. Once you've dispatched your third, feel free to help me with mine."

A tall, slender man in a dark cloak appeared and walked through the horde of tiger hunters. He clapped his hands, then paused and bowed respectfully.

"Master Soshir, welcome to imperial Moriande."

The swordsman straightened from the first Wolf form. "You are most kind, Kaerinus. I remember your healing touch at last year's festival. I have yet to decide if I should thank you or not."

"Thank a *vanyesh*. I think not. We have unfinished business."

"We can finish it here and now."

"Tempting, but His Imperial Majesty Nelesquin the Ninth awaits."

"The Ninth?" Moraven returned both of his swords to their scabbards. "There were not eight emperors of that name before him, nor have their been any since the time of his death. How comes he by that designation?"

"This you will have to ask of him." Kaerinus spread his arms. "He knows you came here to kill him, and has sent this escort to make sure you get the chance. But, first, he wishes you to be his guests at a very special event. You'll be able to see it clearly from Quunkun, I assure you."

"And what would that be?"

The *vanyesh* smiled. "The destruction of the rest of Moriande."

"Put your sword away, Ciras. We have an audience with the Prince."

Kaerinus led the procession to the Bear Tower. An imposing structure, it had been built due north of Kelewan as a miniature copy of the Imperial capitol. Quunkun functioned as the Virine embassy and housed the Virine Prince on state visits.

The tiger hunters maintained a respectful distance, save one or two who growled and came closer to jab with their spears. Moraven ignored them, but Ciras batted a spear aside with his metal arm. The clang surprised the wildmen, and attracted the attention of their masters. They put a stop to further displays of bravery, which made the trip quicker.

Kaerinus conducted them up the broad sweep of stairs to the Crown Chamber, which featured a scaled-down version of the Virine throne. A wretched-looking man sat at the base of it, bound to it by a slender gold

collar and chain. A celestial disk backed the throne, re-
calling the days of the Empire. A half dozen *kwajiin*
flanked it left and right.

Nelesquin, thickly built and bearded, sat on the
throne. He wore a gold robe and a simple crown. His expression brightened for just a heartbeat, then his eyes
narrowed and he straightened up in the chair. He flashed
a smile.

He was big enough that, even seated, he would have
been quite impressive, save for what had been done to
the wall behind the throne. The Virine penchant for murals had been given full vent in the chamber, displaying
heroic scenes from Virine history. The chamber's rear
wall, however, had been completely whitewashed. Over
that, a fairly simple map of Moriande had been drawn
and a tall, slender man with white hair stood by, apparently intent on continuing his work.

Nelesquin rose to greet them. "My dear brother. So
kind of you to visit. You've brought a friend."

Moraven bowed, though neither deep nor long. "Ciras
Dejote, of Tirat. Once my apprentice, and now
jaecaiserr."

"If you can't kill me, he will?"

Ciras lifted his chin. "I came merely to witness my
master's victory." He carefully slid his scabbarded sword
from his robe's sash and set it on the ground.

"I regret then, Master Dejote, to author your disappointment." Nelesquin waved a hand toward the tower's
northern wall. "Behold my masterwork."

Ciras' flesh tingled as magic played. Where no window had existed before, the northern wall drew back.
Two small pillars, splitting the vista into three parts, pro-

vided an unobstructed view of Moriande centered on the Dragon Bridge, yet extended wide enough to display the entire length of the river.

Nelesquin smiled. "The conquest of North Moriande begins now." He turned and nodded to the white-haired man. "Master Anturasi, please."

The man bowed, then his icy blue eyes rolled up in his head and he picked up a brush.

Keles sat bolt upright in bed. He threw off his night-clothes. The cold air shocked him. His flesh felt as if it were on fire. He understood immediately what that meant.

Ever since the river had started to narrow, he'd felt magic pulsing through the land. That pulse had become a pounding, like a spike being driven into his skull. It amazed him that tables and chairs were not bouncing. He shivered, less now from the cool air puckering his flesh, than from identifying the magic's source.

Qiro.

He lay back down, closed his eyes, and forced his consciousness within. He sought the pulses and visualized them as waves crashing on the shore of the moat at Tsatol Pelyn. He pushed inside the waves, joined them, and they propelled him into a new world.

He found himself a giant standing astride Shirikun. The moons combed his hair. Below him people scurried about, tiny points of light, twinkling like stars.

Contempt filled his grandfather's voice. "You have finally decided to defy me openly."

Keles looked up. Qiro likewise rose as a giant above

Moriande. His blue eyes had become novae that blazed with cold intensity. The old man appeared hale and hearty—years younger than when Keles had last seen him.

He extended a brush toward the river.

"No. Stop."

The unholy light in Qiro's eyes flared. "By what stretch of the imagination do you believe you can command *me*?"

"What you are doing is wrong."

"Wrong? *Wrong?* How dare you?" Qiro doubled in size and glared down at him. "I am Qiro Anturasi. I created this world. Nothing exists unless I make it so."

"That's not true." Keles steeled himself for Qiro's fury. He hated the timorous note in his voice. He felt like a child again, cringing as Qiro berated one of his cousins. He'd always vowed he'd not find himself on the sharp side of his grandfather's tongue.

And yet here I am.

"Not true? No? Who are you to say so? What are you, Keles?" Qiro's angry words cut Keles' flesh. "Are you anything that I did not make you? I taught you all you know, but you have been a poor student."

"No, I have learned more than you know."

"Have you?" Qiro's tone sharpened. "I saved your sister from death. You couldn't do that for the woman you loved, nor your *mother*."

"No, but . . ."

Qiro's laughter battered him, knocking him clear of Moriande and into the new northern swamp. "No qualifiers. No explanations. No excuses. You are nothing. This world is mine. I do with it as I wish."

And though Keles knew it was impossible, Qiro dipped his brush in the Gold River, and began to paint in stone.

If not for the urgency burning in his breast, Dunos would have felt ashamed of himself. Horns blared and drums pounded, calling everyone to their posts. People shouted orders. The thunder of marching feet and the groan of ballistae being cocked echoed throughout the city. Something was happening. Something terrible. He should be there alongside Ranai and Deshiel.

But his master needed him.

Dunos had never known anything more clearly in his entire life. If he didn't follow Moraven Tolo, all would be lost. He believed that with the pure and innocent conviction unknown to adults—the loss of which too often goes unlamented.

He ran into the Inn of Nine Fishes and plunged into the sewers. He swam to where he found the rope and, taking hold with his good hand, began the long journey beneath the Gold River.

Chapter Fifty-four

4th day, Month of the Bat, Year of the Rat
Last Year of Imperial Prince Cyron's Court
163rd Year of the Komyr Dynasty
737th Year since the Cataclysm
Grijakun, North Moriande
Free Nalenyr

Perhaps they were right after all, that taking Grijakun for my command post was tempting fate. Prince Cyron stood in its upper reaches, staring southeast toward the place where the Wolf Bridge had once stood. Though it was impossible, some invisible agency was plucking each stone from the river and layering it in place, re-creating the bridge. The stones appeared to be fluid—indeed, drops of stone fell back into the river or coated supports like wax on the side of a candle.

Magic raked ragged claws over his flesh, and Cyron surrendered himself to it. He retreated to his matrix and watched it shift. He reached out, sending troops east, re-orienting siege engines, searching for more lines. Across the river, another matrix existed. Life pulsed along it, too. Thousands of lights burned on that side, massing at the Wolf Bridge, the Tiger Bridge, and the Bear Bridge.

"Our strength is in one place, they come at another."

The last bit of the Wolf Bridge solidified. A howling horde of half humans poured across in a torrent so violent that some of Nelesquin's troops were crushed to death against the bridge's side rails. Broken bodies cartwheeled through the air, then splashed into the water.

Part of that force dashed north, following the city walls, but the majority struck west along the River Road. The broad avenue allowed them to spread out. A few bled off into side streets, but most charged forward, intent on securing the Tiger Bridge footing. Magic was putting that bridge together stone by stone, and another slavering mass of wildmen waited to sprint across.

The Empress' Bodyguards hit the wildmen just after their leading edge had swept past Black Moon Road. The Voraxani blasted into the enemy on their metal mounts. Their charge carried halfway to the river before slowing. The warriors then cut west, bursting through the wildmen. They galloped another fifty yards, wheeled about, and charged again, breaking the wildmen and scattering them into the city.

But by then the Tiger Bridge had risen again from the depths of the Gold River.

Another horde raced north.

The bridges rose from the river as Qiro Anturasi painted them onto his map. I measured the distance to him. I could cross it in seconds and cut him down. The *kwajiin* might prove a minor inconvenience, but the cartographer would die.

Nelesquin eclipsed him. "I've not forgotten you, my friend. I know how you think. Cyron's defenses might work if Qiro draws no more bridges." He smiled. "I've felt it, too. He's found his talent and mastered it. You might be right, but he won't get a chance to finish what he's started."

I cocked an eyebrow. "You're not carrying a sword. You can't stop me."

He gestured. Ciras' sword rattled across the floor, then rose to his gold-sheathed hand. "If you do not mind, Master Dejote, this will do."

"Would it matter if I did?"

"No." Nelesquin chuckled and bared the blade. "Oh, very good. This one has tasted you before, Virisken."

"Not when it was in your hand."

Nelesquin cast the scabbard aside. "Use both of your swords. I'll let you."

"Draw the circle."

Nelesquin nodded and blue flames encircled the center of the floor. He stepped through them and bowed respectfully.

I entered the circle and bowed in turn. I would not dishonor the art because I had no respect for the man. Yet he seemed completely unconcerned at facing me. One sword against my two would have been suicidal even for another Mystic. But Nelesquin was more than a Mystic swordsman. He had mastered magic.

I straightened and he came for me. He slashed wildly, more Turasynd-styled fighting than any civilized discipline. His robe fluttered, flashing, his blade whistled. I ducked, dropping to a knee. The draw-cut with my right hand should have taken his right leg off at the knee.

He leaped above the cut, whirling through a somersault at once majestic and graceful. He twisted in the air, then landed and drove back at me. He lunged, I parried. I had to whirl away, just escaping a slash at my back. I leaped above another slash that struck sparks from the floor.

Landing, I drew my other sword and aimed a cut at his head.

He ducked that one, but I knew he would. The sword in my right hand whipped forward. It caught Nelesquin's sword arm at the elbow in a cut that would sever it cleanly.

Dunos' head broke the water's surface and he gasped. He sucked air in, quenching the fire in his lungs. Then he waited, listening, but all he heard was the echo of water in the sewer tunnel. He waited until he caught his breath, then sloshed forward.

He paused at the iron ladder set in the wall and looked up. He would have started climbing, but a flicker of color further on caught his eye. He stared at it. It grew larger, dancing through the air, then settled on his left hand.

"What are you doing here?"

The glowing green-and-black butterfly didn't reply. It beat its wings softly, then launched itself deeper into the sewers. It flew on about ten feet, then hovered, waiting.

Dunos followed. He worked the oilskin cover free of his sword, then bared his dagger and tucked it into his left hand. Aside from the squealing of rats, the dripping of water, and his own sloshing, things remained quiet. Above people were running to and fro. It was easy to imagine that some of the dripping was blood running from the streets.

But blood didn't concern Dunos. War didn't frighten him. What he dreaded most in the world was failing his master. Moraven Tolo had given him the sword. Moraven Tolo had led him in battle. He'd made Dunos Prince Iekariwynal's bodyguard. He'd trusted Dunos and he'd made him a promise.

A promise I'll help him keep.

The butterfly fluttered around another iron ladder, so Dunos mounted it. He climbed carefully. His left arm had never been much use in climbing, so he just kept it ready with the dagger, and the butterfly perched on his shoulder.

Dunos pushed a wooden grate off at the top and emerged into a tower garden. *Tzaden* vines had overgrown the place. Dunos didn't care for *tzaden*-flower tea. His mother had all but drowned him in it after his arm withered, and the scent of the flowers made him a bit nauseous.

The butterfly flew to the tower. It disappeared through thick vines.

Dunos shrugged his shoulders, bared his sword, and headed into the shadowed precincts of Anturasikun.

The fight is over! That thought echoed in Ciras' mind as Moraven Tolo struck. The younger swordsman watched dispassionately despite knowing the Prince's forearm would fly across the room, taking the sword with it. Blood would gush and then, with another quick cut, Moraven Tolo would take Nelesquin's head.

Ringing loudly, Moraven's blade rebounded from Nelesquin's arm. The slashed sleeve revealed a golden exoskeleton wrapping the Prince's limbs. The blade had cut flesh, but the wound did not bleed.

That is not possible.

Nelesquin stepped back and tore away his rent sleeve. He probed the wound with a finger, then smiled. "You see, you cannot kill me."

Moraven Tolo dropped into fourth Dragon, both blades at angles and forward. "I can blind you. I can take your tongue out, and I'm willing to bet there are other parts that aren't shielded. Let's end this."

The two of them flew at each other, a golden bear battling a fearsome tiger. Blades blurred, the skirling of parries becoming a constant hiss broken only by the whistle of missed slashes or the clang of sword on sword. Bits of fabric floated free as near misses carved cloth instead of flesh.

Ciras watched slack-jawed. Warriors flowed from Wolf to Dragon, Tiger to Scorpion, Crane to Dog and back again. Blades licked as flame, missing by hair's-breadths. It seemed impossible that they would miss, but somehow a warrior would flow around a crosscut blow or twist away from a slash. They'd become two beings of energy, mixing, twisting, and flowing around each other.

And then the pattern broke. Moraven spun down on his knees and thrust both swords forward. The blades plunged deep into Nelesquin's guts and the points emerged from his back.

The Prince roared with fury and brought his sword

down twice. The hilt cracked Moraven's right arm, then his left, breaking his grip. Nelesquin's sword flicked out once more in a slash that should have taken Moraven's head off, but the Prince shifted at the last second. Instead it laid open Moraven's right breast and shoulder.

"You are most tiresome, Virisken!" Nelesquin plucked one sword from his belly and cast it aside. He followed with the second. "That is a fault of your birth. Tainted blood. And you dared think you could be Emperor? You're a fool. You always have been."

Moraven raised a broken arm to staunch his bleeding. "I killed you before."

"Yes, yes. Crow about the last battle. You've not won this time." Nelesquin retreated to his throne and sagged back, leaving Moraven alone in the circle of flame. "I should kill you now, but I want to watch her face when you die. You'll end up in Hell together, along with your Prince Cyron. Actually, he should be there by now, and the last hope of Moriande goes with him."

There he stood, Prince Cyron. One-armed though he was, a tower of strength in a hive of chaos. Clerks ran in, ministers, too, bearing reports. The Prince didn't even deign to look at them. Some he touched, some he just waved at, then issued orders like divine pronouncements. The same clerks turned and fled, hastening to follow orders they couldn't even be certain they'd heard.

Prince Eiran sat beside Cyron. The Helosundian took the papers, read them quickly, and sorted them into piles. He probably didn't even recognize it in himself, but he was understanding what each paper said based on

Cyron's understanding. He had truly learned well from the Naleni Prince and was capable of mastering the same art as Cyron.

It really didn't matter.

Minister Pelut Vniel moved through the chaos unnoticed and unchallenged. He, too, had mastered arts, and one was the art of *belonging*. No matter where he found himself, he could make others believe he belonged. No one would question him.

No one would stop him.

He reached Cyron's side. "Highness, do you remember the knife you sent me?"

Cyron's eyes blinked.

Pelut Vniel drove the knife straight into Cyron's heart.

And twisted.

The butterfly had led him on a bit of a chase through the tower. It ended in a room that Dunos entered through a four-foot-high passage. The room's far side had a semicircular lattice of gold bars cutting it roughly in half. Beyond the bars lay many treasures. Chests of spices filled the air with exotic aromas that made it easy to forget about *tzaden* flowers and sewers. Exotic weapons were stacked here and there amid chests of gold coins. Dunos imagined the butterfly might have brought him there so he could choose a better weapon, but that was a waste of time.

He'd never give up the sword Master Tolo had given him.

The butterfly alighted on the gold bars, but a buzzing

sound beyond it focused Dunos on the human skull mounted on a pedestal. The skull had been covered in gold and set with gems. Dunos guessed it might have been pretty. He didn't like the empty eye sockets, didn't want anything to do with it, but the skull buzzed.

He came right up to the bars. The buzzing resolved itself into words. "You are most tiresome, Virisken! That is a fault of your birth. Tainted blood. And you dared think you could be Emperor? You're a fool. You always have been."

Dunos snarled. "He's not a fool. My master is not a fool!"

The skull didn't answer him. It just stared at him, the bared teeth a contemptuous grin.

Anger boiling over, Dunos raised his withered left fist high and brought it down as hard as he could. The skull cracked, then bounced off the pedestal. It spun slowly, the jaw falling free, then hit the floor. It exploded, spilling the black and white stones filling it all over the floor.

Dunos looked around, then nodded. "No more stupid buzzing." Then he shivered.

There *was* no more buzzing, but he seemed to remember that, when he hit it, the skull screamed.

Chapter Fifty-five

4th day, Month of the Bat, Year of the Rat
Last Year of Imperial Prince Cyron's Court
163rd Year of the Komyr Dynasty
737th Year since the Cataclysm
Zhangjian (The Place Between)

The trek across the last of Chong-to was accomplished with a minimum of effort and few losses. Warring bands crippled their enemies, then held them in thrall, enjoying their pain. It was hardly conduct that would win release, but this new consolidation of power occupied the bands enough that they let Jorim's army travel unmolested.

Jorim passed first through the shimmering veil that separated the First Hell from Zhangjian. The Place Between served as an entryway to the realms of the supernatural. It lay parallel to the physical world, and was everything it was not. Dark and empty, without form or substance, it proved unsettling for everyone. Something supported their feet, but no one could tell what it was. Shimik tried to dig in it but didn't get very far. Riders had to dismount to lead reluctant beasts, and the Nighfor found it too disorienting even to attempt to fly.

The gateway to the Heavens awaited in the distance and this made Jorim suspicious. "There is no reason for the perception of distance, save that someone wishes us to feel far from our goal."

Talrisaal nodded. "Nessagafel."

Pyrust did not let the plane's featurelessness daunt him. He formed his army up, using the Naleni and Amentzutl troops as his center, with the hart-cavalry split on each wing, and the lizards flanking them. The Nighfor waited in reserve, along with the hammer-headed apes.

Something glimmered ahead in the darkness. Jorim started to run, but reached it in two steps. Crumpled in a bloody robe decorated with bats on the wing, Tsiwen lay largely still. Pinpoint wounds from ant bites covered her visible flesh. Her throat and face had been raked with thorns. Her robe covered her belly, but she'd clearly been disemboweled.

Jorim dropped to a knee and felt her throat for a pulse. The gesture was ridiculous. Tsiwen had no more need for a pulse than she did a physical form. Talrisaal appeared on her other side.

Jorim looked up. "You wanted to know why Nessagafel didn't know I'd escaped him? She took my place. I can't imagine . . ."

"Magic works here. I can help her."

"Please, do." Jorim caressed her cheek. "We'd not have gotten even this far save that she fooled him."

"But not for long enough, Wentoki."

A young man materialized past Talrisaal. He was the child Nessagafel had been, now grown. He stood naked save for a black ring around his little finger. "You have been quite audacious, my son. I have not had time to fully assess the damage you've done. But it matters not, since I will unmake all of this. When I start over, I'll bring you back and make a special Hell just for you."

He raised one hand and Tsiwen twitched. Her eyes jerked open. She flew upright, limp as a puppet, her intestines tangling in her legs. With every finger Nessagafel flexed she danced—at times clumsy, others seductively, all the while her head lolling and jaw bouncing open.

"I told you I gave you compassion because I did not need it. I lied." His other hand came up and Nirati appeared, hanging by invisible strings. "I gave it to you to cripple you."

Bones cracked. Nessagafel doubled in size. He sprouted a second pair of arms and raised those hands as well, bringing Nauana and Anaeda Gryst into his dancing troupe. The ancient god laughed, his fingers flicking. The women capered through farcical dances, then dashed against the ground like discarded toys.

"That is it, isn't it? You're just a child."

Nessagafel's head came up. "This, from you? You clothe yourself in flesh and play among mortals. You are the child wishing he could fight alongside his toy soldiers. All you ever sought to do was imitate me, but you never could. You never allowed yourself to set compassion aside. You hoped it would make you superior when you clearly were not."

"I'll set it aside now."

"You, fight me? Here? Now?" Nessagafel's puppets disappeared. "You are a man. I am a god."

"But you are limited." Jorim stood. "By the ring. By your fear."

Light flashed for a second, blinding him. When vision returned he found his companions arranged in a circle around the two of them. They watched horrified, hands pressed to an unseen barrier. He took heart in Tsiwen's appearance—her entrails had been replaced. This gave Jorim hope.

Nessagafel leaped at him, all four arms wide, his fingers sprouting claws. He roared soundlessly, yet vibrations thrummed through Jorim's chest. The murderous fires in his eyes flared, licking up over his forehead, and he descended.

Jorim pushed panic away and grasped the *mai*. The key to working magic had always been to find the *truth* of something. He gathered the magic and, clapping his hands, launched a sizzling sphere. Argent lighting wreathed the ball. It blasted into Nessagafel's chest and exploded. The god flew back, slamming into the invisible wall. The lower pair of arms burst into flames and fell away.

The ancient god crouched at the circle's edge. "You want to see what I truly am? Your mistake."

For the tiniest part of a second, too small to measure, Nessagafel revealed his true nature. His physical form became transparent—nothing more than a vessel for his essence. Sounds echoed in colors, light dripped, textures sang. Emotions, hundreds of thousands of them, vibrated like plucked bowstrings, each a needle scraping over his consciousness. Nessagafel was the stuff of hopes and dreams and fears and hatreds, of love and lust and despair. Understanding even one strand of his being would take eternity, and yet uncounted strands coiled in him.

Then Jorim was down, his robe shredded, his chest bleeding.

Nessagafel, wearing the form of a Viruk, stood over him and raised a clawed hand. "All you need to understand of me, Wentoki, is that I am the one who has destroyed you."

His hand fell.

Chapter Fifty-six

4th day, Month of the Bat, Year of the Rat
First Year of the Restoration of the Imperial Court
163rd Year of the Komyr Dynasty
737th Year since the Cataclysm
North Moriande
Free Nalenyr

A burst of magic exploded out from Anturasikun. It blasted Keles flat, washing him in invisible fire. The flames condensed, locking him in a transparent shell. He lay there, immobile, mocked by the smooth motion of the moons.

For a moment he considered giving up. It would have been so easy. Down, paralyzed, facing magical manifestations of Qiro's fury, it seemed a fight he couldn't win.

It seemed every bit as hopeless as the defense of Tsatol Pelyn.

Keles' hands tightened into fists, dispelling the paralysis. It felt as if his flesh was cracking. He flexed muscles and worked joints, letting the shell fall away in bits.

Rolling to his side, he came up on one knee and, for the first time, took heart.

Whatever had knocked him down had likewise staggered Qiro. His grandfather's image had shrunk again to match his own. The brush had vanished, though two bridges stood complete and a third was rebuilding itself. Qiro clutched his head and muttered in his beard.

"Oh, dear, oh, dear. It's all wrong."

The land shuddered. The river's narrowing stopped and began to reverse itself quickly. Shock waves rocked the city. The change came in fits and starts; a bit would move here, a bit there. The earth tore. Roads collapsed. Towers wavered.

"Stop, Grandfather!" Keles rose and vaulted the city's north wall. "You're destroying everything."

Qiro looked up, horror on his face. "Oh no, Keles. I must make it all right. This is wrong. Is this what you've gotten up to?"

The ground shook again. Towers cracked. Keles reached out, steadying them with magic. In an eyeblink he read the structures and the forces working on them, reinforcing their strengths.

Yet even as he blunted his grandfather's work there, Qiro set about other tasks. More of the bridges started to reconstruct themselves. Nelesquin's troops were already pouring north. Tens of thousands still packed the streets, waiting to cross.

Keru fought at the Bear Bridge and Rekarafi with them. Nelesquin's hordes came on, mindless and unmindful of the havoc the Viruk wrought. He fought using a spear and had scribed a circle around him in blood and flesh. Warriors clawed slippery bodies aside to engage him.

To the east, the Voraxani fought. Archers on rooftops volleyed arrows into the wildmen. Naleni troops and Desei conscripts manned hastily erected breastworks, stemming the spread of the wildmen, but columns threaded deeper through alleys and side streets. Other squads hunted them down, sparing no sector from combat.

Qiro had focused on the Gold River's flooding. He raised a new bank, cutting off the outlet Cyron had opened. Keles magically forced the water back into the narrow river channel. A wall of water twelve feet high poured through Moriande, passing beneath the Dragon Bridge. It did not, however, spare the resurrected bridges. Caught in its fury, the Bear Bridge vanished instantly. Grey water splashed, gushing up onto the River Road, scattering troops and washing away Rekarafi's gruesome monument. The wave swept wildmen and stones down, blasting through the Tiger Bridge. It likewise evaporated, then the whole boiling mass of stone and corpses melted the Wolf Bridge as if it were a construct of rotten wood and children's dreams.

"Oh, no, Keles, look what you've done!" Qiro's voice reflected the horror on his face. "I have to fix it all."

Here and there, with no order or reason, Qiro made adjustments. A bridge started to rise. The riverbank retreated, then thrust forward again. Land folded in on itself, becoming pocket worlds from which odd creatures began to emerge. The land erupted in boils, and blood seeped to the surface. Qiro would see that and react to it, compounding the problems, warping the land well beyond even the time of wild magic.

Keles fought against panic. Everything his grandfather was doing was wrong. Keles constantly referred back to the land as it had been when he traveled with Ryn and that knowledge made it easier to repair the damage. But still he was just reacting to his grandfather's increasingly bizarre efforts. Qiro had lost all pretense of sanity. However he was seeing the world, it wasn't in a manner that allowed him to make things right again.

He's forcing me to react. He's controlling what I do. Keles recalled his conversation with Tyressa. If all he did was react, he could never gain control. He had to link the present to the past, reasserting what was right and true about the world. That would make it harder for Qiro to alter things and easier for Keles to fix them.

But what? What can I do? He reached out, flattening a volcano before it could explode and crack the continent. *I need to anchor the world.*

Then he looked up and smiled.

Summoning all the magic he could, Keles Anturasi reached out and caught the black moon. He ripped it from its celestial path. Heedless of what Qiro was doing, he pulled it down. The stone warmed and Keles sealed it in a mold he shaped from his memory of Virukadeen.

He guided the luminous rock back toward the Dark Sea. Beyond it, from Ixyll, wild azure magic arced out, striking the vast mountain like lightning. And below, the islands flew into the air. They floated around the mountain, not yet restored to their former glory.

The transformed moon settled into the Dark Sea basin. Water should have flooded all the land, except the mountains accepted that part of themselves that had been ripped away so long ago. The earth sealed itself, and springs and rivers flowed again through Virukadeen.

With the black moon returned to the earth, exhaustion seized Keles. He went to a knee. Magic still played around him but he could not muster the strength to work with it.

Qiro stood over him, a palsied hand trembling on his shoulder. The old man looked west, wonder on his face.

"It's so beautiful, Keles. That is the way it should be."

Then Qiro fell over and his grandson's world went black.

Chapter Fifty-seven

4th day, Month of the Bat, Year of the Rat
First Year of the Restoration of the Imperial Court
163rd Year of the Komyr Dynasty
737th Year since the Cataclysm
Quunkun, South Moriande
Imperial Nalenyr

The magic that pulsed through the city drove Ciras to his knees. Moraven Tolo sagged forward, his head down, almost as if bowing to Prince Nelesquin. Kaerinus staggered back, and Qiro Anturasi sagged against the wall, slowly slumping to the floor.

Those who did not know *jaedun* remained unaffected and even appeared shocked as the others recoiled. The magic echoed in Ciras' head like a high, piercing shriek. He clawed his flesh-and-blood hand through his hair as if to brush the sound away, then a new sound invaded.

Laughter.

Nelesquin sat on the throne and looked at his right arm. His fingers came away red. He held his hand up, studying the blood, rubbing a thumb over his wet fingers, and he laughed. "I'm bleeding, Kaerinus! My soul has returned. I'm whole again."

The big man stood, roaring. He pumped his left fist in the air and clearly sought to bring his right arm up, but it failed to move. Alarm registered on his face, but only the left half. The flesh of his right cheek remained immobile and began to blacken.

"What's happening?"

Kaerinus pulled his cloak about himself. "The toxin in Prince Pyrust's ring. You sealed the wound, but you did not neutralize the poison."

"Fix it."

"No, my lord."

"What?"

Moraven lifted his head. "You thought the Empress had *one* spy in your *vanyesh*. She had more."

"No. *NO!*" Nelesquin plucked the sword from his right hand and raised it in his left, charging at the kneeling swordsman. "I will see you in Hell, Virisken!" He whipped the blade down.

Ciras caught it in his metal hand. "Not with my sword." He tightened his grip and wrenched the blade to the left.

Nelesquin looked down, contempt registering on the left half of his face. "You are nothing."

"Fitting last words." Ciras slammed his fist into Nelesquin's breastbone. The sternum snapped as the punch crushed the Prince's heart. Ciras pulled back and jerked his sword from the dying man's grasp.

Nelesquin wavered for a moment, then pitched over backward. Gold bones clanked on the ground, poking at odd angles through his robe. He lay there, staring sightlessly at a mural that depicted him as a god.

Before the Prince had even begun to collapse, Ciras rotated his wrist and transferred the *vanyesh* blade to his left hand. He reversed it, holding it tight along his forearm. The tip extended past his elbow. He raised his arm, catching the first *kwajiin*'s cut easily, then jabbed metal fingers into the man's throat.

Ciras spun and parried, then stabbed back with the *vanyesh* blade. Sparks flew as a blow glanced from Borosan's handiwork. A stab ignited fire in his thigh. Another parry, a lunge, then a twist, narrowly avoiding a crosscut slash. The sword's pommel crushed a face. A slash sent a head spinning. Before it bounced the second time, the last of the *kwajiin* clutched at a pulsing wound in his groin, then stumbled back, tripping over Nelesquin's body.

Kaerinus knelt beside Moraven Tolo. Purple light played and the swordsman gasped. The *vanyesh* laid a hand on each broken arm. More magic flowed and the limbs straightened, but the hands clutched weakly at nothing.

Ciras slashed the chain binding Prince Jekusmirwyn to the throne. "You are free, Highness."

The man still cowered. "Is he dead? Are you sure?"

"Poisoned. Heart crushed. He's dead."

Jekusmirwyn crawled forward and picked up a *kwajiin* sword. He tested its edge against his thumb. Apparently satisfied, he sawed away at Nelesquin's neck. "I'll take his head. Just to be sure."

Ciras recovered his scabbard and slid the *vanyesh*

blade home. He joined Kaerinus and Moraven. "How are you, Master?"

"I'll be fine. I need time to recover." Moraven smiled.

Ciras nodded and looked at his metal hand. "Master Gryst will be proud his work killed Prince Nelesquin."

"As well he should be. He's a wise and clever man."

"One of several it has been my privilege to know." Ciras hooked his metal hand beneath Moraven's armpit and stood. "Come, Master, let's find a way home again."

4th day, Month of the Bat, Year of the Rat
First Year of the Restoration of the Imperial Court
163rd Year of the Komyr Dynasty
737th Year since the Cataclysm
Zhangjian (The Place Between)

Chapter Fifty-eight

A glowing hand caught Nessagafel's wrist, stopping the claws inches from Jorim's face. The Viruk ripped his hand free, then backhanded the man who'd stopped him. He spun away from the blow, rebounding from the unseen wall.

Jorim stared disbelieving. "Prince Cyron?"

The Prince dabbed at the corner of his mouth with his left hand. He smiled. "I hardly expected to find you here, Master Anturasi." He flexed his fingers. "Nice to have this back."

Behind the Prince, Shimik dug furiously at the ground, trying to squeeze beneath the invisible wall. The others made no attempt to hide their surprise at Cyron's appearance. His presence meant he was dead, and that betokened misfortune in the mortal realm.

Jorim gathered his legs beneath him and prepared for Nessagafel's next attack, but the ancient god was not coming for him. Instead, he held his clawed hand up. He rotated it forward and back, as if mocking the wonder with which Cyron had studied his own hand.

The ring that had bound him had vanished.

Nessagafel's laughter started low. He spun as it rose and stared straight at Talrisaal. "It was you. It wasn't my children who bound me with that ring. It was you, the Viruk. You did it."

Talrisaal nodded slowly. "You were bound with something that existed before you did. We bound you with Virukadeen."

"Existed before I did? Hardly." Nessagafel studied his talons. "It does not matter. Virukadeen has been returned to the world. I am free, now, to do as I will—as I have long intended."

"No!" A ragged beast appeared from the darkness. A length of broken chain trailed from the collar around his neck. Grija vaulted the invisible wall, teeth bared. As he flew he took on his full aspect—at last strong and fearless.

His white fangs snapped shut.

On air.

Nessagafel caught him by the throat. Grija struggled, trying to bite, trying to scratch, but Nessagafel tightened his grip.

The wolf whimpered.

"Grija, poor Grija." Nessagafel slowly shook his head.

You were my first child, so I shall do you the honor of letting you go first again."

The ancient god stroked the wolf's fur. It shimmered as his hand passed, then slowly evaporated. With each caress, more and more of Grija disappeared.

Worse yet, Jorim found it more difficult to recall Grija. Fresh memories dimmed. Old memories faded. Jorim found himself wondering how the wolf had gotten into Nessagafel's hands and by the time he realized he didn't know, the wolf had vanished and Jorim was uncertain what he'd been wondering about in the first place.

The ancient god turned to Jorim. "It was easy with him because I knew him so well. With you it will be more difficult, Wentoki, but you will be forgotten soon enough."

Jorim stood, drawing back. "I won't go easily."

"Fight all you want, it won't matter."

Jorim's flesh tingled hotly before he'd even begun to grasp the *mai*. Bits and pieces of his memory began to dissolve. Things he needed went missing. Words lay on the tip of his tongue. He saw people staring in horror, but couldn't remember their names. He raised his hands, trembling. He wanted to ask for help, but who and how eluded him.

"You could have joined me, Wentoki, but all is lost now. As you unravel, I learn it all. I know everything."

Jorim staggered and fell, suddenly having forgotten how to stand. He struggled to rise. "There's one thing you don't know."

"No? Intrigue me, and perhaps I shall let you linger."

"I didn't make the Fennych to kill the Viruk."

Nessagafel's eyes narrowed. "Then why . . . ?"

"I made them to kill *you*."

Shimik squeezed into the circle, having shifted hi shape to get under the wall. He coiled like a snake and growling, launched himself. Nessagafel spun, his righ arm coming up. He deflected the Fenn.

Shimik's serpentine body coiled around his arm an tensed. The limb snapped loudly. The Fenn's thick fu blunted the Viruk's slashing claws, while Shimik's claw dug in at the shoulder, shredding bony flesh. The Fen lunged again, his neck growing longer. His serrated teet sank into Nessagafel's throat. He tore most of it fre with a jerk, then burrowed back in. He clung tightly eve as Nessagafel went down.

He didn't stop gnawing until the ancient god's hea rolled free.

Chapter Fifty-nine

4th day, Month of the Bat, Year of the Rat
First Year of the Restoration of the Imperial Court
163rd Year of the Komyr Dynasty
737th Year since the Cataclysm
Zhangjian (The Place Between)

Cyron rolled to his feet, staring at the severed head. "Is he really dead?"

Tsiwen, having regained her color, nodded. "As dead as it is possible for him to be."

Pyrust stepped forward as Shimik slid from the body and wriggled to Jorim's side. "But there is no god of Death. I know this. There never has been."

Tsiwen opened her hands. "Death, just like life, appears to operate independently of a patron god."

The Viruk nodded. "Death existed before Nessagafel. A god of Death, were one to exist, would be the harvester of souls, arbitrating who is allowed to return to the world."

Cyron frowned. "Then without such a god, Nessagafel could return."

"As long as there are those who worship him, he could return. Only a god of Death could prevent it."

Nirati crouched beside the body. "You needn't worry about his returning. I won't allow it."

Cyron shook his head. "You can't just appoint yourself a god."

"I didn't have to. Nelesquin created the Durrani and they worshipped me. Even now, if I listen, those fighting in Moriande offer prayers so they will not disgrace themselves." She stood. "I shall be the goddess of Death. Nirati the fox. And I shall keep Nessagafel in a grave until the last of his followers comes to me."

Tsiwen turned to her. "This is not a pleasant choice you are making."

"You don't understand, sister." Nirati smiled easily. "All my life I sought my talent and never found it. Yet the one thing I did well was die. Death is my talent, and rebirth is the gift I can give to those who deserve it."

Pyrust nodded. "I trust, in time, you'll find I deserve it."

"I find you already do. Rebirth, and an even greater reward." Nirati waved a hand and Pyrust vanished.

Cyron stared at her. "You have taken to your powers quickly, Nirati. A talent indeed."

Nirati bowed her head, then gestured again and Nessagafel's corpse disappeared. "If you will excuse me, there are a few things to which I must attend. It would help me, brother and sister, if you could do something about the war."

Nirati faded and Cyron stared after her. His eyes narrowed. "She said 'brother and sister,' but looked at me, not Jorim."

Tsiwen linked her arm through his. "He is still her brother, and so are you, now."

"What?"

"How is it that you came to be here, Cyron? Only a god surrendering a mortal sheath can appear here upon death."

"I am no god."

"People worship you. They attribute miracles to you." Tsiwen led him toward Jorim. "You saw the offerings they left in your name, incense burned, relics displayed in those shrines. To those people, you *are* a god."

"But what am I the god of?"

Her laughter came softly to his ears. "You are the god of your talent. You are the god we need. Nessagafel created his children to amuse him, but as it is on earth, so it is in the Heavens. We became a bureaucracy beneath him. You reformed the bureaucracy. You are Cyron, Prince of gods. You unite us and rule over us, bringing order to Chaos and paradise to the world."

"I don't believe it."

"That's the joy of being a god. *You* don't have to believe. Others already do. Just listen."

Cyron paused for a moment, and the voices did come to him. Prayers of thanks, panicked prayers asking for help, desperate prayers, and grieving prayers. Hundreds of thousands of voices, and not just human, but Viruk and Soth and creatures that Cyron never even knew existed.

And one desperate voice, coming from a few feet away.

Nauana knelt there, cradling Jorim's head in her lap. She stroked his forehead, wiping away her own tears. Shimik sat beside her, holding Jorim's hand. The bleeding had been stopped and the gashes healed. Jorim breathed steadily, but stared up blankly.

Cyron crouched and took his other hand. He patted it. "Jorim. Jorim Anturasi. Wake up."

Tsiwen squeezed Cyron's shoulder. "He doesn't hear you."

"I don't understand."

A tear rolled down Tsiwen's cheek. "Nessagafel started to unmake him, but Jorim fought. He gave up little pieces of himself to protect the core. He's in there, somewhere. Only he doesn't have the words to communicate. He's a child again, an infant."

Nauana wiped her eyes. "But he can learn?"

Tsiwen nodded. "Yes, he can learn."

Shimik grinned with a mouthful of golden teeth. "Jrima, Shimik learna, learna big."

The dark-haired woman again stroked Jorim's brow. "I shall take Tetcomchoa back to Nemehyan. I shall teach him. We all will. We will give him back his mind."

Anaeda Gryst glanced over at Cyron. "I will take them back on the *Stormwolf,* if I have your permission, Highness."

"It is no longer mine to give, but I think it is an excellent idea." Cyron nodded. "Please take Nirati's army with you and leave them on Anturasixan."

"Anturasixan?" The ship's captain eyed him suspiciously.

"A large continent. I doubt you'll miss it."

"Very good, my lord."

Tsiwen beckoned Talrisaal to her. "You would go with Wentoki to help them care for him, no?"

"It would be my pleasure."

"And I would grant you leave to do that, if you would do something else for me first."

The Viruk bowed. "Whatever you command, Mistress."

She gestured. A hole opened in the blackness. A simple garden appeared, with flowers in bloom and brightly colored birds singing in the trees. Cyron recognized things, then realized memory was an artifact of his mortality. His *knowing,* on the other hand, came from his new office.

Talrisaal staggered. "The garden. That was my home on Virukadeen."

"So it is again. A gift from Wentoki's mortal brother."

"A *man* did that?"

"Indeed. You might be cautious about whom you enslave in the future."

The Viruk nodded. "Why do you show me this, Mistress?"

"This is a man's gift to the Viruk. I show you the garden so you will go there. I wish you to be my gift to the Viruk, to welcome your people back to their home."

Talrisaal smiled. "Those flowers, the blue ones, they made us fertile. There were no more when Virukadeen died."

"Then I suggest, Talrisaal, you spend your time well and recover all you need to know about child rearing, for that shall no longer be a lost art among the Viruk."

"Forever shall I praise your name, Tsiwen, and pray often for your wisdom." Talrisaal stepped through the window. Before it closed, he bent to sniff the blue flowers and smiled.

Tsiwen smiled. "Do you approve, brother?"

"You're wise enough to know I do." Cyron grinned. "But now, the war. Nirati wishes it stopped. Is there a way we can do this easily?"

"Easily, no." She took his hand in hers. "Spectacularly, oh, yes."

Chapter Sixty

4th day, Month of the Bat, Year of the Rat
First Year of the Restoration of the Imperial Court
1st Year of the Jade Dynasty
737th Year since the Cataclysm
Quunkun, South Moriande
Imperial Nalenyr

Though Kaerinus had sealed my wounds and healed the broken bones, I was in no shape to fight. My arms still ached—full healing would take time. While Ciras had killed all the *kwajiin,* he'd not escaped unscathed. The chances of our getting to North Moriande alive were slender at best.

Neither I nor my companions were sanguine about our chances of survival, but we'd not voiced our doubts. I staggered to my feet and Ciras gathered my swords. I glanced at Nelesquin and made no effort to hear what Tekusmirwyn was whispering in his ear. "Will he remain dead this time?"

Kaerinus nodded. "This time there is no escape. Back

then he had me separate his soul and hide it in a vessel. With it removed from his body, he couldn't be fully dragged into the Hells. I'd put it in a ruby. Others transferred it from item to item until one of the *vanyesh*, in honor of Nelesquin, bound it to his gilded skull."

The magician pointed at Qiro Anturasi, who lay slumped, drooling, against the wall. "Qiro visited Tolwreen and was given the skull to bring back here. He labored under its influence and created the place where Nelesquin could be brought back to life. Neither he nor Nelesquin knew where the soul resided, however. I did not know until recently—Qiro's own magic masked the work on the skull. I still would not have known, save that I saw it in Qiro's trophy room."

Ciras frowned. "Why didn't you destroy it then?"

"It would have killed me to do so—such was the magic I'd used in the first transfer." Kaerinus opened his hands. "I had once worked for Nelesquin, and willingly. I began to doubt him after I worked the spell and he began to murder those who took custody of his spirit after me. Then I returned to the Nine and saw what had been unleashed, but by then I could do nothing until I located the person who could kill him."

I raised an eyebrow. "Who was that?"

"The boy, Dunos." Kaerinus smiled.

The Gloon's words came back to me. *This mission can only be accomplished by someone who should be dead.*

"You recognized how special a child he is, Virisken. He destroyed the skull. That broke the link between Qiro and Nelesquin."

Another voice, a familiar one, spoke. "It also broke the link between Nelesquin and a fallen god, Nessagafel."

My jaw dropped open as the man materialized before us. "Prince Cyron?"

"In part, yes." He clapped his hands once to emphasize how he had changed. "Nelesquin somehow fell under Nessagafel's sway. His works in the mortal realm aided Nessagafel's campaign to upset Heaven and start creation all over again."

"How do you know...?" That question seemed ridiculous. "Your arm?"

Cyron smiled. "There have been many changes, my friends." He gestured and Nelesquin's body rose in the air. "Do you mind if I borrow this?"

"If it pleases you."

"For the moment it does." He plucked the head from Jekusmirwyn's bloody hands. "Thank you."

I, like the others, bowed.

By the time I straightened up, he had left the tower and grown to the size of a giant. He soon dwarfed the largest of Nelesquin's creatures and kept growing. Until we moved toward the portal in the north wall, all we could see was his kneecap and the black robe festooned with stars that covered him.

Cyron's voice boomed. "Behold Nelesquin, the man who would have been Emperor."

The corpse rested in the palm of his hand, with an arm and both legs dangling from between his fingers. We could not help but stare as the head floated above the body. Nelesquin looked like a broken toy, void of all power and pride, but suited to pity.

"He strove to upset the balance on earth, and thus sought to overthrow the reign of the gods. For any man to do thus is a crime against the Heavens, the Hells, and

the mortal realm. His efforts have not pleased us. Those
who supported him were deceived. Unto them no blame
or guilt attains. All should realize that their own sins are
known to Nirati the fox, and when they are taken, she
will mete out justice in ways wonderful and terrible.

"Those who opposed Nelesquin are heroes. They
have pleased us and their rewards will be in keeping with
their efforts."

Cyron, whose robe contained the circle of constellations on the breast, reached up into the sky, plunging his
hand into a mass of stars between Quun and Chado.
Cyron's fingers stirred them. They blurred, then slowly
resolved themselves into a new constellation—a crown.
A different-color star burned on each of nine spikes to
the crown, but at the brow, other stars formed an eye.

A wave of nausea twisted my guts. I looked up again.
The stars on Cyron's breast matched the Heavens. And
though I thought I remembered having seen him stir the
stars, even more strongly I had the impression that
the stars had *always* been that way. In fact, the legend of
the stirring of the stars was just that—forever connected
with the god of the New Year's Festival.

A woman in a robe with a bat crest caressed my brow
and my confusion ebbed away. "There is value in many
legends—so much so that the truth beneath them is often unimportant."

I bowed. "Praise to thee, Tsiwen."

The goddess of Wisdom returned the bow. "You will
go to Anturasikun and rescue your companion. There
you will see a map of the world. Master Dejote already
knows of the Helos channel. The land north of it is being
overrun by the Turasynd. You will lead an army of *xi-*

dantzu, kwajiin, and Imperial soldiers to repel them. In gratitude, the *kwajiin* will be given Deseirion."

"And after that?"

Tsiwen smiled. "I have found it the height of wisdom not to ask what the future holds, but to venture forth and discover it. There is a new order in Heaven, and on the earth. This does not mean, however, that the need for heroes has vanished, nor that villainy has disappeared. The new world, you will learn, has much in common with the old."

Chapter Sixty-one

4th day, Month of the Bat, Year of the Rat
First Year of the Restoration of the Imperial Court
1st Year of the Jade Dynasty
Shirikun, Moriande
Imperial Nalenyr

Keles listened to what the god Cyron had said and felt magic wash over the world. He still retained the sense of reality he'd had when traveling with his father, but it seemed as if a thin veil had been laid over everything. Cyron had been a Prince in Nalenyr, but Keles seemed to remember that the Prince had been named for the leader of the gods.

He fought to retain his memory of the world as it had been. The Gold River had been wider. Virukadeen had not always been there. Nirati had been his sister. These were facts, and should have been immutable, yet the world seemed to want him to remember things differently.

The door to his chamber opened and the Empress Cyrsa walked in. "I am glad to see you awake. I thank you for what you did."

"How do you know?"

She smiled. "Mystics are always attuned to *jaedun*. You dragged the moon from the sky."

"I had to make the world right again."

"And yet, you sense the changing, too?"

"Cyron is now a god and no longer a Prince. My dead sister is now the goddess of Death?"

"There will be many more changes." Cyrsa smiled easily. "When I returned to the Nine, I paid the finest minstrels to write songs vilifying Nelesquin and creating a certain picture of who I had been. The truth of what happened back then no longer mattered. People acted on what they *believed* happened."

She gestured toward where Cyron had stood astride the river. "By the time you have grandchildren, the story of the world will have changed. Nelesquin will be remembered, but only as a dissident Virine noble who sought to overthrow the Empire. He was, of course, insane. He claimed he was the Nelesquin of legend."

"This will become the new truth because you will spend money to make it so?"

"In part, yes; and I do not regret the expense. Consider me vindictive if you will, but my efforts will really not amount to that much. You have been trained to observe. You pay attention; but for many people the world extends no further than their daily travels take them. Though they know the Five Princes exist, show them a map and they could not locate them. What does not immediately affect their lives does not matter. It comforts them to assume that things have always been the way they are now."

Keles shook his head. "You're telling me that the illusion is more important than reality."

"Only because so many people are incapable of handling reality." The Empress opened her hands. "Here is a question philosophers ponder: if the world was created just this moment, and you with it, complete with your memories, what part would the past play in your daily life? How much would the past matter?"

"Well, there is no past, so it cannot matter. I would be acting based on my memories of the past."

"Which are false."

"Yes."

Cyrsa smiled. "And if all memories were one hundred percent accurate, this would not be a problem. They are not, nor are they *facts*. Yet people trust rumors, memories, and dogma more than fact. This means, whether it pleases you or me, perception becomes reality."

"But not if I enforce facts." Keles touched a hand to the book of maps at his bedside. "I have the world here, cataloged. This is fact. If I show it to others, if I educate them, they'll know reality."

"No, Keles, they will know *your* reality. They will make it their own, and it will have weight and momentum that will shape the world." Cyrsa shook her head. "You are a creature of precision and logic. Those who are not will create their own worlds and live within them. And, in many ways, that will be best, since they are incapable of handling what we know to be true."

Keles hugged his knees to his chest. "You sound as if you will acquiesce and join them."

"The gods do offer powerful inducements." Cyrsa rubbed a hand over her stomach. "I am pregnant. It will be a boy. His name shall be Pyrust."

"Congratulations." Keles' throat suddenly grew thick. Thoughts of Tyressa and his mother and Nirati flashed through his mind. "The gods have been kind to you."

The Empress nodded. "And kind to you, Keles."

She opened the chamber door and, smiling, waved two people in. "Please forgive me for monopolizing him."

"Nothing to forgive, Highness." Siatsi Anturasi laughed aloud as she swept into the room, her husband in her wake. "A little waiting won't kill us."

Only as the skewer impaled him did Pelut Vniel recover full memory of his death. He'd driven the dagger deep into Cyron's chest. He'd watched the life go out of the man's eyes. Blood dribbled from Cyron's mouth, then the one-armed man collapsed.

Pelut had spun, his arms wide, ready to accept the accolades of the ministers for his act of salvation. Prince Eiran, enraged, eclipsed his view. The Helosundian grabbed him by the armpits and, in one motion, pitched him from the tower. He fell, arms flailing, and dashed his brains out on the street below.

Men he didn't recognize bound his hands and feet, then lifted him into the fire. His flesh sizzled. Pain came in waves, ever increasing. He spun and grew dizzy. He shut his eyes and found he could not open them again.

Then he began to moan. "Why me? Why me? Why me?"

"Because, Pelut Vniel," answered the man roasting be
side him, "you were ambitious and you failed."

Pelut shook. "Prince Nelesquin?"

"Emperor Nelesquin, you fool." The man hissed as the
sound of a knife being sharpened filled Pelut's ears.
"That's right, cut deep. Those who are here shall feast
well now."

Four days of his mother's fussing over him had Keles
feeling well enough to stand on Moriande's walls and
watch the Expeditionary force heading north. The Keru
and other Helosundian warriors joined them, while non-
combatants remained in Moriande and prepared for
their journey. Desei troops went as well, leading the way
for Naleni and Durrani troops. Even the Voraxani went
along on their metal mounts, and a great many *xidantzu*
rode north with them. The warriors were united to drive
the Turasynd back into their wasteland, and they were
hopeful that Viruk might come up from the south and
aid them in their mission.

Keles smiled. Princess Jasai stood beside him, looking
radiant. At the Empress' order Jasai and Keles had married. Bards had already begun to sing of their romance
and the harrowing escape from Deseirion. In the song
they'd been fleeing the Turasynd. Warriors had already
promised to chase them back to the Wastes in their
name.

The Princess, deep in conversation with his mother,
didn't notice him looking at her. The two women were already as thick as thieves. Jasai's child would be Siatsi's
first grandchild, and nothing would be too good for him

Somehow the identity of the child's father had gotten lost, though the songs gave Keles full credit.

Ryn Anturasi, standing on the far side of Siatsi, was speaking with Borosan Gryst. The two of them shared a fascination with *gyanrigot* and had begun to collaborate on a number of projects.

A minister approached Keles. "The Empress requests a word with the Prince."

Keles turned and kissed Jasai on the cheek. "I shall return."

She smiled and squeezed his hand. "I will miss you."

He slipped his hand from hers and walked along the wall to the watchtower. The *gyanrigot* guards parted. He jogged up the wooden steps, then bowed. He held it a long time, certainly longer than required of a noble before the Empress.

She returned the bow and held it just as long. She straightened up and smiled. "I received your missive last night. I've read it and burned it. Obviously I concur with your plans, though I am reluctant to allow you to leave the Empire."

"It is the only way it can be, Highness." Keles stepped beside her and studied the army columns. "The channel north of the Helos Mountains has become a river fed by Virukadeen. It's right where a river should be. In a generation or two, no one will remember it wasn't there."

"This is especially true since you are taking the Helosundians to Anturasixan."

He nodded. "Tyressa never liked her people pining for what they had lost. They always were victims, now they will be in a new land that will allow them to shape their own destiny. I will take Desei there, too, and others who lost much in the war. They can all start over. A new land for a new beginning."

"A new beginning for you and your family, too?"

"Yes. Ulan will remain here. The House of Anturasi will still create the finest maps and charts in the world. The Empire will not lose that."

The Empress smiled. "We just lose the ability to shape the world."

"Hardly, Majesty." He turned around and pointed south toward the cranes lifting rocks into place to rebuild the nine bridges. "People are already shaping the world."

"But you could do all that work by imagining it."

"Yes, I could impress my sense of reality on everyone, but I won't do that." He shook his head. "They need to build their world. If they do not sacrifice, it will have no value for them. If they know I can save them, then they will not work to save themselves. People who do not look to the future really have no future. They're just waiting for the rot to set in."

She arched an eyebrow. "But the power you possess, do you not find it tempting to use?"

"I've seen what that power can do to the world. I've seen what it did to my grandfather." He looked down at his hands. "I know it can be used for good, but I also know that I am not smart enough to figure out every single consequence of using it. For that reason, I won't."

"Not even if using it to make a single flower blossom would put a smile on your wife's face?"

"No. I have done too much already. I wish to go to Anturasixan with my family. I will care for my grandfather until he dies, then enjoy my grandchildren."

"The gods may have other plans for you."

"If it pleases them." Keles smiled. "I remember when two of them were human—one of them my twin. They have been kind to me so far, and I hope they shall remain so in the future."

Epilogue

32nd day, Month of the Bat, Year of the Rat
8th Year of the Jade Dynasty
6th Year since the Turasynd War
Imperial Road South, Nalenyr

The nearly blind old man leaned heavily on his walking stick as he crested the hill. "There it is, Moriande, the grandest city in the world."

"I know, Grandfather. We live there now, remember?"

Matut nodded. "Of course I remember, Dunos. I remember many things. You may think me just a doddering old fool, but I remember coming this way with you and your father. And I remember a swordmaster, looking something like yours, but not as grand. Empress' consort and all."

"No, Grandfather." Dunos looked back to where Moraven and Ciras were helping a carter push his wagon up the final bit of the hill. "I'm sure he wasn't as grand as my master—as any of them."

"And I remember this place."

"Yes, Grandfather, the bandits." Dunos looked north again, as three figures slipped from the wood to block the road.

Matut squinted. "You shouldn't have said it, Dunos. You gave the gods ideas."

The centermost of the bandits, wearing a robe that had once been white with a red bear rampant as the crest, rested hands on the hilts of both his swords. "Welcome to the Imperial road. I and my companions keep it open and free of bandits. I am sure you wish to show your appreciation."

Dunos stepped forward and bowed. "I am *xidantzu*. I wish harm to come to no one. These people have traveled with my masters and me. They are under our protection. It will cost you nothing to walk away."

The bandit laughed and his scruffy companions joined him. "You're a boy with a withered arm. I'm not afraid of you. I'm Turren Xandao. I'm ranked Superior, so you and your masters should just run off. I'll let you pass, but not the others."

"I am Dunos Ameryne, of *Serrian* Jatan. If you wish to fight, name your terms."

"To the death, pup." The man laughed and drew both his swords. "I'm not afraid of you."

"Not yet." Dunos slowly bared his blade. "Draw a circle."

About the Author

Michael A. Stackpole is an award-winning novelist, game designer, computer game designer, podcaster, and scriptwriter. Raised in Vermont, he moved to Arizona in 1979. In his spare time he enjoys playing indoor soccer and dancing (swing and salsa). To learn more, please visit his website at www.stormwolf.com.